Titles by Tess Farraday

SNOW IN SUMMER
SEA SPELL
SHADOWS IN THE FLAME
TUMBLEWEED HEART

SNOW IN SUMMER

TESS FARRADAY

JOVE BOOKS, NEW YORK

HAUNTING HEARTS is a registered trademark of Berkley Publishing Corporation.

SNOW IN SUMMER

A Jove Book / published by arrangement with
the author

PRINTING HISTORY
Jove edition / February 1999

The Penguin Putnam Inc. World Wide Web site address is
http://www.penguinputnam.com

ISBN: 0-515-12475-3

A JOVE BOOK®
Jove Books are published by The Berkley Publishing Group,
a member of Penguin Putnam Inc.,
375 Hudson Street, New York, New York 10014.
JOVE and the "J" design
are trademarks belonging to Jove Publications, Inc.

PRINTED IN THE UNITED STATES OF AMERICA

10 9 8 7 6 5 4 3 2 1

Acknowledgments

When I was thirteen years old, my family moved from the small dairy town where my mother had grown up to a city of strangers. Leaving generations of family and friends was miserable and I hated our new house—except for something abandoned by the last tenants: a huge waterlogged copy of the complete works of William Shakespeare. In that first lonely summer, *Snow in Summer* began.

Barclay Wheeler, my extraordinary English teacher at Pioneer High School, brought Shakespeare's words alive for the first time. Rex Henriot, the director for the Syracuse Repertory Theatre, on loan to the California Shakespeare Festival, allowed me to reblock the fencing scene for a Hamlet with a torn Achilles tendon only after making me believe Shakespeare's characters were real people. I thank both for lessons I'll never forget.

I'm grateful to a bashful fire chief for kindling my fictional fire and telling me how to catch the bad guy; to Chris Platt for continuing to be my faithful critique partner as her own writing career skyrockets; and to Catherine Bennett, mistress of Melrose Plantation for her patient and friendly consultations on heirloom roses.

Most of all and always, my love and thanks to Cory, Kate, and Matt for everything.

Prologue

A swirling fog shrouded the camp on the day Christopher Gallatin would die. Fog obscured the fire from the crouched cook, the horses from their squires, and the wakening soldiers from each other.

Christopher Gallatin, Earl of Swanfort, wished the fog were thicker yet. He had one boot in the stirrup. Try as he might, he could not swing his other leg up over his warhorse, because a scullery maid clung squawking to his boot.

"Don't go!" the wench wailed.

Hooves dancing, Gallatin's stallion rolled his eyes white.

"Girl, let go." Gallatin kept his snarl low. He'd not draw attention from the other men or ignite the stallion's battle fury. "I'd—" Gallatin shook his leg at each word. "—mount—my—" She clung like a very monkey "—horse."

A temptress moon shone through the mists long enough for the assembled men to see his plight. A soft tide of laughter made Gallatin shake his leg until the girl finally lost her grip.

Feeling every bit the brute, Gallatin saw her hands flail and rags flap as she tumbled like a beggar's bundle.

She came up babbling.

"Treachery." A pale face smaller than his palm showed beneath the faded fringe covering her eyes. Thin fingers sawed at the trinket about her neck. "By my troth, sir, and by this griffin's eye—be wary of the Spaniard's *treachery.*"

The maid's charm was no griffin's eye, only a bead of amber threaded on a leather thong. Still, she stroked the stone as if it were a Papist's rosary. The boldness in her words made him think her older—in her teens, perhaps.

Finally mounted, Gallatin turned his stallion in calming circles, pretending not to listen. Why should he humor the girl Aragon had snatched from the Court kitchens, then cast off like the lowliest callet?

Gallatin fingered the rose-worked hilt of the Toledo blade Aragon had awarded him. Though Gallatin had been assigned to question Aragon's actions, he could not. Could not because he was a novice at deception and because purveying secrets to the queen's spymaster smacked of dishonor.

Still, Queen Elizabeth's cause was just. And royal favor brought royal obligations. The hoop swinging in Gallatin's pierced earlobe proclaimed him no less a queen's man than Sir Walter Raleigh, her seagoing pirate.

In Gallatin's mind, Aragon had only turned traitor to his sire's Spanish blood. This dawn, he obeyed the English heart inherited from his mother. He would lead an attack on a camp of Spaniards set on murdering the queen.

Fingers set like claws, the maid tugged at Gallatin's stirrup.

"He esteems you not—" She stopped as Aragon, the very one of whom she spoke, rode ghostlike into the misty glen. His high-mettled mount steamed as if he'd already galloped to London and back.

"Shall I lop its head off and end its yowling?" Aragon nodded toward the wench. "Then our position might remain secret and you might join the others."

"Nay." Hot with humiliation, Gallatin met his general's eyes. Swanfort blood pulsed bluer than Aragon's. Beshrew the man if he expected an apology.

Confrontation thrummed between them until Barrett rode into the clearing.

Dew jeweled Barrett's hair and a smile tilted his lips. "Leave off wrangling with your doxy, Kit, and—"

Custom accorded second sons jocularity in their lives, but Barrett had gone too far. A touch of spurs brought Gallatin's warhorse nose to nose with Barrett's.

"She's but a child, brother, as you could see, were you not so intent on holding me up for the amusement of others."

At once Barrett lowered his gaze. "Peace, Kit, 'twas only a jest." He bit his lip, then added, "A poor one."

"As you say."

When Barrett faded into the forest mist, Gallatin very nearly called him back. In battle, harsh words could be the last between brothers.

Nonsense.

Suddenly stealthy, men and horses jostled in the creamy fog and joined ranks. Aragon had discovered the Spaniards' camp in a tree-choked slash in the earth. The queen's troop had only to ride in and rout the Spanish dogs.

Barrett would lead. Gallatin and Aragon would guard the troop's flanks. By the time the moon had made its full month's circuit, they'd have ridden home with good tidings.

Gallatin gathered his reins and closed his ears to the maid's weeping.

He shrugged beneath the straps of his breastplate and cursed the womanish sentiment which made him loose a ribbon lacing his doublet. "Child, come hither. Quickly, now."

Her spirit had not fled with her tears. Her idiot necklace was clenched in the fingers of one hand, but she shook a scolding finger at him with the other.

"You've no time left for nagging." Gallatin leaned from the saddle and brushed a lock of fair hair from eyes of startling blue.

"What's your Christian name, child?"

The maid's harsh sniff covered a sob. "M-Miranda."

He knotted the satin ribbon around her hair.

"Fie. No tears while you wear Swanfort blue, Mistress Miranda."

She drew herself upright. Though two convulsive sobs pelted through her, she shed no more tears.

"The griffin's eye will bring you back, safe," she whispered, "to me."

"Well." Gallatin squared his own shoulders. He cleared his throat. His betrothed had offered no such sweet wishes. "Now Miranda, get you far behind the lines."

The stallion blew a snort of complaint as Gallatin wheeled him and rode off at a canter.

He didn't look back.

Following scents of crushed herbs and grass, Gallatin aimed his mount after the others. There was no path, only a narrowing gap descending. No birdsong. No morning light sifted through leaves overhead. It grew ever darker.

Gallatin's gaze strayed across the ravine. On a cliffside leagues away he sensed movement, but as long as Aragon held his flank, all would be well.

Ahead, a horse nickered and Gallatin's belly clamped. Battle-tested mounts never made such mistakes.

Buffeted bushes, snapping sticks, and the stutter of split hooves on rock heralded the approach of a stag. Antlers high, it exploded into their midst, with foam flying from its panic-wide mouth.

Wrong. Three thundering heartbeats underlined the word, until a thought took hold: No beast bolted toward its enemy.

Unchecked murmurs rose from his comrades. All hunters knew a stag ran from the approach of many horsemen. Unless even more pursued it.

Fate sliced time so thin, Gallatin had drawn his sword and lain low, cheek against his stallion's neck when a force like Lucifer's hammer struck his spine and all sound ceased.

Unable to twist away from the power piercing him, Gallatin clutched for his reins. In smothering soundlessness, his chest plate thrust forward over his stallion's mane and flattened ears. A neck-snapping tumble, and Gallatin's temple collided with damp earth.

Feathered fetlocks of another horse brushed Gallatin's lips.

Rumbling shook his jawbone. Forest dark tightened around him, as he saw a vision.

A girl child ran along a misty ridgetop and a ribbon of Swanfort blue streamed from her hair.

Chapter
One

A garland of daisies crowned his enemy.

Unseen, Gallatin strolled around her. He considered a face painted with April sunburn, chestnut hair, a slender throat, and fine flanks as if she were a filly up for bid.

A comely wench.

Comely as hell and just as welcome. Damme! Why couldn't his enemy be a man? Across seas and centuries, he'd searched for the ancient silver box she'd just hidden under the red kirtle laced over her gown. If a *lad* had possessed that treasure, Kit would have sliced him under the ribs with a dagger, then cast him in the dust.

He didn't forgo bloodletting because he was troubled by fears of eternal damnation. God clearly found Gallatin's earthly travails amusing. At times, he felt sure he heard the Supreme Being chuckle.

How it must amuse Him to watch a heartless specter ponder how to claim that silver box without harming the girl. Christopher Gallatin, Earl of Swanfort, had not fallen so low in the past four hundred years that he'd leave beauty a-bleeding.

6

She stood in a peddler's stall draped with gaudy red and yellow ensigns, surrounded by acres of pine-strained sun and shadow, screeching vendors, and break-bone games of chance.

"Lemon tarts!" called one peddler. "Sour as sainthood, sweet as sin! Luscious lemon tarts, here!"

This girl's very silence attracted a throng. Sorrel glints danced amid the crisscrossed braids of her hair as she waited for the fairgoers to hush.

"Toad in the hole, hale and hearty sandwich on a stick!" That vendor's croak distracted only a few who stood waiting to hear the girl speak.

Gallatin moved to the rear of the gathering and materialized in human form. No one noticed—they all watched her hands skim above a display of intricate silver boxes, all copies of his.

Once his foe spoke, the crowd was hers.

"Harken to an Elizabethan legend—the death of the Earl of Swanfort." With a voice rich as burgundy wine, she told the tale quite badly.

He'd expected as much. Since his appearance on this continent, Gallatin had haunted dozens of such "renaissance faires," searching for his treasure. From Connecticut to this glen in California, they were all of a certain sameness. They offered a mishmash of food, fashions, and folderol, purportedly from his time. A charitable man would grant all this had occurred somewhere, during some renaissance. Gallatin was not a charitable man.

Suddenly he turned even less so. A cowled and gray-bearded masquer clipped Gallatin's shoulder without apology. Gallatin's fingers twitched toward his dagger, then he shrugged. The pretend priest was no one of import. He merely resembled a blackguard who'd been breakfast for worms long ago.

'Zounds, now he'd missed the storyteller's prattling account of his death. Not that it mattered. He'd wager she made no mention of the flaming anger which consumed him as he struggled on the end of a pike, helpless to retaliate.

"Pardon me?" The storyteller's blue eyes met his, though

he had not spoken. Her fingers shielded the hollow of her throat.

Gallatin's stare held the cold of ten thousand nights in limbo, but the wench didn't flinch. She gave a self-mocking shake of her head, as if she'd imagined his interruption, then continued.

Hmm, what of *that*?

". . . to spare Arabella the sight of her beloved's corpse, a battlefield funeral took place . . ."

Ah, such wretched news for the carrion birds.

The crowd pressed closer for the bloody details. Few noticed the modest tug she gave the white smock slipping down her shoulder, or the sleight of hand to assure herself that the silver box—*his*—remained in its warm hiding place.

The girl had read his thought, but was she a witch? He'd seen a crone stoned for hexing her neighbors' cattle and a dog hanged as a witch's familiar. The storyteller might be a thief, but he could not take her for a witch.

With the inherent grace of noble birth, Gallatin wended his way closer. He would have that box.

". . . brother, Barrett, drew the earl's sword from his sheath . . ."

Ye gods! His rapier had been ready, in his hand. No unsheathing to be done by Barrett or any other!

The smoky aroma of sausage drifted from a peddler's stand and Gallatin inhaled like a hound. What a lost blessing was food!

"The hilt's intricate filigree depicts the family's loyalty to the Tudor rose . . ."

Why, Aragon had cadged that sword from a dead Spaniard!

Yet she bewitched the mob, telling how Barrett, weeping, snapped the blade free and pounded the sword's hilt into a box just big enough to house his brother's heart. She noted Barrett had given the box to the earl's sweetheart, Arabella.

Ah, yes, Janus-faced Arabella. And Barrett, the new earl, who'd bowed to false whispers of treason and disowned his elder brother. Not that betrayal pricked Gallatin. The two were long since worms' meat.

The throng nodded as the storyteller said the box—patterned like silver tapestry—had been passed down through generations in Britain, India, and finally the colonies, taking on mythic powers until it gained a suitably romantic name: the Graveyard Rose.

'sblood. Not one word of the treachery that killed him.

Quick to duck the storyteller's pitch for her wares, the audience drifted away, holding hands and intense conversations.

In life, Gallatin might have chuckled. The girl was a poor peddler, indeed, if she couldn't gull this lot.

"... replicas handcrafted by a famous San Francisco artisan!" she shouted after them, then slammed her palms on the table in frustration.

He stood to one side of her booth, screened by greenery. She hadn't sold a single box. Surely she would sell him the true one for the proper amount of coin.

From habit, Gallatin eased a finger beneath his starched white ruff. He suspected time had not changed the strangling properties of ruffs nor the smothering heat of black velvet doublets, but ghosthood allowed a few boons; he felt neither.

Exhaling, he turned invisible and slid into the booth behind the wench.

He stood close enough to touch her, so why didn't she shrink from his deathly cold? Gad, she shifted her weight to her heels, as if she would lean against him.

The top of her head did not reach his chin. She smoothed tendrils of vivid chestnut hair back toward the coiled braids, exposing a nape so milk-white and small it put him in mind of a dove.

Rubbish. She was his foe. The silver box warming to her body contained his very *heart*! By force or by guile, he must have it!

Right under his nose, a few locks of her hair strayed loose and stirred a waft of lavender. The herb, dusty green with nubs of purple, had scented his bedding in the long-past days when he'd needed sleep.

Her fingertips drummed the table. They were alone.

What a shame he could move objects only in his corporeal

form. Still, it would take but an instant to shift shape, push her forward over the table, slip the box from beneath her kirtle, and vanish for all time.

Gallatin took in the scents of pine and sausage, of lavender and girl. With eternity looming, he felt less urgency to leave this rough country for paradise. Or hell.

And then their seclusion was breached by the gray-cowled cleric. He'd returned to plague the storyteller and could not see Gallatin lurking.

"I need one of these after all." Flashing false whiskers and lupine teeth, the cleric tapped her arm.

Not that the cleric's claim on her flesh—his *foe's* flesh—unsettled Gallatin. The maid's hesitant laugh did not disturb him, nor did her effort to hide the skin at her low neckline.

And the storyteller *was* a maiden. Death at thirty had afforded Gallatin time aplenty to learn the cow-eyed look of naïveté. Now he wondered why he'd once prized that condition called virginity.

He'd given up swiving long ago. For the first hundred years, he'd relished the task of keeping his ghostly form substantial enough to perform. With grim humor, he recalled the fright he'd given one lively light-skirt.

When a man was set on lovemaking, his concentration sank to one level. A ghost was no different, except that the rest of him faded to nothing. Gallatin's technique had improved with practice and, for a time, he'd prided himself on it.

But the appeal of swiving had faded. Compared to a man's, his ghostly senses were limited. He could see and hear well enough, could smell the sharpest scents, but just as he had no flesh, he had no sensation.

"He must have been insufferably arrogant." The storyteller passed one of the replica boxes from hand to hand. "The earl, I mean, to think Arabella would welcome such a grisly memento."

Arabella? The mistress whose kiss-swollen lips swore that she would be the keeper of his heart? Gallatin had thought the gift quite fitting—nothing worth shuddering over, as the storyteller was doing.

Drawing himself up with self-importance, the cleric—a man of very ordinary stature—prepared to speak. First, feeling a ghostly chill, even if the maid didn't, he chafed his arms as Gallatin moved to stand beside him.

Peering at the maid over the cleric's sackclothed shoulder, Gallatin noted the cat-in-cream curl of her lips and realized she'd pretended squeamishness to hold her customer's interest. Clever girl.

"Heart burial was commonplace." The cleric's scholarly air blinded him to her trick. "With foreign battlefields and the lack of refrigeration, one couldn't be lugging home entire corpses."

The cleric babbled on, and the girl's left eyebrow quirked. She smiled as he sorted through the boxes.

Gallatin admired her spirit. As if she'd felt his esteem, her eyes fixed where his should have been. She seemed about to speak.

Gallatin looked away and heard her stumble, as if his gaze had held her upright.

"You must have other boxes," said the cleric. "This shipment is from Aurora Cantrell, in San Francisco, am I right?"

"Aurora Cantrell." She repeated the artist's name, then glanced at a stenciled cardboard container. "That's right."

"And you didn't sell any earlier?" The cleric's thumb rubbed the metal, as if seeking dents left by the butt of Barrett's dirk or searching out splinters from the deck of Her Majesty's ship *Godolphin*. But no modern man knew those secrets.

Finally, paper bills and coin changed hands and the cleric departed.

"Cold red apple wine-o!" A vendor's cry tempted the girl to purchase a cup and drain it. She blotted her lips as a merry-eyed woman in a white wimple approached. "Andi Fairfield, you're a godsend—"

Fairfield. How cloyingly poetic. Odd how the diminutive of "Andrew" suited this female. And what an utter waste of time to notice.

"—for filling in. I hated to ask, what with the mess Dinah left behind."

"Hi, Jan." The storyteller leaned across the width of the table to embrace the other woman. "Don't give it a thought." Andi swung open a gate and admitted the woman to the vendor's booth, where they hugged once more. "I love Heart's Ease, and Aunt Dinah's offer came at a good time."

Gallatin sensed a testing in her words. Damme, when had he grown so dull that women's matters sparked his interest?

"If you want to talk, the coffeepot's always on. Half our business is coffee." Given the maternal way Jan passed a hand over Andi's hair, they were friends of long standing.

"I'm eager to see your shop. Dinah said Blake came home to help run it."

"Help?" Jan's hand wavered in a considering motion. "She hasn't changed, Andi, and with six of us sharing the upstairs and Blake recovering from a really foul divorce, let's just say we've *got* to work something out."

The woman then proceeded to make excuses for the sister she'd just criticized. Kit had forgotten the vagaries of family life.

"That's why she wasn't at the funeral," Jan said. "Can you imagine suing another lawyer, your partner, for divorce? And her twins are staying with *him* until school's out."

"But the shop's staying alive?"

"Barely. After the old theater burned, I took over." Jan clasped her hands together before her lips, hiding a wide smile. "And I have to say the place looks great. And even if she's still ricocheting between here and San Francisco, Blake's head for business has saved us. Sparrowgrass might not have videos or a mall, but at the sign of the Dancing Goat, you can get espresso, books, and hibiscus straight from Honolulu."

"I can hardly wait."

Again, Gallatin thought there was more in Andi's hand-squeezing enthusiasm than her words conveyed.

"You run along home and finish unpacking," Jan absently accepted money for a box she'd sold without interrupting their conversation. "You took a Graveyard Rose for yourself, didn't you?"

Andi pulled at black threads peeping from beneath the hem

of her kirtle, then dangled a plump gold velvet bag for approval.

"Good. It's become such an art-cult thing. They were selling like hotcakes this morning." Jan scanned the heap of unsold boxes with a surprised expression. "You're an English teacher, after all—you should have one." Jan shoved tendrils of dark hair back inside her wimple. As Andi moved to go, she blocked her way. "You're not walking home?"

"It's barely two miles."

"Okay. Um, Andi, don't be surprised if help comes calling. He's a hunk."

A hunk. The description sounded raw coming from a lady's lips and Andi's yelp of protest made it clear she agreed the word was crude.

"Don't glare at me." Jan held her hands out, palms first. "Dinah hired him."

"I'll *un*hire him." Snippy as a goose, Andi jerked the drawstrings tight on the gold bag which held his heart. "I spent yesterday taking stock. Heart's Ease doesn't need major repairs. Scraping, sanding, painting, and the gardens need weeding and watering. I can do all that. I'll tell you what, though," Andi pointed a considering finger at Jan. "There're some neat-looking old roses trying to come back to life, out by the fence. Maybe you could give me some advice on reviving them."

"I'd love to get my hands on Dinah's roses, but I won't be distracted from the subject of Rick," Jan said. "I shouldn't have called him a hunk. He's a junior college teacher and neighbor who got close to your uncle Jason, toward the end, and he's taken Cisco under his wing, training him for varsity football." Jan stifled a grateful grimace. "I couldn't fire Rick."

"But I could. Don't worry, I'll be nice." She kissed Jan's cheek. "I want solitude and I *don't* want to waste Dinah's money. Although, if your hunk knew about horses—"

"You shouldn't be out there alone."

Jan's fingers sawed at a silver cross necklace.

The Divine Prankster certainly meant to test Gallatin this time 'round.

"Sparrowgrass isn't like it used to be," Jan said. "There've been a few break-ins. And other things."

As Andi's arms crossed, Jan gave up. "Well, Rick's house is just across the ravine. Your folks' old place? That puts you between him and us."

"I'll raise a white flag if I need you." Andi winked, slid the bag to the crook of her elbow, and set off, away from the fairgrounds, with the stride of a female who had absolutely no intention of asking anyone for anything.

The slope of Daffodil Hill gleamed paintbox-green. The pines bristling its crest stood still, though the daffodils along the lonely lane swayed as Andi passed.

A distinct tug pressed the velvet bag against her wrist. The sensation felt odd. Well, it was only Saturday. If she could tough it out until midnight, maybe this weird week would end.

Monday morning, she'd arrived to find a substitute teacher writing his name on her chalkboard. Then Lincoln High School's principal escorted her to his office and closed the door. Steepling his fingers sincerely, Mr. Sterling announced that Miranda's "unfortunate accident involving Coach Santos" had made her presence "disruptive to the educational process." Her principal had advised her to take her accrued sick leave. Immediately.

Andi had wandered as far as the parking lot before the principal's last words penetrated. Suddenly her vintage Volkswagen looked unfamiliar and her fingers forgot how to insert the ignition key.

He'd said, "The school district will reevaluate your position in September."

By nine o'clock Tuesday morning, she'd downed too much coffee, made a list of grievances, and scheduled an afternoon appointment with the teachers' union representative. At ten past nine, Aunt Dinah had called.

Dinah's "darling Jason" had finally lost his battle with lung cancer. Exhausted and leaden-voiced, Dinah brushed aside condolences and begged Andi to attend the Thursday funeral.

She'd agreed, certain educational injustice wouldn't vanish while she was gone.

Wednesday, Dinah had called back and changed everything. First, she apologized.

"Honey, your mom didn't tell me about Domingo. She said I had my emotional hands full with Jason, and, God love her, I did, but I am sorry about your young man. And that's why I'm going to make you a proposition."

Next, speaking on a cellular phone as she packed, Dinah insisted she could not remain at Heart's Ease without Jason. She planned to drive directly from the funeral to Los Angeles and board the first ship bound for someplace she'd never been.

"You just tell your principal that there's only a few days left of school and unless he's an inhuman jerk he'll grant you a bereavement leave."

Before Andi could reveal the depth of her principal's "humanity," Dinah had decreed that her niece simply had no choice. She'd be doing them both a favor by house-sitting Heart's Ease. If Andi wanted, she could help renovate it for sale in the fall.

"*Sell* Heart's Ease? Aunt Dinah, I'd rather evict Mom and Dad and sell *their* house!"

Dinah had managed a weak laugh over the cellular's static. Then she'd hung up, leaving Andi to convince herself a lot could happen before fall.

In the meantime, Heart's Ease was hers.

Andi had quelled the unseemly jolt of joy by paying every bill that had been gathering dust atop her desk, stuffing a summer's worth of clothes into two suitcases, and packing Rosencrantz and Guildenstern, her goldfish, into a tip-proof crate. Last, she'd dropped off the keys to her condominium with her parents and kissed them good-bye.

Only when she'd left the freeways behind and her Volkswagen labored into the Sierras did she let herself rejoice at a girlhood dream come true. For one summer, the curious old mansion was hers. Though nothing could erase that night of horror and its aftermath of stares and snickers, Heart's Ease might help.

Last night, forty-eight hours after Dinah's final call, Andi had busied herself hanging clothes in the closet of Dinah's guest bedroom. As she moved in, she resolved to rise above her curse. She could do that by becoming totally self-sufficient.

Alone, she would feel no giddy romantic highs and no soul-sucking lows. She would welcome the middling pleasure available without men.

Now, Andi stepped carefully between the railroad ties. The tracks marked the last level ground before the ascent to Heart's Ease.

Last night's decision had been a good one. This morning, the pressure in her temples and the darkness lurking at the edge of her vision had vanished. Taking tea and a croissant on the veranda at dawn, she'd uttered a prayer of thanksgiving, and even Jan's emergency summons hadn't fazed her.

Once she'd rummaged through Jason and Dinah's basement for a costume, Miranda had even had fun. Until she began her recitation of the Graveyard Rose legend—and saw him.

Swordsman slim, looking every bit the Renaissance rogue, he was easily the best-looking man at the fair. Maybe the handsomest in California. Not made-up movie-star handsome but real-life tough, like a cop. Except he couldn't be. His black hair, which shone in the sun, nearly reached his shoulders. For a heartbeat she'd questioned her decision to remain solitary.

Her hesitation ended the instant she met his disparaging black eyes. Tension, as if she'd tried to slip past a hot stove or a hedge of poison oak, clamped her stomach. He knew.

Now, a huff of wind brushed Andi's skirts, bringing the lush scents of Heart's Ease.

Steer clear, buddy, she told the arrogant face floating in her mind's eye. Typhoid Mary, Bonnie Parker, and Mata Hari are amateurs next to Andi Fairfield. None of them ever mastered the kiss of death.

Andi yanked at the estate's black wrought-iron gate and almost dropped the velvet bag again. Magenta sweet peas had twined the gate closed between her comings and goings.

Clanking the latch back into place, Andi stood still, listening. Had she heard a footfall? Dinah's house waited alone on a dirt road which dead-ended at its gate. And if the hardworking Rick lived in her parents' old cottage across the ravine, he'd be traveling by four-wheel drive, not afoot. No one else had any business here.

Compared to Andi's urban neighborhood, the countryside had lots of puzzling noises. She might have heard a swallow nesting in the eaves above the red letters which spelled out "Heart's Ease." Perhaps the wind had shifted and brought the brook's prattling. Or maybe she'd startled quail into scuttling for cover.

Andi negotiated the overgrown path toward the mullioned front door, and Heart's Ease reared up before her. Like a grand dame caught wearing a muumuu, the Victorian structure peered through a vivid jungle of wildflowers and unmown grass.

Its red trim had faded to pink and it needed whitewash, but it remained striking. Restored to resemble the set of Jason's most successful movie, a vampire epic called *Heart's Ease,* the house had twelve large rooms, a rambling wraparound veranda, and a few secret passages.

A melodious neigh floated from the sloping acreage behind the house. Trifle, an aging horse who'd starred in three of Jason's movies, presented a challenge to Andi's self-reliance. Feeding Trifle required a knack for chemistry. Two flakes of this and a half measure of that, not to mention vitamin drops. If she wanted to sell something, why hadn't Dinah chosen the geriatric horse?

Clouds smeared the sun as Andi lifted her hem to climb the front steps. She'd resolutely left the door unlocked. This was not Los Padres. It was Sparrowgrass, home of the West's last lynching, where burglars respected their neighbors. Or at least their stubborn insistence on the right to bear arms.

The door harp bonged her entrance. Inside, Andi squinted up at the little ornament. Shaped like an Irish harp, it had tiny wooden balls that struck its strings each time the door opened.

"You're history," she muttered. "Soon as I find a screwdriver."

Wind ruffled a sheet across the living room's polished hardwood floor. Before departing, Aunt Dinah had draped the furniture against dust. Added to the dwelling's creaks and moans, sheets made Heart's Ease look like a haunted house, and Andi had snatched them off the instant she set down her suitcases.

She'd meant to fold them away, but the lingering odor of Jason's cigars had forced her to fling wide every window before the post-funeral guests arrived.

Except they hadn't. Dinah had insisted on a small wake at the church so Andi could take up residence immediately and privately.

Overhead the floor creaked. "Kitty, kitty?"

Lily, the queenly white cat who'd decreed herself the true mistress of Heart's Ease, was deaf. Still, she always sensed Andi's footsteps. Whether she deigned to appear was something else entirely.

"Be that way." Andi unlaced her kirtle, decided modern-day vests were a vast improvement, and stretched.

A rapid patter down a hidden staircase convinced her that Lily was still indulging her pique over Dinah's departure. Or she'd gone to the basement to skulk and swat mice.

Andi gathered an armload of sheets, crossed the great room, and flicked a light switch beside the basement door. As a child, she'd feared the basement. She blamed older cousins, who'd delighted in crouching behind trunks and cast-off costumes, poised to roar as they snatched her bare ankle. Now, as the hinges squeaked, Andi scolded herself. It was just another room.

Steep stairs descended into a cavernous space smelling of cedar and mothballs. She started down.

"Lily?"

Overhead, fluorescent lights sputtered, then glittered on her aunt's sewing machine, a pair of ornate candlesticks, crossed swords on wall hooks, and a huge chest-style freezer, which hummed an electrical greeting.

Dinner. Andi dumped the sheets.

The freezer, stacked deep with condolence offerings, sent up wisps of cold.

Unaware of Dinah's getaway plan, neighbors had come to Heart's Ease expecting to find a widow too distraught to cook. Dinah had wrapped each dish in industrial-strength foil with an informative stick-on label, then stashed it in the freezer.

" 'Gina's tuna noodle casserole—C+,' " Andi read. " 'Jan's *chicken* lasagna—excellent,' 'Black Forest torte by Lizbet: eat first!' " Andi snagged that package and balanced it against her hip.

Shaking her fingers against the cold, Andi looked up as something brushed the door at the top of the stairs. It opened an inch wider.

Lily must want company after all. "What would you say to a little tuna casserole?"

"Sounds great." Any words the male voice uttered after that were covered by the thump of frozen casserole hitting the floor.

Andi started to lunge upstairs to confront the intruder, then stopped. The stairs were steep and flanked by river rock. Neither side had a handrail. One shove and she'd be face down on the concrete floor with a broken nose. Or neck.

So she braced herself. Swung with sufficient energy, a frozen torte could be lethal.

"Sorry." The man wore khaki pants and a yellow knit shirt. His face remained shadowed as he extended his hand. "I *did* knock. Really."

Andi recognized the voice, though the citrus aftershave was fresh and he'd removed the monk's robe. She could see the same white smile he'd worn while buying a Graveyard Rose replica. Now the smile looked a bit sheepish, but that didn't mean she would trust him.

"I'm Rick. We saw each other at the Renaissance Faire?"

"Hi, Rick. What the hell are you doing in my house?"

Though light haloed his head from behind, she still couldn't see his eyes and he still blocked the doorway.

"Jan said you knew I was— I, uh, would've introduced myself at the fair, but I didn't know it was you. Not 'til Jan told me.'' He rubbed the toe of one Nike against the back of his pant leg.

Andi held her breath to keep from talking. Silence was a technique which wrung the truth from most teenage miscreants, but she'd never wielded it against an intruder.

''Jump in here anytime,'' he said. When she didn't, Rick uttered a half laugh. ''Dinah said 'a short blonde,' and you're not short. Or blond.

''Look, I'm the professor Dinah hired to paint the house.'' He shrugged and gave a lopsided smile. ''I'm the only guy in town with a ladder tall enough to reach the top story and I'm beginning to feel pretty self-conscious shouting down into the basement.''

Beside her, Lily lapped at a tiny rip in the foil wrapping the ruined tuna casserole. In front of her, a downright attractive man fretted over her next move. ''Okay, get out of the doorway and I'll come up.''

Heart still beating at a frantic pace, Andi shouldered past him and led the way to the kitchen, feeling smug. She'd not only handled the situation, she still had a firm grip on the torte.

Five minutes later, Rick uttered the only words which could have kept Andi from firing him.

''It's not like I need the money.'' He stood on the front porch, fidgeting with a bulbous black thumb ring. Then he jammed his hands into his pockets. ''It's just that Jan's having a tough time with Cisco, her oldest son.''

Oldest *living* son. Andi closed her eyes, grateful for Rick's ignorance.

''No felonies or anything, or I wouldn't have him helping me.''

''All right.''

''Male bonding is often a good way to avert bigger problems.''

''All *right*, but only the painting.''

Rick appraised her front porch rafters, festooned with cobwebs. ''If you say so.'' He shambled down the stairs, sidestepping a warped board. ''See you tomorrow.''

Rick strolled through the dusk, giving an amused squint across the front acre of weeds, then got into a white van and left.

With arms crossed, Andi walked the path toward Trifle's paddock. She'd hitch up the horse and plow the whole freaking yard *under* before asking his help.

Then she remembered the hayloft. A country gal would have inserted her fingers between her lips, produced a piercing whistle, and summoned Rick's high-rise ladder.

But Andi's mouth had turned too dry to whistle.

Next to the corral, dark, erect, and immune to Trifle's nuzzling, stood the stranger from the fair whose harsh eyes made Andi certain he knew her secrets.

Gallatin knew he must stay here long enough to find his heart. But he would remain no longer. He had no interest in the tangled life of Andi Fairfield. It must be a pretty coil, indeed, if a mere boy like the one named Cisco hated her. He'd told his mother as much at the fair.

"How can you talk to that bitch?" Cisco's dark face had contorted as he stared after Andi.

Jan had sent him off with a simple scolding. Though Gallatin desired to school the boy in manners, he had no time. No time, either, to discover if Andi deserved the designation.

But just now, with hot soil and weeds cooling around him, with swallows fluttering from the rafters and summer night coming on, he marked a faint desire to stay on Earth. He blamed it on the horse.

Though the desert-blooded mare was past her prime, she awakened memories of a time when his legs controlled a ton of volatile animal, a time when his hands knew the delicate fingerwork that would aim an enraged warhorse. With the fat worked off her belly, the mare would be splendid. If only he had time.

Gallatin listened to voices leaving the main house. In minutes someone would heed the mare's hunger cries. Gallatin considered the tiny barn and the apartment above it. Dark and cobwebbed, it appeared the perfect dwelling for a ghost.

By Satan's bones, he had time. He had *eternity* and nothing to do with it.

The keeper of his heart approached.

Thin as parchment, the mare's nostril vibrated, alerting the girl. Andi, head slightly cocked, costume skirts billowing, ignored the warning.

She saw him, right enough, and yet she, a frail female, approached a soldier superior in strength, agility, and wit without hesitation.

Gallatin cleared his throat. "Miss Fairfield, I'd like to rent your carriage house."

"It's not for rent." Quite suddenly her words were edged with fear.

Why? His Renaissance Faire doublet came as no surprise, and no trick of light revealed his ghosthood.

"Have we met?" Her hands perched on her hips, making her question the furthest thing from romantic enticement.

"No." The horse picked that moment to nudge Gallatin forcefully in the spine.

Beshrew the mare. She'd made Miss Fairfield smile. He'd have no smiling. Only business and the recovery of his heart.

"The carriage house has no electricity, no heat, but plenty of mice. You'd hate it."

"On the contrary. Its windows are large," he countered, "I do well enough by candlelight, and I'm quite tolerant of cold. And rodents." Why the devil didn't she ask his occupation, his age, or record of debt? "I'm a writer." That alone should explain all manner of eccentricity.

"What do you write?" Her slight inclination forward made scent of lavender rise from her once more.

"Tales of glory from the age of Elizabeth. You see, all the studios I've investigated have too much chrome and plastic. Hardly conducive to the proper mood." He almost regretted her gullibility. She fancied herself intelligent, the match of any man, but no man would be so easily snared by curiosity.

"Fiction or nonfiction? Shakespearean—?"

"Please." Gallatin shuddered like a wet dog. Why must

that scribbler be the only Englishman these dimwits glori-
fied? He turned his attention to the mare.

"You don't like Shakespeare?" Andi laughed. The sound
put him in mind of larks joyously in pursuit of gnats.

Rubbish. Better he should explore this bump on the
horse's neck than converse with this girl. And yet, she
awaited a polite response.

"Love and royal intrigue, fairies flittering—"

And then she interrupted him. *Him*, a far greater authority
on that pitiful player than anyone living.

"Perhaps the people of his time were more superstitious—"

"Hardly."

Ah, the mare's bump was only an old scar.

Andi tapped her slipper and shook her head in the self-
mocking manner he'd noticed at the fair. She appeared quite
convinced. In faith, he'd swear his handling of the mare had
persuaded her.

She surrendered. But boldly.

"If only for the conversation, sure, I'll rent you the carriage house." Her glee should have made him wary. "Two
hundred dollars a month, but only if you take care of this
animal." She gestured toward the horse.

"You fear the mare?"

"No, I just don't know anything about horses. I'm a city
girl, Mr.—"

And here he should fill in his name.

"Kit Gallatin." What a silly wench to talk and laugh so
freely with a stranger. He extended his hand.

"Miranda Fairfield."

For the blink of an eye her palm pressed his. He could
not wait to be rid of it.

Grinding lust erupted at her touch.

Hell and damnation, if she didn't possess his very heart,
he would vanish and leave her gaping.

"Don't you find it curious, Miss Fairfield, that you've just
completed business dealings with a man you do not know?"

"Suffering from buyer's remorse already?" Level as any
warrior's, her blue eyes held his, then faltered on the mare.

"One seventy-five and horse care, Mr. Gallatin. Take it or leave it."

Couldn't she hear the gauntlet she'd thrown down? Didn't she know that dares provoked a man?

"I will take it." Somehow his voice stayed steady as he turned to face the horse.

Raw power agitated each particle of his being. Braced and restless, he fought this flash of madness. And lost.

Kit Gallatin had not wanted a wench for more than two hundred years. But he vowed to the Creator who'd toyed with him for centuries that he'd not depart Earth without having this one.

Chapter
Two

A flight of blackbirds dark as his mood fled before Kit Gallatin. All this chill night, he'd haunted the estate from flowery gate to outbuildings. He should have spent the hours inside the house, searching for the silver box, but an ancient code of courtesy kept him out.

Sunrise touched the black pines in the ravine behind the house, promising to turn them green. He passed through the back fence, traversed the overgrown side lawn, and climbed the front steps. Then he considered the door.

Sliding through solids wasn't painful, just tight, like fitting through the neck of a garment shrunk by washing. The doorknob turned at his touch, hinges creaked, and he'd nearly entered when his essence stirred a discordant bong.

Kit jerked back into the chill morning. For an instant, welcoming scents of soap, tea, and candle wax had swirled around him, but the girl had set up some sort of accursed ghost alarm.

Dawn-dewed grass brushed by as he stalked toward the back of the house. On the right, Heart's Ease was flanked by the mare's corral and the carriage house atop her barn. On the left, a hedgerow sheltered quail and dowdy brown squirrels. Kit rounded the back corner of the house, averting his gaze from the footpath bisecting the grassy slope to a tree-choked ravine that stirred evil memories.

It was better to concentrate on the windowpane before him. Within, a white cat and a red geranium sat on a round table. The cat gazed at him, unblinking.

"You don't see a thing, bloody rat-catcher, so look away." Muttering, Kit stared up at an open window on the next floor. Early breezes scraped a copper rain gutter against the house and billowed pale curtains out to taunt him. Andi had taken his heart into her chamber and clearly meant to sleep all day.

Warm and complacent, the white cat showed its pink tongue in a yawn. The furry pest would skitter on the doily, upend the geranium, and topple the lamp if he flowed through the window. Kit returned to the front door, braved the bonging, and entered.

Eyes sweeping every table, shelf, and bookcase, Kit climbed the spiral staircase. The cat abandoned her perch to dash between his heels. Together, they crossed beams of multicolored light streaming through the stained-glass windows.

Gallatin followed a waft of lavender and found Andi sleeping in a curtained bedstead. Tasseled cords caught back white swathes of fabric facing east, and though the window stood open, the bedroom corner was warm.

Kit blamed his night of wandering in the stabbing Sierra cold for his need to settle into the window seat. Once seated, he savored the view of Andi in her sunny cave.

Honeyed light rubbed the smooth skeins of her hair. For the first time, he saw them let loose, autumn-hued tresses long enough that a man might nestle her head on his shoulder and measure the locks to his fingertips. White sheets drifted to the plank floor, revealing Andi's sleeping gown. High-necked and bibbed with tucks, it looked like a child's gown in all ways save one. Twisted and hiked to her hip, the gown showed a glorious thigh, knee, shin, and pink-painted toenails. Kit might have credited them with his sudden dizziness if a ladder hadn't slammed through the open window and struck him from behind.

The blow didn't hurt. It disturbed his concentration. Kit wheeled, grabbed the ladder top, one side in each fist, and gave it a shake.

"Christ, Rick, I'm falling!" a stranger shouted.

What a fair greeting to the Sabbath. The profane yell justified Gallatin's wrath, but he regretted waking Andi.

Her long legs peddled, then swung off the bed. She tripped on a sheet before sweeping up an armload of clothing and bolting for the head of the stairs.

"I said they could paint." Andi seesawed faded blue breeches up beneath the gown and talked to the preening cat. "Not bash the side of the house at six-thirty in the morning."

She reached for the gown's hem and Gallatin turned from the immodest display.

"Golly, it's cold out here. Who turned off summer, Lily cat?"

Still facing her bedroom window, Kit heard the garment skim past her rough breeches and smooth skin. A zipper, snap, fingers fumbling with cloth, then the sound of bare feet padding down the stairs. When she'd passed beyond hearing, he ransacked her room.

He lifted the white linens, peered behind and beneath the oak bedstead, and opened the drawers of her clothes cupboard. He found a plethora of faded blue breeches, small stretchy shirts, and female underpinnings too filmy for a man's hands. But no silver box. Irritation at the delay supplanted satisfaction at her cleverness.

Outside, the ladder banged into position a second time.

"See if you can reach the top of the window frame with the sandpaper. I'll hold you steady, Cisco."

Gallatin ignored the men. Cisco had defamed Andi. Rick had trapped her in the cellar. Now they climbed Andi's house, cursing. Their penance would come. No deity, not even one presiding over these rude times, would tolerate such disrespect.

Kit had raised his hand to tap the ceiling, sounding for an

attic, when the cat sidled through the open closet door and vanished. Kit followed. Inside the closet, he found dresses. Behind them, a door nailed shut. How had the cat had passed through?

Kit knelt. He worked his fingers into the frame and a shadow in the darkness opened. The nails were sawed off inside, leaving the nail heads to fool a casual observer. He wondered if Andi knew of her bedroom's secret staircase.

Rick left Cisco high on the ladder where he couldn't eavesdrop. Rick needed a private talk with the mistress of Heart's Ease, and he might as well have it before she peeled off her negligee in favor of clothes. Once he would've pegged Andi Fairfield as the flannel pj's type, but the gossip in Sparrowgrass said he was way off base.

Rick gave the waistband of his shorts a tug and rapped on the front door. Andi must have the true Graveyard Rose. Rick didn't believe artist Aurora Cantrell's nerdy little apprentice had the nerve to double-cross him. Slipping the true box in among the shipment of replicas was a small price to pay for physical safety. Rick blew his cheeks out and knocked again.

No, the nerd had done it. Rick had just been a little late showing up to retrieve it. His buyer wouldn't tolerate tardiness. Neither would Renetta.

Sweat pricked Rick's armpits. He needed the true box by July 4. It didn't matter how he got it.

Last night, he'd planned to replace the Graveyard Rose with his replica while Andi was in the basement. The decrepit mansion had so many creaks and groans, she hadn't heard a thing. But she'd already lost the damn box. Or hidden it.

He knocked again.

"Just a minute." Andi's voice echoed through the cavernous great room before she opened the door. "Rick." Her feet were bare and her tone was decidedly ticked off. Her baggy jeans showed a quarter inch of skin above the waist snap. "Do you country boys always start work before dawn?"

Her toes squeaked on the polished floors as she wheeled away. "Come on in and have some coffee."

The coffee was too strong, and only one egg sputtered in her skillet. A saucepan held something laden with onions, tomatoes, and maybe peppers. Enough to gag a man this time of the morning. *If* he'd been invited to eat.

"I should have warned you we'd start early." He watched her poke a wooden spoon at the concoction. "I teach summer school from eight 'til noon during the week, so I wanted to get a good start today."

Rick smoothed his close-cropped blond hair, wondering why she'd neglected to do the same. She clearly hadn't used a mirror to plait that untidy braid, and her gingham shirt needed the touch of a hot iron.

Brushing past him to a bowl full of glop, she seemed unaware that an eligible man stood in her kitchen. Instead of primping or flirting, she leaned back against the counter, rolling a ball of dough between her palms.

"I'm going to start doing that myself. You know, getting up with the chickens." She flopped the dough from one hand to the other. "I'm starting a compost pile today, I'll weed everything by Wednesday and have a vegetable garden in by next weekend."

"Pretty ambitious." Rick stifled a laugh. Los Padres's sexy sweetheart sounded more like Johnny Appleseed. "But save your energy on the vegetables. From what Dinah said, if the crows don't eat your seeds, the deer nibble off the shoots."

"Really? Crows and deer? Wow." Andi smiled, but he was more satisfied by the way she startled at a crash somewhere outside. "What do you suppose—?"

"Probably Cisco. You know, Jan's kid?" He nodded toward the back of the property. "I've got him up on a ladder, sanding window frames."

Andi's eyes rounded and her breasts rose as she caught and held a breath. Last night she'd had the same reaction when he mentioned Cisco, but why? The kid was a trouble-maker, but in Sparrowgrass his mom and aunt had halos, so no one said much about the kid's problems. Rick watched Andi fret.

Blackmailing Aurora Cantrell's apprentice had been easy. He'd bet it would be even easier to find out why Cisco Kern had Andi spooked.

Bleak, cold, stiff. Despite the warmth of Dinah's yellow kitchen, Andi felt as if she'd stumbled into a snowy sinkhole.

"Cisco came with you today? Great." Andi flicked water onto the black griddle and watched the droplets dance, blocking memories of Clint. "I haven't seen Cisco since he was a baby." After the funeral, Cisco had hung on her skirt, asking, *C'int? Where C'int?*

Andi flipped the cornmeal dough off her palm onto the griddle. Rick appeared so morbidly fascinated, he might have been watching a python swallow a hamster. If he couldn't recognize a tortilla, perhaps he wouldn't notice her uneasiness over Cisco. And that was just fine.

As soon as Rick took himself off, she would savor the breakfast she'd planned while tossing and turning, battling nightmares. With a plate full of *huevos rancheros*, a barely begun novel, and the sunny deck, she'd be safe from memories of Domingo and Clint.

"Now, why did I think I'd find your Graveyard Rose on the mantel?" Rick's voice drifted from the living room.

She shouldn't get so preoccupied she didn't notice men coming and going. "No, but you can feed the goldfish while you're in there." She searched for Dinah's spatula. "I think I—" Gingerly she flipped the tortilla with her fingers. "Ow." Where *had* she put the box? "I haven't decided where to display it. I might send it home."

"That'd be a shame." Rick sauntered back into the kitchen. "It sort of seems like the kind of thing Jason would've gotten a kick out of."

He jammed his hands into his pockets. The habit reminded Andi of the odd ring he'd worn yesterday.

"Hey, Rick."

Andi's stomach couldn't have plummeted more precipitously if she'd stepped off the rooftop.

Cisco Kern was his brother's clone. Clint at fifteen had let the same caramel-colored hair drift over toffee-brown eyes. The resemblance must chill his mother, except for one thing. A permanent sneer lifted the left corner of Cisco's mouth.

"Cisco Kern, I'd like to introduce—" Rick began.

"I sanded the window frames and shutters in—"

"—Dinah's niece, Miranda Fairfield."

"—back. Shall I start on the front?" Cisco's stubborn malice convinced Andi he'd heard all the worst tales of his brother's death.

How could he *not* hate her?

Rick had rescued her from having to make conversation by giving a "just between us adults" grimace as he'd herded Cisco out front. Wrapped in one of Dinah's shawls, Andi ate breakfast on the veranda overlooking the estate's colorful, run-amok front lawns.

Now she wended her way through the straw-filled barn, set on doing the Right Thing. It was barely eight o'clock and her boarder wasn't supposed to take residence until afternoon. She stamped up the steep steps. Her fistful of rags and the broom balanced riflelike against her shoulder guaranteed she'd be back out in the sunshine straightaway. All the same, Andi wished her parents had stressed good times over responsibility.

"I never wanted to be a slumlord," she admitted to Lily. "The well-preserved proprietress of a French *pension*, perhaps, but not this."

The white cat sat to the left of the carriage house doorway, cleaning a paw with enough vigor to block Andi's words.

The door had no lock and its tarnished knob turned at a touch. Andi peered inside and exhaled. Except for a silver skim of dust, the carriage house lived up to her childhood memories.

The barn's steep staircase emerged in the middle of a living room–kitchen decorated with more red, white, and blue than an election-year convention. Patriotic bunting draped two dusty windows. The pine floor wore a collection of faded bicentennial throw rugs. One of them, positioned in front of the apartment's sole sink, commemorated the Freedom Train's stop in Sparrowgrass.

Past the sink lay a sleeping nook with a bare metal cot. The striped mattress that she and her cousins had abused with jumping when they made this their playhouse lay balanced on the rafters overhead. Andi leaned across the cot, swung the window outward, and rested her hands on the sill. Below, she saw the corral, rear veranda, and ravine.

After spying on adults from that window, Andi and her cousins had retired to the opposite end of the room, where they lolled in a 1950's restaurant booth, swilling milk and chomping smuggled cookies.

Andi touched a brass tack on the red leather upholstery and polished a clean place on the window next to the booth. Since the barn and carriage house abutted the hillside, the view here showed nothing more than foliage, spreading yellow and flat against the glass.

Cobwebs floated overhead, stirred by an unseen breeze that sent Lily frisking into the room. Andi brushed her fingertips together and considered her chore. Since Dinah had obviously stayed abreast of housework in preference to yard work, Andi figured she wouldn't need much more than an hour to dust, sweep floors and ceilings, and splash around a little pine cleaner for effect.

"For the price," Andi said to Lily, who'd risen on her haunches to paw at floating dust motes, "I should make him clean it himself."

Kit stepped free of the cat's paws. It ran contrary to his purpose to spew a loud, mouth-filling oath into the loft room, but he wished the puss would cease her sharp caresses. Moreover, he wished Andi Fairfield had some idea of her place.

Kit would doff his manners quick enough if she proposed such work to him. He understood her reluctance to toil among cobwebs. In life, he would have summoned her a squadron of scullery maids. But clean the place *himself*? How dare she allow the idea to cross her mind, let alone her lips? Faced with such humble labor, he'd consign the place to the spiders.

There were plenty of them. Kit scanned the open-beamed ceiling. Heaven protect him. One could fall, legs wriggling, right through him. He shuddered, wondering how the dreadful little atomies had earned Andi's mercy. Each time her broom threatened a spider, Andi dangled a dust cloth for it to climb. Then she shook the cloth out the hillside window, intentionally freeing it! He'd misjudged when he said she was no witch.

Satisfied with the tidiness she'd wrought, Andi set her broom against the wall and vaulted onto the metal bed. With feet braced apart for balance, she reached overhead. The boyish breeches cupped her buttocks in a way they would never have fit a male. Her blue shirt lifted to show the satin channel of her spine. Then the mattress tipped off the beams.

"Lily cat, get out of the way! Get—!" With stubborn insistence, Andi clutched at the mattress as it took her over backward.

He could catch the falling mattress or the girl. Kit's decision didn't take a particle of the concentration he needed to materialize.

One arm snared Andi's middle as her feet slipped forward and the back of her head slammed his face. In another time, his nose would have bled like a cut ox.

Though his rearward, stuttering steps were undignified, he kept them both upright. Andi's back slanted across his chest. The flesh at her middle resonated with a heat he'd forgotten. He set her on her feet, away from him, but didn't release her. She showed no eagerness to escape.

His fingers made dusky shadows, indenting the flesh on each side of her waist. He felt her warmth.

Why not take her now? Lust unfurled in his belly. Even if he'd imagined the sensation of softness and warmth, he'd vowed to bed her before vanishing with his heart. *Why not now?* She faced away from him, her stillness an invitation. Any moment, she would gaze back over her shoulder, meeting his eyes with a doe's silent eloquence.

Her fingers manacled his wrists and removed his hands from her waist. With emphasis.

"Thanks." Andi faced him. "I'm pretty clumsy."

For the first time, Kit noticed the freckles marring her ivory skin. "Knowing that, whyever would you chance such an unwieldy burden?"

Her shoulders bunched at his jest and her eyes focused somewhere between his shoulder and ear.

"I didn't hear you come up."

"You were admiring your handiwork."

"And . . . ?" Now her humor returned. Andi raised both brows and lifted her hands, palms up.

"And?" He repeated, at a loss.

"And, it looks wonderful," she suggested, rotating one hand like a wheel gaining speed.

It did not look bloody "wonderful." A gentlewoman's cushioned chamber looked wonderful. This looked acceptable. For a monk's cell. But the wench prattled on.

"And, I've whipped it into such great shape you couldn't possibly pay such paltry rent. And, in appreciation, you'd love to take me out for a cappuccino."

"No." By the Virgin, he would not ask the meaning of *cappuccino*. Hadn't he heard of a tropical monkey of that breed? Did her penchant for odd creatures extend beyond spiders?

And why had she suddenly bitten her lip?

Guilt flickered amid his lust, but it was quickly doused. Never had he wished to leave his mark on a woman, but he'd felt growling satisfaction at his fingerprints fading on her waist. And those toothmarks vanishing from her nether lip. What if he'd left them?

For four hundred years, sex had been a parlor game, a challenge of staying solid long enough to pleasure a wench though he felt no sensation on his skin, because his flesh was illusion. He'd tried to dismiss yesterday's reaction to her handshake as imagination, a buzzing in his brain, and no more. But he had felt her curving waist and he ached to feel more. 'Zounds, why her and why now?

"Want to help me carry this thing outside so we can beat the dust out of it?" Andi feinted a kick toward the mattress.

"Why would I want to do that?"

"Gee, I don't know. To make good on that charming English accent?'' Andi bent, hefted one corner, and slogged like a beast of burden toward the stairs. ''To prove chivalry's death throes have been exaggerated?''

Damning himself with curses old and new, Kit brushed Andi aside, dragged the mattress downstairs and into the yard below. He didn't understand half of what she'd said.

Trifle shied as if he hauled a monster. She capered sideways and swiveled her heels in a kick. Summer warmth hovered over the paddock dirt. A magpie flashed an indigo-streaked wing as it deserted a pile of horse droppings.

Andi's retort had sounded half complimentary, half disappointed. To feel disappointment, she must have high expectations. Perhaps he'd bed her today, after all.

With a distinct lack of logic, she beat the mattress with her filthy broom. Noon sun fired her hair into unseemly brightness. She stood back and rubbed her cheek, making a smear of gray dust.

Kit glanced around. By the scuff of sandpaper, he could tell that Cisco and Rick had moved their ladders to labor over the front shutters. In this backyard of deep grass and hedgerow, Kit and Andi were alone.

He approached her with a menacing mien. She stood firm. He thought again what a warrior she might have made, then blamed his idiocy on years of peace.

He lifted the mattress, filling his arms so they wouldn't embrace her, but his eyes still searched hers. She didn't fear him, didn't—alas!—want him. She studied him with the worst sort of curiosity

''Charming English accent,'' she'd said. Clearly that was flattery. The mattress wobbled and he tightened his grip, pondering how a man ''made good'' on charm? He carried the mattress back toward the barn, mounted the stairs, and left the dust-smudged ragamuffin behind.

His interest in her was carnal. He didn't give a fig for her flattery, or her disappointment.

He pitched the mattress upon the metal cot frame and lay down upon it. A sunbeam slipped through the roof's shingles overhead as he recalled this morning.

This morning, the secret staircase had muffled her words.

He couldn't make out her meaning, but her tone was lush. It put him in mind of an Oriental carpet patterned in crimson and azure. It recalled a pear with blushing golden skin, sitting in a dish of pewter. None of the images matched her milk-maid appearance.

Kit closed his eyes against the vision of Miranda Fairfield and her eyes of Swanfort blue. He'd find that box tonight, take his heart, and embrace the afterlife he'd earned, regard-less—

What if, after all, *this* was it?

Kit swallowed a sardonic laugh. Gad, what if he'd weath-ered hundreds of years in limbo, only to land in this fresh hell devised by Satan himself? What if Black Ned sat back, chortling and smoldering, even now, at a ghost haunted by a mortal woman?

Chapter Three

Most people would consider it impossible to get lost in a town with one main street. Andi lifted her foot off the gas pedal, listened to cicadas chirring in the heat, and wished the road weren't too narrow for a U-turn. It was—and flanked by thorny pyracantha bushes, too. She had no choice but to drive the half mile to the driveway up ahead, then back out. How fortunate that half a dozen bare-torsoed men had turned out to watch.

They'd take her for a tourist. A dumb one, since a single road left Sacramento and lanced straight through Owen to Sparrowgrass. There, a driver turned right to bounce along the dirt road that dead-ended at Heart's Ease. Only volunteer firefighters turned left.

With the Volkswagen slowed to a crawl, she got a good look at the volunteer crew. Goodness. Andi briefly considered playing with matches, then told herself to knock it off. She'd made this wrong turn while considering similar self-indulgence.

To escape Kit's indifference, she'd awarded herself a cappuccino. She *deserved* a mimosa, but buying orange juice and champagne at Brown's grocery would stir up gossip. Aunt Dinah always claimed that if you didn't know what to make of your neighbors, you had only to ask Gina Brown.

Indulging an appetite for store-brewed coffee was bad enough, but champagne? It was just what Sparrowgrass old-timers expected of city girls. They couldn't guess that Andi Fairfield's deadliest vice was romance.

Kit didn't like her. He'd called her clumsy. He'd recoiled as if helping her was beneath him. He'd snubbed her suggestion that they go out for a cup of coffee even though he'd dressed again in Renaissance costume, clearly bound for the last day of the fair. Just what was it she found attractive about him?

Not his permanent frown. Not the bearded jaw set hard against the world, nor the shadowy eyes that brightened only with skepticism.

Why did she imagine she could change that?

Andi pounded the heel of her hand against the steering wheel. As if a deaf cat, an old horse, a ramshackle estate, and a sordid past weren't trouble enough, she wanted to play emotional missionary to a world-weary Englishman. And what happened when he learned the truth? Sooner or later someone would get a phone call from Los Padres, or a fax. Modern technology meant juicy gossip was only a computer click away.

Kit's sarcasm was already honed killing-sharp. She didn't want it turned against her.

Even when he'd touched her—okay, *caught* her—during her dance with the falling mattress, she'd sensed a barrier between them. He could be somebody's runaway husband or a gentleman thief.

As her front wheels hit the lip of the driveway, the shirtless men polishing an already gleaming fire engine turned their eyes away from an extension ladder which rose with mechanical precision toward the sky.

The VW's engine died at the same time a parti-colored Great Dane loped down the driveway with a thunderous "woof."

Perfect. Andi turned the key and restarted the engine as

the dog's black-and-white muzzle entered her open window.

"Gertrude!" A tanned man, red hair silvered at the temples, grabbed the dog's collar. "Sorry. She wants to be the firehouse Dalmatian."

"Aren't they a lot smaller?"

"Gertrude has a warped self-image." As his head tilted toward the Volkswagen's engine compartment, Andi noticed it was a swarm of freckles that made his face appear brown. He smiled. "Need directions?"

"No, I just moved back into town." Andi jiggled the gearshift. Reverse vanished as the men moved toward her. "I took a wrong turn looking for a shortcut."

"You must be Dinah's niece," he said. As his voice faded under the others, Andi thanked the silent voice of propriety for making her wear white jeans and a black T-shirt with turquoise beads instead of a tank top and shorts. She hid behind her sunglasses and tried to follow the comments of guys set on checking out the new female in town.

"Aren't you a teacher in Los Padres?"

"Hey, that back road you wanted? Out of your driveway, turn right next time, left looks right, but it's not."

"You know, I was out past your place the other day and you ought to cut the brush back from around the house—"

"At least you've got composition shingles—"

"Those blasted wooden shakes on the old place down the road will catch like kindling—"

"You'd be in a fine fix if we had to bring an engine down there." A balding man in overalls pointed a bony finger. "With just the one road in, you'd be trapped."

Gertrude's freckle-faced master winked, sympathizing over the meddling nature of small towns. Gertrude slurped a washcloth-size tongue across Andi's cheek.

"I'll take all that into consideration." The Volkswagen finally slipped into gear. "Thanks!" Lurching down the road, she nearly missed her turn again. Not from scrubbing at her sloppy cheek but from gawking.

A couple passed in a flash. Andi kept her foot on the accelerator. She might have imagined a woman arched into a tangoesque backbend in the shade of the cottonwood tree while a man gripped the thigh around his waist. For sure, though, she'd seen a tipped trash can, ripped garbage bags, and dozens of beer cans.

Andi checked her rearview mirror. A wooden sign on chains identified the Hangin' Tree Bar, the one place in town the cousins had been forbidden to explore.

An arm-thick rope dangled from the cottonwood and a plaque labeled it the site of a 1901 vigilante hanging. In two generations, it became the toughest dare in town to swing back and forth on the rope until you had the momentum to kick the bar's back door. Then you dropped, rolled, scrambled upright, and fled before the bartender opened the door and yelled.

If you made it as far as the air-conditioned lobby of the Crest Theatre and had a witness to prove your bravery, you were guaranteed summer stardom.

In Andi's fourteenth summer, the day before Clint Kern died, he'd witnessed her daring. Had Clint had a chance to tell his mom they'd celebrated by splitting a red Nehi soda at the Crest?

Main Street was clogged with Renaissance Faire–goers. As traffic inched forward, Andi noticed the Crest marquee was gone. Burned, Jan had said, but Andi recognized Wolcott's Hardware and Feed as the old five-and-dime with a new name. Three women in high heels and Sunday dresses stood talking near an old iron hitching post. Wolcott's would probably have the fertilizer she needed to start her compost pile.

Two trucks stopped in the middle of the street while their drivers talked. The silver Toyota throbbed with music that was all bass, and the Suburban in front of Andi was packed with kids.

Andi rocked in her seat as tourists wearing shorts and cameras slipped between the Suburban and her front bumper. The Suburban's back window was opaque with gummy handprints.

"I just want a lousy cup of coffee."

She loved Heart's Ease and hated the thought of selling it, but right now she'd swap ten minutes of rustic peace for a freeway and drive-through espresso.

Andi glanced toward one end of the field where the Renaissance Faire was in full swing and spotted a log house. New or newly restored, it bore a sign announcing DR. NOAH LINCOLN. She couldn't tell if he was a veterinarian or a physician.

"Shoot!"

The Suburban had driven down the block and angled into the single slot in front of the Dancing Goat, Jan's shop. Andi slowed, took in the river-rock store with its front-door portrait of a joyous goat festooned with flowers and ribbons, and smiled.

After walking three blocks back to the Dancing Goat, Andi's cheeks ached. She'd smiled at everyone who claimed to recognize her from childhood or Jason's funeral. Only Gina Brown, whom Andi recognized by her crown of silver braids, hadn't spoken. She'd glanced up, then gone back to sweeping the walk in front of her grocery. When Andi looked back, Gina had been staring after her, tapping her temple with an index finger, no doubt trying to recall Andi's transgressions.

A troubadour sipping iced coffee and balancing a lute held the door for Andi to enter the Dancing Goat. She had a full minute to appreciate the remodelling of the Crest's lobby.

The aroma of fresh bread and coffee mingled with greenery and roses. Mismatched wooden tables and chairs cluttered the space between the door and a chrome counter in the rear, where Jan's gleaming brown pageboy bent over a cash register. A blackboard listed Hot Cross Buns as today's special. Portraits of Dancing Goat classics—Hangtown honey buns, focaccia, and coffee—were hand-painted on the walls and framed with scrap lumber. Yellow roses filled odd containers ranging from a copper teakettle to a polished cowboy boot.

"Wow, Jan, this is—"

Tapping footfalls heralded a child with chocolate-smeared hands. He grabbed Andi's knee and swung around her leg as if it were a flagpole. His poufy-skirted twin followed, patent leather mary janes rapping each of Andi's toes.

"Cami, Cody, get back upstairs!" Jan ordered. "Melissa, I thought you—"

"Sorry, Aunt Jan." A teenager with wheat-colored hair rolled her eyes as she shambled down the staircase. "I was just trying to change and they—" Aghast, she stared at Andi's jeans and turned professional. "I'm so sorry. What were you going to have? Dancing Goat would be glad to serve it to you, on the house."

Jan came out from behind the counter, scooped up the twins, and balanced one on each hip. "It's okay, Melissa. This is Andi Fairfield. She's here for the summer, and even though you two haven't met, she's practically family."

While Jan scolded the twins, Andi mustered a smile for Melissa, but she felt sick, wondering where Melissa fit on Clint's family tree. Had she been deprived of a brother? A cousin?

Jan set the twins on their feet. The dark-haired, rosy-cheeked imps couldn't be more than two years old, whereas Jan must be nearing forty. The Kerns were known for embracing even the inconvenient aspects of their religion.

Jan pointed at the stairs and patted the twins' diapered bottoms. "You two stay up there and mind Melissa. Do you hear me?" With feigned chagrin, they trudged upstairs. They broke into a run as Jan turned to Melissa. "Where'd they get the chocolate?"

Melissa shrugged and followed.

"Which one of you urchins ate my eclair?" Blake Kern knotted an obi at her jumpsuit waist as she passed the stampeding twins.

"Not me, Mom." Melissa held up denying hands.

Blake smiled and tousled her daughter's hair in passing.

If Jan was wide-hipped Juno, Blake was Pan. No more than five feet tall, she wore aggressively short, unstyled hair, which managed to show off great bone structure untouched by makeup. She was exactly the sort of woman who kept eclairs at hand, yet never gained an ounce. Blake had been that way since they'd gobbled candy hearts and jelly beans in first grade. She'd stayed that way through the summers they spent together after Andi's family had moved to Los Padres.

Blake stopped on the bottom step.

"Well, Miranda Fairfield. It *was* you in my rearview mirror." She reached out to clasp both of Andi's hands.

Had Blake changed? Andi remembered her parents' excusing Blake's neglect of their old friendship as a symptom of grief, until Blake's scorn had turned ugly.

One Christmas they'd met in front of Brown's grocery. Andi could still feel her hopeful smile snuffed by Blake's muttered "You had my nephew thinking with his hormones instead of his head—a real femme fatale." Andi wondered how long she'd stood there, clutching a carton of eggnog against her chest.

"It was me." Andi squeezed Blake's hands and stepped back. "You look great. What have you been up to?"

The routine inquiry left her tongue before she remembered Blake's bitter divorce. Blake endured the remark with tact and a shrug.

"How far away did you have to park?" Blake slid behind the counter and drew a glass of plain soda.

"A couple of blocks." Andi breathed deliberately. Blake *had* changed, and Andi longed to mend their friendship. "But the exercise is good for me. I haven't run a step since I got here."

"Hauling around all that guilt's got to be good for burning a couple hundred calories a day."

"Blake!" Jan gasped. "You knock that off!"

A wave of light-headedness drowned Andi's hope.

"Sorry." Blake forked fingers through her hair, raising a coxcomb. "I'm sorry, honey."

Andi shrugged and feigned interest in the chocolate smeared on her jeans.

"Fat lot of good Mass did me." Blake grimaced.

"Don't go blaming the church," Jan scolded. "At twenty-six, you should've outgrown that misery-loves-company mentality. And, if you'll pardon me, Andi, you shouldn't be so sensitive. Not that it's your fault. Your parents should have kept bringing you back every summer to face this 'guilt.'

"Because *I* had to face it every day," Jan said, repositioning an African violet near the cash register, "I finally figured out it was an accident. An *accident*." Despite her words, tears stood in her eyes as she cleared her throat.

Blake gestured toward the array of coffee beans and machinery behind her. "Do your worst, Andi. I'm buying."

"A double cappuccino would go a long way toward regaining my good graces," Andi managed, but she wanted to duck away from Jan's motherly arm. She wanted to run.

"Blake's husband called this morning," Jan whispered, giving Andi a parting squeeze as she advanced on a nearby table and pinched a brown leaf off a philodendron.

"*Ex*-husband." Blake's hiss mingled with a plume of steam from the espresso machine. "He left the church, me, *and* the kids, for a nineteen-year-old bimbo with pierced nipples."

Andi made an involuntary grab at her chest. "Ow," she said, then took the proffered cup of coffee.

"You know what he told me? 'Piercing stimulates erogenous zones.' " Blake wiped the cream steamer with vicious swipes. "This from a man who, in ten years of marriage, never indicated he'd ever *heard* of—" Blake's fury froze. She flicked the towel and nodded past Andi's shoulder. "Hi, Gina. What can I get for you?"

"You know, dear, a cup of Constant Comment. A tea bag, no fancy loose tea." Gina Brown's ladylike dresses and powdery perfume indicated a traditional grandmother, but her gray eyes would suit a fighter pilot. "And one of your Hot Cross Buns."

"Coming up," Blake said.

"Miranda, I haven't seen you since the funeral." Gina straightened her lace collar.

Andi didn't say it had only been four days or that she'd just passed Gina on the sidewalk.

"I mean to *talk* to," Gina added.

"Is your column in the paper today, Gina?" Jan interrupted. "I meant to show Andi that Sparrowgrass has its own correspondent to the *Owen Canyon Times*.'' Behind Gina's back, Jan mouthed an incomprehensible message, then carried a flat of seedlings away from the sunny front window.

"Only on Fridays." Gina carried her tea to a table and motioned Andi to a chair.

"The column's called 'Hangtown Tattletale,' right?" Blake asked.

" 'Tattler.' " Gina bobbed her tea bag. "The paper titled it."

Andi settled on a blue stool, blew across the foam on her coffee, and scalded her tongue with the first sip.

"I hear you have a gentleman friend staying in Dinah's carriage house."

Children's feet stampeded overhead. Andi felt the warmth of three stares. Then a shadow crossed the window and shaded her with an odd sense of relief.

"Actually, he's a total stranger."

June sun danced on the gold shoulder stitching of Kit's black doublet. How she knew it was he, since the dark figure framed in the Dancing Goat's window turned to watch the festival across the street, Andi couldn't say.

"A nice enough stranger," Andi lowered her voice. "A British writer suffering from writer's block."

"Ohh?" As Gina's tone ascended, she garroted the last drop of liquid from her tea bag. "Poor man."

"It seemed like the neighborly thing to do and an opportunity to make a little extra money for Aunt Dinah."

Neighborliness and Dinah were indisputable icons. Even Gina gave a grudging nod.

Outside, Kit shaded his eyes, looking down the street. In profile, he reminded Andi of textbook sketches of Sir Walter Raleigh, explorer, pirate, Queen Elizabeth's suitor . . .

"It's a good thing to have a man on the grounds." Gina tapped the table to draw Andi's attention. "We've had our share of trouble lately, and a woman alone can't be too careful." Gina craned her neck to see what was keeping her Hot Cross Bun.

"Rick's helping out." Jan wielded a watering can over her seedlings.

"Temporarily." Andi thought of Rick fidgeting in her

early-morning kitchen. If salsa made him squeamish, she didn't want him defending her against burglars.

"Friend to widows and orphans everywhere." Blake placed Gina's pastry next to her tea.

"Now, Blake Kern, Rick has been a helpful soul since he was a boy." Gina adjusted the doily beneath her roll. "Why, he was only a teenager when Sadie Williams got down with that broken hip. We all should have done more, but Rick was the one who did."

"Out of the goodness of his heart, I'm sure," Blake said, then her eyes followed Kit as he paced in front of the store.

"He deserved that cabin she left him," Gina insisted. "Your old place, Miranda, down the road from Heart's Ease . . ."

Andi remembered how the cousins had leapt the brook, then sprinted through the dark woods to visit Sadie in "the Williams place," a cabin Andi's parents had shared before she was born.

". . . how he helped the Smiths when this theater burned and they lost that archive of valuable old films! And look how he befriended Jason and your own nephew." Gina issued a last *tsk* at Blake before shifting her attention. "Miranda, is your writer a helpful soul?"

"I'm not sure. 'My writer' is sort of a recluse."

Kit couldn't have heard, but he wheeled toward the window, face grim above his snowy ruff, black mustache bracketing a frown that brought Andi to her feet.

"What's *his* problem?" Blake stood with one hand on her hip, Gina pressed against her chair's ladder back, and Jan set her watering can on a table.

"As a matter of fact, that's my boarder." Andi strode to the door. "What if I ask him inside to meet all of you?"

Bloody hell. Kit Gallatin sweltered under the dreadful California sun, longing for a dank and lonely grave. Ending this instinct to safeguard certain mortals would be the best part of eternal rest. Alive, he'd defended no one but himself. And his younger brother, Barrett, of course. In afterlife, he'd fretted over fragile Sarah, gently reared and stranded in a heathen land. But Sarah had needed him. *This* flushed and hearty wench, swinging out of the tea shop doorway with her braid over one shoulder, needed no champion.

A strand of turquoise pebbles hung around her neck and swayed across her bosom as she summoned him. "Kit!"

In all the centuries of his life and death, had any woman called him so? No, he was sure not. Mother, Arabella, and Sarah had all called him Christopher. Comrades-in-arms and fellow pub fighters had yelled for "Kit," but they were four hundred years dead. The wench set herself amid odd company.

"Please." Childishly, she tugged his arm until he followed. "Come inside and convince these ladies that you're a hardworking writer with no designs on my virtue."

Would that it were so. But he couldn't keep his fancy from offering portraits of her sprawled on his cot, painted with slants of sunlight spilling through the roof onto her just-conquered flesh. The image struck him speechless.

"Kit Gallatin, this is Gina Brown."

He awarded the old woman a nod.

"And Jan Kern, and her sister, Blake."

"Ladies." He bowed over each hand. One smelled of earth and greenery. That would be Jan, whose hair curved like the locks of a Court page. The other hand was scented with pastry crumbs and doubt.

Blake scrutinized him with raised eyebrows. "May I get you some tea, Mr. Gallatin? Or coffee?"

"Thank you, no." Pretending to consume food or drink galled him when it smelled this appealing.

"A writer," Jan mused. "I didn't know the carriage house had power."

"And if Jason wired it, it'll blow Heart's Ease's fuses, then knock out your hard drive." Blake frowned. "If I were writing a book, I wouldn't risk it."

"Precisely why I've come to town for paper and ink." Kit touched the leather bag knotted at his belt.

Picking pockets was no more a thing of the past than dishonesty. He'd caught two cutpurses working the holiday crowd. With a nimble touch, he'd filched the money, returned it to fools who never knew they'd been robbed, and kept a small commission. After all, he must purchase food, clothing, books, and shaving gear, all the trappings of this indulgent society. And he must pretend to use them, until he found the Graveyard Rose.

"All right, Andi," Blake winked. "You can keep him."

As if he were a mongrel pup! Ire bristled along Kit's spine as the jesting grew worse.

"He looks safe enough." Jan gathered plates from a littered table. Kit presumed she didn't see his fury. Miranda had no such excuse.

"Harmless"—her lips barely parted from the blue-gray cup—"as a fly." Her eyes taunted him over its rim.

If night had shrouded the streets or fog choked a nearby alley, he would have rushed her outside, taken her to the wall, and made her withdraw that "harmless."

Alas, the sun shone. That old betrayer made him wait, but when Kit Gallatin got his revenge, oh, how he'd enjoy it.

Andi avoided potholes and steered the Volkswagen around rocks studding the dirt road which led to Heart's Ease. Jeans and button-front shirts, boots and T-shirts advertising Walcott's Hardware and Feed were mounded on the passenger seat beneath notebooks, yellow pencils, and paper bags full of fruit.

Kit had welcomed shopping help, spending a small fortune on the items she suggested, but she'd felt his anger all afternoon. Even after his glare subsided, Andi was careful to keep their hands from bumping, their elbows from touching. They'd walked from the Dancing Goat to Wolcott's to Brown's grocery in silence grown brittle, as if they were braced for a quarrel.

Andi steadied a sack of oranges before they avalanched to the floor mats. Kit had accepted transport for his purchases, but he'd edged away from her car as if he sensed something malevolent. He refused a ride, insisting he needed the walk home.

He *had* said "home." Andi smiled, then realized the front gate stood open. The five-pound sack of fertilizer, destined for her compost pile, slid off the backseat as she braked. She'd asked Rick and Cisco to keep the gate latched.

Whiskers twitching, Lily greeted Andi and considered the Volkswagen's aroma.

"I agree," Andi told the cat. "But if it's all the same to you, I'll get this stuff out"—she lifted Kit's purchases—"before I see if it's sprung a leak that's filling my car with manure."

Clearly insulted, Lily batted a stone between her front paws, then twitched her tail and preceded Andi to the house.

Rick had folded his ladder and gone, and there was no sign of Cisco. They'd sanded the red shutters and window frames down to pinkish brown and left the smells of sandpaper and paint dust mixing with that of cooling grasses. Though the five o'clock sun still shone, the house sat in the loneliness of dusk.

Something moved at the upstairs window.

Andi dropped a bundle of pencils and retrieved it. When she looked up again at Jason and Dinah's room, there was nothing. Maybe one of the swallows, winging through the air to a nest under the eaves, had caught her eye.

Instead of bringing Kit's parcels inside, she detoured around the house, through the back gate, to the barn. Lily sat on a fencepost, tail curled around her feet. Trifle followed along the fence, head bobbing as she snorted in hunger or greeting.

New to the landlord business, Andi figured it would be less invasive to leave Kit's purchases at the foot of the stairs. Arms free, she paused next to the corral to glance up at the curtains billowing from her bedroom window. She should have Rick hang some screens. Anyone with a ladder could bypass the front door and let themselves inside.

Andi staggered a step as Trifle nudged her shoulder.

"Watch it!" Unruffled, the white mare swished her tail, blinked huge brown eyes, and extended her muzzle for a pat. "Oh, all right." Andi touched a finger to the thin skin between the horse's nostrils. It felt like velvet. "But don't think this means anything."

Trifle blew through her lips and leaned forward into a

doze. As a swallow dove past, toward the stream, Andi squared her shoulders. What had she noticed which made her reluctant to enter the house?

"Quit stalling, Fairfield."

Lily leapt down and followed at Andi's heels, until Andi stood in the middle of the yard. She cinched her arms around her waist and stared up.

She *had* noticed something. Eyes narrowed, Andi tapped her foot. Then she saw it.

Chapter
Four

Late that night, Kit eased open the lid of a quilted window seat, taking care the hinges didn't squeak. *Firewood. Drat!*

He understood why Andi was disturbed. In her absence her home had been disfigured.

Kit lifted the cushion from a sea-green chair as he mused that though the house hadn't been marred permanently, Andi viewed it as an assault.

Atop the chair, he placed three couch cushions, then slid his hand over the exposed areas. Nothing.

Dropping to his knees, Kit lifted the chair's skirt. He peered into darkness marked off by wooden legs and felt the bottom of the furniture, in case she'd taped the box in place above the floor.

Kit did not comprehend his own anger, since the vandal—assuredly Cisco—had not damaged or stolen the Graveyard Rose. In the clumsy way of young males, he'd rubbed off some ornate lettering of the house's name and made one sloppy addition to leave his crude message.

Squatting, Kit parted the fireplace screen and peered up the chimney, but his mind's eye sent back a memory of the space under the house eaves. "He r asS," Cisco's creation had said.

Kit blinked the image away. Brushing soot from his fingers, he considered a gilt-framed landscape hanging above the couch. It hung quite flat, and yet there might be a cavity behind it, deep enough to harbor his heart.

Of course, there wasn't.

Arms spread wide, he gripped the frame and positioned the wire stretched across the back of the painting into place above the hook. Then he remembered Andi's stiffness as she'd entered the house, the slowness with which she'd opened a can and heated soup. Sitting at one end of the long wooden table, she hadn't protested when the white cat leapt onto the tablecloth, then ate 'til her belly swung with each lapping.

What of it? With that demand, his grip loosened and the painting's corner slammed the wall. Bedsprings squeaked overhead and something hit the floor. Kit cursed. So what if he'd given Miranda a scare? In the end, he would find his heart and vanish. Better for both of them if the end came tonight.

What if she crept downstairs to discover that Kit Gallatin the writer was a housebreaker? His specter's affliction made it impossible for him to move things while invisible. Ghosthood had not been planned for the convenience of the ghost.

He strode past the kitchen. Since the clashing and clanging of pots would bring her running, he would search there later. Just now, promise flickered behind a closed door off the main room. Gripping it with the whole of his hand, to muffle sound, he turned the doorknob right and pulled. Left, and pulled. He lifted it, jiggled it. Still nothing.

Locked! Marry, that boded well for his search.

Outside, the mare nickered, and Kit wondered who she greeted.

Then he caught a patter of cat's paws on the stair. Kit leaned through the locked door into a gentleman's study. Even his blunted senses twitched. The male resident had fouled the room with years of tobacco. No wonder the den was kept locked.

Last night, during his basement search, he'd come upon a cluster of keys hung on hooks beneath crossed swords, but he had no need of a key. The stair tread squeaked once more, and Kit grimaced as he stepped through the oaken door.

Andi threw her book against the wall. Bestseller list or not, the author was a fraud. The heroine's husband, father, and dog had perished and Andi did not care. When she'd found herself wishing a piano would plummet from the sky and put the never-say-die twit out of her misery, Andi surrendered.

The clock said 3:14.

Storming into the house after her first glimpse of the graffiti, she'd nearly sprained her index finger punching in Jan's telephone number, then hung up before it rang. She'd paced laps between the great room and the kitchen, hit Redial, drew breath to tell Jan her son, Cisco, was an out-of-control punk, then slammed down the receiver

By midnight, she'd removed the child-induced smear from her white pants, working with such energy that she might have scrubbed a hole in them. She told herself she should jog a few miles to blow off steam, then called herself a coward because she hadn't. She'd tasted tepid soup, sorted through Dinah's stack of home-and-garden magazines, and considered driving home to Los Padres. Finally, she'd eaten the chocolate eclairs Blake had forced on her.

Now, Andi ground the heels of her hands against her eyes. The chocolate had pushed her over the edge. By the time she crawled into bed, she'd sunk into a bog of self-pity. Her eyes felt gritty with old tears.

Lily had curled up on her bed at about two o'clock. Too lazy to retrieve the paperback she'd left on the veranda, Andi had snagged this glossy hardcover from behind an arrangement of dried flowers.

The first time her attention wandered, she'd imagined the door harp's trill, then dismissed the sound as Lily's purr. Still, she'd wished the only telephone weren't downstairs.

A squeak came next, and a puff, like something soft hitting the floor. If she dialed 911, where would it ring? Owen

Canyon, twenty miles away? Sacramento? She'd sat with her spine against the headboard, knees tucked under her night-gown, listening and wishing Lily's ears would twitch to con-firm the sounds. Deaf Lily slumbered on, with breathy feline snores.

For another half hour, Andi subjected herself to the book. Then Lily sprang awake and fixed her eyes on the doorway.

"What do you think, kitty?"

Lily quaked with focused attention, then vaulted off the bed.

"Wait for me." Andi swung her bare feet to the floor and scanned the bedroom for a weapon. Not that she needed one. After teaching high school for three years, she recognized a mean-spirited adolescent prank.

She snagged a flashlight from beneath the bed. Because of the unreliable wiring, Dinah stashed one in every room.

If Cisco planned to scare her with a creepy-crawly through Heart's Ease, the little jerk was in for a surprise. Ms. Fair-field's "teacher voice" could make varsity linebackers wet their pants.

At the head of the stairs, Andi depressed the flashlight's On button. Nothing happened. Could she shake some life into the batteries? As she tried, a doorknob turned down-stairs.

Oh, hell. Andi took a step down and stopped, toes curled against the bare wood. What if it wasn't Cisco? Jan had mentioned burglaries. So had Gina. By now, everyone in town knew she lived alone.

She'd craved self-sufficiency. No giddy highs, no leaden lows. No safety, either.

A doorknob had turned, but to which downstairs room? The kitchen flowed off the great room. The veranda opened off of that, through a sliding glass door. Jason's study door was closed, but locked. The only key hung on the basement wall.

With cold fingers, Andi gripped the flashlight like a base-ball bat and crept toward the office. A gasp blocked her throat as she caught movement at the window, then recog-nized her own reflection.

The sight reminded her she wasn't alone. Downstairs windows stood open to the summer breeze. If she screamed, Kit would come running. Wouldn't he?

Lily paced in a grapevine step outside the office door. The metallic rasp of a file drawer convinced Andi that Cisco had somehow broken in. But why? Andi rushed toward the kitchen telephone. Let him tell it to the police.

Then the rustling stopped and she felt a pulse of compassion. She'd contributed to this kid's messed-up mind. Must she give him a police record too?

"Cisco? Get your butt out here." Andi's voice boomed with authority. "If I have to call your mom, you are going to be *so* grounded." Andi gave the doorknob a twist, but Cisco had locked it from inside. "Okay, time's up. I'm calling the cops."

Yowling, Lily shot back from the door. Andi grappled along the hall wall. Light. Where was the damned switch? Her fingers skittered over rough knuckles before something slammed her to the wall.

A concussion shook her. Could a bomb be silent? No sulfurous cloud rolled down the hall, but warmth seeped through her nightgown. No flames consumed the air, but weight forced her ribs inward and breath fanned her cheek.

Amid the shadows, she saw nothing. No Cisco, no explosion, no intruder set on rape. Andi closed her eyes. Black and gold swirled behind her eyelids. Sightless, it all made sense. A hallucination couldn't flatten her back to the wall or graze her lips so gently.

"Kit?" Recognition scratched her nerves, but she didn't understand it. As the flashlight hit the floor, Andi struggled. "Kit!"

The weight lifted. She pushed off from the wall and darted to the end table that held the phone.

Dial 911. Panting too hard to talk, but they can still trace the call. Just dial.

"Wait, *wait*." She broke the connection, keeping the receiver clapped to her ear. What could she say since there was no one there?

It wouldn't matter. A levelheaded officer would survey the

premises and ask if a window stood open in Jason's locked office. Probably it did. He'd ask if a breeze could've ruffled papers inside. Probably it could.

If she told him about the rasping file drawer, he'd mention the copper rain gutter shifting in the wind, then suggest that for her own peace of mind, she ask someone to stay with her.

"No." Andi hung up the phone. She already had a weird reputation. She wouldn't add to it. "Okay." She held her hands out from her sides, as if balancing. "I was probably sleepwalking."

Just because she'd never sleepwalked before didn't mean she couldn't. She switched on the kitchen light and thought of coffee. It was almost dawn. She put the kettle on, ground some coffee beans, then walked back into the great room and waited for some explanation to occur to her.

The kitchen's light outlined the couch, green velvet chairs, the coffee table and phone. Rosencrantz and Guildenstern hung motionless in their bowl on the mantel.

Andi relaxed one shoulder, then the other. While she tried to unravel this nonsense, she really should get the key from the basement and check the office.

Maybe she'd wait until daylight.

She glanced toward the east-facing window. Her reflection surprised her again, but this time eyes glimmered back amid her gown's whiteness.

As her hand jerked up to cover her mouth, a hump of darkness dropped below the window frame.

The snap and rustle of weeds carried through the open window. Trifle uttered a sleepy neigh, then bolted. Andi heard the mare's chest hit the fence.

This time she gripped the phone hard, waited for an operator, and asked the Owen Canyon sheriff's office to send someone out to take a look around.

That kiss.

Her lips had parted for him. He'd felt their welcome and their warmth.

Kit couldn't climb the steps to her veranda, couldn't answer her call for help, couldn't stay corporeal until he dispelled this awe. He tightened his fists, set his jaw so hard his skull creaked. Except—he had no skull. Such logic did nothing to banish that kiss.

He'd meant to frighten her, knowing bloody well he couldn't pull her to him, couldn't mold her mouth to his, not while he was invisible. It had been her doing. And he'd felt a trace of what it was like to be touched by a woman. He'd stood near and somehow, *she* had drawn him in. As if he were life-sustaining breath.

Kit considered the graying sky and a sprinkling of stars living out their last minutes before dawn.

God's truth, he'd meant to stop.

Miranda. The name strummed like lute strings, reminding him of a truth just out of reach.

Miranda was no beauty. Her cheeks were tinted by too much sun and her hands gestured ceaselessly. She was no lady, entitled to his chivalry. It must not matter that he'd failed to respond when she called for his help.

Kit's spirit swirled down into the dark ravine. He counted himself dashed lucky that no one stood near enough to hear his sigh.

Dinah would have a terrible time selling Heart's Ease if Andi broke her neck falling from the upstairs window, so she clung to the window frame with one hand and daubed a wet paintbrush on Cisco's handiwork with the other.

As dawn broke, her arm muscles twitched. She'd almost finished her touch-up work when a truck growled down her dirt road. The huff of air brakes at her gate signaled the arrival of the volunteer fire department. Without sirens.

Andi thought of the noisy, crowded *efficiency* of cities. In Los Padres, a fire engine wouldn't respond—an hour later— to a report of an intruder.

"Hey, there, honeybunch, you're not planning to jump, are you?" A tie, pressed shirt, and dress slacks created such a disguise that it took the Great Dane, leaping from the truck like a cow over the moon, to tip Andi off.

The freckled fireman who'd been so friendly yesterday leaned against the hood of the fire engine.

"Miranda, I'm Noah. Y'all called Owen Canyon for help?" His arms crossed loosely at his waist. His drawl seemed more pronounced, his kindness more deliberate, than it had yesterday.

"I called the sheriff, not the VFD. I had a prowler." She released her grip on the frame and eased back inside, placing both palms on the sill.

"That's it." His tone coddled her, as if the step she'd taken away from the ledge, were momentous.

"I called two *hours* ago. If he'd been a chain saw massacre-ist, I'd be sushi by now." A twinge of guilt fled as she rationalized that he'd provoked her sarcasm by treating her like a kindergartner.

"Miranda, why don't you come on down and open the door for me?" He pushed off from the truck and took a slow stride closer.

Suddenly his patience and calm repetition registered. Woman with a history of death, destruction, and guilt calls for help. When help arrives, she's hanging out the upstairs window in her nightie. At least he'd come alone.

"Hey, Noah. I'm not up for suicide. Let me get dressed and I'll explain."

"I won't peek, hon. Meet me at the door. Now."

"Yeah, well, my coffee'll taste better if you have to wait for it." Andi ducked back inside, but not before she saw a tan Suburban bumping down her road.

Reinforcements, damn it, and the Suburban looked familiar. She jogged to her room, sent the nightgown flying, slipped on a cut-off sweatshirt and khaki shorts. A glance at the mirror said she'd better take a minute with her hair, so she wouldn't look like something folks kept locked in the attic.

Outside, tires crunched and a woman's voice mixed with Trifle's neigh. Gertrude the dog loosed a thunderous woof.

Andi took the stairs fast, shaking her head. Double damn. The circus had come to town, and once again Miranda Fairfield was in the center ring.

It turned out Noah Lincoln was not only a volunteer fire-fighter but also the town doctor. And because the Owen Canyon sheriff's office was twenty miles away, he'd been deputized to handle Sparrowgrass's rare law enforcement needs.

He'd been savoring a bagel at the Dancing Goat when the call came to respond to Heart's Ease. Blake had followed in her Suburban.

Watching Noah watch Blake, Andi wondered if he had hopes for a romance. If so, they were doomed. Blake stood, holding a cup of coffee, while Noah sat on a bench, considering a clipboard full of multilayered forms and watching her from the corner of his eye. Blake ignored him as she tried to pin the vandalism and skulking on someone besides her nephew, Cisco.

"You don't want to rule out your new boarder."

At the suggestion, Noah glanced up with a combination of disbelief and pity.

Blake caught his expression and bristled. "As the prowler, at least. As for the—" she gestured. "I said I'd repaint it, whether Cisco did it or not."

"Now, Blake, no one's saying—" Noah began.

"They'll cover it today, anyway. They just started white-washing and they'll be back this afternoon," Andi said. "Don't bother."

"No bother." Blake squeezed Andi's shoulder. "You've got some scrap lumber around, don't you? Let me just letter something for you to nail up there. We've got the fire truck . . ."

"I could run the extension ladders up and hammer it on," Noah agreed. Then he turned back to Andi and his youthful smile faded, leaving him sun-wrinkled and looking every day of forty. "I'm a little concerned about whoever's snooping around. You wouldn't borrow Gertrude, I suppose?"

His concern felt good. Instead of suggesting she'd heard a raccoon or a figment of her imagination, Noah had checked beneath the living room window. He'd found a partial footprint amid the crushed weeds and believed her. Of course, she hadn't mentioned the heavy embrace and phantom kiss. One asked only so much of a white knight.

"Thanks, but no. I feel Lily radiating disapproval right now."

"I figured." Noah stood, pocketing his pen. "Just the same, I'd like to see some screens on these windows, a dead bolt on the door, some kind of rod to block the sliding doors to the back veranda, *and*,"—he raised his voice—"I'm not happy about that basement. I can't quite figure that old crawl space out back."

Blake dismissed Noah's worry with a wave. "You know how Jason was with all his secret stairways and weird passages. That's probably just an entrance that goes nowhere. I swear, Andi, you're probably safer because of them. Any burglar'd get lost. The only people Jason gave guided tours to were the kids."

"Like Cisco." Andi drained the last of her coffee.

"No, but—wait, you're right." Blake brightened. "Cisco must know how to get inside without trying the window."

"Well, someone was in the office." Andi insisted.

"Check to see if anything's been disturbed." Noah moved down the veranda stairs. "If I didn't have office hours starting"—he grimaced at his watch—"twenty minutes ago, I'd poke around, myself.

"Hey, y'all heard there's been a black bear and cub sighted near the brook, right? Watch out for her." Noah leaned one hand against the fire engine. "Since Blake's making you a new sign, I'll give her a ride back out here tonight. C'mon, Gert, that cat's not going to play."

Andi expected Lily's disapproval to be visible, but when she glanced toward the open front door, the cat was dancing on her hind legs, paddling at the air as if reaching for invisible butterflies.

Christ, the girl was a workhorse.

Rick looked down from the ladder and watched Andi swipe the back of her hand at hair straggling loose from her topknot. An hour ago she'd been batting cobwebs down from the rafters over the veranda. Now she smeared dirt and sweat across her temple, adding to the general mess she'd made of herself while kneeling and tending the weed-choked flower beds bordering the house.

He cut in white paint around window frames that he meant to paint barn red. He'd leave the broad expanses to Cisco. After a morning of wind sprints and weight lifting, Cisco wasn't up for detail work. In fact, compared to the kid Rick had had working for him last summer, Cisco wasn't up for much of anything.

Cisco was bright enough. Most physical tasks, you only had to show him once. Like most kids, he refused to ask questions, just bulled ahead rather than suffer the embarrassment of admitting he didn't know everything.

Outlaw spirit was missing, though. Aimed at someone he held a grudge against, like Miranda, he would do the odd bit of malicious mischief, like yesterday's creative writing exercise. But Cisco got no kick out of lurking.

Rick needed a partner who was willing to freelance, to make it up as he went along, because Miranda wasn't playing the game. She came and went at odd hours, refused to fall for his boyish charm, and didn't even sleep when she should. She'd scared the crap out of him last night.

Moving his head a couple of inches, Rick watched Miranda weeding. He looked right down the sweat-sheened cleavage of her turquoise tank top to the edge of her bra.

He dipped his brush and held it, hovering, until a single drip plopped on the rise of her right breast. He turned back to make sharp, professional strokes before she swore under her breath. He felt her eyes on him, accusing, assessing, finally deciding he was such a nice guy he couldn't possibly have pulled a prank like that on purpose.

Last night he'd been sure he finally knew where she'd hidden the Graveyard Rose. It had come to him at an inopportune moment.

Renetta got a kick out of screwing his brains out in her own bed, while her husband served drinks in the Hangin' Tree, just across the parking lot.

There was nothing Renetta wouldn't do, with a smile on her face. He couldn't wait until he and Renetta split. Fourth of July, he had a buyer for the Graveyard Rose. Then, while her husband slung drinks at the community steak fry and fireworks display, Rick and Renetta would take off.

A couple days later, they'd be in Townsell, New Jersey, where Renetta had grown up. She wanted to show him the place behind the bleachers at her old high school, where'd she first learned she had a thing for football coaches.

She'd been doing a little illegal motion of her own when he'd remembered Dahlia Smith, owner of the ill-fated Crest Theatre. Dahlia didn't trust banks, so she kept cash stashed in a spare refrigerator in her apartment over the theater. She'd heard refrigerators were the only things guaranteed not to burn in fires. She kept the thing as a vault, empty of food, full of valuables, such as the rare films she and her husband, Smitty, had collected.

If only someone—she'd blamed forgetful Smitty—hadn't left the refrigerator ajar the night of the fire.

Remembering, Rick had slipped out Renetta's back window, making plans to slip in through Miranda's and check out the basement freezer.

He couldn't believe he hadn't thought of it immediately. She'd been down there that first evening she got the silver box. While he'd been searching upstairs, she'd been stashing it in the freezer.

Last night he'd made a mistake. Before slipping into the hidden crawl space, he'd glanced through Andi's back window. She'd been standing right there in her long white nightgown, staring back at him like a freaking ghost.

And then she'd gone and called the cops. Luckily, the call had been funneled to hell and back before Noah's emergency radio had gone off. Noah and half the working folk in Sparrowgrass, Rick included, had been breakfasting in the Dancing Goat when the alarm sounded. Most of them just shook their heads over that crazy Fairfield girl. Her folks had always seemed so levelheaded.

Rick figured he was in the clear. Noah was a lot better doc than he was a deputy. Even those folks who blamed Cisco had to admit Blake made a good case against that

Englishman, Gallatin. Rick had been itching to get Gallatin gone. Now he reconsidered.

Rick had counted on using Cisco as his fall guy and had no compunctions about it, but Sparrowgrass protected its own. Gallatin might be surprised by the mess he'd walked into.

Andi stomped to make the soil fall off her knees. She pulled a burr from her sweatshirt and considered her dusty sandals and the black dirt caked under her fingernails. She really wanted a shower, but she'd decided against it. If she knocked on Kit's door trailing cobwebs and smelling of compost, he couldn't very well think she was coming on to him.

A good landlord would notify Kit that his domicile wasn't quite the haven he'd assumed. She would not fidget with the feeling that he should have heard her whispered call for help. A good landlord would simply march into his apartment and explain that a trespasser had come creeping around last night and, oh, yes, the deputy sheriff might have pegged Kit as a suspect.

"Knocking off for the day?" Rick rounded the corner of the house, balancing paint trays. Sun glinted off his blond hair.

How did he stay so clean? His gold polo shirt was unspotted by paint, and his Nikes might have come right off the shelf.

"Taking a break." Andi fought the urge to cover the sunburned skin above her scooped neckline. "You?"

"I've got some Cokes in a cooler. Cisco and I are going to sit in the shade for a few minutes. Want to join us?"

"No, thanks." Andi licked her dry lips. All day she'd put off saying anything, but now was the time. "You probably heard I had a little excitement last night."

"I did. I can't believe that happened here." Rick blushed, as if shouldering blame for the town. "Could've been a transient, I guess, but most hitchhikers stay near the main road."

"I was talking about the graffiti."

"Graffiti." Rick tilted his head. "I didn't hear about any graffiti."

"While you were up on the ladder today, you didn't notice that 'Heart's Ease' had been painted over?"

"Isn't that sort of the opposite of graffiti?" Rick chuckled. "Cisco cut that in for me yesterday after I left. He just didn't finish the job."

"By 'cutting it in,' you mean like you were doing around the window frames? Painting the white right up to the edge where you're going to use the red, right?"

Rick nodded. "That's right." His smile applauded her understanding of the fine points of painting. "I'm sorry I didn't tell him not to paint over the lettering."

Andi studied the paint she'd daubed over the estate's slandered title. She believed Rick, of course. She was only weighing the best way to punish Cisco.

Her teacher's brain reminded her that some kids would do anything for attention. Good attention or bad, it didn't matter. So she would just ignore the infraction. It should drive him nuts.

Rick cleared his throat, filling the silence. "It *is* my fault."

"No problem. Enjoy your Coke. I've got to go tell my renter to keep an eye out for prowlers."

She'd pulled a handful of purple and pink sweet peas off the back gate, when Rick called out, "Is Gallatin your boyfriend?"

A warm breeze tickled the sweet pea tendrils against the inside of Andi's knee, but the cottonwood tree's leaves didn't so much as shiver. Andi blamed her own quaking hands and asked, "Would he be sleeping in the carriage house if he were?"

Rick grappled with a paint tray. It dipped and spilled a brush onto the grass. As he straightened from retrieving it, he raised both brows. "With a gal like you? I guess not." Then he walked away, whistling.

Swell. Now word would get around that she was not only loony and dangerous but a tramp as well. And she'd *bet* she was the only twenty-six-year-old virgin in town.

Without a glance toward Cisco's laddertop clatter, Andi strode toward the barn.

People believed what they wanted to believe. Witch, black widow, or whore, they could call her anything, and facts wouldn't deter them.

The facts were that two young men had died in two un-related accidents. Accidents, as her mother and countless sur-veys had concluded, were the leading killer of males under thirty.

Here, she was miles away from Domingo's death. And twelve years past Clint's. The stares and whispers she'd dreaded hadn't come, except for Cisco's, and teenagers didn't scare her.

At Heart's Ease, hard work and country silence could scrub away guilt and nightmares.

Once she reached the shade of the barn, Andi leaned for-ward, hands flattened on her thighs. Amid the straw, a seg-mented gray sow bug flicked its antennae to get its bearings, then blundered on. Andi straightened and took a deep breath.

She was no magnet for malice. No danger to Kit or anyone else. Every logical brain cell said so, but as she climbed the stairs to Kit's loft, she shivered and wished for the glare of sunlight.

In the dark at the top of the stairs, a door opened and Kit was silhouetted against the sunny apartment beyond. Blink-ing, Andi offered the handful of sweet peas.

He hesitated, then took the flowers and bowed her toward the red booth. It was a courtly bow, more suited to yester-day's black velvet than today's jeans, and it was made with-out a whiff of mockery.

The red leatherette gummed to the back of her legs, while Kit stood outlined against the windows over the cot. She could tell his hair was loose, a little disheveled, but her sun-dazzled eyes couldn't bring him into focus. Tomorrow she'd definitely wear sunglasses.

He moved closer and gestured with the flowers, his usual arrogance creased with confusion.

"A housewarming present," she explained. "Welcoming you to the neighborhood." Surely they had similar traditions in Britain.

"Ah." His close-cropped black beard moved with the word.

"You could put them in water."

He nodded. As he turned toward the cabinet over the sink, Andi's elbow bumped a lined legal pad that lay face down on the table. A pencil, its tip beveled in a way indicating that it had been sharpened with a knife, sat nearby. She'd never interrupted an artist at work. She'd love to read whatever had him so muzzy and distracted.

A cabinet hinge squawked and Andi looked up, afraid he would catch her snooping.

Kit peered at the meager collection of dishes and glassware as if he hadn't seen them before. Perhaps he'd been too preoccupied with writing. The brown bags of fruit still sat on the kitchen counter.

As he took down one of Jason's cast-off "highball" glasses, filled it with water, and plunged the viney sweet pea stems inside, Andi watched him move.

Despite the beige T-shirt stenciled WOLCOTT'S HARDWARE AND FEED and half tucked into fresh jeans, despite the haphazard way his jeans rumpled over the Western boots he'd insisted on buying, Kit moved with a sharp formality that belonged in another country, or in a ballroom, not in a cramped apartment over a barn in Sparrowgrass.

His chest expanded, but he didn't speak, only shifted at the discomfort of being studied. She'd seen handsome men before—her basketball-playing brother ran with a pack of professional athletes. Why couldn't she stop marveling over the incredible counterpoint Kit's broad shoulders made to his slim waist and hips?

He clunked the improvised vase onto the table with an odd expression of achievement. "Miranda."

Her name startled them both.

"Sorry. What did you say?" She scrambled for an excuse as he loomed before her. "I'm a little groggy from being up late and doing yard work all day." She patted the back of his hand to reassure him that she was neither scheming nor dozing off.

He refused reassurance, reversing his hand to capture hers. "Last night, did you call to me for help?"

His grip took all the warmth flooding down her veins to where their hands joined. "Not me."

"No?" His hand tightened.

"I did have a prowler. Someone was walking around outside the house."

"A prowler?" Within the brackets of his black mustache, Kit's lips pressed together. He released her hand.

"More of a Peeping Tom, really."

He muttered something profane as he turned away.

"Maybe, subconsciously, you heard something. Thanks for the thought."

Andi watched him pour five oranges from their sack. As he kept them from rolling off the kitchen counter, she flipped the yellow pad over.

She looked up as he took a cutting board from a hook and drew a knife from its chopping-block holder. While he considered the blade, she read the carefully printed title: "Courtier in Exile: The Lifelong Musings of an English Gentleman."

She looked up in time to see him test the knife edge with his thumb. "Careful," she warned, but he didn't glance her way. Right behind the squirm of her stomach came a question.

How should she tell this stuffy gentleman he was a suspect in such an ignoble crime? It would be easier to accuse him of masterminding a jewel heist.

He balanced the knife tip on the cutting board. The heel of his hand lowered the haft. He halved the orange with the grim precision of a headsman. "Nothing more than a Peeping Tom, you say?"

The knife rose again, to carve the orange into quarters. Judging by the hard turn of muscle at his jaw, his teeth were gritted as he awaited her answer.

The last time she'd seen a jaw clenched with such fury it had been Domingo's. Driving to a beachside motel, determined to give up virginity that had become a burden, she'd developed cold feet.

"Decide." Domingo had slammed his fist against the steering wheel but kept his eyes on the darkness beyond the windshield. "Are we going on or going home?"

Coward that she was, she'd whispered, "Home."

Domingo had jerked the steering wheel into the start of a furious U-turn, collided with a commercial linens truck, and died.

Kit tapped the knife blade on the cutting board. "Nothing more than a Peeping Tom?" He repeated.

How on earth could he know she hadn't already given him the truth?

He steadied the orange with his other hand. When he finally looked up, his eyes' furious glitter gave way to a coaxing softness. She could learn to like this man.

If Domingo and Clint had taught her nothing else, they'd taught her that she didn't have time—*no one did*—to shunt aside life's treasures.

"I dreamed you were kissing me." Andi's topknot wobbled with silly indignance, but damn the man for pushing and pushing until the words all but choked her. "How long are you going to make me wait?"

Kit sucked in a hissing breath as the blade fell. In a single stroke, it sliced through the orange and three of his fingers.

Chapter
Five

. . . Upon these dates, the Queen dispatched missives allowing that she would offer King Philip's rebellious subjects sanctuary. Little could she know that such beneficence would lure Aragon and his traitors to our shores.

In masquerade as one such rebel, Aragon offered to school such of the Queen's courtiers as she saw fit to submit, as musketeers to equal Spain's. Such a one was I.

Misfortune decreed Aragon should fall under the spell of the lunatic Infante Don Carlos. Philip's sole heir might have turned misfortune to his advantage, for he held his sire's affection. Alas, he was more depraved in spirit than distorted in body.

What manner of man boils live hares for sport? What monster cuts his own steeds to hear them scream? And whips innocent maids to feed his lechery?

69

> *Don Carlos, who rejoiced in giving away secrets of*
> *the state, lusted after his own mother. Don Carlos,*
> *whose evil withstood the trepanning of his skull,*
> *earned the loyalty of Aragon and ordered the killing*
> *of our Queen's men as proof of that loyalty.*
>
> *Even after the Infante's death, Aragon persisted, as-*
> *sembling a secret troop of Castilian pikemen for an*
> *ambush of such gullible gentleman as I ...*

Kit forced himself to read each word over as the slap of
Andi's sandals descended the steps from the carriage house
to the barn to the yard. The very sound reproved him.

In his mind's eye, Kit saw how Miranda's little backside
had churned in the short pants. She'd had garden clippers
jammed in a back pocket. Even imagining her breasts swaying inside the tight blue bodice didn't dim the echo of the
words he'd wrung from her.

"I dreamed you were kissing me." Her face had flushed
redder than sunburn, her graceful throat had tensed, forbid-
ding her next words' escape, but it failed. "How long are
you going to make me wait?"

By Christ's bones! Kit raged at his reaction. He had no
blood to make male flesh rise to those words. Not then. Not
now.

The fever Miranda Fairfield roused was impossible. Even
if some mountebank's curse let her touch transcend his
ghosthood, he sheltered no tender feelings toward her.

So, he had scorned her innocent confession with a sneer.

"How amusing," he'd said, then fended off her pity for
a nonexistent wound from the knife that had slashed, harm-
lessly, of course, through his hand.

Then he'd ordered her to leave.

He shouldn't have let her in at all. Scratched by the wire
frame for a compost pile and dirty as a peasant, Andi Fairfield had invaded his domain. Yet he'd treated her as he
would a lady. Better, come to that, than he'd treated his be-

trothed, though Arabella had been patrician from her marble complexion to her blue-blooded buttocks.

Even though Arabella was long since dust, Kit felt a twist of discomfort at her memory. The jet-haired minx had kissed him and used him kindly in life. In his earliest days of ghosthood, he'd returned to his betrothed and found her entwined with a new love. Speaking of Kit's death in breathy gasps, she'd called him a heartless whoreson and said he, a traitor, deserved his family's scorn.

If only this storytelling hadn't kindled memories of that other Miranda. Long ago, that abused but plucky scullery maid had warned him of Aragon's treachery and promised that her amber bauble would bring him safely back to her.

Nonsense. Amber held no such magic. Still, weren't boxes which carried a voice away from the place it spoke magical? Yet tape recorders, televisions, and radios existed. And what of refrigerators, which had ended meat brined or spiced to hide the taint of rot? More to the point, what of ghosts? In life, he'd scoffed at specters.

Kit forced himself to sit at the odd table. He scribbled a few sentences describing his death, a topic he was heartily sick of, before he thought of her again.

If Miranda's touch had caused a flicker of sensation, it must be what these people called static electricity. He would not be fooled. After four hundred years, he would never again feel a woman's hands trace the muscles he had molded by sword and horse. But if there were a mortal woman who could stir such sensation he would seize her. Kit Gallatin was no monk sworn to celibacy. If Miranda could cup his face and he could feel each finger, if she ran the soft pads of her thumbs over his lips, reminding him of what lips could do, he would run down the steps after her and ravish her now.

Would that the dratted cat chose now to intrude upon his isolation. He might make a test. He knew the creature felt his touch. This morning as he'd begun writing, she'd curled purring on his lap and he'd dashed her off. Had he felt her fur?

Tests be damned. Better to trust the science of this age.

Better to deem the crackling from Miranda's hands a dance of invisible energy.

At the sound of thrashing, Kit walked to the window. Squatting, snipping, ripping, and tossing, Miranda attacked the barbed blackberry bushes at the edge of the woods path. Working off the humiliation he'd inflicted, the girl overlooked the thorns that slashed her forearms and hands. She didn't spare Cisco a glance, even when he folded his ladder. When fair-haired Rick loaded his van, shouted farewell, and drove off, Miranda worked on.

Her scratches bled, trickling and merging until her skin wore a disturbing red lace. It was proof that he had no heart, for he stood and watched from the window until twilight.

Then he returned to his tale, not because it demanded telling but because he'd seen her eyes' trespass and knew she'd read more.

He flexed fingers long out of use for such a task. Soon he would be gone. If he left this manuscript behind, perhaps Miranda would understand.

> *At first there was no word of my death. In the battle's aftermath, it was clear that the entire company, all but a few, had fallen to the Spaniards' pikes. Once found, I was mourned. Barrett fell to his knees beside me. As if in grievous pain, he entreated God to explain. He displayed a decided lack of piety, this lad who'd never before questioned afflictions from God's hand.*

That day, Barrett had loved him. Who had turned the lad's loyalty and convinced him Kit was a traitor? No matter. Today Kit wrote the story of his death. That day, Barrett had shown a brother's devotion.

> *Then Barrett turned workman, snapping off my sword and using its hilt as a basket. For a time, he ignored the pike in my back, then snapped off its haft as well, leaving a blade where my heart should be. And well*

*he should have. That blade has served well to cut
through such briars as this endless life is made of...''*

He wrote nothing of the espionage which had brought
death instead of glory.

Darkness crowded the room by the time he heard Miranda
move through the long grasses toward the back gate. Her
footsteps paused, as if she stood staring up at his dark windows. Then metal struck metal. The gate closed and Kit's
blunt pencil moved on.

*Barrett found a skillful apothecary to embalm my
heart, then wrapped it in silk, in coarse cloth, and finally housed it in the box, which he finished and buffed
to a glow.*

Kit stopped. Now that Miranda had departed, he climbed
down to feed the hungry mare. He should make her earn her
fodder. Tomorrow, mayhap he would.

Inside the house a light flared on, followed by a frantic
sort of music. Should he follow Miranda about the house,
see if she took out the Graveyard Rose and threw it against
the wall in a fit of rage? If she knew what it contained, she
might, but of course she didn't know. Faith, he rather thought
she'd eat and fall asleep, having vented her temper on the
blackberry bushes.

But she only adjusted the discordant music to bawl louder,
and the singer decried his lack of satisfaction. When Andi
came into the yard, she carried a glass tinkling with ice. The
screen door slammed behind her, but not before he heard her
whisper snatches of the song. She moved about the yard,
checking the wire-framed compost pile—for what, he could
not imagine. She trailed hoses, considered a pair of sticks
she believed to be rosebushes, and turned on sprinkling de-
vices, working until she stumbled with weariness.

•   •   •

Oh, no. Andi sat straight up in bed.

Coyotes' yips had penetrated her sleep, spurring recognition of the dread which had hammered her dreams.

She glanced at the glowing numbers of the clock. Midnight, and she hadn't seen Lily since this morning, when she'd snatched her off the mantel before she could knock Rosencrantz and Guildenstern to their deaths.

Wait—think, Miranda. The white cat must have twined around her ankles once tonight. Cat food must have rattled in Lily's dish or boards signaled her stalking of imaginary prey. Andi's nearly terminal plummet into humiliation must have kept her from noticing. That was all.

Her instant infatuation with Kit had pushed her into blurting what she wanted from him. She'd hoped for passion, spontaneous combustion.

Oh, God. Andi hid from herself, face in hands.

Nevertheless, she was tough. She would pretend Kit was nothing more than a convenience. Like a paperboy. He fed Trifle and paid her for the privilege. She'd never drooled over the paperboy.

Night wind billowed her curtains as the coyotes' barks turned joyous, then slid into a howling chorus. Poor deaf Lily wouldn't hear them. Andi cursed her inattention to the nature specials she'd seen over the years. Maybe coyotes wouldn't touch a hapless house cat. Or maybe their cries celebrated a midnight snack.

''Lily!'' She searched the house, hoping the cat would feel the vibrations of her footsteps or her shouts.

Moonlight streamed through the cottonwood tree as Andi moved outside. A warm breeze shifted branches, changing hues from gray to glowing. In each shadow she imagined the flick of Lily's tail or the bob of pointed ears.

''Lily!'' Beneath the chugging chatter of the large sprinkler, she heard a rustle of dry daffodil stalks out near the front gate. She tugged her oversized football jersey toward her knees, skirted the sprinkler's spray, and pursued the rustling as crickets stilled around her.

Was that faraway hoot an owl? Heavens, she'd bet a good-sized owl could pluck up a cat. Andi shuddered at the image of huge overhead talons flexing, then gripping. And Lily would be incredibly visible, white against the midnight fields. Country nights were filled with danger for a little deaf cat.

Something big hit the fence.

"Lily?"

Big, but not big enough to be the bear Noah had mentioned. Rick had said deer munched down the rows of Dinah's lettuce, and this impact had sounded about that size. The thud might have been hooves hitting the top fence rail, but what if it were a coyote, hunting Lily in her very own yard?

"Lily cat! Here, kitty." Andi wondered if a coyote would battle her for the cat. Unlikely, but she hoped Rick had remembered to close the gate to the road. "Lily!" He had. The latch was in place, doubly secured with twining sweet peas.

Lambent light silvered the long grass that snatched at Andi's legs as she trudged back toward Heart's Ease. She considered the area between the gate and the front door and vowed to cut the grass tomorrow, even if she had to buy a mower. It couldn't be more than half an acre.

Like ice-cold Uzi spray, the sprinkler zapped her across the chest, then moved on. Andi started to wrap her arms around herself against the chill, but her jersey was soaked. She held her arms out from her sides and ran tiptoe for the veranda, seeking shelter from the breeze.

She peered around the dark porch, hoping she'd left a blanket or sweatshirt on the porch swing. She didn't dare go inside. If Lily finally decided to come home, she wanted to whisk the cat indoors fast.

No blanket, no sweatshirt. She climbed onto the porch swing and pushed her hair forward, wishing it covered her wet front. She pulled her knees up under the faded red jersey and locked her hands around her knees, trying to form a tent of warmth.

She was working hard not to let her teeth chatter and not to feel sorry for herself when Kit appeared on the veranda.

His broad-shouldered form, looming so suddenly out of the night, should have frightened her.

"Have you seen Lily?" Andi jumped up so suddenly, the porch swing smacked her behind the knees.

"The white cat?" As he moved closer, moonlight showed him dressed all in black, a tailored shirt and black jeans. Though he'd banished her from the carriage house, Kit's presence was a comfort.

But not a warm one. A cloak of cold attended him, as if his icy demeanor had turned to actual temperature. Andi sank to the top step, fingers curled around opposite elbows.

"Y-you wear a l-lot of black," she managed between shivers. Really, she should have chanced two minutes to run inside and change.

"What *should* I wear?"

"Don't tell me I've of-of-offended you again." She almost hoped she had. If he insisted on maintaining a cool distance between them, why did he keep coming around? "Black is fine." He stood so near she looked up the side seam of his jeans. "It looks good."

"Suits me, you mean?" He sat beside her and steepled his fingers, considering them, not her. "And my evil temperament."

It was the closest she'd get to an apology from this arrogant Englishman. "Wait." She held a hand out, though he sat silent. "Did you hear something?"

"A flutter of wings." Kit skimmed his hand across the board porch.

Of course the entire veranda should be sanded and every plank revarnished, but that was not her immediate concern. "Do you think an owl would eat a cat?"

Kit jabbed his index finger against a splinter as if testing its point, then answered, "Not without considerable yowling and commotion."

"It's not funny. I'm so afraid I've killed Dinah's cat. I can't get in touch with her—Dinah, I mean—because she's taking my parents on a cruise to Mexico."

She unwound a lock of hair in which she'd twisted her finger. No need to act like a despairing child. "Dinah called tonight, to make sure things are going all right. It should have clicked then, but I didn't realize Lily was gone. So I can't even ask Dinah if Lily has any favorite hiding places. Not that I would. She'd only worry, and she's had enough of that."

As her words dwindled, Andi braced herself. He'd say something cynical and she'd still sit here, because Lily could be lurking nearby, nose to nose with a coyote.

"She's off on a hunt, I'd suppose." Kit waved his arm at the estate's neglected bounty, heaven for a curious cat.

"Maybe," Andi admitted.

"Well, then." Kit prepared to stand. Not once in these five minutes had he met her eyes or revealed why he'd come to her veranda at midnight.

She wanted him to stay.

"It's a good thing you're caring for Trifle—everything I touch dies."

He stiffened.

Apparently she had no shame. It wasn't bad enough that she'd asked this unwilling man to kiss her. Now she was on the verge of boohooing on his shoulder.

"Come, now. If you mean ferns and flowers, they're transitory to begin with."

"No, I actually do pretty well with plants." She bit her bottom lip to keep her mouth shut.

"House pets, then?" Though he looked in her direction, Kit might have regarded her from beyond a cool wall of glass. "It's not so easy to hurt a horse."

Lily's disappearance had apparently jiggled loose the censor in her brain. She didn't ever indulge in confessions like this. She possessed solid adult judgment. She had good sense.

"Two men."

The fragile pane between them cracked.

Kit's sudden concentration was almost physical. "Never."

Andi turned away, clearing her throat. She needed a snappy comeback—or even a lame one. She was sorrier than she'd ever been for speaking.

With a sidelong glance, she caught Kit's stare. Now that she had his attention, it was relentless.

"Explain."

"You have no right—" Her haughty rebuke wavered. "I don't have to explain anything to you, Mr. Gallatin."

"You do."

His was not a sensitive you'll-feel-better-if-you-talk-about-it response. Kit meant he'd force her.

"Well, it's not like hundreds of people don't know." Andi blew her cheeks full of air. Only a few knew about *both*. "You met Jan." Kit nodded. "And Cisco?"

"The boy painter."

"Yes. I— When I was a kid, we used to come here during school vacations. Actually, my parents lived here when I was a baby. All of my cousins came, too. We used the carriage house as sort of a—"

Kit brushed her words aside with an airy gesture. "Miranda, be brief."

"Right." She formulated a shorthand version and rattled it off. "When I was fourteen, Jan's son, Clint, was my boyfriend. It was summer vacation and we were supposed to take the younger kids to the movies, but we left them and sneaked off. We were having a picnic, necking in the sunshine . . ." A sigh rocked through her. "Pretty tame stuff, but he was my first boyfriend.

"Clint looked just like Cisco, only happier. Same toffee-brown hair and eyes. He would've made a handsome man." Andi swallowed. "Anyway, when we finally got around to eating, Clint wanted to pick some flowers for our picnic blanket centerpiece. There were a million flowers past the barbed wire at Daffodil Hill. There was also a bull.

"A big, ugly bull. A Brahma crossbreed, they said, like a rodeo bull. Clint knew it was there. I shouldn't have let him go, but he was stepping between the middle strands of the fence and ducking under before I noticed. I was laying out this romantic little picnic. Crustless sandwiches cut into triangles, radishes cut into roses, sort of, and wineglasses full of strawberry soda. Clint loved strawberry soda.

"He didn't make a sound. I heard the bull huffing. When

I looked over, at first it looked like a bundle of rags. The bull dug his head down, shoveled something up and flung it.'' Andi covered her eyes against the indelible image. ''They said the charge broke his back, so he couldn't run. When I finally got out there, the bull had lost interest. He just . . . he just trotted away.''

The sprinkler chugged and the dry husks of spring flowers chafed against each other.

''Perhaps if you put out some tinned fish.'' Kit gestured toward the yard.

Lily. While remembrance slashed her, Kit had reasoned that the cat would come at the scent of canned tuna. How practical. Fighting off memory's trance, she went to the pantry, opened the can, and returned to the veranda. Kit was still there, silent as she set the can before the veranda steps.

''Lily!'' If she didn't call the cat, she'd wheel on Kit and denounce him as a heartless bastard. How could he deny her a single word of pity?

''And the second one?''

She sat farther apart from him, leaning against a square porch post as night chill turned to simmering anger.

''The 'second one' was Domingo Santos, the track coach at my school. He taught math too, but you should have seen him run. He was a world-class marathoner, made the Olympic trials, then pulled an Achilles tendon, but he ran like a cheetah. His head never moved and his stride was just this fluid surging . . . I think we would've gotten married.

''His mom was teaching me how to cook Mexican food.'' Andi's mind replayed the sputter of onions frying, the smell of cumin seed ground with mortar and pestle. ''Tortillas, *menudo*, the real stuff, not Taco Bell.'' She didn't give Kit time to grow impatient. ''Then Domingo was killed in a car accident. There you have it.''

''Tell me about the accident.''

''I bet this is research, right? Let's see if I can remember what it said in the police report. I went over it enough times, I should probably have it memorized. We were eastbound when he made a U-turn at a high rate of speed and slammed into the back of a truck.''

"Forgive me—I still don't understand."

But he didn't want forgiveness. He wanted gory details. Andi demonstrated the cars' positions with her hands, until frustration and grief overcame her.

"Forget it." Regret and bitter bile boiled up in the back of her throat. "It doesn't matter. Domingo died and I walked out of the hospital the next morning with bruises from the air bags. At his funeral, his little nieces wore their white confirmation dresses."

"Why was he turning back?"

"It doesn't matter."

That had been the worst of it. And she'd told no one else. Not even the paramedics who'd extracted her from Domingo's crushed Camaro. She'd lain on the asphalt, listening to passing traffic, to static from the radio inside the ambulance, not to the profane and dogged search for an airway through a trachea smashed flat, as Domingo's.

He believed her unconscious—that one ambulance attendant making lewd jokes over a smashed champagne bottle and lingerie. Or maybe he handled job stress with such dark humor.

"Did you ask him to turn back?"

"Look, you needled me into saying something stupid yesterday. I'm not doing it again. Just back off."

"Very well." Kit smoothed his hands on the air between them. "But if this happened recently"—he quirked a brow until she nodded—"and the other, what, ten or twelve years past?" Andi nodded again. "In that length of time, wouldn't it be unusual if you *didn't* know two young men who'd died?"

"I don't think so."

"The fact remains, Clint and Domingo"—he pronounced the names carefully—"did rash things young men have always done. Fate catches the unlucky ones. And makes them pay."

"But they did those stupid things because of me. Don't you get it?"

"Why would you want to believe that?" As he moved toward her, Andi scooted away.

"I *do* believe it. Kit, there's something about me that makes guys do stupid things. And then they die." For a minute his expression softened, and she couldn't shrug away from the arm he wrapped over her. "You've heard of the kiss of death. The myth had to start somewhere. With someone like me." His hand closed on her shoulder and he pulled her to him.

"You tried to warn me once before." Kit's voice was a whisper. "I didn't listen then either."

"What are you talking about? If you're trying to distract me, it won't work. Thanks for your concern, but all the evidence is laid out in front of you."

" 'The kiss of death,' is it?" Kit's lips brushed hers so softly, she was more aware of his chest pressing her wet jersey. "Ah, Miranda, you can't hurt me . . ."

His mouth took hers. His arms crossed her back, crushing her to him. "Sweet Jesu," Kit gasped, and he was shaking, *shaking* as if he'd never kissed a woman.

That couldn't be true. His simple kiss pulled her, aroused her with an expertise which contradicted his trembling eagerness.

Andi's eyes flickered open. Some cloudiness seemed to waver between them, making his face indistinct, but then Kit's eyes opened. He looked surprised.

With lips still touching, she slid a hand over his face. She'd never kissed a man with a beard. It felt glossy, smooth. As she pressed the hard bone beneath it, Kit leaned against her fingertips.

Her hand followed the line of his jaw and he snatched a quick breath which made her smile. His faint groan as her hand burrowed beneath his hair electrified her. This was more than appreciation, more than pleasure. Kit loved her touch.

She didn't stop, even when her jersey rode up, baring her thighs to the chill and the veranda's splinters. Even when she feared they might tip backward onto the porch. She didn't stop until she heard Lily's mew.

Kit drew back so quickly, he might have melted from beneath her hands and reappeared standing.

Shame tightened her face. Andi pushed to her feet. Her nunlike reserve hadn't lasted long. One breath of encouragement, and she'd been all over him.

She leaned down to grab the cat, to fill her arms.

His touch caught her as she straightened.

"Sweet Miranda." Without a flicker of scorn, his fingers memorized the turn of flesh at her temple.

Startled by tenderness she couldn't believe, she smiled and squeezed the cat. "A good thing Lily came home when she did."

He touched his thumb to her lower lip. "I would have taken you beyond the 'kiss of death,' you mean?"

Her throat closed. She nodded.

"Ah, yes, and what would have been the cost of that, I wonder?" Sarcasm tainted his words, then vanished. "Tell me the penalty, so I can think whether to risk it."

She shrugged, unable to joke, less able to watch him walk away. "Burst into flames?"

She hated the sound of it, regretted the words even as Kit stopped. He smiled as if they shared a grim secret.

"Very likely, lady, very likely."

Chapter
Six

Curtains flickered at the upstairs window. For the first time in three days, Andi saw him.

Let me spill my secrets. Then serve up the most incredible kiss of my life and vanish.

No problem. Fine with me. Have a nice day.

Kit was there now. To him, one kiss had been simply that. She could act like an adult.

"I must look like a plow horse." Andi leaned against the lawn mower's wooden handle and shaded her eyes to look up.

"Hardly." Kit spoke from the carriage house window. In the midmorning sun she couldn't see his expression. "If memory serves, the horse goes in front and drags the machinery."

Andi turned back with a reluctant smile. She considered the mower's split handle and brownish blades. "I may try that next."

After searching Heart's Ease outbuildings, she'd found the ancient mower in the basement. Lugging it up the stairs had been tough, hefting it over polished wood floors and Persian rugs, tougher, but neither compared to keeping the thing under control. If it hit the smallest obstacle, it bucked forward, rubbing blisters on her palms.

It had taken Kit an hour to notice her toil, but Trifle had kept her company, cantering along the fence, nickering and flinging her mane. Now Trifle pawed the ground, snorting in impatience.

''Suppose you could give this poor animal some exercise?'' When Kit didn't answer, Andi looked up. He'd gone.

The brook splashed in the bottom of the gully as Andi surveyed her efforts. Often she considered ''pride in a job well done'' an overrated delight, but tending Heart's Ease ranked higher than planting a Los Padres window box. She walked the last stretch of overgrown grass, scanning for pebbles to cast out of her way. Once she finished this lawn and the front as well, she would reacquaint herself with the steep path down to the brook.

Maybe Kit would come along. Or maybe he was worn out from writing a red-hot chapter based on her eager cooperation. *Let's see, his right hand would go here, while her knee . . .*

Andi worked her fingers under a fist-size rock. At least Kit's arctic tone had thawed. She pitched the rock toward the blackberry bushes. A disturbed flock of birds fluttered up, almost obscuring the sound of a vehicle crunching down her road.

Andi untied the shirttails knotted at her waist, brushed down the sleeves she'd rolled up, and walked around to the veranda. She didn't recognize the gray sedan bumping toward the house.

Gaunt in a brick-colored suit and tie, a man unfolded himself from the driver's seat and scanned the yard. Holding a sheaf of yellow pamphlets between his ribs and elbow, he scowled.

Andi crossed her arms. Who was he, the county building inspector? She glanced over her shoulder. The patches where Heart's Ease had been scraped but not painted did look a bit scabrous.

Then he moved to hold the passenger door for a young woman cradling a baby.

"Hello!" Andi waved, but he must not have noticed.

Wiping blistered palms on her shorts, she strode toward the couple. The Sparrowgrass version of Welcome Wagon had arrived and she'd mowed the *back* lawn.

"Hi. Oh, what a tiny baby." Andi gazed down at a newborn no bigger than a loaf of bread.

"This is Paul," his mother cooed. Her baggy jumper hung to the tops of the white socks showing above her oxfords. Her tower of dark hair had probably never been cut. "And I'm Lizbet Wolcott."

"I'm Miranda Fairfield, thanks—"

"Welcome—" Lizbet began.

The bony man's throat-clearing halted both their voices and Andi blinked. Barring a rampant sinus infection, the guy was inexcusably rude.

"Miss Fairfield. Brother Dean Wolcott."

His face narrowed from a receding hairline to his brown mustache. Andi recognized him from the volunteer fire department. Yesterday, she'd noticed he was older than most volunteers. Maybe in his late forties, while his wife looked like a teenager.

"Lizbet," he said, "what have you forgotten?"

"Of course." Lizbet glanced toward the car's interior. "As usual, you remember my duties better than I do." She tilted the baby toward him and he shook his head in exasperation. When Lizbet gave a sheepish smile, her pink mouth wasn't much bigger than her baby's.

"I'd love to hold him," Andi offered. Better the infant than that layered confection inside the car. It looked like a wedding cake.

It wouldn't fit in the freezer full of casseroles. Did country folk respond to all occasions with food? That was fine. When Domingo had died, the dead-bolted, peepholed doors in her building hadn't opened an inch.

"Just for a minute." Lizbet pressed the baby into Andi's arms and turned to the cake. " 'Til I get this inside." Lizbet adjusted a doily's edge. "I was afraid the icing would melt in this heat."

Andi settled the baby's wispy hair into her cupped palm.

He was fragrant with baby shampoo, and she wondered how a girl Lizbet's age cranked up the nerve to bathe this delicate little being.

As Mr. Wolcott's chain saw throat-clearing signaled his desire to move toward the house, Andi wondered where Lizbet had found the courage required for baby Paul's conception.

"I'm afraid the house is a bit of a mess." Andi took the steps to the veranda with extra care. "I'm still getting used to the fact that Heart's Ease doesn't have a dishwasher."

Lizbet gave a sympathetic chuckle. Brother Dean Wolcott's grunt said he wasn't surprised.

To center the cake on the table, Lizbet moved aside a newspaper, a handful of wilted wildflowers and a paperback mystery with a particularly lurid cover.

Not that Wolcott noticed. He was inspecting her sink, which held a knife rimmed with mustard from last night's sandwich and a glass pitcher flecked with orange pulp.

"Shall I make coffee? I've got some fresh beans from the Dancing Goat."

"We don't indulge in stimulants," Wolcott said. "In fact, I've brought a selection of tracts. They might help you reconsider such practices."

As Lizbet took the baby, Andi had no choice but to accept the yellow sheets. Photocopied onto paper too flimsy for good reproduction, the top article was titled "Desecrating Your Body's Temple." It bore Brother's byline.

"Oh, you wrote these. How great. So, 'Brother' is a, um, religious designation."

"Everyone calls him Brother," Lizbet bragged.

"Which church are you affiliated with?"

"I'm self-ordained."

"I see."

"We're building a church behind the hardware store." Lizbet jiggled the waking baby. "We'd love for you to join us for worship some Sunday."

Without apology Brother decoded her hesitation. "Like Dinah, you're probably a Methodist. Little better than Buddhists, in the eyes of the Lord."

"Maybe some herb tea?" Andi filled a kettle and set it on the stove. Brother hovered at her elbow.

"Jason, your aunt's husband, was a godless man. If he'd allowed any devout dialogue, I might have helped him." Brother shivered. "The timbers of this house are drenched in his sin, his heathen Hollywood offense." He rubbed his arms as Andi reached for a tin of tea. "If only he'd received me into his sickroom."

"Dear?" Lizbet made an owlish readjustment of her wire-rimmed glasses. "Hide your light under a bushel just this once."

Lizbet rubbed her baby's cheek with her own. Brother slipped a chrome implement out of his pocket and cleaned his nails, drawing attention to nicotine-stained fingertips.

So, Brother had once been a pagan, Andi mused, then rushed to cover her cynicism.

"It really *is* a gorgeous cake," Andi said. "I'm almost afraid to cut it."

"A Lady Baltimore layer cake." Lizbet shrugged as if it had come off a grocery store shelf. "I'll be glad to give you the recipe. And to cut it."

Andi brought a knife, plates, and told herself to relax. They were only welcoming her to the neighborhood.

"I used raisins, figs, and hazelnuts, but you can use any kind you have around." Lizbet wielded the knife without scattering a crumb.

Brother bolted down his serving and moved toward the great room hearth, hand passing before him as if feeling for drafts. Andi and Lizbet ate, watching the baby's pink fists unfurl as he wakened.

"Hel-*lo*!" The baby's arms jerked and the door harp trilled. "Does a girl need an engraved invitation to drop off a gift?" The husky voice was unfamiliar.

Passing a window, Andi saw a powder-blue convertible parked next to the Wolcotts' sedan. "Come on in."

She already had. The woman smoking in Andi's doorway held a bowl against her hip. "I'm Renetta Duncan."

Renetta Duncan brought to mind black-and-white stills of

young Sophia Loren. But Andi would bet Sophia had never tattooed lips around her navel.

"I'm Andi Fairfield. Thanks for—"

Delivering the bowl without a glance, Renetta shrugged a scuffed purse off her shoulder and sauntered past.

Andi headed for the refrigerator. It would be cruel to set Renetta's offering next to the Wolcotts', but Lizbet eyed the passing bowl before it was stowed.

"Yum," Lizbet said. "Lime Jell-O with—"

"Lime Jell-O." Renetta squinted toward the great room. "Hey, Brother, how they hangin'?"

Andi slammed the refrigerator in time to see Renetta poise her cigarette over a plate.

"No ashtrays?" Renetta asked.

"Sorry. This is a flammable old house."

"Don't I know it." Renetta stubbed the cigarette out on her palm. Lizbet gasped and hand contracted into a fist. "The VFD's been talkin' structure fire here since I joined up. Isn't that right, Brother?"

Brother came to stand beside Lizbet. "It's something we consider with all old houses, but we're more concerned about entrance and egress." He reached for the baby.

"Which means you'd have a helluva time getting your VW past the engine if we were coming down this road. Just ask Brother, our fire science expert. Reads every textbook he can get his hands on."

When Brother jounced the baby instead of responding, Renetta added, "You might call him a fanatic."

"A fanatic on fire science is exactly the guy I'd call if Heart's Ease were burning," Andi said.

Brother's accidental smile faded as Renetta brushed off the tip of her unsmoked cigarette, then, in a leisurely fashion calculated to hold Brother's disapproving eyes, wedged the cigarette into a back pocket.

"If he hadn't heeded the Lord's call, Brother would be a firefighter," Lizbet said, then whispered, "I don't think they're contradictory, do you?"

Andi didn't want to be in the middle of this dispute. "Renetta, how about some cake?"

"No, thanks." Renetta slid her hands from her ribs to her thighs. Andi couldn't recall meeting a woman so enamored of her own flesh. "Hey, aren't Rick and Cisco working for you?" Renetta scanned the great room and the stairs.

"In the afternoons," Andi said. "after summer school."

"Almost forgot this." Renetta worked her fingers into a front pocket. "From Ralph. My husband—the bartender— sent you these." She plucked three yellow coupons from a rubber-banded packet.

Andi took the coupons. Lizbet cocked her head to see the Hangin' Tree logo and offer of half-price drinks. Brother cleared his throat, again.

"Thanks. Tell him I'll come by."

"Better get going." Renetta mimed a yawn. "Ralph does like company for his afternoon nap. Don't bother walking me out."

But they all did, and when Jan arrived in the dusty wake of the other cars, Andi was sitting on the veranda's top step.

"Might want to keep your distance," Andi called. "I think I've used up all my cordiality."

Jan rolled back the van door. "Don't be pleasant on our account." The twins spilled out in such a tangle, Andi couldn't tell which was Cami and which was Cody.

"Watch me do a cartwheel!"

"Hey, lookit this!"

"No, *me*. I take gymnastics. Watch *me*."

"Hey you two, *heel*." Jan skirted the threshing legs, bearing Blake's hand-painted sign and a bag. Dark heads gleaming, the twins pounded up the stairs, headed for the house. "Wait just a minute."

The twins stopped. "Sorry." Cody jerked his thumb toward the open door. "Can we go find Lily?"

" 'Please, Miss Fairfield,' " Jan prompted.

"Go ahead. She usually sleeps on my bed. Upstairs."

"We know."

Jan cleared the way for their tennis-shoed stampede. "Stay away from the windows," she shouted after them. "This house doesn't have screens."

Jan pointed to the house's freshly whitewashed top half.

"It's looking good." She plopped a brown bag next to Andi. "Greek salad with feta and olives. And iced teas for us." Jan lifted two foam cups and poked straws through their lids. "You look like you could use it."

"Very subtle. Thanks."

"I see you had company. What did you think of the Addams family?"

"The—?"

"Brother and Lizbet—Morticia and Lurch. That's what Cisco calls them. Sometimes the kid is pretty perceptive." Jan worked her straw up and down until it squeaked. "You don't really think he trashed your house, do you?"

"No," she lied. "Not that I wouldn't understand." Andi lifted Blake's sign. "I like this better than the original."

"Because if you do, don't pay him. Or tell Rick not to."

"Jan, it was a prank. No big deal." She fingered the plaque's beveled edge. "I thought Dr. Noah was going to bring this back, with Blake."

"Isn't he cute?" Jan turned an ear to the muffled commotion inside the house, then continued. "A really nice guy. My mistake was telling Blake I thought so. My approval is lethal where men are concerned. I swear Blake married that loser just to spite me."

Lethal where men are concerned. She didn't need a psychiatrist to analyze why the words reminded her of Kit, but why did desire spike through her as if he still gripped her shoulders?

"Hey, do you have time to check out those roses for me?" Andi led Jan to the well-weeded beds and spindly plants.

Jan squatted to finger the dark foliage and upright stalks.

"It's hard to tell just now, but the Lamberts, who lived here before Dinah, had a bed of Apothecary's Roses."

"I don't remember any Lamberts."

"You weren't born, Andi. I used to ride my bike over for Mrs. Lambert's sugar cookies and she'd tell me about her flowers. If these are the roses I'm thinking about, they go back to the Middle Ages. Monks kept them for some medicinal purpose, and that healing power is probably why they weren't allowed to die out."

Jan's finger hovered above a solid green shape. "Mrs. Lambert called them Mad Gallicas, too. The colors are wild. When this opens, it could be bright pink or purple."

"Really?" Andi looked around the estate. Slowly, it was improving. "I'd love to get these going for Dinah."

"Don't get your hopes up." Jan rocked back on her heels. "Ever since I've been reading about heirloom roses, I've started 'seeing' them everywhere."

Andi pulled a threadlike weed from the rose's base.

"So, speaking of monks, and prayer, is there any way she can find out?" Jan asked.

"W-who? B-Blake?"

"Gina." Jan lowered her voice. "Can she find out about your accident? Not that it would count as news anyplace except Sparrowgrass, but she was in this morning, talking about how you've pulled your life together since Clint." Jan's sigh replaced a hundred words of reproach. "Gina's found a hobby, and that paper's desperate enough to take anything. I swear, they even make up the classified ads."

"Mama! Maaa—"

Jan was up before the second cry ended. Andi ran behind her.

"That man wouldn't let us go upstairs!"

"*What* man?" Jan demanded.

"Tell him we can go upstairs! Miss Fairfield said so. We can, too!" Cody shouted over his shoulder.

"What man?"

Wind stirred the cottonwood. It didn't bring relief, only more heat, and Andi knew, before Cami pointed and said, "That man."

Of all the bloody luck. Through some lapse, he'd allowed the twins to see him. He'd felt invisible as air, but they'd begun gibbering the instant he blocked their pursuit of Lily as she leapt onto the window ledge.

Now he positioned himself on the path up to the veranda. Purposely visible, he stood behind Jan and Andi. He glared at the little wench who pointed with such assurance. He should have let the little beasts fall.

Smiling, Andi came to stand beside him. Sun had tinted her shoulders red and cast a sprinkling of freckles over her cheeks. The lines of muscle in her arms begged to be stroked. And she brought him a flurry of scents—fresh-cut grass, sugar, woman—though he should smell nothing.

The rank rot of a battlefield, yes. The reek of clotted milk or the stench of a boar's den, certainly. And rarely, food wafted directly beneath his nose. His ghostly senses could translate those. What was Miranda's mystery that he caught faint lavender on her skin?

"You thought you saw this man upstairs?" She took his arm.

"I think not. My muse has wielded her lash quite zealously this morning." Kit cautioned himself to school old cadences from his tongue. "I haven't stirred from my work since Andi woke me with her lawn mowing."

Cody tugged on Jan's blouse, untucking its hem from her jeans. "It's him, Mom."

A gentleman might have soothed them with an explanation, no matter how false. Kit brushed off such nonsense. He was no gentleman, only a spirit which had been one. As Jan prattled to her children, he didn't smile. As Andi searched with secret, darting glances, he gave her no assurance about that kiss. He asked permission to take the mare out and took his leave.

He didn't know when the visitors left, only that Andi began mowing where he couldn't watch. He heard the rolling, chopping blades and the occasional metal-on-rock impacts. Cisco and Rick arrived thereafter, just as Kit turned to saddle the mare. So, of course, he could not depart.

Would they finish with their infernal scraping, their clashing buckets, and slaps of paint before he found the box? Would he have one day alone with Miranda, a day to savor her touches and tears before all senses were snuffed?

He heard Rick speak to her.

Leaving the horse, Kit transported himself to the veranda. Ah, Rick was stooping to see what the mower had hit. Undamaged. Oh, yes, do you say so? Or is it your blackguard's way to crouch at her feet, reveling in her nearness? And now the Spaniard asked for ice and Miranda gave him a wafture of her hand, telling him he was free to take ice from the house and cake from her table.

'sblood! He could despise Miranda for allowing Rick in her private rooms, but he would not follow. Why should he?

Kit halted the pacing he did not recall commencing. Rick mounted the steps to the veranda. What a surprise if Rick felt a hand vee over his throat. And close.

Kit's presence was surprise enough. He saw Rick's arms come alive with gooseflesh. That was enough. He was no threat and no Spaniard. True, his light features echoed Aragon's, but that was all. Better to watch the dark-skinned youth.

From his ladder, Cisco studied Miranda as a man might a wolf. That fascination with something dangerous and beyond control.

Miranda's mower struck with a metallic clink.

"For crying out loud." She squatted and forked her fingers through a tangle of weeds.

"What is it this time?" Rick hadn't stayed in the house for long.

"A square nail," Miranda displayed it. "It looks old, doesn't it? What did you think it was?"

"I was hoping it was your Graveyard Rose."

"Out here?"

"You're sure you took it inside, then? Doesn't matter. I just hope you find it. Here, I brought you some ice water."

Rick watched her tilt her head back and swallow. The intensity of his gaze pulled Kit off the veranda. Still, Rick seemed harmless enough. Any man would stare at Miranda.

"Yo!" Rick rattled an insulated bottle.

Cisco descended the ladder like a monkey, then shambled across the half-tall, half-tamed lawn.

"You guys are doing a great job." Andi set her empty glass on a fencepost. "How long, d'you think, before you're finished?"

Kit smiled. Miranda echoed his longing for privacy.

"She's trying to get rid of us, buddy." Rick elbowed Cisco.

It was as close as Kit had seen Cisco come to Andi. She didn't meet his eyes overlong. She didn't address him directly, merely treated him like a creature she'd lured to hand.

"We're taking a football break. Want to toss it around for a few minutes?" Rick didn't open the door to his white van, simply leaned through the window to snag an oblong brown ball.

Rick and Cisco threw the ball back and forth, leaping for it, contorting faces and twisting torsos to keep from missing it. The focused joy in their activity reminded Kit of childhood and sparring with Barrett.

Miranda watched, too. She unhooked the grass catcher from her mowing machine, carried it to a wire frame in the yard's corner. She poured in the clippings, carefully as a cook, but her eyes watched Rick and Cisco.

Rick noticed. Holding the ball between fingers and thumb, he feinted toward her. "Wanna play?" Rick's gesture brought Cisco's groan to a halt.

"No, thanks."

"C'mon." Rick's tilted head caught the sun, making him look more boyish than Cisco. "We'll take it easy on you."

The grass catcher hit the lawn with a clank.

"You'll do what?" She strode toward them. "Take it *easy* on me? I guess you couldn't know I was the only girl on my block."

Rick tossed the ball and she caught it. "Not bad."

"No condescension, *Coach*." Andi sent the ball spiraling back.

Rick caught it with a muffled grunt and hurled it to Cisco.

"My parents forced my brother to make the guys be nice to me, too, so you can swallow your patronizing, self-esteem-building remarks. I know them all."

Cisco's throw came at her like a bowman's bolt. She caught it, fired it back. When it zipped through his fingers, Andi crowed, "Good effort."

With a bored air, Rick set up to catch Cisco's toss and threw the brown ball low, toward Andi's knees. She dove and rolled to her back, still holding the ball. Next, she lofted the ball high.

Squinting into the sun, Rick missed it.

"Nice try," she shouted.

Her excellence was outside the natural order of things. Still, Kit approved. The males muttered and growled as Miranda bested them. Each time they fumbled, she offered a palliative so patronizing that Cisco's sneer finally faded and he laughed.

When Rick turned from dropping the ball back inside his van, he slung his arm over Andi's shoulders. "Good going, girl."

Kit thought he might strangle the man, pressing gristle against windpipe until Rick's legs quit pumping like a rabbit's.

But Miranda must share the blame for this betrayal. She allowed Rick to hold her so, close enough that he'd feel heat from her cheeks' flush. She stood as Rick's arm grazed the moist sheen of her shoulders.

She all but cuckolded Kit Gallatin before his very eyes, but he knew how to remedy this sickness.

The mare danced in her paddock, eager for the saddle, accepting bit and bridle like a gift.

Kit mounted with a forgotten grace and felt the shudder of the mare doffing her milk-sweet temper. Hooves stuttering, she awaited his permission to explode.

Within sight of the stream, he gave it, urging her to prove herself. Forelegs reached, muscles slid against taut hide. With hands and weight defined by his own concentration, Kit guided a ton of running horseflesh.

Like wagon spokes, the mare's legs reached and planted and reached. How simple to lean so she avoided a fallen branch. How natural to clap heels to her ribs and lean his face to her flying mane. How exhilarating, that beat of silence after she launched herself over the brook. And then landed, square and true.

Kit pulled the mare toward a winding path that led to a house hidden in a glade.

He'd been bred for this, trained for it, meant for it. Born

a horseman, not a fop who fussed with lutes and sonnets. Let these mortals believe what they liked. He knew a great airy chain held order, from queen to the lowest mite. He knew his place upon it. The day he'd forgotten and taken spying as a way to renown, he'd been cast into Chaos.

He would not err again. Destiny had decreed that he ride hard into the darkness, alone.

Chapter
Seven

Tall and pointed as a letter A, the house stood centered in a glen. Reddish boards, round metal chimney, curtains drawn. Nothing untoward. The birds' stillness and Trifle's crab-stepping annoyed Kit.

"Daft old beast. Do you think we've stumbled upon a warlock's lodge?" He rode past the clearing and tied Trifle to a stout branch.

Trifle was a satisfactory mount. Her smooth gaits and spirit pleased him. She moved to rub her face against him and Kit stepped away. In spite of her fire, she was a bit too much the pet.

Animals reacted predictably to ghosthood. Horses, for instance, didn't mind what manner of man commanded, so long as he knew what he was about.

Kit drew slow breaths, dematerializing before he stepped into the glen. He listened for a warning bark.

Dogs took him for a strange sort of human. They bristled and circled, growling and cautious, until he spoke. Then, all but the worst wagged their tails and romped. Kit walked toward the house. It appeared deserted, except for a black cat rising from the shade near the front door. With the exception of Lily, cats dismissed his difference.

This one paused, tail lashing. One paw pinned a pale-bellied lizard. It lay dead, front legs raised in supplication. With gentle jaws, the cat took it up, then trotted into the forest.

Though no sign or mailbox identified it, Kit knew he'd found Rick's house. Paths were raked and the porch swept with forced tidiness, and he'd heard both Jan and Rick indicate how near he was, in case of emergency.

Is that what this was? The emergency of a suitor green with jealousy? Nevertheless, he would waste ten minutes to assure himself that Rick was no threat to Miranda.

Silvery carpet yielded underfoot. A narrow gray couch faced two matching chairs, but no table stood between them. Didn't a professor need papers and books? He saw none.

He checked the ceiling overhead and glanced behind doors. He found nothing remarkable. Still, a man who'd died from a cowardly rearward attack never forgot. He reached a small kitchen and ran his hand down long tile counters, unmarred by a single crumb.

Damning a man for cleanliness could be nothing but jealousy. Yet, something here felt wrong. *Tick.* The hand of a pewter wall clock twitched to the next minute, startling him.

His renewed sense of smell detected something which was not quite ammonia, nor camphor. The morbid odor made him swallow.

Nonsense. He'd swallowed nothing but his pride. He hadn't pursued a fugitive to this door, or come searching for goods purloined. Like a mumblecrust old woman seeking gossip, he looked for reasons to distrust. A nobleman should come armed with a better excuse than the sight of a man's hand on a willing woman.

Kit had passed partway through the front door when conviction seized him. Any secrets would be hidden from view of the idle visitor.

He followed more silvery carpet past a neat blue bedroom, a bathroom with lavender towels. Upstairs, the A-frame formed a loft. The carpet before him was bathed with crimson light. Maroon taffeta draped the windows, luring him into a macabre museum.

In two centuries of afterlife, he'd sensed no other specters. But here, their shuffling and suffering pressed close. The room was filled with relics of death.

Checking behind the door, he found a gravestone of weathered granite. The mason had chiseled willow trees weeping before a setting sun, but the name of the dead was missing.

To his right, he saw a glass case divided into compartments. Rings, brooches, and lockets lay on white satin, but all the jewelry was black. One ring bulged with a winged death's-head. Another ring bore a coffin, complete with a skeletal inhabitant and the initials A.H. Where the bony arms crossed, the ring's black paint had rubbed away to show gold. A jet brooch with dangling beads featured the coin-size portrait of a man with a drooping mustache. Intricate lettering framed the portrait: "Prepared Be to Follow Me."

"Unprepared, but present all the same," Kit muttered. "So, this is where he works." He considered the modern desk, its computer and clipboard full of paper. He opened one drawer and found a bundle of fragrant candles. The drawer beneath held glass vials filled with herbs. He eased the drawer closed and stared at three framed floral designs in shades of brown, hung above the desk.

Kit leaned on stacks of books, bringing his face near enough to scrutinize the art. Not oil paintings, not ink sketches. Bits of hair had been inlaid like brushstrokes to imitate petals.

They must have been arranged with a jeweler's tiny tweezers, but what was this? He drew back suddenly, bumping the desk chair.

Auburn braids no wider than his little finger twined beneath the glass covering the middle picture. A light spot in the center proved to be a primitive photograph. Waxen in death, lay a woman of middle years.

"Sweet Jesu." Kit smoothed his beard.

Had some grieving husband commissioned this violation? Had sorrow so soaked his brain that he'd forgotten all women had vanities? His dear could not pat her collar into place nor arrange her lips in a smile. Memorializing her with locks shorn and pasted onto an effigy seemed cruel.

Kit's hands closed on the books and frustration elbowed pity aside. The titles included words he did not know: *thanatology* and *euthanasia*.

And then he saw the Graveyard Rose.

"Pigeonholed!" Kit withdrew the replica from an open-faced nook. "By my soul, it's not even silver." He weighed the filigreed box in his hand. Unlike the true Graveyard Rose, this copy had a slyly disguised and hinged top.

The hilt of his Toledo sword had been hammered shut around his heart. This impostor was more utilitarian. He heard something shift within it.

Often, he'd wondered how he would feel, opening the Graveyard Rose to find his withered heart. But this was only a replica. It probably held candy or sealing wax. Kit flipped the lid open.

The necklace glimmered back at him. Did Rick deem this piece unworthy of a place in the glass-topped case?

He lifted a gold chain with lopsided links and lowered the trinket to the hollow of his hand. Half a broken heart. He rubbed his thumb over the inscription on the back of the charm, held it to the murky light and read, "Death parts united hearts."

Quite the reverse of the usual drivel. What a perfect bauble to leave Miranda, in memory of their kiss. Of course he wouldn't filch it. Even a ghost's honor was worth more than sentiment.

He replaced the necklace in its box and would have stowed it, except for a wrinkled paper in the niche. As he removed it, a door closed downstairs.

Odd that a thin slip of paper, printed with mechanical letters, bore such tidings. It was not the confirmation of money to be paid on July 4 for the Graveyard Rose that stunned Kit. Nor was it the ungodly sum of money. It was the name. A name which belonged on hell-singed vellum.

At the sound of raised voices, Kit replaced the paper and set the box atop it. A tussle shook the house as he drew a centering breath, lost form, and drifted down the stairs.

On the silvery living room carpet, Rick shucked the shirt off a whore.

Whore she must be, rocking on all fours above the man. Face hidden, she suckled at his ear. Mediterranean dark waves fell short of her shoulders. Rick's tugging had bared the length of her serpent-supple back.

"Find it." The female loosed Rick's pants, shoving them lower with knees more adroit than most women's hands.

"I've looked everywhere." Rick grabbed a handful of her hair, pulled, and bit her exposed throat. She cried out and twisted, showing an obscene etching on her stomach.

Kit fixed his eyes on the rug beneath his feet. If not for Miranda, he'd leave them rutting.

"Why didn't you search when you came back?"

"Asshole. What did you think I was doing? Really looking for my purse? While you were out there copping a feel?"

It took no imagination to unravel the vulgarity. Why had he left Heart's Ease so precipitously and what had happened after?

More grunting, the rasp of more garments shed, then there, on the silver carpet, a telephone with no cord or supportive instrument, rang. They ignored it.

"I kept her busy while you were inside. I'm just keeping her off balance."

Kit valued cold control, but damme, if Rick spoke of Miranda, while he prodded his whore, that was reason enough for murder.

"Shut up." The whore's order cut across Rick's moan. "Again. Do that again and hurry. That's Ralph." She gestured vaguely to the telephone. "He's wondering why I'm so long at the bank."

"She won't tell me where it is."

"I said shut *up*." The whore gasped, then fell to crooning. "That's better, baby. It's just that we've got no time, baby. I'm leaving, and I want you with me."

"She'll give me the box."

And then, you'll die. All reasons to keep this cur alive would end, once Kit had his heart.

"Do what you have to, but if I ever see you groping that nicey-nice little schoolteacher again, I'll tell Noah everything."

It would signify nothing, the death of such a bitch. If he grabbed that neck and shook her, it might silence her foul mouth.

Kit turned substantial.

He flexed his fingers in a killing grip, but pale-haired, fastidious Rick had finally stopped the whore's mouth, and Kit could stomach no more.

Through dusk's veil, Kit saw Miranda watching from the back veranda as he broke cover, galloping up from the ravine. She wore a proper skirt, long and filmy. It billowed as she moved to the rail and smiled.

He and the horse complemented each other. He knew that, but he felt more than pride. He felt her eyes' caress and remembered her touch.

Now. Tonight.

He must find the Graveyard Rose and let Rick know it was gone. That accomplished, he would truly and permanently die, ending Miranda's danger.

The girl had tried to protect him from herself, a harbinger of death. Her misplaced mercy tempted him to live, but playing the suitor to Miranda Fairfield would be as cruel as the braid-bedecked photograph was.

In him, Andi would have no lover. The shoulders she'd held belonged to a puff of English dust. The kiss which thrilled them both came from lips long dead. Like Sarah, she would find Kit Gallatin's truth grotesque.

Above him, Miranda leaned folded arms on the low railing.

"You're back."

Kit touched his heels to Trifle. Though Miranda's position looked boyish, it should afford him a lovely view of her breasts.

As Kit raised his hand in acknowledgment, she stood straight, ending his voyeur's view. Still, he drew rein. Trifle fought the restraint. With her corral in view, the mare wanted to be rid of him.

But Miranda's smile stayed him. Her wide eyes bid him welcome, though both hands twisted in the gauzy blue skirt. Nervous and hopeful, Miranda was really nothing like Sarah. Though less gently bred, Miranda was more fragile. His truth would break her spirit. Therein lay a goad for honor.

"All you need is a suit of armor and a sword."

"I'd give much for a sword."

How many centuries since he'd severed a head from a neck? He wondered if he still had the knack, for he knew one in dire need of lopping.

"Skirmishing, even with shadows, is quite good exercise," he explained.

"I have a sword in the basement." Openly pleased, she gestured back inside the house. "Do you want it? Actually, I think there's a couple of them."

"Truly?" He craved a real fight and Rick's blood on his hands.

"Come on in, I'll show you."

"I'll just put the mare away."

Trifle got short shrift. Stripped of gear and rubbed down with a handful of straw, she bolted from his slap on her rump.

Lucky he didn't want the basement as a trysting place. All rock and hard floor, it offered no attraction except privacy.

Very well. He would talk with her a bit, enjoy her touch if she granted it, but he would allow no grazing of lips or breasts and definitely no kissing.

Kit spared a glance at the round mirror swaying from a leather loop in the stable.

Once, maids had thought him handsome. Though browned by exposure, his skin was unmarked by disease, and his hair and beard were free of vermin. The blade which had slashed beneath one brow in his first battle had left a scar, but he'd kept a pair of eyes colored so dark a brown they hid the black of his pupils. He'd been comely enough on the day he died, and had remained so. Only honor kept him from seducing her.

He smoothed the sides of his beard, remembering that gesture from Miranda. While their lips touched, her fingertips had pressed his whiskers and skin. Faith, he'd felt her touch in his jawbone.

She would do it again. She was as eager as he and wondering why he'd mentioned nothing of Monday's moonlight kiss.

The kiss was a farewell to living. Nothing more. Though randy as the greenest boy, he wouldn't take her. And there lay the greatest irony: Miranda's curiosity brewed the headiest love potion he could imagine.

'Zounds, he must remember his honor.

Even before the overhead lights sputtered on, Andi decided the basement seemed less sinister with Kit along.

He preceded her down the steps. "This is how it's done." He glanced back over a shoulder too broad for the white linen shirt. "If brigands are lurking, they'll bash me first. If a serpent's coiled on a step, I'll dispatch it for you."

Andi smiled at Kit's archaic cadences. He was really getting into the Renaissance period of his book. No wonder he wanted a sword.

When he stopped without warning, she slammed into his back.

"And if you fall, lady, I'll pillow your landing."

Wouldn't *that* leapfrog a few awkward moments? Not once today had he met her eyes, but a graceful plunge would take them past the point they'd left off.

As Kit surveyed the sewing machine, the unlabeled cartons and retired Nordictrack, Andi tried not to consider the perfect couple-size dimensions of a braided rug the color of orange sherbet.

Even the headless, plastic-draped mannequins looked dashing, swagged in their period costumes.

"Ah." Kit lifted a sword from its rack and settled it in his hand. He rotated his wrist in turns that made the sword hiss, then aimed it toward the floor. He muttered as he gazed down his arm, along the blade.

"What?"

"Not balanced for defense." Kit cocked his elbow, held his arm in line with his torso, and advanced on a mannequin. "More of a ceremonial sword, perhaps."

"Jason probably used it in a movie. Jason—my uncle," she clarified, but he wasn't listening.

"Why do you sigh?" Kit faced her, the sword drooping from his wrist.

"No reason."

He accepted the lame explanation, replaced the sword, lifted down another, and moved it in an air-whipping figure eight.

"Much better. By the way, I do like your garb."

Andi smoothed her rayon skirt and straightened the waistband over the sleeveless shell. "Thanks. I'm having company for dinner."

A quizzical smile raised Kit's brows.

"Rick's coming back after he cleans up. Would you like to stay?"

"Thank you, no."

She told herself she wasn't taunting him. Not really, but if he'd concluded their kiss was a faux pas, why shouldn't she? If Kit was her boarder, not her boyfriend, why were his black eyes narrowed in fury?

"I won't keep you." Kit bowed stiffly. "But I would borrow this sword, if you've no immediate use for it."

"Go ahead."

He stepped carefully past her for the stairs, as if brushing her arm would burn him.

Before Andi followed, a metallic glitter stopped her. She plucked one of her silver and turquoise earrings from the basement floor. She'd last seen Lily batting it across the bathroom floor. Shaking her head, Andi pocketed the earring. She'd only taken three stairs when Kit turned.

Unsettled by his sudden nearness, Andi almost retreated a step.

"Those Graveyard Rose boxes you were selling at the fair. Do you have one here?"

First Rick, now Kit. Maybe the damned things *did* have some mystical power. "I did have one, but I've misplaced it.'' She took the chance to squeeze past and up the stairs in front of him.

"How is that possible?"

"I just put it down somewhere." Andi held the door, watching him climb. He looked suddenly weary, but it wasn't her fault. "Why do you ask?"

"I didn't get a good look at those you were selling, and I've heard they're something of a legend in the States."

"It'll turn up." She switched off the basement light and closed the door.

"What are you cooking?"

"Me? Nothing."

As they passed through the living room, Kit stared toward blank windows that looked into the night.

"So, this paragon even cooks. Thank you for the sword, Miranda, but remember, men are not always what they seem."

When Cisco followed Rick through the front door, Andi felt relieved that they were a threesome. Together, Cisco and Rick plopped armloads of grease-stained bags onto her kitchen table.

"Quick! You don't want to eat these cold." Rick spurned her neat place settings and ripped through a sack whose logo advertised the Ground Cow in Owen. Inside lay a mound of wrapped hamburgers. "I almost bounced poor Cisco through the roof, trying to get back before they congealed."

"You got that right." Cisco lifted pouches of french fries out of another bag, then scattered catsup and mustard packets. "God, my mom never lets us eat this stuff."

He crammed a wad of fries into his mouth and, belatedly, removed a cap studded with a button which read, I READ BANNED BOOKS. Andi's English teacher heart applauded, but she didn't compliment him. Her approval would ruin his mood.

They ate in companionable silence, except when Lily entered the kitchen, bristled at the visitors, and streaked out of the room as if squirted by a hose. Then they all laughed.

Once wrappers and soft drink cans had been cleared away,

Rick produced a Scrabble board and spread it across the kitchen table as if they were a family.

Though Cisco sat with arms crossed and head tilted so that a glossy hank of hair obscured his eyes, he had a great vocabulary.

" 'Abjured'? With a triple letter score for the *j*? Wow, Cisco, not bad. You're ahead, 172 to my 130 and your coach's 55."

One corner of Cisco's mouth lifted, before he leaned his head into his hand, shading his eyes from view. "Like that's a real big deal?" He yawned.

"English teachers don't like to get skunked by a—what will you be next year? A sophomore?"

"A junior."

They finished the Lady Baltimore cake and half the Jell-O, and Andi had started a second pot of coffee when Rick remembered tomorrow was a school day.

"Eight o'clock's going to come pretty early." He thumped Cisco's shoulder.

"What if I ditch?" Cisco lurched to his feet and pretended to square off.

"If you cut class, you're dead meat." Rick pursued Cisco into the living room and tackled him. The boy hit the floor with a *whump*. "No favors for friends." He pulled Cisco to his feet. "And no wrecking your employer's furniture."

Hoping she would see deer grazing in the moonlight, Andi turned off all the house and outside lights as she walked them to the veranda.

"Listen." She held up a hand. The sprinklers' patter cast a quiet spell over the night. "Sometimes I get deer in the yard. I hear their hooves hit the fence when I surprise them."

For a few seconds, they waited. Even her Volkswagen was silvered with moonlight.

Cisco emitted a snort. " 'Night." He shambled toward Rick's van before mumbling, "Thanks."

Andi blinked as Rick slipped an arm through hers.

"I think you've made a conquest," he whispered.

"A dent, maybe. Not a conquest." Andi heard the radio

blare on in Rick's van. A bass throbbing joined the other night sounds.

"He finally told me what it is he holds against you."

His vagueness grated.

"Anyone in town could've told you I killed Clint Kern."

"That's not exactly what he said." Rick squeezed her arm, but it gave no comfort.

"Close enough. Pretty creepy, huh?"

"Sad. Unlucky. I wouldn't call it creepy."

"Thanks, but it's still a good thing you two are almost done with painting."

"While we were up on the ladders, I was taking a look at the roof. Those shingles are pretty old. You could have a mess, come winter," Rick said.

"They're not leaking now, and I won't be here when they do." Andi felt a twinge. It had been years since she'd seen Heart's Ease covered with snow. "That'll be the new owners' problem."

Moonlight dappled the path, but the cottonwood's shadow made a black bar before them.

"Thanks for a nice night." Rick jingled the keys in the pocket of his khakis.

"You're welcome. Thanks for all the work on the house."

"Dinah's paying for it."

"Okay, then—for the cheeseburgers."

"You're welcome."

A night bird worried in liquid tones. When Rick moved to kiss her in the cottonwood's shadow, out of Cisco's sight, Andi let him. The kiss fell on her cheek.

"Better go in." Andi shrugged out from under his restraining arm. "I'm getting seedlings in the morning. Jan said to be there before nine." She'd taken two steps toward the veranda before she called back, "Drive safely."

No need to think he'll crash after a silly little peck on the cheek. Not with Cisco in the car, please.

She bustled through the front door and closed it behind her. In the center of the living room she stopped.

More than an errant breeze chilled her. More than a window left open or a gust down the chimney flue. She'd shut the basement door, but Lily might have bumped one of Jason's trapdoors ajar. Andi rubbed her palms together, then closed her icy fingers inside her fists.

What if the Peeping Tom had watched for Rick's van to depart? She turned slowly, checking each window for a dark silhouette.

Her bare toes hit the leg of a table that Rick and Cisco's wrestling had jostled out of position.

"Damn it!" Andi flounced down onto the couch, then bolted upright, eyes straining through the darkness to see what was there. Nothing. No cat, no lurker, no source for the sudden warmth which had supplanted the wintery cold.

She was nuts. It was a reflection of her instability that she actually thought something was there, when the couch was empty. She flicked on the light.

Lily's paws pattered down the staircase from the bedroom and she leapt into Andi's lap.

"Good kitty." Andi stroked Lily's smooth white length. Stealing earrings must be a sign of acceptance.

People in town would do the same. Curiosity about the city woman, about the girl who'd killed Clint Kern, would slack off.

People would find other gossip to amuse them. Maybe a mouse would scamper across the bread counter in Brown's grocery. Brother Wolcott and his teenage bride might prove to be cousins. And Renetta, with hungry lips tattooed around her navel, had to be a scandalmonger's dream.

Sparrowgrass was checking her out. That was to be expected. Her one lurker had been Cisco. That, too, was logical.

Her feeling of being watched was nothing but the result of guilt and paranoia. No matter how real it seemed, nothing angry had been waiting inside her house.

Chapter
Eight

Slamming his fist into a wall might dam his fury, for now. Kit wondered how two days had passed since her betrayal—that moonlight kiss from Rick could be nothing less—and he felt even more desire for violence and pain.

Sword in hand, he crouched in a fencing position. He feinted at air, advanced, retreated, lunged at the pillow he'd hung from the rafters.

Rick could eat her food, but Kit had no appetite.

Rick could keep his body substantial while he rutted in mindless sex, but Kit had to concentrate to keep every boundary solid.

Rick could give her a child.

That last revolted Kit more than a maggoty chop. But it would not happen. Miranda was no fool.

Kit lunged again and ripped the pillow's cover. What meager satisfaction. The blade hungered for the heart of an opponent. Oh, what joy to rip that pulsing organ from his body, knowing that paltry boy lacked the nerve to get it back!

Kit cast the foil away, letting it roll until its bell hilt struck something with a clang.

When she'd come back into the house, lips fresh from Rick's, she'd stood in the darkness, afraid. Seared by her betrayal and her fear, Kit had searched Heart's Ease all night. And again yesterday, through the night until dawn.

Why hadn't his heart called out to him?

Though he'd never reclaimed his heart, his passport to eternity, he'd never had trouble finding it. In the days just after death, he'd materialized within reach of it many times, but he hadn't mastered the otherworldly coordination to grab it.

Years ago in India, he might have taken it as he materialized beside a paisley-draped table on which it sat. His hand had been poised to grab it as Sarah entered the room. She'd believed him a thief. She stood wide-eyed as he lied, then her beauty delayed him. Her need detained him. Her revulsion very nearly destroyed him. Leaving without his heart seemed a fair bargain for survival.

Now, salvation lay in that bloody house and he could not find it! Each time he thought he felt its summons, he ended tracing Miranda's steps, from basement to kitchen to bed, and found nothing.

His preoccupation had less to do with lust and more with worry. Rick, still reeking from his whore—in spirit, if not in fact—had kissed Miranda. She'd guessed nothing of Rick's plan to gull her innocence. Kit's brain turned the same page again and again. Each time, he saw Rick kissing Miranda.

Picking up a tablet of paper he'd brought for his "novel," he settled in the red booth and propped his elbows on the table.

He poised the pencil and started a list:
1. Rick set on thievery
2. Miranda must be told—before I find box—depart
                    —before Aragon determines to . . ."
   . . . *hurt her.*

Aragon was base and ugly-spirited. Driven by greed and frustration, Rick Aragon could harm Miranda.

Aragon. The slip of paper in the villan's desk had confirmed what instinct should have known. The son of a son of a whoreson.

It was unnecessary to ponder such an outrage.

Kit chewed over the simplest solution. He would repeat what he'd heard in Rick's cottage. It was up to Miranda whether she believed him.

Kit turned the pages back to paper he'd already inscribed with his past. He'd left off with Arabella. His lips twitched at the thought of that female who'd proved females did quite well on their own.

> *Dark, lit only by candles, my lady's chamber smelled of spiced wine and sex. James, he to whom she'd newly given her affection, had departed, codpiece flat, still assigning the disposition of her money.*
>
> *Though the day blustered outside, Arabella's chamber was warm. Myself, cold as ice since Aragon's betrayal, I embraced this warmth. Leeched newly innocent by death, I strove not to scare Arabella. I should not have troubled overmuch.*
>
> *"Love, be not afrighted. It is Christopher, your betrothed."*
>
> *At that, she rose on an elbow, hair of purest jet streaking the crimson coverlet, cheeks rubbed red by another's beard.*
>
> *"Burdensome shade!" quoth she. "Restless spirit! James swore thou would return for thy heart." Her rough words smelled of clove. "You don't know what's chanced, I've news that will exorcise thee faster than any priest."*
>
> *Mayhap fear made her cruel.*
>
> *"Aragon's returned, professing thou the traitor. One who believes him is Barrett. He's lopped thou from the family tree. Thou might have died at birth."*
>
> *It was then I felt the aching summons of my heart.*

*My heart lay hidden in its coffer, beneath a great
pile of dress and underskirts. No. 'Twas not hidden,
neither, but cast aside in Arabella's hurry to have her
coney coped.*

"But give it to me and I will depart."

*I accounted it generous so to vow, the cow being
too stupid to fear for her immortal soul.*

*"Fie, I'll not." Arabella tossed her hair, baring her
bosom to taunt me. "I'll sell it to purchase knightly
trappings for James and his horse."*

*And though the Lord requires nothing of us but that
we return the love He so freely gives, mention of the
knave's horse set me swearing. I condemned her, upon
whom I had cast all my care in life, for her fickleness.*

*And when I sought to take my treasure, which meant
naught to her and all to me, I could not. Arabella
laughed. I called her a cheating whore. And regret it
I do not.*

• • •

Could atmospheric pressure tighten around you like a
noose? Andi raised her face to the shower's needle spray.
Ragged from work, her hands snagged as they passed over
her wet hair. Scrubbed until the dirt under her fingernails
was wedged there for good, they looked like hell, too. But
she didn't need prom-smooth skin.

What she needed, wanted, *desired* was a Weed Eater.

She'd weeded the old roses with care, but plots around the
estate could take a less delicate approach. With rake and
shovel, she'd reclaimed Dinah's garden from the weeds and
wild grass. Her fingers ached from uprooting every shoot of
errant vegetation. Yesterday in town she'd spotted a dandelion with the audacity to show its yellow face in a cracked
sidewalk. She thought nothing of stopping to tug at it until
Dr. Noah strolled out of the Dancing Goat and cautioned her
to bend her knees and squat if she didn't want to hurt her
back.

A Weed Eater would mow down that thicket by Trifle's corral, clearing a raised hump of sunny ground perfect for a corn hill. As it was, the Early Glow corn seedlings shared the basins she'd formed from trowel and mud. Flanked by basil, tomato, and zucchini, the corn would have to be thinned after it sprouted. She'd planted seeds for three kinds of lettuce, radishes, and scarlet runner beans too, which should scroll up the chicken wire fence by July.

She'd taken Jan's advice and covered the beds with a layer of straw to hold in moisture and deter birds. Gathering straw from Trifle's barn, Andi discovered that Kit Gallatin had not been keeping his end of their bargain.

Not surprising, really, since Kit, who'd given her the most tender kiss of her life, hadn't shown his pompous face for three days.

Not that it mattered. She'd sworn off giddy highs and esteem-eating lows. If he happened to see her mucking out Trifle's stall, she would be coolly polite.

Andi cranked the shower off and dressed without toweling dry. An engine's sudden silence and a ratcheting emergency brake said Cisco and Rick had arrived for their last day's work.

Maybe.

Andi traced her toe over a fissure in the bathroom linoleum. Had it widened since yesterday? Maybe Sparrowgrass had shaken with a subtle series of earthquakes. She imagined brushing her teeth one morning, the floor dropping, plummeting to the basement . . .

"*Then* what would I tell Dinah?"

As if she'd heard, Lily shook a well-licked paw, vaulted off the laundry hamper, and mewed her concern.

"Never mind, kitty." Andi pulled her hair up in a sloppy topknot and made a kissing sound toward the cat. "The fall alone will kill me."

The shower's refreshment clung until she reached the veranda. Rick stood in the driveway, smirking.

"Where's Cisco?"

"I gave him the day off, since we're pretty near done." He leaned against his van, arms crossed and smiling.

"Is something going to jump out of there?"

"Not exactly." He slid the door open, grappled inside, then presented something long and unwieldy.

"A Weed Eater. Wow!"

"A friend covered my class so I could drive into Cloverdale—"

"I've got to plug it in."

"Here's an extension cord," he shouted as she ran toward the veranda's electrical outlet. "It's ready to go. I bought some extra line. Hey, take it easy. Do you know how to run the thing?"

"How hard can it be?" The machine roared off the ground, whirring like a helicopter. "I'm going to try it out in back." She took a few steps and stopped. "Did you pay for this?"

"It'll be on Dinah's bill."

"Good." Though it wasn't wrapped in fancy paper, she couldn't accept such an expensive gift.

"You should wear safety glasses."

Because Rick's caution made her feel guilty, she flicked the switch to off and squeezed his forearm. "Thanks."

Summer silence made it sound like more than simple gratitude. Hot gusts of wind broke the afternoon's sealed heat.

Oh, hell, he was going to do it again. Andi grappled with the Weed Eater so Rick's kiss only grazed her cheek.

"Storm coming in." Rick squinted toward the horizon. "Want to drive into Owen and have a real dinner tonight?"

"I'm exhausted," Andi yawned. "I couldn't do a real dinner justice."

"Gina's frozen pizzas aren't bad. I could pick one up and come back about seven."

"You know what you *could* do?" Andi fidgeted, eager to slash weeds. "Something weird's going on in the bathroom. There's a crack in the linoleum, and it's gotten wider just since yesterday."

It was an odd sop to throw a guy acting like a suitor, but it worked.

"Great. I'll take a look before I gather up my painting stuff." Rick gestured toward the house.

"Go ahead. I'll be around back." She considered the distance. "I think the cord will reach."

The door harp trilled.

That hadn't been difficult. In his eagerness to get at the bathroom floor, he'd forgotten about dinner.

Andi hefted the heavy orange extension cord in a coil over her shoulder. She paid it out slowly, working toward the thicket beside Trifle's corral.

By evening, gray-bellied clouds spilled rain between Heart's Ease and the western mountains. A steady drizzle soaked her black tank top until, fearing electrocution, she unplugged the Weed Eater and fled to the veranda.

Thunder rumbled as she pulled on the pink flannel shirt she'd left on the steps that morning. She watched the storm move closer.

For no reason, it annoyed her that Rick's van remained parked next to her VW. Why hadn't he taken a quick glance at the crack and gone on his way? Maybe she'd turned into a hermit—she didn't feel like going inside until he was out.

As the wind freshened, Trifle jogged around her corral. Andi stood up slowly, feeling both knees catch. Still, cleaning Trifle's stall wouldn't be hard. By the time she finished, Rick should be gone.

Hands on hips, she stood in the barn doorway, glanced at the staircase up to Kit's apartment, then surveyed the dim stall until a sudden shove sent her forward a step.

Andi choked back her gasp. The animal had startled the heck out of her.

"Sorry, sweetie." She grabbed the cheek piece of Trifle's halter, turned her toward the corral, and clucked as she'd heard Kit do. Snuffling, Trifle went.

Quite pleased with her growing equine expertise, Andi dusted her hands together and studied the stall once more. It would be better if she had overhead lights—and if she knew what she was doing.

At least the upstairs horse expert wasn't standing by, giving advice. She hadn't even heard a creak from overhead.

She latched open the top half of a Dutch door and considered the wooden shelves. Curry combs, wicked-looking curved implements, rags, all sorts of liniments, and a radio.

Though the barn had no electricity, some thoughtful soul, probably Jason, had brought a transistor radio out. Hoping its batteries were fresher than those in Dinah's upstairs flashlight, Andi adjusted the dial. Finally static cleared with a sawing of fiddles and a blaring down-home voice.

"K-H-O-S, broadcasting live from the Cooper County offices in Owen, California. Kay-hoss, for the cowboy in all of us."

Twanging guitars might just put her in the mood for shoveling manure. "Thanks, Jason," she muttered, resetting the radio on its shelf.

She selected a rake, thinking it was probably weird to thank a dead man for providing music on a rainy day. Come to think of it, though, she wouldn't mind such a legacy, even if the prevailing station was country-western.

Humming, Andi cleared the soiled straw into the corral, shooed Trifle once more, then sprinkled powdered lime from an apparently antique shaker can. Was it Jason who'd told her lime "sweetened" the floor beneath the straw? She'd bet it just killed bacteria.

Half done. She turned the radio up to hear a haunting ballad about a rodeo cowboy, then shucked the flannel shirt and searched for a pair of snips to cut the wire on a fresh bale of straw. Finding none, she knelt and wrestled the wire loop off with her bare hands. When it sliced her knuckles, Andi cast it aside, making a mental note to get rid of it so Trifle didn't ensnare herself.

A footstep?

Whistling applause greeted the opening bars of the concert version of "Stand by Your Man," and Andi kept watching the stairs as she scuttled out of her undignified position, but no one stood there.

That was a good thing, because though her voice was better suited to lip-sync, Andi crooned along with Tammy Wynette.

She separated flakes of straw and scattered them.

If the rain continued, Trifle would love this cozy corner in her barn.

The pitchfork made a serviceable air guitar until she started separating flakes of straw and scattering them. Then she began to sneeze.

As rain blew in the window, her serenade grew froggier and punctuated with sniffs, but Andi layered the straw good and deep.

Then she drew in a lungful of straw dust, faced the curious horse, and belted out the last words. "Thank you," she said modestly, then executed a final bow before baling wire caught her ankle and she whumped forward into the straw.

This time the applause wasn't wildly enthusiastic and it didn't come from the transistor radio.

Andi thought she might just stay face down in the fresh straw. She would get used to the stalks piercing her tank top and stabbing her chin.

"Quite the lark, are you, Miss Fairfield?"

It *would* be Kit, lowering himself into the straw beside her, tugging the back of her tank top until she sat up.

He sat cross-legged, facing her. "I've never heard the song before. Still, I think I applaud the sentiment."

"But the performance left something to be desired?" She suggested with a sniff.

"Indeed." Kit leaned his right shoulder against the stall wall.

Nothing like a critic to clear the sinuses, she thought, but the barn's watery gray light softened his fierce features as his black eyes filled with her, then lowered. He lifted her battered and wire-sliced hand as if it were attached to a princess.

And then, he didn't kiss it, exactly. Keeping his eyes on hers, Kit raised her scuffed knuckles. He brushed them back and forth over his lips, drawing breath as if each move aroused him.

In her corral, Trifle stomped a hoof.

"So," Andi began, "you must have been busy the last few days."

"Worried," he admitted. "About this Rick character." He released her hand. "Have you asked yourself why he's excited about fixing a bathroom floor?"

"What are you talking about?" She pronounced each word with deliberation.

When she'd lingered in the yard to tell Rick about the floor, when Rick kissed her cheek, had Kit been watching? He couldn't have, not without her noticing him. His window faced north, not west.

"Rick is pleased because he'll be working inside your house. Alone. While you muck about outside with your plants, he'll ransack your belongings, looking for the Graveyard Rose."

"That's ridiculous." Andi made fists before her hands darted up in frustration. "Those boxes are a dime a dozen. You saw them all over the table in that booth. They're a fad. Soon you'll be able to buy one in shops from Long Beach to Long Island."

"Not like that one."

"They're all the same. They were made by the same artist."

"No artist formed that one, Miranda. Didn't you notice how it had broken in some places, while the castings, the copies, just appeared to be broken? The first box was made of a basket hilt, pounded with the butt of a left-handed dirk." Kit rubbed the space between his brows as if it pained him. "Somehow, you got the true Graveyard Rose, battered into shape by Barrett."

Even if Kit Gallatin had run across the facts in his historical research, even if he were an antiquities dealer, for crying out loud, he wouldn't know so much? Would he?

"They wouldn't have let me take the original. Besides, why would the original be in Sparrowgrass?" Exasperated, Andi slapped her palms on her thighs. "Why are we even talking about this?"

"Because Rick made a vow to his doxy that he'd do whatever he must to take the Graveyard Rose from you."

Rick and his doxy. She looked away from Kit and frowned. Other than actors, English teachers, and dachshund breeders, how many people used the word *doxy*? Even allowing for complete involvement in his novel, Kit was a most perplexing man.

Outside, the cloudburst had ended. She tried to imagine Rick plotting. Intermittent plops fell from the rafters as she wondered if junior college instructors had doxies. Andi smoothed tendrils of escaped hair toward her topknot, then took the whole thing down to wind up again.

Kit mistook her silence for tranquility. "I must say I'm baffled over why you'd permit a man like him access to your person."

"*Access?*"

Kit nodded, smoothing his beard. "It's a diversionary tactic, of course, and frankly, I'm a little disappointed—"

"Get used to it."

"I beg your pardon?" Kit blinked. His arrogance faltered.

"Get used to disappointment, because I don't care what you think."

"Shhh, of course you do." Kit's hand slid down her loosened hair.

Andi did not find the gesture soothing.

"Excuse me, but you are my boarder, a virtual stranger." She touched her breastbone. "We have a business relationship."

Kit's chin jerked up and he raised one brow.

"I don't know what British backwater you've been in for the last three decades, but I have a news flash for you. Smart, independent women think for themselves. That chattel thing? It sort of ran its course."

Kit's sputtering produced no sound that resembed words, so Andi finished, "And *I* think I'll choose the men I'm with."

Only his grasp on her upper arms kept her from falling backward. He lunged so near, his brow almost struck hers. "You're right. It's bloody well time you were with a man. And it had bloody well better be me."

"Oh, now wait—"

His grip shifted. A forearm supported her spine. A hand cupped the back of her head. Both protected her as his lips forced her down to the straw, beneath him.

No. If she screamed it, Kit would stop.

"No." As she spoke against his lips with the faint breath

he'd left her, "no" sounded like a languid complaint. When Kit's hand burrowed under the black tank top, worked between them and lifted her bra, she felt heat rather than flesh and bone. Her second "no" sounded like a mew.

"Oh, yes, Miranda."

She'd never noticed the syllables of her name. They rolled off his tongue, muffling her mind's logic.

"What are you doing?" Andi knew she was not asking *him*. Still, it was Kit who answered.

"What I should have done long ago."

Andi shook her head, trying to reactivate thought.

He trailed a hand across her brow, through her hair, and forked his fingers through her outflung hand.

He'd said . . . what? *It bloody well better be me.* She pulled her lips away.

"This isn't about me, is it?" She struggled to sit and settled for Kit leaving her lips free to speak. "This is a guy thing, like dogs quarreling over a—"

"Please don't say that." Kit's forehead wrinkled. He rolled to one elbow, looking truly pained.

Confusion replaced Andi's irritation. "I was going to say, 'quarreling over a bone.' "

"Oh. Go on, then."

She laughed at how completely he'd derailed her thoughts. She'd been braced against his arrogance, and instead his eyes had glowed with something very like respect.

Far off, she heard the door harp and then the jingle of keys. Kit must have heard too, for he stood, pulling her up by one hand, though her arms tensed with a need to clamp him close.

Kit sensed that too. He stayed so near, her bare kneecaps brushed his jeans. Clearing his throat, he picked straw out of her tank top. Then his arms linked around her waist and he looked down at her.

"You're wrong. In all the history of the world, Miranda, nothing has been more *about you*. He's"—Kit jabbed a dismissing hand toward the house—"beneath contempt."

Her eyes stung from staring so hard at him. She felt dizzy, about to topple forward, yet she couldn't look away.

Just an inch, she raised her arms and Kit's lips slanted across hers. His chest bowed, his arms gathered her in a protective invasion as, open-handed, she touched his shirt.

She must try to think. The whirring start of the van's engine meant something. Tires rasped on dirt. It meant they were alone.

She surged closer to Kit, kissing him, knowing she needed to get closer to him, but fighting the dark, steady pulse coursing beneath her skin. It spread deeper, under her ribs, then bloomed hot beneath her heart.

"I *will* please you," he vowed.

"Oh." Andi felt her head sway, felt his lips graze her neck. "I know." She tried to laugh, to find one drop of humor to dilute this drugging flood. Then he pushed the black strap off her shoulder.

"God, Kit." Her voice peaked as her eyes fluttered open. Searching for that bright awe she'd seen before, Andi opened her eyes.

Sun sifted through the beams, gilding dust still floating from their scuffle. Her hands fell, suddenly empty.

Kit's face, marked with profound sorrow, wavered before her.

"Forgive me, Miranda," came his voice but by then he was gone.

Chapter Nine

Kit had heard of impotence. Around midnight campfires, soldiers had few secrets, but tales of personal disaster always surfaced as *other* men's misfortune. Those poor sots lost male power at the critical moment, felled by drink or age or unlovely partners.

None of these problems plagued Kit. And no momentary droop approached the humiliation of *vanishing* from the circle of Miranda's arms.

'sblood, what degradation. All because he must concentrate to maintain a solid shape. In God's holy name, *how* might he concentrate when the wench set him afire?

He wanted to sling through the forest, whack trees, swear, shout, rage at this hell. But no gentleman would escape hell and leave Miranda behind, weeping.

Be a man, Swanfort. Materialize and tell her the truth.

And how might that truth go?

My body, not your beauty, failed us. Come to that, love, it wasn't quite my body, either. That earthly vessel was left afield for magpies and daws to peck at. Only my heart, a grisly memento, remains. That heart is in your house, wherever you mislaid it!

No, he must not blame her. Miranda already believed herself guilty of much mischief.

A pitying laugh nearly broke from him as he watched the wild-eyed lass stamp her foot. She rubbed her arms as her eyes searched among the beams. She'd find nothing.

"Not even bats, Miranda." He materialized, sitting on the stairs behind her.

She startled and shouted. "Am I nuts?"

She didn't turn at his voice, though, only watched Trifle clop back inside the barn to lip the fresh straw.

"No, you've been set upon by a most inconsiderate specter."

Miranda didn't listen. Though he appreciated the graceful arms bared by that scrap of a black shirt, though he felt foggy all over again, staring at her blue-jeaned backside, he wished she would turn around.

"Maybe something's wrong with my eyes. Cataracts. Don't they make your vision cloudy? Or what if I knocked myself out when I tripped? I bet that's it." She turned slowly, and her glance darted around him, not meeting his eyes. "Then I dreamed you were here. Did you revive me?"

"I did not, because you did not lose consciousness." He reached out to her, palm up. "I did kiss you."

Her hand closed on his, hard. He thought of eternity—cold, dark, and solitary. He must kiss her again.

"But wait." She released his hand. "Just *wait* a minute, Kit. How did you vanish?"

"I told you, Miranda."

"That's just not possible." She waved her hands in outright dismissal. "Unless it's like mind control. Hypnosis, hooked into what I told you about Clint and Domingo." She slid a finger across her lower lip, musing. "You *took* that confession, then wiggled your way into my mind."

"Do you believe that?"

She considered the barn floor and shook her head.

"No, you're an arrogant jerk, not a sadist."

"I never thought to thank you for such words." He exhaled and let her pace.

Finally, she strode back to him. She set both hands on the rise between his shoulders and neck. Only gradually did she lean forward, trusting him with her weight. He pressed out with all the force of his being. Touching him, she would feel strong solidity.

Her sorrel hair curled around her chin. It looped across her cheek and teased the corner of her mouth. Her eyes of Swanfort blue implored him to explain once more.

"Forgive me, Miranda. If I could have taken my heart without vexing you, I would have. But, no, you must needs slip it down your bodice. And I cannot move the physical world without turning physical myself." He felt her hands, cold on his shoulders. He *felt them.* "To take the box, I would have had to turn visible and unlace your kirtle. I might have knocked you to the dust. Certainly, I would have frightened you."

Still she said nothing. Her eyes, glazed and weary, held on his face. Kit raised his shoulders, filling her palms.

"Miranda, I am a ghost."

"Are you sure?"

The tilt of her head indicated she could not be convinced. All the same, he nodded.

"That's just not possible. Stop me if I'm repeating myself." She covered her lips, stifling a rather unbalanced giggle, then started back a step and stared at the boards overhead. "You *died* up there. I'm going to walk up the stairs and find you dead."

Miranda's arms circled his shoulders and nightmares filled her eyes.

Ye gods, what evil made him enjoy her mourning?

"You'll not find my remains." He edged out of her path. "See for yourself, lady."

"I know I'm going to find a body," she said, but already disbelief was crowding out pity.

He must act quickly.

"Take my hand, Miranda. Walk to my loft. I vow you'll see no corpse." He held tight to her chilled hand.

Lechery counseled him to tug her up the stairs, through the door, and pull her atop him. Once astride, he'd show her the liveliest ghost in Christendom.

Instead, he escorted her as he would the queen, with all due reverence.

The door creaked in frightening fashion and her hand clutched tight. What irony that she found his presence comforting! He gave Miranda a soul-testing ordeal and she gave him trust.

She inspected the premises, taking note of the counter with its arrangement of oranges and purplish sweet peas. Though they'd begun to wilt, he'd kept the glass filled with water.

She stepped over the fallen sword, crossed to the cot, smiled at—he knew not what. But then her legs trembled. She lowered herself to the cot and closed her eyes. Without looking, she touched the indentation in his pillow. She heaved such a sigh, it rocked him with uncertainty. Lashes of rain hit the window above his bed, drawing Miranda's attention to the darkening sky. It interrupted her reverie and banished her weakness.

She pushed herself to her feet. She walked to the shower and parted the curtain. If she noticed the soap was dry and smooth as the floor of the shower itself, she said nothing.

Stiffening as if she'd caught a whiff of sulfur, Miranda crossed to the oranges and stared. Four sat uncut, skins starting to pucker. He'd slashed the fifth one into quarters that day she'd said she'd dreamed of kissing.

"Why haven't you eaten these?"

"I don't eat, Miranda. I have no need of sustenance."

"That day the knife cut through your fingers, it really happened, didn't it?"

"Of course." He spread all ten fingers wide. "They're illusion, just like the rest of me."

Kit expected a sigh for the flesh she couldn't possess, but her mind veered elsewhere.

"You lied, saying I'd seen wrong. That made me feel really dumb, Kit."

"It was too soon. I didn't feel I could tell you the truth."

"And you were skulking around in my house. Never mind

Rick and the Graveyard Rose. *You* were following me around. *You* grabbed me outside the study.''

"I don't deny it, Miranda, although 'grab' seems unfair, given your response.''

A slip. Oh, he'd slipped badly, bringing rosy shame up in her cheeks. She gathered herself to storm away, but the apartment was so very small that she had to pass him. He caught at her arm.

"I never breached your privacy for sport." He held her when she would have pulled away. "I never looked upon your nakedness.''

She took a shuddering breath and bent her gaze so far down he saw her nape.

"And I never touched your skin secretly." He trailed one finger on the velvet softness of that small white nape. "Never without your permission.''

"Until today." She flung her hair back in a stinging mass. "I'll concede you one thing, Kit. I'm as deranged as you are. Logic keeps telling me not to believe your lies, but I want to. My brain is spinning out excuses so fast, even I'm amazed.''

A bitter laugh twisted her lips, then dropped away. She bounced from disbelief to sweet compassion to fury.

Kit stopped her. "If you plan to number each of my transgressions, you won't sleep this night.''

"*Then* you said how amusing it was that I wanted you to kiss me." Miranda's breath came fast, as if she'd been running. Or making love. "How do think *that* made me feel?''

She struck his breastbone with the point of her index finger.

"Don't," he warned, grabbing her finger. "Don't do that.''

"Let go.''

He did. He was so far gone with a green boy's lust that the squirming of her finger inside his hand aroused him. Well, he knew how to scatter lust and tenderness.

"Mistress Miranda, may I beg forgiveness for all my sins at once? Or will you have me on my knees the livelong night?''

That rocked her back on her dirty tennis-shoed heels. Ah, yes, sarcasm was a good, familiar creature. It served him well.

"That won't be necessary." She crossed her arms. "I blame myself for trusting a stranger. You warned me, but I didn't listen." Each set of nails bit into the flesh of her opposite arm. "I'd like you to find another place to live. It's only fair to give you two weeks' notice. After that, I want you gone."

Andi paged through the Services section of the phone book.

She was not "in denial," and she wasn't practicing "avoidance," or whatever pop-psychology term they applied to sensible behavior. She was "getting on with her life," choosing not to mull over the words of the madman living in Dinah's carriage house. She sipped coffee, read the paltry information on shore-to-ship calls, and dialed "o".

She didn't believe Kit, exactly, but Rick did seem overly interested in her Graveyard Rose. Before she set him free in Dinah's house, she would ask Dinah how she felt about him.

"Operator."

"Hi. If I needed to call a cruise ship, what would be involved?"

"First call the marine operator and give her the ship's number—are you all right?"

With a gasp, Andi fielded Lily's jump into her lap.

"Yes. Sorry." She pushed the cat off the phone book, crumpling the thin pages.

"Are you looking for that number?"

"Um, no. I don't have it yet."

"Call the cruise line and see if they give out the number for non-emergencies. This isn't an emergency, is it?"

Let's see, a ghost told me this guy couldn't be trusted . . .

"Not exactly."

"I should warn you, those calls are very expensive."

Lily vaulted back to the couch and feinted a paw at Andi's

coffee cup. As Andi lifted it out of range, Lily considered the fishbowl on the mantel.

"How expensive?" Andi walked to the end of her telephone cord. Rosencrantz and Guildenstern glubbed peacefully.

"I can't quote rates, ma'am. You'll have to call your own long distance carrier and—"

Simultaneously, a scratch sounded at the front door, Lily swelled into a spitting puffball, and the lights went out.

"Gotta go. Thanks." Andi juggled the receiver back into its cradle.

Thunder rolled and the scratching came again. Certainly Kit was above pulling such a prank. She listened, wishing she hadn't felt him vanish. That sensation made his lie almost credible. One minute she'd been lost in a kiss, the next she'd been alone.

She wasn't alone now. A yodeling whimper came from the other side of the door. It was some sort of animal, in distress.

Andi edged open the front door and a gust of wind pushed it wide. Behind her, windows and the basement door shuddered in their frames. And then she was faced with a monster dog.

"Down!" Something wet and huge collided with her stomach, knocking her aside. "Hey!" The Great Dane filled the room with a one-beast stampede. "Gertrude!"

Lily hissed, couch legs screeched on the hardwood floor and something tumbled off the mantel. Not the fish! Andi stayed against the wall as the animals ripped around the great room, through the kitchen, then pounded up the stairs.

After locating the flashlight, Andi held a match to an ornamental candle and made her way to the mantel. Rosencrantz and Guildenstern were alive.

Overhead, boards squeaked. A giant "woof" reverberated and Andi heard her bed buck. She imagined muddy paws redecorating her room. The dog probably had her telephone number on her collar, but Andi had no intention of blundering up the dark stairs into ambush. She hauled the phone book closer to the flickering candle and peered at the ant-track print until she found Dr. Noah Lincoln's number.

He answered before the second ring. "Damn, I'm sorry she bothered you. Gertrude is terrified of thunder. I let her out to take a—"

"I'd bring her home, but I have no idea where you live."

"You'd have a tough time getting her into your VW, assuming you could get her out from under your bed."

"Under my bed?"

"She hides. She's not howling, though—that's good."

"Howling? Why should she be howling?"

"Gertrude's not the bravest dog on the block. Let me grab my keys and pager and I'll be right over. Just pray all the thunder we're going to get has passed over."

Gertrude the hellhound howled, thunder rumbled, and Andi paced the veranda. It was only seven o'clock, but she was exhausted. As soon as Noah collected Gertrude, she'd make herself a sandwich and sleep. She refused to think about how the power failure would ruin the freezer full of casseroles.

Headlights bobbed down her driveway, heralding the arrival of Noah and the fire truck. Draped in a yellow slicker, Noah splashed through the mud slurry, carrying a plate covered with foil.

"That girl does hate a storm." Noah shook his head at Gertrude's howling. "For your trouble." He extended the plate.

"Cookies? They smell wonderful."

"I'd tell you to have a look, but it's dark as the inside of a cow out here. Any reason you've got the lights out?"

His tone simmered with suspicion left from the last time he'd paid her a visit. That time he'd thought she was about to jump from the upstairs window.

"Chocolate chip?" she asked, preceding him into the house.

"Fresh-baked. What about the lights?" Noah flicked the switch just inside the front door.

"Power failure, I guess."

''Nope.'' Noah advanced to the kitchen and jiggled another switch. ''Think I would've noticed.''

Andi lifted the foil and inhaled. Maybe if she improved her diet, she'd stop imagining that flesh-and-blood men could be ghosts. She took a bite gooey with chocolate. Then again, it was Saturday. No one started a diet on Saturday night.

''Where's your fuse box?'' Noah shucked his slicker, pelting her with raindrops.

''The basement?'' Andi enunciated past the chocolate.

''That's a good bet.''

Suddenly Gertrude's baying stopped.

''Storm's past.'' Noah laughed. ''Why don't you give me that?'' He took the flashlight and slipped through the basement door.

Feeling sheepish for accepting rescue and relieved to hear him moving around with such confidence, Andi waited. Outside, the copper rain pipe shuddered against the house. Inside, the lights flared on and the appliances recommenced their normal humming.

Andi applauded and flicked on the basement light. ''Thanks. That must be a land speed record for replacing a fuse,'' she congratulated as Noah stomped back up the stairs. ''You don't look very pleased.''

''Did you have the cartridges pulled for some reason?''

''It wasn't a fuse?''

''Cartridge fuses.'' Noah gestured as if grabbing a handle. ''Heart's Ease has old cartridge fuses, and two of them were pulled out, lying on the basement floor.''

Fear snaked down Andi's spine.

''Can't blame this one on the cat.'' She swallowed hard, trying to marshal a cool chuckle.

''When did the lights go out? Never mind.'' Noah glanced at the kitchen clock. ''Sure you didn't pull them for anything?''

As if she'd forget. She wanted to shout with anger, but she whispered, ''Like what?''

Someone had done this on purpose. Someone had hidden in the basement, then plunged her into darkness.

Cisco. It was just the sort of prank he'd pull. Like the

graffiti, like lurking around doing the Peeping Tom thing.

"Wait, Rick was working on the bathroom floor." Andi matched her fingertips, delving for an answer that didn't involve the teenage boy with the rare smile. "And I used the Weed Eater all afternoon."

"Naw, they weren't blown. They were pulled *out*." Noah fiddled with a knob on his pager. "Mind if I take a quick look around upstairs?"

No matter how angry he was, Kit wouldn't have tried to scare her. Even as he'd confessed his ghost delusion, he'd chosen his words carefully, avoiding grisly explanations.

Andi listened as Noah's boots tracked mud into every upstairs room. Not that she minded. She heard Gertrude's tail thump as he coaxed her out from under her bed. If not for Gertrude, Andi wouldn't have called Noah. She would have been alone with the intruder.

Tail wagging, Gertrude sauntered into the great room beside her master.

"Why don't you let me take you over to Jan and Blake's for the night?" Noah suggested.

Before Andi could answer, the teakettle screamed. She laughed and bolted toward the kitchen. "I was making a second pot of coffee when the power went out. Want some?"

"Sure."

An hour later, Noah hadn't repeated his offer to take her to town. At his pager's summons, he had returned a patient's call and prescribed baking soda baths for the itch of chicken pox, while Andi reset the clocks.

Now, as they sat at the kitchen table finishing the chocolate chip cookies, Andi decided the combination of doctor and deputy sat well on Noah Lincoln. He clearly loved his small-town practice and the adrenaline surges that came with police and fire calls.

Still, she wondered why he stayed. Was he biding his time, waiting for her to admit she'd pulled the fuses to bolster her prowler story? Or waiting for bad guys to pop out of her pantry?

Andi yawned. Her nerves were unjangled by coffee and cookies and she didn't fear Cisco, but she needed sleep.

A muffled crack sent Gertrude crowding under the table.

"Hot damn. What d'you suppose that was?" As Noah stood up, Andi noticed he didn't have a gun. He turned off the kitchen lights and peered out the front window. "You seen any sign of that bear I told you about?"

She winced. "I sort of forgot about it."

"Well, I think she mighta left you something to remember her by."

The downpour had stopped, leaving the night warm and fragrant with green things. Rain dropped from branches and one cricket chirred alone.

"Not a bad night to be a bear," Andi said.

"Yep. I bet it was her," Noah said.

Part of the VW's windshield lay sprinkled inside, but most clung in place, like a glass etching of a spiderweb.

Noah stepped gingerly. Glass crunched as he squatted and checked beneath the car.

"You're not expecting to find a bear under there." Andi rubbed her nape, trying to still the primal prickle of warning.

Noah checked the car's interior. "Have any food in here?"

"Not for a couple of days."

"Must've caught scent of the flowers and mistook 'em for supper. What d'you plan to do with all of them?"

"Flowers?"

First Andi thought of the seedlings in their watered basins. Then she followed the flashlight's beam as Noah swept it over the interior of her car.

Armloads of daffodils lay scattered over the backseat. A few decorated the driver's seat. One fell onto her tennis shoes as she opened the passenger side door.

As a girl, she'd loved daffodils. She'd planned a church bursting with daffodils for her someday wedding. But that had been a long time ago, before Clint was gored to death on Daffodil Hill.

Chapter
Ten

Balancing a laundry basket of wet clothes on her hip, Andi jogged up the stairs from the basement. Sunbeams streamed through Heart's Ease. Outside, there were no puddles, no dewy grass. Only wisps of moisture, cooking up from the ground, recalled last night's cloudburst.

Yesterday's strangeness, from Kit's confession to her broken windshield, might never have happened.

A meadowlark warbled as Andi crossed the veranda. She glanced down the driveway on her way to the clothesline.

Her cracked windshield testified that yesterday was no illusion, but what about Kit?

All through the night he'd guarded her. She tried not to believe it, but Kit's warm shadow had overlapped her fitful sleep, as if he sat at her bedside. He'd appeared in her dreams, sometimes grieving, sometimes smug. As dawn glowed through her eyelids, she'd felt him snug against her back.

She'd stared at the wash of sunlight brightening the rosebud wallpaper the boy cousins had despised. She saw birds' shadows pass. Nothing disturbed her conviction that Kit was near. Except that when she'd reached back to touch him, he was not there.

He might be gone for good. She had, after all, evicted him. How ridiculous. What had they quarreled over? The way he'd chopped his fingers and lied about it? Her skepticism over his ghosthood? No, the quarrel had erupted because she was embarrassed.

Andi plopped the heavy laundry basket on the grass beside the clothesline.

What was the danger in believing Kit a ghost? *That* would explain the midnight encounter outside Dinah's office. *That* would explain a room quaking with jealousy over Rick's haphazard kiss.

If she could believe Kit, his ghosthood was different than ghosthood in the movies. Things didn't go hurtling around the house, thrown by an invisible force—because Kit had to turn visible to move material objects. But *could* she believe him?

Andi snagged a pair of damp cutoffs from the basket and fastened them to the clothesline with wooden pins.

Many intelligent people believed in angels. Was there really so much difference between ghosts and angels?

She hung another pair of shorts, a T-shirt, and her white nightgown. Then her stomach plummeted and Kit's words echoed.

It's bloody well time you were with a man and it bloody well better be me.

Alone behind her screen of clothes, Andi's face flared with warmth. Kit's words didn't prove him a ghost, but they eliminated the possibility that he was an angel.

The basket was heaped with bedding. Last night, after Noah departed, she'd gathered the daffodils from her car and dumped them in her compost pile. After that, she'd staggered upstairs to stare at the mess Gertrude had created by dragging blankets and sheets under the bed. Andi had stripped off the muddy linens and remade the bed practically in her sleep.

Now she hung a peach-colored blanket lengthwise, using half a dozen pins to keep it above the grass. Moving to the last strand of clothesline, she glanced at Kit's window. It glinted with a reflection of blue sky.

Her brain punished her, forcing her to recall words more seductive than his hands. *I will please you.*

No doubt about that. Andi uttered a silent whistle and kept her knees locked against buckling.

She stood on tiptoe to pin a sheet. With the peach blanket behind and the sheets in front, she was hidden. A hot breeze gusted up from the ravine, shaking the blackberry bushes, fluttering the sheet against her legs.

The blackberries' rustling stopped. The sheet drifted toward her, rippled around her waist, and veiled her.

Andi closed her eyes. With no one watching, she indulged the fantasy of Kit's hand tracing her features through the sheet. Confusing, confounding, arrogant man.

Suddenly, he was there. His shadow didn't show through the sunlit sheet, but his arm wrapped her waist. She waited, expecting him to pull her forward. He didn't.

Because he couldn't.

He couldn't move objects without turning solid . . . oh, Lord. Trusting a truth only a madwoman could believe, Andi stepped forward until her chest pressed his. He felt hard and fit, absolutely real.

As his grip loosened, she opened her eyes to see him standing before her, brushing the sheet from his shoulder.

And yet he hadn't been there before. She'd heard no footsteps approach. *No one* had stood there. She knew it.

"I never would have guessed laundry bred lechery," he mused. "But I think I might tumble you here, in a nest of these sheets spread over warm grass."

Arms crossed, eyes mocking, he took her breath away.

"How do you think of things like that? And how," she whispered, "can you say them?"

"A courtier knows weapons of both love and war." His joke ended in a sigh. "What a pretty mess we've come to, Miranda."

Kit brushed her hair back, kissed her forehead, then stepped away and squared his shoulders. "At least I can manage so chaste a kiss and remain substantial."

The bitterness in his observation jarred her.

"I'm glad," Andi said. His answering smile, white inside the dark beard, dazzled her before it vanished.

"As am I, but it will come to naught." Kit raised the sheet as if it were a velvet curtain and bowed her through.

They walked down the path to the brook. When their hands brushed, he claimed hers and touched it to his lips.

Seated on a boulder, Andi watched him pace. He wore jeans and his feed-store T-shirt, but he strode with a grace she didn't recognize. Maybe the grace of a courtier.

A bird cried overhead and Kit glanced up. "I miss hawking. Imagine it, Miranda, sitting in a church with light pouring through stained-glass windows to gild the feathers of the falcon perched on each noble's embroidered glove." Kit shook his head.

"What else do you miss?"

He caught her sympathy and bristled. "No good will come of remembering, I say. Rewriting destiny is not possible."

Neither are ghosts. She didn't say it, but she watched Kit's shadowy eyes and saw how pride pricked him each time soft feelings showed. That was when he turned cruel and sarcastic.

"What if you caught one of these hawks and trained it?"

"Your tender heart would shrink to see her sitting on a fencepost, shredding a hare, fur from flesh."

She couldn't deny he was right, but if his emotions soared along with the hawk, she would encourage him to try.

His shoulders shifted as if something had slipped down his collar. "Will you speak of last night's misfortune?"

He meant fuses pulled to trap her in the dark, the broken windshield, the daffodils—not the sound of her damned panting as he caressed her.

"No, I won't. You need to get back to work—"

"God's bones, Miranda. The novel was a ruse. I've told you why I'm here and what I search for."

"—and I have to drive to the hardware store and see if Brother Wolcott can do something with my windshield." She stood and brushed off the seat of her shorts.

Across the ravine a car door slammed.

"It was no bear, you know." Kit's attention focused on the sound of approaching feet.

"Thanks. The flowers tipped me off."

That got his attention.

"What has caused this mockery?" he asked.

Rampant hormones? Delight that a ghost couldn't die from her kisses? A call to fill all the blanks of his empty life?

She said none of it, since the footsteps jogging nearer must be Rick's. From the boundaries of Heart's Ease, through the brushy ravine, to the old Williams place was under a half-mile and the brook marked the midpoint.

If Kit really believed Rick was the worst sort of thief, she must keep them apart.

"Come help me tape some plastic over the windshield before I go." She tugged Kit's wrist. "If there's another downpour this afternoon, my car's going to fill up."

Kit didn't stir. His stance turned lazy but balanced. As his eyelids drooped, Andi knew she'd seen nothing like it. Kit was focused on a hidden core of violence.

"Andi!" Rick shouted, nearing the stream.

The left corner of Kit's mustache twitched before she turned.

"Hi. Did you leave school early again?" Andi maneuvered between the two men.

"No, my students are doing fieldwork." Rick stepped past, hand extended to Kit. "I've seen you around, riding the white horse, right? But we haven't met."

"Christopher Gallatin." Kit's use of his full name and his grudging slowness to clasp Rick's hand reminded Andi that handshakes had once been an act of faith. By engaging his hand, a man implied he trusted the other not to stab him.

"Kit volunteered to help with Trifle, since I don't know much about horses." Andi gritted her molars until they squeaked. Neither of the men listened. They were bristling like hounds.

"Rick Aragon." Rick hurried to withdraw his hand.

"Aragon," Kit weighed the name. "You're a Spaniard, then?"

"Maybe. Way back." Rick flexed the fingers of his right hand.

"Oh, I'm quite sure of it." Kit withdrew his hand, slowly.

"My family's never really been into genealogy. Though we did have a guy in the Revolutionary War." He gave Andi a lopsided grin. "Wrong side, though."

"And which side would that be?" Kit's accent intensified.

Rick laughed and tipped both palms out, ignoring Kit to face Andi. "Did you say something about fixing your windshield? Can I help?"

There was no way in hell she would have turned her back on Kit if she'd been a man. But Rick did.

"A bear broke my windshield." Andi caught Kit's faint nod of approval. "Noah warned me one was in the area."

"You found bear tracks?" Rick's hands came to his hips. "Did you have food in the car?"

"Earlier," she explained.

As they walked back to the house, Andi expected Kit to return to his apartment, but he continued to walk beside her. When they stopped at the Volkswagen, Kit watched Rick.

Rick leaned his head through the driver's window. "You shouldn't drive it. I'm not sure it's safe."

"I concur," Kit said.

How nice they'd found something to agree upon.

"Thanks, guys, but I could drive to town blindfolded."

"I don't think Brother can do anything with this." Rick spoke with the assurance of a native. "ABC Glass did some display cases for me. I could drive the VW into Owen and have them take a look. Unless *you* want to?"

"That's quite all right," Kit's tone disdained the task, but Andi heard wariness, too.

If Kit had lived in the 1500's, he'd never seen a car, let alone driven one. Andi recalled his grace riding Trifle and the easy elegance with which he'd tested Jason's old sword.

"I can drive it in. Besides, I need chicken wire for fencing. The deer trampled my basins and nibbled the seedlings. If I don't break that habit now, they'll be calling it their private buffet by August."

"This is deer heaven. You're asking for failure, Andi," Rick said.

"Doesn't that seem odd, with a bear on the loose?" Kit mused.

Rick ignored him yet again. "I'll take the Volkswagen and you take my van."

"No, you just got me the Weed Eater."

"It's no big deal. Make me dinner if you want to thank me."

She didn't want another reason to thank him.

"My van drives just like a car," Rick said. "Besides, what're you gonna hit in Sparrowgrass?"

When Rick gave Kit a conspiring wink, she had no choice. Certainly, she could drive his van. If Kit hadn't groaned, Andi would have enjoyed taking the dare.

Standing up to taunts would be Miranda's downfall. Defiance was a dangerous trait in soldiers and deadly for females.

Hazarding all to prove bravery, Miranda had taken him, a stranger, into her carriage house. He'd seen her walk into darkness to investigate sounds. She squelched instinct and womanly softness in favor of logic.

As she took Aragon's car keys, Miranda didn't guess she'd been manipulated by a man with the bloodlines of Judas. Kit shouldered the burden. He must protect her from herself.

But damme, how he hated cars.

At least horses dumped a man on earth. Kit pressed his palms to the lap belt, as Andi stomped on the van's stopping mechanism.

"Damnation, Miranda!" His neck snapped with surprising discomfort. "You'll send us both through the glass. Do you think to shatter another windshield?"

The jarring was so intense, he wondered why he hadn't lost shape. She left him no time to ponder.

"You expect me to break into Rick's house?"

"Of course not. I'll go through," he explained, "and open the door from inside. It's simple enough." He settled himself and regarded the road. Miranda continued to stare. "Go ahead.'' He gestured toward the street. ''Keep driving.''

''Don't tell me what to do. You've never driven a car in your life!''

Or death, he thought. Then he realized the import of her statement. ''Miranda, you believe me.''

''I didn't say that.'' She lowered sunglasses to cover her eyes and sent the van forward.

Kit rejoiced. In spite of his failure and Miranda's logical self, she believed him.

His senses returned with tormenting fury. His fingers recalled the thick glossiness of her sorrel hair. His palms knew her ribs seemed covered with velvet. Every nerve knew the wanton weight of her breasts.

''You can quit smirking,'' Miranda said. ''I'm considering the *possibility* that you might be telling the truth, but the odds aren't in your favor.'' She took a turn and warmed to her subject. ''I'm an intelligent modern woman. I'm a teacher. I'm a Christian—''

''Oh, yes, let's have that one on, shall we? I was a lifelong Christian, too, love. Years of self-denial, prayer, occasional whipping and fasting to seal my faith. But when I was killed fighting for my good Christian queen, what happened? My corpse was not buried in hallowed ground and I'm doomed to wander.''

A sigh burned Kit's throat. He could not forget that this accursed wandering had brought him to Miranda.

''Couldn't they bury you at a crossroads or something?'' She braked to let a covey of quail scatter. ''I always heard that where two roads came together, forming a cross, that could serve as hallowed ground.''

Perplexed, Kit told her, ''Hallowed means 'blessed.' ''

''I *know* what it means.'' With a squeal of tires, she turned onto Sparrowgrass's main street.

''Apparently not,'' he said.

He didn't deserve that poisonous look or the cold alacrity with which she parked, entered the hardware store, and ordered rolls of fencing, posts, and staples to be loaded into the van.

Her temper might improve after coffee at the Dancing

Goat. Then he'd remind her that the papers in Rick Aragon's study showed he would steal the true Graveyard Rose by July Fourth.

"Might want to check the pressure in that right rear tire," said the man loading Andi's wire.

"Thanks." As Andi stooped to look, Kit saw the workman appreciate her tight shorts. Kit strode quickly to her side.

As the dolt backed off, Andi returned, frowning, to the van. "Tire gauge. Glove compartment?"

She found the instrument, applied it with apparent skill, then shrugged. As she returned it to its compartment, Kit gazed at the park where he'd first seen her and the structure identified as the doctor's office.

Suddenly, her distress slashed through Kit so intensely that his form wavered.

Careful, bloody careful. Kit glanced down the street. An elderly man on a bench before the post office rubbed his eyes. Kit forced solidity to his fingertips, up his forearms, elbows. All was well.

"Miranda, what is it?"

The van door was open and she sat in the passenger seat, a yellow slip of paper in her hand. Her eyes moved over the paper again before she handed it to him.

Daisy May Florist had written a receipt for two dozen daffodils, and though they hadn't inserted the purchaser's name, clearly Rick had bought them.

"I thought it was Cisco," Andi said.

It wasn't jealousy Kit felt as questions rained over Miranda's blue eyes. And not quite pity, that she faced such disillusionment. He wondered how she'd placed faith in Aragon.

A cold spot between his shoulder blades reminded him.

Kit leaned across her and replaced the paper in the compartment. As he secured the latch, Miranda's cheek pressed his shoulder. He heard her swallow.

"I guess this makes me pretty stupid."

"Lady," he began, then faltered.

It was well he couldn't meet her eyes. He already felt as insubstantial as smoke.

"Miranda." He focused on the van's interior, faded black plastic, cracked and peeling. "How could you not believe in a bone-and-blood man like Aragon, when you've come to believe in me?"

Her breath stirred the hair he'd bound at his nape. He steadied his feet on the curb and glanced toward the hardware store window in time to see the watcher.

Behind a display of orange and black boxes, the gaunt man called Brother watched. He shifted a folded newspaper, end over end, as he stared at them.

Kit helped Miranda alight from the van and released her hand immediately. "Now, please introduce me to the pleasures of this potion you call 'cappuccino.' "

Chapter Eleven

Round gray rocks and pale mortar made the Dancing Goat look old, but in Kit's opinion the door painting of a goat wreathed in ribbons was quite modern.

Blake and a swirl of children nearly trampled them as the door opened. Blake wore high-heeled shoes. Moss-green makeup shaded her eyes.

"Blake!" Miranda greeted as Kit held the door.

The other woman bit her lip and squeezed Andi's arm. "Hang in there, hon," Blake said.

"What?" Miranda asked, but Blake only herded the children down the sidewalk. "Maybe she heard about my car."

To Kit's ear, Miranda sounded unconvinced.

His thought held as they moved into the shop. Pleasure in the aromas of leeks and vegetables, wheaten loaves and cinnamon, was diminished by the stares.

Something was amiss. For one thing, the big-bladed overhead fan clicked like snapping fingers, then spun to a stop as they entered. The quiet had the effect of a fanfare.

Of all the faces turned their way, Kit recognized only Jan's. Overhead lights glinted on her pageboy styled hair as she gave a weak wave from a counter in the rear. All eyes tracked Miranda, but the girl was oblivious.

"Two," Miranda said as Jan gestured with a cup. "You've got a full house today."

"Saturday lunch." Jan faced a steaming machine, pulled a lever and directed trickles of black coffee into tiny silver pitchers.

Kit looked over his shoulder as the fan spun sporadically, puffing a breeze through the sunny spouts of daffodils in vases on each table. He tried to blame his uneasiness on that echo of last night's trouble, but then two middle-aged women leaned their heads together, whispering as they watched Miranda.

Catching his frown, they returned, guiltily, to their bowls of greens.

"You want these coffees to go, don't you, Andi?" Jan's eyes were red-rimmed as she reached for paper cups.

"No way. Kit's never had cappuccino. We'll enjoy it in style. How about a couple of scones, too?"

"Apricot or blueberry?" Jan sighed with resignation.

"Kit?" Miranda looked childishly small as she gazed up at him.

"Fine." He gave her a wad of paper money, then searched out a secluded table.

"Kit, you gave me thirty dollars," Miranda said as they crossed the room. "The Dancing Goat's not that pricey." With her back to the room, Miranda arranged cups, plum-colored napkins, and a thin newspaper Jan had placed on their tray.

Miranda started to speak, halted, then began again.

"Do I look all right? I've got a real wave of paranoia going here."

"You look fine. You're far and away the prettiest woman in the shop." He knew scores of compliments more flowery, but none more true. "I wouldn't be surprised, though, if others have heard of the mishaps at Heart's Ease."

" 'The Mishaps at Heart's Ease,' " Miranda said. "It sounds like a Nancy Drew mystery."

A trace of foam clung to her upper lip. Kit's tongue slid

back against the roof of his mouth, fighting the urge to lick that foam away. And then she did.

"You don't know Nancy Drew, do you?" she said.

Kit shook his head, eyes straying to the cameo-size photograph on the newspaper's folded page. He didn't suppose the elderly woman in the lace collar was Nancy Drew.

Then he recognized her as Gina Brown, Sparrowgrass shopkeeper.

"Don't you like it?" Miranda asked.

Kit drank. Cooperation was less arduous than resistance and the coffee was actually good. Kit was about to tell her so, when Noah Lincoln bustled into the coffee shop. His necktie flapped over one shoulder, his white coat streamed behind like a cape. Overhead, the fan spun to another loud stop.

Noah Lincoln spared Kit a direct frown, then leaned his palms on the table. "Andi, you didn't buy those daffodils, did you?"

He might have shouted for all the good it did to whisper. "Wasn't a bear, either. Goddamn it, I should've secured the scene."

Not a spoon stirred. The Dancing Goat's patrons sat mute. Kit willed the fan to spin noisily to life. It didn't.

"How did you know?" Miranda's voice was a crone's croak.

Noah thumped the headline Kit had spotted. Miranda pulled the paper to her and read. Her growing paleness didn't disturb him. The way she folded forward did.

Kit despised the fact that he could use Noah's knowledge to find his heart and help Miranda. He hadn't forgotten the sound of Rick's whore threatening to "tell Noah everything." That bloody well better mean Noah was a good and careful sheriff. Kit closed his fist and brought it down near the doctor's splayed hands.

"Hell." Noah forked fingers through his rust-and-gray hair. "Want to go someplace else to talk?" He glanced out the streetside window. "Later, I mean. I saw you and ran right out of the examining room. Left a patient sitting there, bare-assed in a paper gown.'' He shook his head. ''*Later*, Miranda?''

''All right.'' Her coffee cup wobbled as if it were weighty.

As Noah left, customers' voices rose self-consciously and Miranda pushed the *Owen Canyon Times* toward Kit. She watched so intently, it was clear she expected him to read while she watched.

Gina Brown's column, Hangtown Tattler, bore a telling headline: TRAGEDY REVISITED.

Not so long ago, a grinning teenage boy rode his bicycle through my petunias. That boy was Clint Kern. Clint had a habit of making silly mistakes.

Clint rescued white rats from the high school biology lab, not caring if he shouldn't.

Clint barreled down Sparrowgrass's first sidewalk on a skateboard, exactly where he shouldn't.

Clint laughed at his new baby brother's antics in church, when he knew he shouldn't.

And Clint fell in love . . .

Kit heard the unwritten echo and covered Miranda's hand with his before reading on.

One day Clint's girlfriend dared him to pick her flowers from a pasture on Daffodil Hill. Heedless of Jacob Webster's Angus bull, Clint climbed the fence and began the search that would end his young life.

Miranda Fairfield, niece to Sparrowgrass's Dinah and Jason Bradford, was Clint's girlfriend. Miranda turned twenty-six this year, and though Earl and Janet Kern never saw Clint graduate from high school, Miranda graduated from college and taught secondary school. She fell in love again and would have married

this summer, if her fiancé hadn't died in a fiery auto-
mobile crash.

In an attempt to gather the tattered shreds of her . . .

The clash of cutlery being cleared distracted Kit and he
realized he'd read enough. He creased the newspaper and
slapped the cameo photograph face down on the table.

"This is rubbish. Sentimental, ill-written rubbish." Kit
kept one hand on the paper while the other lifted his cup.
"Pay it no mind."

"All right." Miranda squared her shoulders with a faint
smile. "Everyone's watching me anyway, right?"

Kit cleared his throat. How should he answer a lady who
met dares head on? Miranda swung her Hydra-bee machinery
with the same determined expression she wore now. He
should proceed cautiously.

"Of course, they're watching. Don't do anything stupid."

"Oh, ye of little faith . . ."

"Pardon me?"

Miranda stood. She pushed in her chair with a screech.

"I said, if they're staring anyway, why not give them
something to watch?"

Kit didn't try to stop her. What bloody good would it do?
He ran the pad of his thumb over a butter knife. The tail of
Miranda's sorrel braid swayed behind her and the blade's
ridged edge pressed a design into his thumb as she marched
toward Jan.

Why would she face a widow who'd had sadness wrung
from her so recently and publicly? Valor, Kit supposed, did
not require intellect.

Jan put down the plastic basin into which she cleared
dishes. She crossed her arms.

"Jan," Miranda spoke too loudly, "how're you doing?"

"To tell you the truth, honey, I've had better days."

Miranda's arms flared away from her body and Kit sensed
the affection building as she reached to hug Jan. Jan did not
pull away as Miranda whispered fiercely.

"I did not dare him," she said.

"I know that." Jan gave a sad smile. "From the day he reached the terrible twos, Clint was a disaster looking for someplace to happen."

As if to underline her words, the fan whirred into action, cooling the shop once more.

Miranda felt like a mummy bound to hide the flesh underneath. She left the Dancing Goat for Brown's grocery. Once inside, she concentrated on collecting ingredients for dinner.

Andi bit her lip against mentioning the Tattler column, though Gina followed her up and down the store's four aisles, pretending to rearrange stock.

Andi frankly did not want to talk with the woman. Small-town journalists ought to have to pass a proficiency test. In the wrong hands the printed word could be a nudge toward suicide.

Only when Gina replaced the tomato in Andi's hand with a "nicer" one did Andi confide her purpose. Gina had a solution for that, too.

"Steak, baked potato, and green salad with French dressing," Gina recommended. "That's Rick's favorite dinner. Leastwise, that's what Sadie Williams used to cook when he mowed her lawn and helped around her place. The Smiths served him the same thing, come to that." Gina gestured down the block, toward the old Crest Theatre.

" 'Our golden boy,' the Smiths called him. He was the only one in town who appreciated their collection of old films . . ."

Andi hurried. She grabbed a basket of blueberries, then a carton of vanilla ice cream. Surely Rick's palate wouldn't find that dessert too exotic.

Andi's gaze stopped on frozen gourmet pizza jumbled next to the ice cream. *Quatro fromage* with pesto. Oh, yes. These she'd have after Rick left.

". . . so when Rick offered to catalog those old films, my, weren't they pleased."

Kit's dark hints and the receipt from Daisy May made

Andi queasy over such psalms to Saint Rick. She reached for a bottle of olive oil.

"No, Andi, get that dressing in the plastic squeeze thing. That's what Rick likes."

Just as well. Her Caesar dressing, complete with coddled egg and anchovy fillets, took time, and the afternoon was slipping away.

"Pearls before swine," she muttered as Gina punched the keys of the old-fashioned cash register.

"Altogether a real helpful soul, isn't he? Easy to confide in." Gina's cheeks flushed, then mottled with embarrassment.

Her reaction made Andi replay the words. *Easy to confide in.* Why had that made Gina blush?

With excessive rustling, Gina rolled the top of the brown bag.

"You going to take that magazine too, hon?"

"Uh, no. Thanks. 'Bye."

Easy to confide in.

Miranda climbed into the van and slung the groceries into the back without acknowledging Kit's raised brow. Had she confided something to Rick that he'd passed on to Gina? Other than the shocking state of her bathroom floor, she couldn't recall a thing.

It didn't matter. Like Kit's eavesdropping, Gina's allusion was flimsy proof. Only the receipt pointed to Rick as a scoundrel.

As Miranda drove the lumbering van back to Heart's Ease, she struggled to find a plausible explanation for the receipt.

"That's it." She slowed the van and turned toward Kit. "Those daffodils were for the Dancing Goat. You saw them."

"Put your foot back on the treadle—"

"Gas pedal. And you *don't* know how to drive."

"—you're blocking traffic."

A white sedan honked and zipped around them.

"Really," she continued, "couldn't that be it? Rick

bought the daffodils for Jan, then Cisco snatched some and dumped them in my car.''

"For what reason?''

"To freak me out.'' Andi drew a breath. The column had triggered memories which clicked past like snapshots. "To remind me I killed a brother he was too young to know.''

"Enough.'' Kit leaned against his seat belt, toward Andi. His hand burrowed under her hair to squeeze her neck.

He had a magical touch. Her stomach spun cartwheels and her muscles turned to mush.

"Miranda?''

Damn. Her eyes. Andi stared past the sun-dazzled windshield. He'd touched her and *she'd closed her eyes*.

"Keep your hands to yourself.''

"Very well.''

"Or you'll—make me swoon.''

"Swoon?'' His chuckle warmed her. "I've not heard that word of late. I never fancied swooning maidens. Though if I could cause it with a touch . . .''

"Don't get cocky.'' Andi frowned at the asphalt unrolling ahead.

"Mayhap *I* should learn to drive,'' Kit said.

Andi swerved back into her own lane.

The front gate stood open and Cisco's mountain bike lay propped against the cottonwood tree. He slouched by a porch pillar, legs sprawled to show how long he'd been waiting.

When Andi turned for Kit's reaction to Cisco's presence, Kit was gone.

Cisco shambled toward the truck, stiffening when he saw Andi.

"Where's Rick?'' He dashed blond bangs away from his eyes. "I thought you were him. He didn't pick me up after practice.''

Earlier, Rick had come bounding across the stream. His class was doing "fieldwork,'' he said, explaining why he was home so early. Had Rick abandoned Cisco, forcing him to find his own way home?

No matter. There was something else she needed to know.

"Rick let me borrow the van while he took my car into Owen."

Andi lifted the groceries out of the backseat before facing Cisco. It was hot enough that her legs were wet from the plastic seat covers. Cisco stood in a patch of shade and didn't offer to help.

"Yeah?" Cisco's fingers teased the hem of his T-shirt, fraying it stitch by stitch.

Clutching the grocery bag with one hand, Andi reached down to pet Lily. The cat arched her back, purred, and twined between Andi's ankles.

"Somebody broke my windshield. On purpose."

The hem dropped from Cisco's fingers. "No shit?"

Kit's disapproval crackled around her. The warm force of him was tangible, and it was directed against Cisco's crude language.

"Oh, man." Cisco studied her. "You're not thinking it was me. Tell me you're not."

Andi waited.

"Look." Cisco pointed toward his bike. "Do you know why I'm sixteen with no driver's license? Because I screwed up."

Andi offered him an opening. "Screwed up, like . . . ?"

"Like Mom told me not to go to Owen with my friends and I went anyway." Cisco's singsong tone said he'd told the story more than once. "And I didn't call." His head bobbed to one side. "*And* I got picked up for painting Owen High's dorky mascot—Owen Otter—Sparrowgrass green."

"What happened to your friends?"

"Don't *say* anything about my friends, okay?" Cisco shuffled over to lift his bike away from the tree. He scuffed his shoe amid the weeds. "See that stuff under the weeds? You should give it a chance to breathe. I don't remember what's it's called, but Mom really likes it. Those little bumps turn into white flowers. Have her tell you about it."

"Okay, I will."

A long sigh rushed through his lips. "Look, the thing is, I can't get my license until July. There's no way I'd do something like break your windshield and get Mom on my case again."

She almost believed him.

But Cisco's denial meant Rick had defaced Heart's Ease. Rick had been in her basement. Rick had vandalized her car. From a teenager those things meant a bid for attention. From a thirty-year-old college professor they meant psychological warfare.

Andi lay in a claw-footed tub, up to her collarbone in hot water and lemon bath salts.

Rick had called to say he'd arrive in an hour, so she'd started dinner, then, with wet hair wrapped in a towel, retreated to the tub. She leaned back, giving her mind the silence it needed to fit these puzzle pieces into a picture.

The bathwater still steamed when a sound startled her into a splash. Had she dozed off? The faceted-glass doorknob turned, jiggled, remained locked.

Kit paced outside the bathroom door.

"I am no spymaster, Miranda," Kit answered a question she hadn't asked. "I can't tell you how to entrap Rick Aragon. But I do know this: Don't be obvious. Don't show sudden interest in him. Don't, by all that's holy, make taking advantage of you *too easy*.

"This is all unnecessary, of course. You have my word he's contracted to sell the Graveyard Rose to someone named Sharif. You have a receipt for flowers used to frighten you—"

"But why? What would that accomplish?"

"He means to flush you from the house and do a more thorough search."

Kit's pacing resumed, then stopped.

"There's another thing. He may not believe you've misplaced the box. He may force you to tell."

"Well, he can't. I've been over that afternoon hundreds of times, and I don't remember what I did with it."

"Tell it to me, then. I left you at the front door."

Andi moved her fingers across the water's surface, remembering. That afternoon she'd noticed some late daffodils bowing, though there was no breeze. Had Kit strode beside her, rippling the flowers as he passed?

"Okay, the front door was unlocked when I came home from the fair. You saw that. So I didn't have to fumble for a key. Besides, the box was under my—" Her gesture sloshed the water around her.

"Kirtle," Kit supplied. "But you're wrong. As you left the fair, you slipped the bag and box out of your kirtle."

"Right. The drawstring was around my wrist and I still had it when I looked in the living room, then stripped the dustcovers off the furniture. After that, I went down to the basement to wash them."

"Was the basement door unlocked? Might you have mislaid the bag while finding a light switch?"

"No, I—"

"Will you leave off doing that?" Kit shouted.

"What?" Andi stared toward the bathroom door, surprised it hadn't trembled at his bellow.

"Moving about in the water. Swishing from side to side as you think. I am trying to concentrate on skulduggery and I can only envision water lapping your—"

Andi swallowed. Eyes closed, she waited.

"—self."

Silence. Only as she released her grip on the lavender soap did Andi notice her fingernails had marked it. She heard a sliding sound, as if Kit's hand passed over the door's surface.

"Now, did you start the wash?"

"I think so."

Her hesitation amused him and he laughed. "Miranda, pray you never have to stand in your own defense. You are a bloody awful witness."

"That's it. I'm getting out. This was supposed to be a relaxing soak, not an interrogation."

"Stay put, please."

Andi sloshed the bathwater good and loud.

"You vex me past bearing." His sigh was audible, a small victory. "Now tell me, mistress, when Rick came, did you still have the box?"

"I was holding a bunch of casseroles and talking to Lily.

I dropped them when he said something." She pictured the opened dish and Lily lapping at tuna casserole. She didn't remember the velvet bag amid the mess.

She slid down until the water lapped her chin. "He might have taken it then."

"Surely you would have noticed *that*. Besides, he might lie to his doxy, but why go through this dumb show of friendship, if not for the box?"

Was Kit teasing or serious?

"You may find this hard to believe," she said, "but he may just be a nice guy. Or, he may find me attractive."

"And yet she doesn't like him," Kit mused.

"Who?"

"The cat, though you've seen him inflict no cruelty on her."

The bathwater bubbled away from Andi's lips as she laughed. Of all the arguments she'd expected from Kit, the testimony of a cat was the very last.

As his injured silence vibrated through the door, she drew the shower curtain to hide herself.

"You might as well come in."

"I think not."

"Oh, right. I locked the door."

"That's of no consequence, Miranda. You know that. It's only, if listening to water stroke you— If I were to look upon you—"

Anticipation did a tickling dance up the inside of her arms. Or maybe the water was just cooling.

"But I suppose *that's* of no consequence, either." Kit's voice turned clipped and arrogant. "Exerting my male prerogative appears not to be an option."

"Maybe you're wrong, Kit." Andi felt wild possibilities well up in her. "Maybe you're not even a ghost. Maybe your heart's inside you, where it's always been and you have amnesia, or some sort of minor, really *minor*, dementia. Or maybe your disappearance, yesterday, was like mass hysteria. You thought you were vanishing, then I thought—"

Andi bent her forehead against her wet hands.

"I won't speak of this," he said, but the door creaked a little, as if he leaned against it.

She felt it stretch between them, a thread pulled taut and ready to snap. They each held one end of hope.

"I'll be nearby, if you need me," he said.

"I know."

"Damme, Miranda! You know nothing of the sort, but tonight, I will be here."

Chapter Twelve

Rick stood in the sliding-glass door open to the rear veranda. From here, Heart's Ease appeared to jut over the ravine. All very picturesque, if you liked rustic splendor. Even the cat, perched on the deck rail, suited the scene.

Andi tended the barbecue, poking at his dinner. A puff of wind made her squint against smoke, then fan it away. She seemed altogether more awkward than usual.

"Doesn't the breeze feel good?" she asked. "And it smells like summer, full of sagebrush and pine."

Rick smelled the cremation of perfectly good beef and a whiff of horse manure.

He swirled the wine in his glass, trying to savor its bouquet. Just as he'd guessed, Andi had purchased a harsh Cabernet to go with the steak. Lucky he'd selected a Gewürztraminer from his own stock and passed it off as a hostess gift.

This time Sharif was making Rick work for his money, but it'd be worth it. Come the *fifth* of July, he and Renetta would be having a real celebration, far away from Sparrowgrass.

"Back, kitty," he said as the idiot cat slapped at his slacks. The second time, her claws caught. Rick squatted to unhook them.

"Sorry." Andi glanced back. "I think she was just being friendly."

Gina's column had done a nice job of softening her up. Andi's undertone of apology proved that. As he walked closer, one sleeve of her white shirt came unrolled. She'd be smeared with charcoal before long.

"Do you ever bake potatoes this way?" she asked.

"Can't say I do."

She'd thrown the potatoes, wrapped in aluminum foil, among the coals. Any cook knew steaks went under the broiler, not on a grill, and baked potatoes were just that, baked in an oven at 425 degrees for exactly fifty-five minutes.

She was about to brush the steak with basting sauce. Although he suspected that the red bits in the sauce were chili peppers, he didn't mind watching her reach for it.

Though clueless about cooking, the woman had a nice butt and her jeans cupped it just right. Choking down dinner would be a small price to pay for a piece of that.

Renetta would never know, either, because Miranda Fairfield was a respectable schoolteacher. If she got it on with a neighbor and he brushed the encounter off as entertainment, she'd call herself a fool and keep her mouth shut. Her reputation couldn't take another assault.

Andi bent her knees to blow on the coals and her jeans pulled tighter. God, he could split her like a wishbone.

Of course, he might not take it that far. Cold wind, sharp as winter, gusted over the deck. He didn't have much time. If sweet-talking and sex didn't work, he'd move on to drugs. Violence wouldn't be necessary.

Andi had that bruised look around the eyes, which signaled she was about to cave in. She'd taken Gina's column hard. According to Renetta, who'd been lunching with her busty girlfriend Tammy at the Dancing Goat, everyone in the place had been gossiping about the Black Widow from Los Padres. Then she'd come in, gone pale reading the Owen

Canyon paper, and finished with a sappy hug for Jan.

The Graveyard Rose was as good as his. A cozy chat about the joys of teaching, a few kisses, and she'd bring it out of hiding.

Unless it was really lost.

That complication would slow him down, but barely. He'd just urge Andi to go home where she belonged. He wouldn't allow her to feel guilty over deserting her post. He'd be glad to stand in as caretaker.

She'd never know that he'd brought in help to search the place once the dust settled in the wake of her pitiful VW.

For $500,000 on delivery, he'd get that antique box before July Fourth. Whatever it took.

"Watch out!" Andi gestured with a long-handled fork.

Wine wet Rick's cuff as the cat launched off the picnic table, straight at his chest.

"Whoa there, kitty."

The words rumbled with the right blend of surprise and warmth, but damn, he couldn't wait to put that little blue-eyed furball out for coyote chow.

Andi forked the potatoes and steaks onto the platter and made her way to the table inside.

Thank God. What if she'd made him eat on the veranda? The wooden picnic table held two citronella candles, things which stank but never kept off mosquitoes. Scratching bug bites was not what he had planned for the evening.

Rick tugged at his shirt collar. It was unseasonably cold. As he followed Andi inside, he shivered.

By the time dinner ended, Andi had certainly blunted his appetite for *her*.

Andi missed school. She missed her students, and she listed their abilities and shortcomings in mind-numbing detail. She even missed scoring their final exams and wondered if the substitute teacher had graded them fairly.

Rick dried dishes and watched her. Andi extended friendship with the same efficient care she gave the soapy plates. She was only thanking him for getting her car fixed.

"All done." Rick folded the dish towel and followed her

glance past his shoulder. Nothing behind him.

Something had made her cautious. The spark sputtering in their moonlight kiss had been snuffed. She was an adult. She knew the dangers of leading a thirty-year-old man on. And yet she'd changed.

He could probably blame Christopher Gallatin, her mysterious boarder. For all Gallatin's British reserve, they'd hated each other on sight.

Not that it stopped him from knocking on the carriage house door to alert Gallatin. Tonight, on his way into Heart's Ease, he'd paused to issue neighborly notice that Trifle was loose on the other side of the stream. The Englishman had sworn and grabbed a rope when Rick said the horse was galloping along a path which eventually curved toward the freeway.

Having Cisco hide the horse had been a stroke of genius. Rick needed no complications. He needed to be able to follow his instincts without interruption. The search should occupy Gallatin all night.

Damn, this house was cold as a crypt. Just watching Andi scoop ice cream made him shiver. Short of going home for a coat or begging a transfer of body heat, he had only one idea.

"It's a little chilly in here." He rubbed his hands together and sidestepped the cat. "How 'bout if I build a fire?"

Andi poured two mugs of coffee.

"That would be really nice," she said. "Then you can tell me about *your* classes."

Oh, joy.

By the time they settled on the hearth rug in front of the blaze, Andi seemed her former self.

"Eat your ice cream before it melts," she ordered.

Really, she was an uppity little bitch. He wouldn't mind taking her down a peg.

Cross-legged, eating quickly, she looked like she intended to take notes on his slice of academia.

"Besides being a coach, I teach thanatology."

Her eyes narrowed. He watched as her mind sifted for a definition.

"Don't worry, very few people are familiar with the term. It's the study of death from all angles: medical, psychological, social. And I add the arts."

Sitting with the cat curled on the lap of her blue jeans, Andi sniffed as if he'd knocked her scholarly little nose out of joint.

"I can't imagine where you'd start with a class like that," she said.

"It just happens," Rick admitted. "And it's almost embarrassing how much I enjoy teaching it. I should pay the college for allowing me to do it."

This time Andi's smile was genuine. "You must be really good at it."

"Most days my students are interested. Some days, even fascinated. For instance, today they did rubbings of gravestones. That's in preparation for the next unit, in which they plan their own funerals."

As Andi recoiled, the cat moved to a position on the couch.

"They estimate costs, write wills, other practical things." Rick unbuttoned his shirt cuffs. When her eyes followed, triumph shouted in his brain. Who'd have guessed *lesson plans* would turn her on?

"You'd probably like the historical aspects better. Have you ever heard of the Society for the Prevention of Premature Burial?"

"Do I want to?"

"It was a funeral tradition during the Victorian period. Relatives sometimes built miniature bell towers above the grave." He formed a pointed roof with his hands. "Then they ran a cord from the bell down into the casket." He pretended to place a rope in the crease between her thumb and forefinger. "If, by chance—"

"I get it." Andi snatched her hand away.

"Probably based more on hope than science."

"Nothing wrong with that." She gave a haughty nod.

He scratched his head, pretending to think of her as a reluctant student. "Know what you'd like? My unit linking modern-day science with ancient legends."

"Try me."

"You're familiar with Poe's 'The Raven'?" He held a hand palm out to stifle her outburst. "Of course. And you've heard crows, kites, and other black birds called harbingers of death, but do you know how the legend came to be?" He waited for the grudging shake of her head.

"Carrion birds learned—oh, at least as far back as the Roman legions—to follow troops of soldiers, in anticipation of the feast which followed."

"Okay, that's pretty interesting." She took his bowl, with blueberries bobbing like survivors in the melted ice cream, and set it on the coffee table with hers.

Then, beside him again, she leaned back on her elbows. From another woman, the posture would be enticement, but he'd better bide his time and be sure.

Rick forked his fingers through his hair. She was still watching.

"One that's harder to accept is based on Celtic folklore." *Right on*, he thought, as Andi sat forward and wrapped her arms around her knees. "You've heard of near-death experiences, but did you know there's a theory that ghosts, banshees, and fetches are actually spirits which were roaming when their bodies were buried?"

Clanking made them both start. The cat had been lapping at melted ice cream and jostled a spoon. So much for mood.

"But you don't believe that," Andi said.

He tilted a hand side to side. "It's not a bad explanation for ghosts."

The color came up in her cheeks. She unraveled her braid, then, with jerky moves, began to replait it. Did he dare tell her to stop? Loose in the firelight, her hair was a rippling Renaissance mane. Downright sensual.

"Meaning you *do* believe in ghosts?" she asked.

"I do." He nodded. "I've had my house exorcised and I told Jason he should—"

"Good Lord, Rick!" She'd abandoned the braiding. "I don't believe this!"

"You should take my class."

"You had your house, S-Sadie Williams's old place, the

cottage where I was conceived, for crying out loud, exorcised of demons?''

''It works equally well with restless ghosts.''

For a minute, he thought her magnificent hair would stand on end, but she crossed her arms and raised one brow.

''Exorcism works even if you're not Catholic? Even if you don't believe? Are you telling me it's *not* the voodoo effect? Like watching someone poke a pin in a fetish and claiming you've suddenly got a headache?''

He tsked his tongue. ''I'd be insulted if I hadn't been through this a hundred times before, Miss Fairfield. But I'm going to give you a minute to relent while I clear these bowls and pour us more wine.''

From the kitchen, he could crane his neck and see her reflection in the back window. From that same window, he'd watched her bustle about in her white nightgown.

He took the eyedrops vial from his pocket, glanced up to be sure Andi still stared into the flames, then squeezed two beads of liquid into her wineglass.

''Another glass of that red stuff?'' he called.

''Yes, please.''

He poured the wine over melted Rohypnol, pleased he didn't need Gewürztraminer's sweetness to cover the drug. ''Roofies,'' were colorless, odorless, ten times stronger than Valium, and cheap.

Timing was critical. He would just keep talking thanatology. The topic of antique death relics, like the Graveyard Rose, would follow naturally, but roofies could work as quick as ten minutes, and he couldn't have her too groggy to talk.

''Need any help?'' she asked.

''Nope.''

Something thudded overhead. Probably the cat. Just the same, he shoved a bowl along the counter, making noise to cover what had better not be Cisco.

The kid was becoming a liability. He'd accomplished his first task well enough, and today's, but he was waffling, barely held in check by hero worship and the risk of a juvenile record.

"Just tidying up a little." Rick swirled the drug in Andi's glass.

Mixed with wine, the Rohypnol could scrub away inhibitions and make her a little feisty and boastful before she passed out. She'd tell him where she'd hidden the Graveyard Rose, then forget everything after that last glass of wine. That was one of the drug's best qualities. In most women it was an amnesiac.

Sadie Williams, for instance, probably hadn't remembered how he convinced her to change her will.

Tonight, he could extract the location of the Graveyard Rose by half-strangling Andi with her own hair. She'd wake up tomorrow morning wondering why she had a sore throat.

And she *would* wake up. He'd refined his knack with dosage since Sadie.

"How about some more ice cream?" he called.

"No, come tell me some more stuff!"

She sounded petulant as a child. Carrying both glasses, he returned to the great room.

God, that hair.

"There you go." He handed her the glass, moved the fire screen, and prodded a shower of sparks from a log. He listened for her to swallow, but when he turned back, Andi was staring at some vague point between the tip of her nose and the hearth rug. The goblet sat beside her.

"What's a"—she cleared her throat to continue—"fetch?"

"Simply stated, it's a spirit projected to another place or time from someone who's still living."

Andi nodded. Her fingers worked up and down the stem of her wineglass.

"Some time-travel proponents claim it's how people are propelled through separate planes. A spirit departs prematurely—perhaps with death or danger imminent—"

He had her nodding, lifting the goblet. He spun the words out, soothing her. *A few little sips, Andi.* She was small. It wouldn't take much.

"—and once the fetch accomplishes his goal, such as finding his treasure or wreaking revenge, he becomes real again.''

Andi went rigid, the lip of the glass pressed to hers.

''What? Not, 'rests'? Weren't you going to say''—she gestured with the glass, slopping a few drops of wine on her jeans—''he accomplishes his goal and his soul passes into the Great Beyond?''

''Remember, these concepts predate Christianity.''

Andi took a long, considering sip of her wine. Rick saw the smooth movement of her throat as she swallowed.

And then a shadow darkened the firelight glow upon her hair.

Christ. A black shirt hung open on Gallatin's chest. His Levi's weren't buttoned completely, and his long hair hung in disorder you attributed to a man who'd come out on top in a knife fight.

His voice rasped. Rough from sleep, booze, or maybe a desire to kick Rick Aragon's sorry ass.

''Is this likely to take much longer?''

Chapter
Thirteen

If a black wave towered overhead, about to batter the breath from her lungs, Andi thought she might admire its ebony beauty in the instant before it killed her.

This Kit was a force. Even if he aimed his rage at Rick, its impact could destroy her.

The floor didn't shudder at his stride. He moved toward her as silently as he'd entered the room. When he reached for her wine, she let go before his hand closed.

He caught the glass and swilled her wine like grape juice.

Rick's satisfied grunt ended as Kit flung the goblet against the fireplace.

One shard still rocked on the hearth as Rick, pale and cautious, backed toward the front door. "Sorry to overstay my welcome."

Kit's glare stopped Andi from uttering the polite protest stalled in her throat.

Rick walked to the door and let himself out. He must have found the keys she'd left in the van's ignition, too, because she heard him drive away.

Kit crossed his arms.

She should launch a few recriminations. How dare he saunter into her living room, half dressed, and scare the bejesus out of her company? She didn't ask, but anger gave her the courage to pluck a willow leaf from his hair and kiss his cheek.

"Zip up your pants, wild man."

With a flurry of irritation, he did so, then walked to the door and stepped through as the Irish harp trilled.

Sudden weakness blurred the room's colors into mud. Andi braced herself against the wall. "Good Lord, Kit!"

Fear for him, *of* him, crashed around her. Believing the concept of a ghost was one thing. Watching him fade through a door was something else.

Hands shaking, she tried to open the door. The knob slipped in her fingers.

Finally the door swung toward her. Kit's handsome face was expressionless as water.

"He tried to poison you," he said.

She wanted to misunderstand, but the words wouldn't form another meaning.

Andi touched her throat. Hers had been a small sip, but Kit had gulped the rest. She gestured toward the shattered goblet.

"You drank it."

"So I did." He made a quick smoothing of his beard. "And now I bid you good night."

"No." She grabbed his sleeve. The unbuttoned shirt came halfway down his arm. "You think it won't hurt you, but you don't know. You thought . . . *I* thought, you could make love to me, and look what happened. I need to watch over you, just in case."

He made no move to adjust his shirt or pull away.

"What witchery makes me stand and listen? You'd have me gelded, Miranda, but I am not a thing which needs 'watching over.' "

Andi's stomach cramped with dread, but she didn't release his arm.

"You watched over me," she said.

Scorn marked his face, as if any dunce knew the situations weren't the same.

"Your mare's got out." He shifted his weight, still letting her cling to his sleeve. "Or been turned out. I must find her."

"*Then* will you come back?"

"Of course."

He answered too quickly, and she knew he was pacifying her with a half-truth.

"To me," Andi insisted. "Tonight."

Kit's jaw shifted to one side. "To you, tonight."

Andi used her hands to keep her lids open and her eyes fixed on the carriage house. Once, she woke with her cheek against her bedroom's wooden windowsill. The next time she woke with a start and slipped toward the floor. That was when she put on a gown, crawled into the curtained bed, and slept.

Though she'd left a light burning, she awoke to a dark room. And Kit. His footsteps moved through her dreams, pulling her into wakefulness. She reached for the bedside lamp, through air that seemed too thick to shove aside.

"Don't bother," Kit said. "I turned it off. It's late and you should be sleeping."

"No." She shoved her hair away with both hands, but her eyes were only half open. "I'm awake."

"Very well."

A silence shimmered between them.

"Kit." Andi managed to hold back the bed curtain. "Come in with me."

He obeyed so quickly, her hands formed an instinctive shield, until he guided her arms around his neck. The mattress dipped beneath his weight as he eased atop her.

Their matched shoulders and knees and lips electrified her. Kit's murmured apology for the bump of her head against the bed's headboard faded as she tugged him too close for speech.

In the dark behind her eyelids it didn't matter what he was or where he'd come from. Their hands strained together, clamped tight. Their chests pulled toward each other. Their hips pressed for the heat beneath her gown and his jeans.

Her toes skidded past his bare feet and the rise of his anklebone as she curled her leg over rough jeans.

"Take them off."

"Damme, Miranda. I can't do what you want."

He sidled away, but her leg curled over his, and he let himself be caught.

"What *we* want," she said.

"All right, vixen. *We.*"

His head nestled on her shoulder, giving her time to think. But his body covered hers completely. She didn't want to think, didn't want him still and scrupulous.

"I don't know how to do this, exactly. You're going to have to—" When her hips trembled against his, Kit groaned.

"Lady, I have spent two days in a dungeon, with limbs clamped in irons. Your torment is worse."

"Should I apologize for wanting you?" In the dark she could talk this way. "You're no fantasy. I can feel your weight. I can feel you here." Her hands flowed from his shoulders, to his waist, and stopped at his hips. "And *that* pressure is real."

Cold lapped between their necks as his chest parted from hers.

"No," she said. His hands pressed the bed on each side of her head. Blood rushed in her ears and modesty flowed away with it. "I don't know what else to say."

He kissed her lips' corners. Too gently.

"You don't have to wait." Did she sound shrewish? Fine. She wasn't offering idle encouragement.

He rocked onto his knees, and she opened her eyes as he loomed over her. His silhouette showed the wrinkling of his shirt. She wanted to rip it off and expose the smooth flow of flesh.

His chest lay bare beneath that shirt. She wanted to touch it, to feel the beat of the heart he claimed he did not have.

He kissed the hollow of her throat before pulling her beside him, to face him. Andi spread one hand in the darkness until she found his cheek.

"Kit, I've never felt like this before."

"Shhh." His finger tapped her lips. "All lovers say so."

"*I've* never said it. Never."

"All right." His hand smoothed over her brow, into her hair. *Lovers.*

Kit would never know he'd been too late to stop her from drinking.

The thought slowed her pulse, but not the hands she skimmed over Kit's jeans and tailored shirt.

"This isn't a come-on," she said, "but aren't your clothes uncomfortable?"

"A 'come-on.' " Kit chuckled. "No, I feel nothing, except where we touch."

She squirmed against him, touching him everywhere. His chest. Hadn't she needed to press her palm to his chest?

"That's new, isn't it? Feeling my touch? Kit, please, tell me."

For a minute she'd been thinking straight, but now, she felt it again. Excitement, an edge of panic, and something hot as anger.

"It's new." His hand slipped along the curve of her flannel-covered waist.

"You're changing back."

"Perchance, but I'd sooner stay a ghost than revert to a four-hundred-year-old—"

"—just know you are. That night when Lily disappeared, and we were on the veranda, I knew it was more than just a simple kiss. Because a man like you—when you touched me—I couldn't believe how you trembled and—"

"Christ's bloody nails, Miranda. Men in this weak time may allow their lust to be chronicled, set down, and recited. I will not have it."

At his embarrassment, Andi gritted her teeth. Stop. Go. Stop. Go. Afraid she might scream, she listened. Outside, Trifle cantered in her corral, round and round in the darkness. Outside, an owl's hoot discouraged her excitement.

"By my troth," Kit hesitated, "it's not just the touch of you. Scents of things are returning too."

Joy overwhelmed her. He could be hers.

"Kit, I—"

Resolve hardened his kiss. Although he didn't say a word, Kit blocked her vow. His hand, at her waist, urged her closer, but Andi struggled away.

"You can't shut me up with a kiss."

Kit pulled the bed's one open curtain closed.

"I'll wager I can, mistress."

His mouth brushed hers but she wanted more. He did it again and again, until frustration pricked her into meeting his lips solidly.

She thought she felt him smile as he mirrored each move, touching her cheek as she touched his, tightening his fingers in her hair as she did his, until she grazed the tip of her tongue against his.

Kit took over. He rolled her to her back and heat flashed across her skin. Andi tugged the shirt out of his waistband and searched the smooth channel of his spine with her fingers. Her head tipped into the pillow at his urgency. And then, he stopped.

As he parted their lips to breathe, Andi heard the unearthly loud sound of her own panting. All the while, Kit's shoulders stayed solid beneath her hands. What did that mean?

Old expertise might let him go through the motions of passion while he maintained cold detachment. Clearly, his concentration hadn't faltered, though he'd called them *lovers*.

"Kit, I do. I—"

"Hush, it's only lust, Miranda."

"Don't talk as if I'm a child. I trust you. I want this."

As Kit's hand skimmed up her neck, impulse made Andi twist to kiss his fingers. She felt his deliberation. She wanted it to stop.

"Wondrous strong lust," Kit admitted. "But pure lechery all the same."

"I don't think so. I can't believe I agreed to marry Domingo without knowing—" She swallowed. "Kit, what if I'd already married him when I met you?"

He ignored the question. Then, unwillingly, he added, "You must have felt—desire."

How could he move away, when just the word *desire* made her want to twine around him?

"No, maybe a little curiosity. But if I'd felt this, I never would have chickened out. I'm the one who told him to turn the car around, remember? I wouldn't go to the motel with him." She wound her arms around his neck, wishing for light to see his expression. "I'm not afraid with you."

She heard him swallow and hoped he understood. In fact, he pretended amusement.

"You're afraid to mate with a man, but eager to embrace a ghost. Please explain the basis for this—what shall we call it?—grand devotion."

If he thought she'd shove him out of bed, or storm off in a huff, he was wrong. When Kit turned arrogant and cold, it meant she'd crept past his armor.

"All right. Example one: When you kissed me just now, you followed me. You did what I wanted."

"It's what a man does with an untried woman." He dismissed her praise.

"And, it was really nice when you found Lily. And paid for the cappuccino."

"By God's—" He inhaled, sharply. "Go on."

"And I relax with you. With Rick, for instance, I felt tense."

"Mmmm, I've heard some women are averse to being wooed with poison."

She kept talking. "And you protected me. Tonight you drank that poison for me."

"Where's the nobility in acts which hold no danger? Drugs aren't likely to kill a man already dead."

It was still brave. She just couldn't explain how.

"Fallen silent already? Perhaps Domingo was the better choice after all."

Andi rubbed her eyes. "I was marrying Domingo—because—oh, it sounds so stupid, but—I was marrying him because I thought it was past *time* I married, nearly *time* I had children."

He pounced on her words.

"Do you dare dream you'll have that from me? I can't

keep hard long enough to swive you, let alone fill you with my babe.''

Outside, the owl hooted once more, underlining the regret beneath Kit's cruelty. Kit had imagined her round with his child, she just knew it.

"Kit, we're in a mess, but it's getting better. You hold me and don't disappear and even if we don't find the box—"

"Are you so base that you'd settle for *this*?"

Did he mean love with a ghost? Marriage which might end in a puff of sulfur?

"For—what?" she ventured.

"Precisely, lady," he said. "So far, the qualities you admire come from a list of seven deadly sins. We have lust, of course," he numbered off his fingers, "touches of sloth and greed—"

"Kit, don't think this is working." It was. Tears burned behind her eyes, but he didn't have to know. "You won't protect me by driving me away."

He flung back the curtain, rattling the wooden rings on the rod overhead, then stood and switched on the bedside lamp.

She pulled her knees up beneath her white gown and blinked under his scrutiny.

He mocked her tears. "So you fancy I'm protecting you."

As if sun slanted across one shoulder toward the floor, Kit's image wavered. Andi told herself it was a good sign. He couldn't lie to her, taunt her, and crave her all at once.

"I can see right through you, Kit, in every way. You're afraid to love me, because it might keep you here, in a place where you don't know everything. Y-you're afraid to let me love you, and even though I don't know why, I still trust you."

Lord, if she'd been panting before, it sounded ten times louder now.

"Why would a ghost choose honor, Miranda? Answer that."

"Because you're the ghost of Kit Gallatin." She stared into his black eyes and didn't flinch when he laughed.

"Don't deceive yourself. I am a *heartless* bastard, Miranda. I always was. I'll do what I must to find that box.''

''I don't believe you.''

Kit's chest moved as if he'd been running. It gave her hope. Andi stood, almost tripping on her flounced hem, and took her last chance.

''Kit, I love you.''

Power crackled around them. Kit took her hand and forced its palm flat against his chest. She stared into his eyes. Energy, invisible, but tangible as electricity, coursed around them, but beneath her fingers there was stillness.

''Get this through your thick pate, Miranda. There is nothing here to love.''

And then, of course, there wasn't.

A rigid tranquility closed around her. She could almost see herself sobbing on the bed, but she didn't. Instead, she lifted the skirts of her gown so she wouldn't trip and sprinted downstairs. At the landing she felt woozy, nauseated. She leaned against the wall until the poison quit twisting her stomach.

Poison? But why would Rick try to kill her? It didn't make sense.

Andi picked her way past Lily, turned on the light, and pulled out the telephone book. The print was illegible, as if she gazed down from a height.

At last she found the A's. Names came into focus.

''Aragon . . . Aragon . . . Richard.''

Yawning, she dialed. If Kit wanted the Graveyard Rose more than anything, she'd call in an expert. Motivated by greed, Rick would help her find Kit's heart. It didn't mean she had to let him keep it.

The telephone rang twice. Then she heard it juggled from its cradle.

''Yeah?''

''Rick, it's Miranda Fairfield.''

In the fireplace, an ash-coated branch broke, spilling red-orange embers.

''Yeah?'' Rick repeated, sounding half asleep.

''What time is it?'' Andi found that the telephone cord

reached far enough that she could warm her hands at the fireplace.

Rick's indrawn breath was almost a snore.

"Two twenty-five. Look, if you called to apologize, forget it. I didn't know Gallatin was living with you."

"Oh, he's not." Andi closed her eyes. "I'm not," she added.

"You feeling okay?" Rick's voice sharpened.

"So, that's why you want to help me look for the Graveyard Rose," she said.

"What's why? Andi, you need to wake up a little if we're going to talk."

"You collect stuff like that for your class."

"Right, and I know other people who do too. There's a thriving business in death artifacts. Auctions all over the country . . . Internet sales . . ."

"Of what?"

"Andi, is Gallatin still there?"

"No, he's looking for Trifle, I think, but he can't find it. He wants me to find it." Andi dropped the phone and retrieved it. "I need to go to bed." She stifled a yawn. "I'll let you know when to come help me."

"That's good. Go to bed—but, hey, Andi, don't hang up."

She dragged the phone toward the couch. She would never make it upstairs. "Okay."

"Make sure you clean up that broken wineglass. Andi?" Rick made an annoying tapping sound on the telephone receiver. "You want to clean that up and take it out, do you hear me? The garbage man comes in the morning, and you want to be sure and get rid of that sharp glass."

Chapter
Fourteen

Beshrew her for a liar.

Kit sat in the shade and watched Miranda labor. For her false vow, she should suffer this farewell.

Face burned red by the sun, she called to mind a peasant. Except, each time she rocked back on her heels, battling rope-thick roots of weeds, he smelled lavender. Just once more, he wanted to taste the hollow of Miranda's throat and fill his senses with lavender.

It would never happen.

Because Miranda trusted him to do what was right, he had crushed her words of love, saving her from heartbreak or ruin or both.

His payment, after her grand confession of love, had been a Miranda who spent two nights pacing, two days grubbing in the dirt, and not a minute with him.

A blue-feathered bird squawked from the cottonwood branches. Miranda looked up and dusted off her palms. Still squatting, she gazed toward the carriage house, but dark glasses covered her eyes. He couldn't read her expression.

Although he knew he'd been harsh, mayhap she longed for him, a little.

Miranda used one dirty finger to stab the glasses back up the bridge of her nose.

"No way," she muttered as she uprooted a tall prickly weed. Then, humming, she disentangled the weed's strangling tendrils from a plant.

Those fingers had traced his spine with a daintiness which made him want more. Those small hands and eager lips had been promise enough, without vows of love. And though no canopied bed had ever felt so right, he'd left her maidenhead unbreached.

Heat clamped his throat. *Not* for another man.

'sblood! The thought had burst from nowhere to madden him. He'd called Miranda base, insinuated that she was a dunce, and laughed at her tenderness because it kept her from cleaving to him. Miranda would be an old woman before she appreciated his gift.

His restraint had naught to do with the chance he might have mucked it up, going all foggy and frail.

She'd fought him. "This isn't working," she'd said, though her tears told another tale. He'd admired her strength and let every drop of admiration whet his cruelty.

Now it was time to go.

No angel coaxed him to seek his heart's summons in another time. No devil pulled him toward Chaos. Miranda had trusted him to do what was right, so he would go.

Kit willed himself to part from Heart's Ease. He imagined his spirit soaring away from Sparrowgrass, California, and summer.

Simple regret halted his ascent. His human senses convulsed with loss.

Sky, wind, rocks. Miranda. For a few weeks, they'd all been his. While Kit's spirit spun away, he watched her.

Glorious, with sorrel hair tossed back, Miranda stood, removed dark glasses, and raised her face. Perhaps his going freed her. Arms outflung, she worshiped the sun as Kit Gallatin's world turned black.

• • •

Chills made Andi jump up and expose every inch of skin to sunshine. Summer was no time for flu, but ever since Saturday she'd felt queasy. Maybe she should ask Gina to check on her beef supplier.

Andi hoped Kit wasn't sick in bed. Probably not. It wouldn't be the first time she'd provoked him. And this time she deserved his anger. What an ungrateful wretch to tell a man of such dignity to "zip his pants." Especially when he'd come to her *rescue*.

Andi dropped the trowel, tightened the band around her hair, and rubbed her arms. All morning she'd tended the roses, and she hadn't been cold until now.

She'd weeded, mulched, and sent the sturdy stems thoughts of the illustrious plant heritage that Jan had revealed. Jan had phoned yesterday to read Andi a passage that said Mad Gallicas were so old they'd probably been used as the first rosaries.

The buds remained tightly closed, but there was a promise in their fragrance, even now, when the sun hid behind a cloud.

A jog might warm her up.

The door harp sang her entrance to the silent house. She climbed the stairs, listening. Nothing moved until Lily, dozing on the bed, raised her head and mewed.

Andi snagged her running shoes, slipped them on, and bent to knot them. When she stood, she felt dizzy. *There's nothing here to love*. In a weird grab of memory, she heard Kit's voice. But they'd never had such a conversation.

Shambling down the stairs, she decided on a flat-out sprint. Exertion might make her remember.

The front gates were twined closed by magenta sweet peas. She hadn't left Heart's Ease for two days. Not since Gina's column. Not since her dinner with Rick. Andi jerked the gates apart, hit the timer on her watch, and started running.

The driveway took her to a trail. She jogged past dry brush and took the turnoff for town. Heat waves shimmered from the asphalt ahead.

Twenty-five minutes out, Andi's chill had dwindled to

coolness. She'd just started toward home when a black Miata pulled up beside her.

Noah Lincoln lowered the tinted passenger-side window and leaned forward. Andi slowed to a walk and waved, not at all sure she had the breath to talk.

"You courtin' heatstroke?"

Andi shook her head and kept walking. Her muscles would seize up from a sudden stop.

"Time-and-temp sign at the bank said it was ninety-eight degrees at four o'clock."

"Small-town doctors sure shut down early," she said.

"Don't let the long evenings fool you. It's after five. Besides, I closed up to play cops and robbers," he said.

Fatigue hit suddenly. Andi leaned her hands on her thighs, catching her breath.

"Want a ride?"

"Only in the fire engine." Andi took a few steps before she considered him again. "Unless you're takin' me in, Sheriff."

"Deputy," he corrected.

She stumbled on a stone. As her ankle twisted, a current of cold returned.

"You feelin' all right?"

"Fine." Andi scrubbed at her eyes, hoping the flush from her run would cover the dark circles.

"Well, you look like you been drug through a knothole backwards."

"Is that your medical or legal opinion?"

"Quit being a smart-ass and get in the car."

His Southern accent made the gibe sound brotherly, so when Noah reached across to open the door, Andi joined him.

The Miata smelled of leather upholstery and dog. By creeping along at three miles per hour, Noah missed each rock on the road.

"Sorry, I'm touchy on that 'deputy' stuff. Once in a while they need a real guy, not a volunteer fireman." Noah maneuvered through her gates. "You gonna talk to me about that night?" He braked and switched the key to off.

Andi stifled her surprise, then reminded herself he meant the *other* night, when someone had cracked her windshield and filled her car with flowers.

"You gonna cuff me?"

"Now, dammit—"

Andi laughed, feeling better.

"There's not much more to tell, Noah, so leave the paperwork in the car." Andi indicated an official-looking clipboard sharing the backseat with a box of dog biscuits and a rumpled lab coat.

Unwinding from the low car, she regarded the deer hoofprints marking the hardened mud around her garden.

"You know, I've been meaning to ask you for some dog hair," she said. "I read that if you twist some into the fence around your garden, it discourages deer. I don't mind if they nibble the occasional zucchini." Andi stopped at the bird feeder she'd suspended from a low cottonwood branch. Empty again. "But if they eat my roses, we'll be discussing a Bambi buffet."

She lifted a jar of cinnamon-orange tea she'd left steeping in the sun on the veranda.

"Dog hair, huh?" Noah followed her inside and slouched on the couch. "Be nice if Gertrude were good for something, but gardening at Heart's Ease is an uphill battle. Old-timers say the house was built smack in the middle of a mule deer wintering plot."

"I'd like to give it a try." She poured tea over ice and took it to him.

"Okay, I'll get you some." He nodded and waited for her to recount the night of the storm.

He listened halfheartedly, apparently more interested in studying the great room. Understandable, since she'd been over this before.

"So, who knew daffodils would wrack your nerves?" He asked.

"Anyone who knew where Clint died." She leaned back, making space on her lap for Lily. "Or how."

"I talked to Jan, and while it's not my area of expertise,

hon, you might ask yourself why you're still carryin' around that guilt.''

"How can you ask?" As Andi crossed her arms and shifted, Lily extended her claws in a gentle reprimand. "I'm a schoolteacher. We don't kill people and get over it. Most cops don't kill two people in a career." When Noah stayed silent, she added, "You read about my other boyfriend, in Gina's column, didn't you?"

"Only two boyfriends between ages fifteen and twenty-five?" He whistled. "Now there's a crime."

The sun lines around Noah's eyes were downright flattering. He was a doctor and not far past forty. If Blake didn't return his affection, she was nuts.

For a minute, Andi forgot you could always count on the good guys to pull the rug out from under you.

"Your boarder, Gallatin. I've been wondering what he had to do with that report of shouts and breaking glass?"

"From who?" Andi asked.

Wrong question. She cursed sleepless nights and faith in human nature. Then she amended her response.

"Shouts and breaking glass? Where, at the Hangin' Tree?"

Noah fished an ice cube from his tea and crunched it before he smiled. "Sloppy rebound, Miranda."

"Okay." She sighed and tapped her foot. "If I explain what happened, will you tell me who 'tipped you off'?"

"Naw, you don't have to tell me a thing." Noah rolled his shoulders. "I should probably go ask Gallatin."

Kit's arrogance would only make things worse.

"Unless you want to tell me what the yellin' was about."

Andi couldn't remember any yelling, but she searched her mind for proof of Kit's innocence.

"Kit hasn't caused any trouble. Remember the other day in the Dancing Goat? How he slammed his fist on the table because you missed looking for the guy who smashed my windshield? He was just acting protective."

"Could've been territorial, not protective. Some men are like that."

Because she'd made the same assertion just days ago, Andi

rushed ahead to describe her dinner with Rick. Noah nodded accompaniment as she insisted the evening was no amorous tryst, but he pressed for the location of the incident.

"And this was out on the veranda," he said once. Then, "And you had dinner at Dinah's old maple table, but how about your ice cream and teacher talk?"

"In front of the fireplace." Andi's throat tightened as Noah moved to stand by the hearth. "That sounds romantic, but it wasn't. I'm sort of *off* men."

Noah didn't ask for details. Instead, he rearranged the fireplace tools.

"Rick's not my type, anyway," she said, as she heard Noah grunt. "Don't you trust him?"

"I wouldn't say that. Now, Christopher Gallatin, is he more your type?" Noah peered around the dusty hearth.

No, my type usually dies after *I kiss them.*

Andi squelched an ironic laugh. "Just the opposite."

"So, was there a fight?"

She rubbed her fingers between her eyebrows, erasing wrinkles of concentration. "I'm trying to remember."

"You're having trouble remembering three nights ago?"

Andi weighed Noah's question. It sounded more diagnostic than accusatory. She nodded.

"You mentioned Gina's column, though."

"I couldn't forget that."

"And when you got home from the Laughing Goat, what'd you do then?"

"I took a bath and made dinner." She watched Noah's eyes narrow. "And I *don't* drink much. Nor do I have a history of blackouts. So, don't ask."

"You didn't go on a bender, even when your friends died?"

"Even then."

"Why don't you come into the office, sometime, just for a checkup?" Noah hung his thumbs in his pockets and shook his head. "You haven't been sleeping much, that's obvious. What about appetite? Temperature?"

"Nothing unusual, except I can't sleep because I'm trying to remember."

"Worrisome," Noah admitted. "What's this, here?" Noah moved the wrought-iron tool holder aside.

"Did you bring white gloves too? If you're checking my housekeeping . . ." She couldn't muster a joke, and when she saw the stained shard of glass, gooseflesh ran down her arms.

"Don't suppose you remember how this got here?" Noah asked.

Andi shook her head. *Why didn't she?*

Even more unnerving was the way Noah started up the sorghum-sweet gab all over again.

"A girl pretty as you—well, sloppy housekeeping's not much on my mind, but I'll tell you what. How 'bout you poke around in the cupboard and see if you've got a Ziploc bag. I'd like to take this with me and have a closer look."

Long after Noah drove away, Andi leaned against a post on the veranda. How could she explain to Kit, when she felt so numb-minded herself?

Trifle's neigh and the rustling of brush came to her on a breeze. It sounded as if Kit were walking up from the ravine.

With no reason to put it off, she strode toward the carriage house. Swallows stitched through the twilight and a tardy hummingbird zipped between the empty strands of laundry line, abandoning the orange trumpet vine for nighttime shelter.

Trifle nickered. Then, as Andi approached, the white mare backed away from the fence, tossing her forelock back from perpetually startled eyes.

"Kit?"

Rustling stopped and she heard only the muted gossip of quail. Apparently she hadn't heard anything but birds, making their last forays before sundown.

Inside the barn, mice scurried into silence. Trifle's manger was filled with dinner, but she stood outside, swishing her tail.

Andi didn't hear Kit's steps moving in the rooms overhead. But then, she wouldn't. She mounted the steps, avoiding a troop of black mountain ants investigating a crumb.

What would she say when Kit opened the door? "Hi, sorry

about the zip-your-pants remark and whatever *else* I said that night. And, by the way, the deputy sheriff wants to talk with you.''

Two steps from the top, Andi noticed the door wasn't closed. The pulse in her neck sprang into panic mode, but she couldn't say why.

''Kit?'' She knocked backhanded on the door as it swung open. ''Are you home?''

And just where would that be? She almost heard his sardonic voice asking the question, but she heard nothing else as she stepped into the middle of the room.

She felt vulnerable standing there, but she was alone. Faint scents of oranges and furniture polish eddied around her, and she noticed how few possessions Kit had brought with him.

The bicentennial red, white, and blue offered false cheer in a room where no one lived. Jeans and a few shirts lay folded on the bed beneath the window which overlooked Trifle's pen. A sheaf of lined yellow paper sat on the table inside the red leatherette booth. The manuscript was written in the same cramped, ornate hand she'd struggled to read before. Beside the pages sat the room's only decoration.

A thorny blackberry cane, its white flowers just beginning to open, shared a water glass with an exuberant spray of trumpet vine.

Obviously, Kit wasn't home.

With serpentine subtlety . . . the chapter began.

A scuff, like a shoe in the bedroom closet, made her start.

She was not about to fling open closet doors looking for him. Instead, she'd just leave. She had no business violating his privacy, except . . . Kit was gone, as if he'd never been here.

Had he been here? Of course, Christopher Gallatin had. Half the citizens of Sparrowgrass had seen him. But Kit Gallatin, who'd skimmed experienced hands beneath her blouse, then disappeared? Kit Gallatin, a ghost set on finding his heart. Had he ever been here?

Andi turned slowly, scanning every wall and beam and rug.

Yes. Until now, she hadn't quite noticed the warm currents and charged atmosphere which signaled Kit's presence, even when he was invisible. But now she knew. Kit wasn't here.

Chapter
Fifteen

Andi tucked herself into the red leatherette booth. Why pretend she wasn't going to read Kit's manuscript? She might as well get comfortable. Besides, the arrangement of flowers hinted that he had meant her to find it and read it.

As she accustomed herself to his random spelling and swooping embellishments, his handwriting grew easier to read.

With serpentine subtlety, Aragon's seed spread through an unsuspecting England. I knew that much when I surfaced from the swirling netherworld which consumed me after Arabella's betrayal.

Though I came back at the summons of my vagabond heart, it was hatred thick as tar which lured me beyond civilization, beyond the reach of my Queen, to India.

At first, only tropical heat made me question my whereabouts. I appeared to be in an English drawing room. Against one wainscoted wall stood a table draped with paisley. Atop it sat a golden replica of the box which held my heart.

Hands numb with cold may close, though the owner does not feel them. Hands clumsy with drink may bat and fumble, but the hands of a ghost whose attention will not focus are useless. I wanted to snatch my heart and vanish, until an English lady showed me my folly.

April blossoms are less fragile and lovely than Sarah Easter. I remember Sarah by her own surname, though she'd wed and borne the child of Anthony Aragon, descendant of my great enemy.

She came upon me in that drawing room, amid dusk's blue shadows, and did not flee.

"Are you a thief?" she asked.

Falling on ears half deaf from a hundred years of Chaos, her voice was unbearably sweet.

"My husband has a post at this fort, you know. It would be a sad mistake, stealing from us." Brave words from a girl alone.

When I did not answer, she studied me as she would a difficult sermon.

I thought I looked rather well, still dressed in a shirt of ivory lawn and a dark doublet with padded sleeves and tapered wrists, the whole slashed to show a bit of scarlet lining.

"Are you a disbanded soldier? A gentleman adventurer?" Sarah's moon-pale hair tilted to one side. "That red silk in your waistcoat looks a bit like a tart's petticoat." Then a worse horror struck her. "You are British?"

Because I conceived the whole truth would affright her, I nodded. Even dead, I was an Englishman.

Her hand shook as she gestured at the doorway and

*said the voices without belonged to Anthony Aragon
and two English officers.*

*She took care not to mention Jamie. I didn't know
of him until later. Even a lark leads a cat away from
her nest.*

*I erred. I should have taken the box and vanished
before Sarah asked me to stay. From other rooms, we
heard the brush of bare feet, the clink of dishes, the
guffaws of men at cards. Sarah pled cowardice. She
dared not order tea for a stranger.*

*Her voice, her lily skin, and the undeserved friend-
ship she offered were refreshment enough.*

The uppity little witch.

Andi let the tablet fall back on the table. She'd gripped it
tightly, turning pages to catch the fading light from the window. Now she stared at the hillside just inches outside the
window. Instead of a rusted latch and double-paned glass
fogged in between with moisture, she saw upper-crust Sarah,
criticizing Kit's clothes, then keeping him as a pet.

"It happened centuries ago," she muttered, but she
thought of a short story she taught each year in freshman
English. Its depiction of colonial India echoed Kit's story.
She thought of bloody revolts and scanned the manuscript
for a date, then shook her head. She should worry over the
scurry of mice in the walls, not fret over Sarah, who was
long since dust.

The place was Fort William, Calcutta, India.

*"A world away from Surrey," Sarah called it, and
added, "Only unalterable matrimony holds me in this
heathen place."*

*When Sarah's husband bid her attend him, I left. I
might have vanished before her eyes, but I could not,
any more than I could resist exploring.*

*India spread a feast before my starved senses. Sarah
saw with the critical opinions of a lady. For her, India
was purgatory. Even deprived of taste and touch, I rev-
eled in India. My eyes devoured sights like a starved
man swallows fruit.*

*I followed well-chaperoned Sarah through the
streets and bazaars of Calcutta. Where I saw black-
swan women bangled with silver, wrapped in silk of
gold-shot lime and violet, Sarah saw whores.*

*"They're temple dancers so wanton, even their hea-
then religion won't have them. Imagine, even people
who worship many-headed, snake-limbed gods have
cast them into the streets."*

*One hot afternoon, I marveled at Indian dwellings
with orange-and-ocher frescoes of amazing striped
beasts. When I said I did not miss gray London, Sarah
gaped in disbelief.*

*"They dwell in mud huts, most of them, and still
look slit-eyed at their betters."*

*Because I wanted to stay, I did not ask how she
would receive intruders on her family's estate in Surrey. And I did not mention the box. Sarah was all I
missed of life, and she convinced me I was all she
missed of home.*

*I found her in cool gardens once. Her son, Jamie,
paddled in a fountain, sailing boats made of leaves,
and I watched, until she noticed and flew at me, enraged.*

*I vanished and we never spoke of Jamie or of my
ghostly state. She did not wish to know. Once I ventured in that direction, asking how she'd come to own
the box. Sarah nearly swooned and she did cover her
lips, threatening sickness if I told the truth of what it
held.*

I fear my hint was vile enough. From that day, Sarah

*pulled her skirts aside when she passed the table it sat
upon. She regarded the box as if it dripped with gouts
of blood. But then, Sarah Easter was a lady. To this
day, I have not known one more exquisite.*

No lady likes a scene, Andi reminded herself. And hadn't
she and Kit made spectacles of themselves while they dis-
cussed his ghosthood in a common stable? Luckily no one
had watched them slam around, hurl accusations and sarcasm, and punctuate their fight with heavy petting.

Perhaps Miranda Fairfield was no lady in the Elizabethan
sense, but she'd trade such immaculate credentials for the
distinction Kit bestowed upon her. She had restored the nerve
endings of a ghost. Andi matched her fingertips against one
another, buffed them together and wished she were touching
Kit.

*I thought it ironic: My killer's heir owned my heart.
Sarah spoke no ill of Anthony Aragon, her mate and
match in blond beauty, but her praise oft sounded like
censure.*

*Coming to India, Anthony insisted his wife stay on
deck, even when their ship was attacked by a French
frigate.*

*"He bade me swim for my life, rather than sink with
the ship," Sarah explained. "And he commanded that
a sea man fetch all our valuables. They must needs be
on deck as well.*

*"As the ship was fired upon, a shell ripped a splin-
ter—the size of a man's limb it was—from the deck. It
stabbed through the Graveyard Rose. And pierced the
sailor carrying its bag, as well. Amid the smoke and
shouting, no one noticed the filigree had been bent.
Once he discovered the harm, Anthony was distraught*

*as if the damage had been done the child in my
womb.''*

One glimpse of glory, Sarah gave me, then.

*Yes, it was the first time I heard of the hilt-fashioned
box called the Graveyard Rose. Yes, the name shocked
and surprised me, but shock faded under the maternal
love shining from her face as her arms protected the
space long since left by Jamie.*

*Mine was never an amorous love. In that moment it
turned to pure longing.*

A breeze wafted past. Andi withdrew her imagination from
the work and looked up in time to see the door waver. Hadn't
she closed it behind her? Probably not.

Outside, it was turning night. The carriage house had no
electric lights, and she didn't see a lantern.

It was almost too dark for reading. She'd just about re-
signed herself to giving up, when the next line gave her the
historical date she'd been searching for. Gooseflesh crawled
over the exposed flesh of her thighs.

*In 1755, Aragon had commissioned a slightly larger
replica to protect the battered sword-hilt box. Engraved with symbols and stories in several Indian di-
alects, it told the exploits of the Aragons.*

*Ye gods! Aragons! I should have destroyed it then
or asked Sarah to surrender it to me. My heart rested
inside a golden glorification of a traitor.*

*Aragon's arrogance did not stop there. I heard him
talk with officers. They detailed the small wars weak-
ening the regions of India. I watched a toast to the
Crown's plan to hold dominion over a dark people and
their riches. I saw a livid bruise on Sarah's cheek,
like a thundercloud marring Easter dawn, after she
refused to play the hypocrite and extend her gloved*

hand to a man who fell somewhat short of being a
maharajah. I . . .

Here, a page had been torn from the lined tablet. Andi
flipped ahead, squinted at the backs of pages and read on,
before she lost the light entirely.

. . . *bejeweled man of nobility took them on a tiger
hunt. Anthony Aragon allowed Sarah to travel safely
on the elephant. The nobleman, whom Aragon called
Ali, rode a gray pony with fiery eyes, and so Aragon
did the same. His hot-blooded bay wore a saddle with
dangling tassels. It was to these that Jamie clung,
seated before his father.*

*I drifted alongside the riders. Somewhere ahead in
the tall grass, the beaters sang. Ali warned Aragon to
leave Fort William.   A reckless youth had come to the
throne in Bengal. He vowed Calcutta streets would run
red with British blood.*

*At the mention of blood the tiger pounced and the
bay horse reared. Shaking his forelock, fighting the
reins, he demanded all Aragon's horsemanship. And
Jamie fell.*

*Sarah's scream raked us. Even the tiger twisted in
its plunge for the pony's neck and in that moment I
went to the child.*

*Of course I feared failure; a ghost is sometimes
weak. Of course I feared discovery; materializing before their eyes carried risk, but I needed arms of my
own to grab Jamie.*

*Cat's claws hook, tighten, and drag. The tigress
would have peeled my flesh down through meat and
muscle to my rib cage, except I did not have one. I
was a shell around Jamie, but I sufficed until the cat*

fell to rifle shots, then kicked as if death gripped her hind legs in a final game.

Leaving without my heart would have been the coward's way. That night, I asked a boon for saving Sarah's son.

She denied me.

Just as she'd shaken with excitement on discovering a thief in her drawing room, Sarah now trembled with rage.

"You may not interfere with my life. You may not show yourself. You must not go—out there."

"Am I your private toy, then?" I had never touched her, but I wanted to shake her frail shoulders. "A secret you would keep at the cost of your child's life?"

"Anthony would have saved him." Her eyes said she knew it for a lie. "You betrayed me."

"Betrayed you how, Sarah?"

"Don't say my name. Ever. You're no more than vapor and wicked thoughts. You must never touch me or my son. Begone!"

I laughed at her.

'Aroint ye!' she'd have said in my time, but 'begone!' worked just as well. Still laughing, I vanished.

With no intention of taking the box, I lingered for a day, in case Sarah showed remorse. In those hours, I saw her discover two maidservants gossiping about the box. One, a wench with a pellet of amber on a string around her neck, had always regarded me kindly, although she could not have seen my form or face. This maid, black-skinned and slight, told Sarah whoever possessed the box would be invincible in battle, and Sarah flushed with fury.

Later, Sarah shouted with glee at her husband's in-

sistence he'd seen a shade. And she hushed sweet Jamie's questions.

She didn't cry because I'd gone. In fact, my leaving made her stronger. When Anthony confided Ali's warning and offered her passage home, Sarah hardened her jaw and snapped that she would not be driven off by anyone, or anything.

For three school years, Andi had taught the short story "Sahib." For three years, she'd guided class discussion of historical context. She knew what came next.

Andi stared at the open window above Kit's bed. Night wind carried the white curtains inside, their fluttering more ghostly than any movement Kit had ever made. She could close the window, but it wasn't the breeze that chilled her.

In 1756 Fort William had been attacked by a rash prince. In summer's blazing heat, hundreds of women and children had been locked in a jail smaller than this carriage house. Only a few had emerged alive, and ever after the place was called "the black hole of Calcutta."

Andi repositioned the manuscript just as she'd found it. She slid out of the booth and listened to Trifle snorting and pawing down below. It was just possible that Jamie and Sarah were fictional characters who'd sprung alive in Kit's imagination.

She'd close the window and get back to the house. Lily would be hungry, and so was she. She wondered if the defrosted lasagna could stand reheating one more time. Tomorrow she would brave the stares and the pity and drive into Sparrowgrass for supplies.

Andi knelt on the bed to pull the window closed. Glancing out, she saw movement. It distracted her from a sticker or burr that pricked her knee. Something drifted near the clothesline. Not deer, not waving branches, not laundry. She'd taken it all in and the lines had been empty just an hour ago.

She glanced at the corral. As she made out the pale spot

which must be Trifle, dozing unafraid in one corner, Andi's fingers found the pin which had stuck her knee.

She didn't need light to read it. It was the sassy button she'd noticed on Cisco's shirt the night they'd played Scrabble. I READ BANNED BOOKS, it said, but how had it gotten here?

Cisco had been in Kit's apartment.

Andi let the idea roll through her mind, but it touched off no avalanche of answers. She'd bet Kit hadn't invited him. And if Kit had discovered an intruder, she had no doubt he'd exacted a phantom's revenge.

Determined to face Cisco, and whatever havoc he'd wreaked down below, Andi slipped the button into her pocket and descended the stairs from the carriage house to the barn.

Her eyes noticed the blue metal baseball bat which leaned in one corner of the barn. She left it there.

As it turned out, the bat would have done no good.

Stalking a woman with her own nightmares was impossible. Andi knew it, but she also knew it was happening. Again. First the daffodils, now this.

Nylon ripped, a clothespin plopped to the ground, and Andi's hands worked like pistons.

"Damn you," she whispered. She grabbed even as she tried to shrink away from what floated overhead, brushing her face. She slipped on grass going wet with dew, and then she shouted. "Damn you!"

Andi's voice echoed over the creek rushing through the ravine as she bolted through the back gate and up the steps to the veranda, her arms full of pink lingerie.

She started a fire and burned it all. It was stupid, wasteful, and as a destruction of evidence, probably illegal. It felt great and smelled awful.

With the fireplace poker, Andi shoved a scalloped lace bra nearer the flames. Lily meowed, twining at her ankles.

"Okay, watch-cat." Andi scooped Lily up and nestled her on her shoulder like a baby. "Is someone coming, or are you hungry?" Andi felt reassured by her own voice.

She stared from the kitchen window, past her own reflection and into the yard. No sign of Noah, thank God. He'd seen the daffodils and the broken windshield. He might believe that a clothesline full of pink lingerie had materialized out of nowhere, but she didn't want to push her luck.

Lily squirmed and made a fluttering sound in her throat.

"Too late for blue jays, Lily cat."

All the same, Andi turned on the outside light so the cat could watch. The Volkswagen sat alone on the driveway. No Miata or fire truck had raced to Heart's Ease. No white van, either.

Burning underwear on a summer night constituted a giant leap past idiosyncratic behavior. Noah might feel compelled to lock her up unless she explained. And she couldn't. Not to Noah, not to Kit, not to anyone. So how had Rick or Cisco found out?

Lily feinted a paw toward the window, and finally Andi saw. A doe stood at the bird feeder, which hung from the cottonwood. Gray-brown and graceful, she reared, twisted, and butted until she finally achieved an angle which let her lick her tongue into the feeder.

"Wow, I am a city girl." Andi marveled at the explanation for her constantly empty bird feeder.

An adolescent fawn wandered away from his mother, past the Volkswagen. Effortlessly, he hip-hopped over the chicken wire fence into her garden.

"Hey!" Andi dropped the cat and rapped on the kitchen window. "Get out of there!"

The doe shied, made a sweeping run toward the garden, and fled with the fawn at her heels. They bolted out the front gates.

Andi had saved her summer salads, but if she didn't walk out and latch the gates, the deer would be back.

Andi pulled a diet soda and the remains of the lasagna out of the refrigerator. It curled up at the edges like old sandals, but she slid it into the microwave anyway.

The machine hummed. The fireplace blaze crackled and smoked, melting man-made fibers certain to burn a hole in the ozone. Flame sputtered and sizzled, consuming a spaghetti-strapped teddy. If she had a shred of conscience, she'd pour water over the entire mess, and soon.

First, though, she had to latch that gate. She sipped her drink. There was no reason not to walk into the yard. Her stalker clearly didn't want a confrontation. What did he want?

It must be Rick, set on driving her off so he could find the Graveyard Rose, but the cruelty felt more like revenge. The lingerie was definitely about the accident which caused Domingo's death.

The phone rang, startling her into taking a huge gulp of her drink. She coughed, carbonation fizzing in her nose, but she didn't answer it. Last night about this time Rick had called and asked when she wanted him to come over and help.

Fix the bathroom floor, she supposed, but she'd told him she had the flu, to give her a few days.

For crying out loud, if she didn't go shut the gate, it meant she was letting Rick, Cisco, or Vlad the Impaler keep her wriggling like a bug on the point of her own fears.

"You stay inside, coyote bait." She slipped through the front door, leaving a complaining Lily behind.

Andi strode to the front gate, latched it, then turned the sprinkler on a dry patch of grass beside the driveway. Something, a lump of mud, maybe, had jammed the sprinkler holes. As Andi squatted to dislodge the goop, she thought the night so warm it felt more like Los Padres than Sparrowgrass.

Blood warm, she thought, as the sprinkler bucked free of her hands. Ratcheting spray slapped her knees, stinging where Cisco's pin had poked her. Water dripped from her bangs onto her cheeks, and she thought of the night Domingo had died.

She'd never known who'd unhooked her seat belt and eased her onto the pavement. When her eyes opened, she'd seen the laundry truck's broken axle, canted so that one tire spun crazily. She'd fought dizziness and restraining hands to stagger upright. Blood gathering on her eyelashes had blurred everything. Everything except the driver's door of Domingo's Camaro. Welded shut by the impact.

That's the way those memories should stay. Welded shut.

Usually they did. Andi stared toward the Sierras, concentrating on their white-draped peaks instead of the sourness in her throat. But one deep breath crammed her lungs with the chemical-laden smoke roiling up from the chimney, and she began to retch, just as she had that night.

Chapter Sixteen

"I almost hit you! God, are you all right?" Blake stumbled out of the Suburban, leaving the headlights on and the engine running.

Andi straightened up from her position beside the sprinkler. The Suburban's front bumper had missed her by inches.

"This is no way to stir up business, Blake." Pain stitched across her stomach. "You're supposed to chase ambulances, not—"

"I swear to God, I didn't see you. Driving this barge, I didn't feel a thing."

Andi held out a hand. "Stifle, okay?"

"Internal injuries? You're all bent over." Blake hefted a Coach bag over her shoulder and turned toward the house. "I'm calling Noah."

Andi swallowed and tried to rally words that would stop Blake. "I was pulling a couple of weeds, okay?"

"In the dark?" Blake circled back and reached inside the Suburban to switch off the key. "Noah said you were sick."

"I'm not sick—"

"In the Kern family we believe doctors over patients, and

I, personally, believe pulling weeds in the dark is a sign of illness." She popped off the headlights. "Why don't you drag your bones inside and wait to see what's in the care package I brought?"

Andi sat at the kitchen table. Warned of Blake's impending arrival, she would have doused the lights and hidden. Her bewildering talk with Noah, Kit's manuscript, and the most recent invasion by someone who knew too much about her past had left her unwilling to spar with Blake.

"What in heaven's name is that smell?" Blake gripped the handle of a picnic basket and her purse had slipped to the crook of one elbow. It swayed, banging her kneecap.

It was the first time since sixth grade that Andi had seen Blake look less than graceful. The sight improved her mood.

"You barbecuing a yak?" Blake sniffed again.

"Lasagna," Andi made her voice faint, hoping Blake would be so overcome with pity, that she'd forget the stench. "In the microwave," she said, but Blake had already opened it.

Blake grasped the edge of the paper plate and frowned at the crispy cube of pasta. Opening the below-sink cupboard, she poised the meal for disposal. "Unless you're emotionally attached—?"

"No, I wasn't even hungry. I was just eating because it was dinnertime."

"It looks like you've been doing a lot of that." Blake considered a loaf of bread through its plastic wrapper. "The mold's a nice shade of teal, though."

"Save it for the birds," Andi began, as Blake took a container out of the refrigerator. "Now that I've smelled whatever it is you've got in that basket, I'm pretty hungry."

"I'm looking for Maalox. I saw you holding your stomach. Maybe even milk. Or juice." Blake peeled back the container's lid, grimaced, and pitched it after the lasagna.

"Listen," Blake turned with hands on her hips. "I don't mean to pick on the poorly, but are you camping here?" She held up a restraining hand. "The *outside* looks great," she added.

Using two fingers like pincers, Blake advanced on Andi. She held up a carton of vanilla yogurt and indicated the pull-by date. Andi winced.

"You're right," Andi said. "I'm having more fun in the garden."

"You don't look like you're having fun." Blake swiped a knuckle under each of her eyes, then glanced up at a noise overhead. "Squirrels in the attic?"

Guilt wasn't going to muzzle Andi's irritation much longer, but she kept her tone level. "No," she said. "It's Lily."

"Thank God. Now, prepare to be coddled." Blake began lifting food from the basket. "Chicken soup with homemade egg noodles, sourdough rosemary bread, and fresh macaroons."

It figured. Since girlhood, Blake had dumped criticism on Andi's head, then wiped it away with a smile that said a friend's faults were trivial. With one awful exception.

Blake poured soup into a copper saucepan and stood stirring.

"I'm kind of embarrassed that you brought all this food," Andi said. "Not that I'd refuse, but I mean, it is your business."

"If Melissa or one of the twins needed tutoring in English, you'd volunteer, right? Besides, except for the soup—which Noah prescribed—it's all today's leftovers. *And*, you're going to be our guinea pig."

Blake cut slices of sourdough and carried them and a plate to the table. She sat, then nudged the plate forward.

"It's something between a terrine and a dip. Its working name is Yuppie Loaf. Jan liked that better than Noah's suggestion, Heart Attack on a Plate." Blake handed over a serving. "Little bites, Andi. It might not be just the thing on a delicate stomach."

"Yes, Mother. Mmmm."

"Sun-dried tomatoes, basil, olive oil, shiitake mushrooms." Blake ticked off ingredients on her fingers. "Fresh mozzarella, white pepper, and toasted pine nuts on top."

"Oh, yum."

"It should be served on a garlic-brushed baguette." Blake licked a manicured finger. "But what do you say we rough it?"

Thirty minutes later, Andi felt sated, verging on stuffed. Best of all, her edginess toward Blake had abated.

Just as Andi refused tea and macaroons, Blake pushed away from the table and stalked in to stare at what remained of the fire.

Until now, Andi had never heard Blake sputter.

"What—? I—"

Although the lingerie had charred before smoldering out, there was no question about what it had been.

Blake sank slowly onto the couch. She stared into the fireplace until Andi sat beside her.

"How sick are we talking, Miranda? I thought you had the flu."

Lily minced into the room, leapt onto the couch cushion between them, and groomed a paw.

"We're all ears," Blake said.

"Someone hung a bunch of strange underwear on my clothesline."

" 'Strange' like peculiar, or just not yours?"

"Not mine." Andi felt herself smile just a little, not from Blake's weak joke but from the fact that she made it.

"Why didn't you call Noah?"

"Blake, are you listening to yourself?" Andi's irritation boiled over. "Noah is a great guy, but he's no cure-all, and he's not much of a cop. Do what you like, but *I* don't need Noah to solve all my problems."

"You're right. You need a shrink. People are vandalizing Heart's Ease. They're hiding in the basement and leaving bizarre Victoria's Secret messages." Blake gestured toward the fireplace. "And you haven't got the sense to be scared. Know what I think? You're eating up the punishment."

"Oh, please."

"Then why haven't you moved out? Or asked someone to stay with you?"

"Because I'm not *that* afraid."

Or hadn't been, until now. Dread made the room darker.

Kit might be gone forever, and though she'd never expected him to rescue her, he had.

Blake switched tactics. "What do you think that means?"

"I know exactly what it means."

"Then tell me." Blake folded her fingers together and slumped back on the couch, mirroring Andi's position. It was probably some lawyer trick to make her feel more comfortable, confiding.

"I don't particularly want to tell you."

If Blake's moment of shock had lingered, Andi might have confessed. Why did it grate so that Blake, in her pressed white camp shirt and khakis, looked so damned competent?

"You should," Blake said. "I promise not to tell Noah, if that's what you want."

From high school dropout to mother of three with a law degree. Poof! For Blake, it was no tougher than tending her manicured nails. And Andi couldn't even manage a summer of house-sitting without making a mess of it.

"You know," Blake's fingers shook as she forked them through her short hair. "Just because I don't advertise it doesn't mean I've never done something stupid." Suddenly her face seemed to melt. "I nearly killed Melissa."

Andi grabbed Blake's forearm. Melissa, her daughter? The leggy blond teenager who'd offered coffee on the house to make up for the twins' chocolate attack?

"I'm sure you didn't mean to."

"*You* didn't mean to. I'm talking serious intent." Blake laced her fingers together, hard. "You'd already moved when I was a sophomore and got pregnant, but you must have heard."

"Whispers," Andi admitted. "My mom and Dinah. . . . And then Mom warned me I'd better finish high school before I got married. I thought she was nuts."

"Well, I ran away before I 'settled down and did the right thing.' I didn't want to marry Bart. I wanted to go to Paris and be an artist and be—*exceptional*."

"Blake, look at you. You are exceptional."

Her lips' twist said it wasn't the same. "So, I ran away. I hitchhiked and got a ride to Fresno, of all places, and got myself stuck there with $22.50 in baby-sitting money. But hitchhiking had really scared me, so I sat in the bus station and prayed for something to happen. To the baby.''

"But Melissa's alive. You didn't do anything wrong."

"I just sat there until Jan came walking off a bus and took me home." Blake rubbed her eyes.

"So you panicked," Andi said. "Melissa's sweet and beautiful and I bet she's smart too."

"Incredibly. And she has the voice of an angel. I see her bopping around the store with her Walkman permanently attached, singing, chirping 'Yes, Mom,' over whatever's pounding through her headphones, and I think, I prayed to un-do her." A single tear escaped Blake's eyes. "So don't tell me about screwing up, Miranda. You never intended for Clint to die, or—" Blake fumbled for the name. "—your fiancé."

"His name was Domingo."

Andi told the story, like a girlhood confidence. She explained the tension-filled weeks before the accident, how late-night phone calls turned X-rated, how Domingo grinned as he brushed past her in the faculty dining room. Finally, feeling cornered, she'd maxed out her Visa card and, one Friday morning, had Domingo open his car trunk for her suitcase full of enticing scraps guaranteed to cover her reluctance and little else.

She hadn't done her students justice that day. Instead she thought of the Camaro, the suitcase, and the drive that would begin as soon as the last bell rang at three-fifteen.

Blake chewed her thumbnail as Andi told how, in shock, she'd struggled to her feet and searched for her suitcase. Domingo had gone in the first ambulance and she'd never seen him again.

Red and blue lights spun atop the second ambulance, turning the scene purple. Emergency radios crackled and a man with a broom began to clear the street of broken glass.

Andi stared at the cat in her lap, but she remembered the street. She remembered the smell of surf. If only the crashing waves had been closer, they might have covered the words of an emergency worker.

"What did he say to you, Andi?" Blake's protective voice startled her.

"He wasn't talking to me. I don't know if he was a paramedic, a cop, or someone sent to tow Domingo's car. I must have been really shocky, because it was like this voice came out of nowhere.

"He didn't mean me to hear. I'm sure it was a way of, you know, defusing the horror—battlefield humor."

"For God's sake, Andi, quit apologizing for the guy. What did he say?"

"He was laughing, so I didn't get every word, but I heard him say, ' . . . champagne, pink underwear, and ol' Romeo, alllll over the highway.' I was on my knees vomiting when they found me and made me lie down on a stretcher."

Maybe it was the chicken soup or Blake's presence, but this time when Andi looked at the smoldering fireplace, her stomach didn't go queasy. Her mind did.

Who knew and what did he want?

Kit came back to himself in a place of crags and open sky. He stood with jogging shoes braced on a sloping pitch of stone. A black ant crawled over the edge and disappeared.

A wind-warped pine bisected the horizon. Beyond, the sun hung like a shilling stuck against the molten silver sky. Just dawn and he already felt the promise of a sweltering hot day.

Bound by wrinkled jeans and black shirt, he wished for a kerchief to bind his brow against this headache. He'd never felt such weariness upon resurfacing. Usually he felt rested, honed to a hunting edge.

Averting his eyes from the sun's glare, he pressed his temples. Discomfort, headache, weariness. What if they added up to life?

He'd known a soldier, Ian, blinded by a blow to the head, who'd turned to dairying. Kicked by a milk cow years later, he'd regained his sight. Each time Kit left one world for the next, he thought of Ian.

What if these fingers bled when he scuffed them against stone? What if this catch in his chest weren't excitement but the effect of altitude? What if he could hold Miranda?

He wouldn't test it. Not yet. First he must know what time this was, and what place.

The western mountains, dark purple and tipped with snow, looked like Miranda's Sierra Nevada range. Kit held to the pine's trunk. Mindful of its roots' tenuous grip on a fissure in the granite, he peered down a sheer drop to trees zigzagging after water.

A squawk alerted him to a young falcon on the ledge practically beneath his shoe. Scents of dust and feathers rose from beating wings, and Kit retreated, lest the bird fall.

"What a fair little thing."

Once, he'd loved hawking better than drink.

"You're not s'large, now?" Kit smothered the talk, chiding himself.

The first falconer he'd known had been an indentured Scot with time to waste on a child's curiosity. He'd taught Kit to handle birds and left a crooning burr as the best means of comforting them.

Small and dark, this bird looked rather like a merlin. A lady's bird. Nonetheless, when a falcon of a perfect age to bring to hand was cast at a man's feet, he couldn't refuse her.

Fierce yellow eyes tracked his motion. Her wings, streaked underneath with brown and black, agitated the air. Her blocky head wore a faint line like an actor's mustache.

She must be hurt, to allow him so near, but he could not see the damage. Kit squatted, making himself small.

Both her wings moved, feathers intact, but the left one kinked with each stroke and the left claw fidgeted in pain.

"Not watching where you were going, lass?"

Vainglorious in new flight, a young bird might slam into a rocky ledge or tree trunk or attack a fat pigeon that fought back.

Kit looked up the gray shoulder of rock behind him. Though he spotted no aerie, he'd wager it was nearby.

Thready and far, a neigh floated to Kit. He'd landed in a time with horses. Could his heart have summoned him backward?

Kit craned his neck. At the margin of black-green trees sat

a peaked roof like the one belonging to Rick Aragon.

Oh, no. He hated the thought, hated it like hell's pains, but he listened to the neigh with the intent of recognizing it.

By Saint Peter's stones, no! It was Trifle's neigh.

Kit shot to his feet. The grating of his runner soles frightened the bird into frenzied flapping.

There, through the trees, Kit saw the whitewashed walls of Heart's Ease. He'd gone nowhere. Not back, not forward. Up was the only place he'd gone.

Kit turned to the rock face behind him. He drew back his fist, then slammed it forward. Smoothly it passed through the rock and came back to him, unharmed. Bloody, *bloody* hell!

Andi latched the gate behind her and drove toward town. She'd spent a full week in hiding since Gina's column, and that was enough cowardice for the entire summer.

For just a minute she thought she saw a flicker of movement in her rearview mirror.

Please let it be Kit—but it was only a swallow, swooping toward a nest under the eaves. She made one mental note to buy birdseed at Brother's, another to give up watching for Kit.

If nothing else, the precise instructions he'd left next to Trifle's grain bin proved he was gone.

Three weeks without driving in high heels made her miss the shift as the Volkswagen jerked into third gear. For her showdown with Cisco, she'd dressed like a teacher: navy shirtwaist, heels, red scarf knotted around her hair.

She couldn't persuade herself that Cisco was responsible for the pink lingerie. He was a teenager. Even if she credited him with a high IQ, mastery of the Internet, and a criminal mind, he didn't have the interpersonal skills to weasel information out of health care professionals or cops. But she still wanted to find out how his button had ended up in Kit's apartment.

Main Street was quiet. Two men in plaid shirts carrying lunch boxes and silver thermos bottles walked as far as the hardware store, then climbed into the back of a pickup truck headed out of town. A woman walking a boxer dog smiled as Andi drew alongside, then looked away, dismissing her as a stranger.

If she believed Kit, only Rick could be the undergarment terrorist. Impatience had nearly driven her to call him and demand the truth, but he'd kept to himself for a week and she was relieved by his absence. Besides, she should be able to figure this out.

Who knew the pink negligee had spilled free of the suitcase and fluttered with a life of its own along the highway? Emergency workers, her parents, her brother, Will, and Rainy and Irma, her two closest friends.

It had been Irma's idea to order lingerie all in shades of pink. Creating a seductive "trademark," she'd claimed, would build Andi's confidence and make Domingo feel like he'd stolen away with a French courtesan.

Irma loved gossip, so it was barely possible she'd told someone, before. But she wouldn't have, in fact, *couldn't* have shared the details of the accident.

Irma and Rainy had flown out of the San Francisco airport less than twenty-four hours after the accident. They'd come to Andi's hospital bedside in tears, offering to delay their departure on a teacher exchange program to Belfast.

Andi had refused to let them stay, claiming her parents as sufficient support, but she'd missed them terribly and wished they'd been there the day Mr. Sterling asked her to take a leave.

Andi pulled up in front of the Dancing Goat. The shop opened at six-thirty, according to the hours painted on the window, and she'd left Heart's Ease about six.

She took Cisco's button from her purse, and sat for a minute, watching Gina Brown hose off the sidewalk in front of her grocery store.

A rap on the passenger window drew her attention to Noah's face. Gertrude gamboled beside him, greeting Andi with a thunderous woof.

"Feeling better?" Noah studied Andi as she climbed out of the Volkswagen.

"Lots." Andi slipped the pin back inside her purse. "I decided to come down and eat an enormous breakfast."

"Good idea."

Her plan would flop if he asked her to join him.

"Where can I buy a newspaper?" she asked, hoping this bid for privacy was neither rude nor too subtle.

"Gina has them delivered early," Noah glanced at his watch. "But Jan usually meets the truck and keeps a couple inside for customers."

The idea of facing Gina gave her chills.

"Sit." Noah watched the huge black-and-white dog drop to her haunches. He backed away a step, still watching the dog.

"Won't she stay?" Andi asked.

"Usually I tie her to a hitching ring." Noah nodded at an iron horse head at the curb. "But once she slipped loose. This morning I can't take a chance. I've got a packed house. Seems half the boys in town went to Scout camp to roll in poison oak. I don't have time to go searching for her."

"Want me to watch her for a few minutes?"

"I thought you were afraid of dogs."

"I am *not* afraid of dogs. That day Gertrude stuck her head in my window and slobbered on me—it was the drool, not the dog."

"No, I just heard—"

"From who? I think I'm doing okay." Andi rubbed behind Gertrude's ears until the dog's pink tongue flopped from the side of her mouth. "Don't you?"

"Yeah. I know, it was Gallatin. Come to think of it, he mentioned *horses*, not dogs."

Every one of Andi's cells came to attention.

"When did you see Kit?"

"Oh, that was a couple weeks ago, right after he showed up."

Andi hoped her disappointed "oh" blended with Gertrude's groan as the dog closed her eyes and leaned against Andi's kneading fingers.

"Is it your job to check out all newcomers?"

"No need for sarcasm, sugar. I offered the man a free checkup."

"I bet. That's how you ended up driving a Miata?"

"I'm a humanitarian. Gallatin looked pale. Thought he might be a touch anemic."

Andi laughed, then staggered as Gertrude's dozing weight shifted. "Go. She's in good hands."

"I'm only getting coffee." He was halfway through the door. "Nothing fancy. Just coffee."

A little pale. Andi laughed to herself. How would Noah, a man of science, face undeniable evidence that ghosts existed?

Noah had better hurry. Her plan was to ambush Cisco before Rick picked him up for summer school.

"Thanks." Noah returned, and Gertrude yelped as if he'd been gone a week. "Hon, I just remembered. Yesterday, a gentleman stopped by the office while I was out. He asked for you. Tammy—that's my front desk gal—said she knew you lived just out of town, but she didn't know where."

A gentleman. A series of male acquaintances clicked through her mind. Few qualified as gentlemen.

"Except for you and Rick, I—"

"No—no, he was from out of town. An office type, kind of soft." Noah patted the air just out from his belly. "Said he was in Owen for business and wanted to stop and 'see how you were holding up.' "

"He said that?"

Domingo had two brothers, but both worked construction. No female would describe them as soft.

" 'How I was holding up'?" She repeated.

"Tammy was real clear about that. In fact, I'm afraid— Lord, that girl ought to be working for a veterinary—she showed him Gina's article, but turned out he'd already seen it."

"My dad's out of the country and my brother knows I'm at Heart's Ease." Andi squinted across the street, thinking. "And none of the guys I dated before Domingo—"

"According to Tammy, this one was 'father age.' " Noah paused to wave.

A girl with blond ringlets and breasts suspended by something sturdier than a mortal bra jogged by in purple shorts.

"And Tammy would know," Noah added.

"I'm stumped."

"Okay," Noah said. "You eat something healthy. Let's see what we can do about your memory."

Andi blew her cheeks full of air and let it out with a sigh. She had a crummy little recall gap, not amnesia.

The aromas of coffee, cinnamon, and buttery baked goods rushed out as she opened the Dancing Goat's door. Then Noah yelled for her attention once more.

"Andi, don't worry." He had stopped in the middle of Main Street. He sidestepped a cyclist who pedaled past, waving, and his shout had attracted the undisguised stare of the lady with the boxer. "If he comes back, I won't give him directions 'til I give you a ring."

Until then, it hadn't occurred to Andi to worry.

Chapter
Seventeen

"You're not letting Noah do his job, you know." Blake gave Andi an owlish look, then pulled the handle on the espresso machine.

"Do you want me to?"

In light of last night's exchange, Andi had warned Blake that she meant to ambush Cisco and pump him for information. Rick had mentioned that the teenager usually ate breakfast at the coffee shop. She considered it the perfect setting to ask Cisco why she'd found his button in Kit's apartment.

"No. Even though that"—Blake nodded toward Andi's closed hand—"doesn't amount to evidence, it'd set Noah on Cisco all over again. Jan could use a breather between crises."

Blake glanced toward the cafe's only customers. A thirtyish couple in hiking boots had spread their table with maps. Even though they seemed oblivious to gossip, Blake lowered her voice.

"I'm just *saying*," Blake continued, "this doesn't feel like a prank, Andi."

It wasn't. The trouble could only be meant to scare her away from Sparrowgrass. Andi took the tray and arranged breakfast on a table facing the staircase that rose to the family quarters.

Two mothers, two teenagers, and a set of twins lived upstairs "like rabbits in a warren," Blake said. Andi sidestepped a twinge of guilt to contemplate breakfast.

Fortified with Irish porridge and a raisin-studded scone, Andi was sure she'd have enough calories to beat Rick to the Graveyard Rose. Determination to be *the one* to give Kit back his heart would drive her harder than Rick's greed would drive him.

Footsteps scuffed down the stairs and stopped. Cisco's T-shirt was blinding white—in compensation, Andi would bet, for voluminous jeans with a chain looping out of one pocket. She couldn't tell what Cisco muttered as he saw her, but it didn't sound like a celebration.

She gave him five minutes to down a bowl of cereal and a pile of pastries, while she skimmed the newspaper. Then, as he crumpled a napkin, Andi raised her hand in a leisurely wave.

"Hey, Cisco, I'd like to talk to you." She could almost hear his heart plummet.

"My ride will be here in a minute." Cisco gestured toward the alley behind the block of Main Street shops.

"You've got time." Blake didn't meet her nephew's betrayed look. "Rick's usually late."

Cisco walked toward her table, then stood, arms crossed, his weight all on one leg. "Yeah?"

"Sit down for just a sec." Andi plopped the button on the edge of a lace doily, and Cisco's face brightened.

"Cool! Where'd you find it?"

Andi's accusations stopped short.

Cisco plucked the button from the table and stabbed it through the cotton of his T-shirt. "Thanks a lot."

His wasn't the reaction of a burglar who'd left clues behind. Not that she couldn't be fooled, but wouldn't even a hardened criminal blink at such a confrontation?

"Wow, I thought I'd had it since then, but I guess I lost

it when we played Scrabble.'' Cisco shrugged. ''Like when Rick tackled me on your floor.''

''No. I found it in my carriage house.''

Cisco frowned. *''Where?''*

''In the apartment over the barn, where Kit Gallatin's staying.''

His hands flew up, then fell to his sides as his protest faded into sullen acceptance. ''So?''

''You tell me.''

The door tinkled open. As Gina Brown entered, Blake called, ''Just tea, Gina?''

Cisco sniffed. ''Gotta go. If I miss my ride, I'm screwed.''

''I'll wait with you.'' Andi grabbed her purse. ''Hi, Gina.''

She used long strides to follow Cisco down a hallway, then into a kitchen bright with polished aluminum.

Melissa mouthed lyrics to the song on her Walkman as she tucked tart-size pastry into rippled tin cups. She ignored Cisco until she saw Andi.

''What'd you do now?'' Melissa held her floury hands above the pastry and shouldered off an earphone. ''Like, spray-paint her cat?''

Cisco responded with a gesture, then hit the back door, jeans flapping, as Andi caught up.

''I am shocked, Cisco!'' Melissa shouted after him. *''Shocked—''* The closing door cut off her words.

Sparrowgrass's single alley smelled of wet cement and petunias. Dumpsters were painted chartreuse and flower beds flanked the side opposite the shops.

''I didn't do it.'' Cisco glanced up the alley. ''Whatever got done, it wasn't by me.''

''I didn't accuse you of anything.''

''Like you weren't even *thinking* I broke your windshield, when half the people in town are saying I did. Dr. Lincoln is, like, he can't take his eyes off me. He knows where I am when Mom doesn't. And Renetta gives me this bimbo raised-eyebrow look.'' Cisco had to reach halfway to his knees to put his hands in his pockets. ''Well, I didn't do a thing. I told you, another month without getting Mom mad and I have my license.''

Andi nodded. Cisco's motive for staying straight still rang true. A license meant freedom, a passport to the real world, especially to a small-town boy.

"So, how did your button get in the carriage house?"

"Ask that guy who's living with you." Cisco shuffled and his cheeks flushed. The double entendre had been intentional, but he couldn't quite carry it off. "Or Lily. Dinah says Lily is half pack rat. She bats things around 'til they end up someplace weird."

Cisco peered toward an approaching vehicle. When he saw it was a yellow VW van and not Rick, his shoulders hunched.

"Jeez, last time I was out in the carriage house," Cisco rolled his eyes heavenward, "was when Mom made me take the twins for a tea party, while she and Dinah planted a little window herb garden for Jason, to make the room smell, you know, not like medicine and stuff."

Down the alley, the VW van stopped and a man with dreadlocks unloaded a mound of clothing and approached the hardware store.

"If half the people think you broke my windshield," Andi mused, "what do the other half think?"

Cisco's slow grin warned Andi, but not enough.

"Rick and Brother think Heart's Ease is haunted."

Blood rushed in her ears and a metallic taste made her swallow. *Kit.* What could they do to him?

Nothing. He was dead. No one could hurt a ghost. But Brother fancied himself a minister, and Rick . . .

"Rick thinks it's haunted?"

"Jeez, of course. Don't you know what he teaches? I just work out with him, running and stuff, but I'd never take his class. It's hellaweird."

Thanatology, he'd said, and she hadn't given it another thought since the night Kit backed him down.

Thanatology. Andi considered the concept as if she could pass it from hand to hand, weighing its meaning.

With a whirring clatter, the VW bus pulled up.

"In this town, you know of anyone who'd take custom

clothing on consignment?'' The driver wore wire-rimmed glasses and a smile. Reggae music and incense wafted from the bus.

"No way,'' said Cisco. "Brother has that farmer junk, but nothing else. Try Owen.''

"Been to Owen,'' the driver said, "but maybe you'd like a look.''

In seconds he was out of the van, lifting garments for their perusal. A crimson cloak hemmed with gold stood out from tie-dyed tops and crocheted caps. Island rhythms throbbed like a pulse as Andi reached for the plainest garment in the bunch. The driver sang along.

"Hand-stitched by a woman who knows what men want most.'' His head dipped side to side, still keeping time as he slipped the shirt off a hanger and draped it over Andi's hands.

Smoke-blue corduroy, fine as velvet, had been fashioned into an ordinary shirt with wooden buttons down the front and at the cuffs. How brazen to think of it touching Kit's bare shoulders.

"And look-at-this.'' The words accompanied drumbeats he improvised. "And look-at-this,'' he repeated, pulling out a retractable rack of jewelry.

Beads and chains and nose studs she could resist, Andi thought, so she'd take only the shirt.

"Oh, wait.''

He seemed oblivious, shoulders swaying, eyes dreamy behind the wire-rimmed glasses as Andi reached for a rough leather necklace strung with a single bead. Dark gold and round, the amber was warm to her touch.

Like magic, it came loose from the tangle of baubles. Andi held the amber to the sunlight, dangling it at eye level. She had to have it.

She peered into her purse. If she bartered just a little and asked Gina to run a grocery tab, she'd still have enough left to buy birdseed.

"No more. I haven't had a paycheck all month.'' Andi gave him all the cash in her wallet, blocking the sound of her own wistfulness.

The driver folded the shirt in half, over the amber amulet. He laid them in her arms like an infant.

Loaded down and satisfied, Andi turned.

"Cisco, isn't this—"

She looked down the alley, both ways, and at the Dancing Goat's back door, but Cisco was gone.

Working quietly on the mountain, Kit ripped his black shirt, thread by thread, into a rough square. In order to do it, he had to remain substantial, and the falcon detested his human nearness. She expressed her displeasure with the scream of a Bedlamite.

She must be hooded. Deprived of her keenest sense, she wouldn't harm herself with desperate movements.

He didn't need a project beyond finding his heart, but he was loath to refuse Nature's gift.

Left on the ledge, the falcon would fall prey to a predator less careful than he.

No less cruel, perhaps, since she was born free and he meant to keep her captive. But he wouldn't cause her pain by seeling her eyes, in the old way.

The needle-and-silk-thread seeling of a gyrfalcon's eyelids, had turned his stomach when he was a child. He could not commit the act. If she doffed the hood and escaped, so be it.

Kit poised, tossed a crumb-size pebble aloft and, as her eyes tracked it, he pounced. He used the rest of his shirt as a net, swooping black night around her before she flapped backward off the ledge. He held her to his chest, so she couldn't fight and ruin her bad wing.

Peck, rip, tear, but she didn't squawk as he tied the makeshift hood in place and knotted jesses made of a shoelace around her legs.

Hooded and tethered, she shivered. Kit knew wrapping her once more would be a mistake.

"You're not cold, are you, lass?"

Her head tilted, beak working against the opening he'd left in the hood. Her wings beat and talons grated on stone.

Tomorrow would bring a decision. He could try to tame

her here, where she tasted freedom in each breath, or he could return with her to Heart's Ease.

Miranda would interfere, of course. Kit stilled a smile, realizing he looked forward to the flush-cheeked, brows-knit scolding she would give him. He missed her. And a few days were naught compared to the eternity he'd meant to abide alone.

The falcon fretted. Manning, this next bit of work was called. It meant lingering until the falcon lost her fear. Eventually, through nearness and greed fed with bits of meat, she'd tolerate, ay, even enjoy, his presence.

He'd brought Miranda to hand without trying. She fought him on only one thing, this matter of love.

If his senses were coming back . . .

If he could not leave her . . .

A man without a heart could not love her, but by God he could please her. In that cool, curtained bed, in his carriage house cot beneath misplaced windows and slanting walls, on that sunny veranda . . .

The falcon vibrated with suppressed energy. He'd take her home to Miranda and tame them both.

"Kinky." Andi looked over her shoulder into the mirror and twitched her hips. Dressed in a short denim shift she'd found in Dinah's discard drawer, with a red bandanna tied over her hair, Andi was by-golly ready to clean house.

Whistling "The Impossible Dream," she descended to the basement. Since the fuse incident she'd felt ill at ease here. Just for drill, she should make herself stay an extra five minutes.

But she didn't. She sprinted back up the stairs, balancing a push broom, a squirt bottle, and towels from a rag bag.

She started on the veranda. After sweeping, she climbed the low wall, one arm twined around a pillar, and swiped at cobwebs.

Next, she slid cushions off the couch, chairs, and window seat and piled them on the lawn. She dragged every rug out of the house, but when she tried to clip them to the clothesline for a beating, their weight nearly brought the entire ap-

paratus down. Coughing and blinking, she shook them
instead.

By then, she'd worked past masochism into enthusiasm.
Though she had the entire downstairs swept, vacuumed, and
dusted by noon, she'd seen no sign of the Graveyard Rose.

"Witnesses." She sneezed as she addressed Lily. "We
need witnesses to this drudgery."

In reply, the cat reared up on her hind legs, hooked her
claws over the freestanding fireplace screen, and pulled it
onto the clean floor.

"Thanks for reminding me." Andi spread newspapers and
cleared all manner of black and gray stuff out of the fireplace.

She was less tolerant when Lily started batting a blackened
chunk of wood. "Beast," she said, as it sailed like a hockey
puck across the clean floor. "You don't even have the de-
cency to get dirty."

Unperturbed, Lily licked the pink pads of one paw.

Whatever had happened in front of the fireplace that night,
it hadn't included the Graveyard Rose's incineration. Andi
found no sign of metal, melted or not.

She tapped her fingers on the hearthstone. A dedicated
reader of classic and popular mysteries should be able to
figure this out. Where did one hide things? In "The Purloined Letter," Poe extolled hiding in plain sight, but Dinah's decorating ran to bright landscapes and antique
candlesticks. The box would stand out. Besides, if the box
had been set out on an end table, she, Kit, or Rick would
have spotted it.

In thrillers, bad guys often lurked overhead in tree limbs
or barn beams. Andi looked, but there was no molding or
wooden gingerbread suitable for disguising a silver box as
big as her fist.

She'd lost the damned thing.

Andi bundled the newspaper full of ashes out to the trash.
She started three sprinklers as she walked back, telling herself that was *it*. She would do no more outdoor work.

Walking past the garden, she ignored the half-empty bird
feeder. Then the phone began to ring.

Andi sprinted to answer it.

"Mom! Where are you?"

Scratchy words and intermittent beeps punctuated her mother's sentences. ". . . ashore . . . your father . . . *de Gatos* . . ."

Through a combination of shouting and intuition, Andi figured out her parents and Dinah were having a wonderful voyage. Its high point was food.

". . . champagne and chocolate . . . Lobster Thermidor and saffron rice . . . waiters in starched white . . ." By the time a sound like crumpling cellophane cleared, Mom had switched subjects. "Dinah wants . . . house—but first . . . how *are* you doing?"

Apparently nothing could garble a mother's sympathy.

"I'm doing fine. Settling down, sort of."

Even Mom couldn't take the news that Andi was falling in love with a ghost.

". . . Blake?"

"We're getting along, almost like the old days. I think things are kind of healing." Andi swallowed hard.

Why did this always happen? She could go months without crying, and then one word from her mother launched her into sentimental tears.

"Oh, baby, I'm glad."

"Don't make me cry. I've been cleaning house and the dust on my face will turn into mud."

Another burst of static interrupted as her mother apparently handed the receiver to Dinah.

". . . something terribly wrong with the connection. I thought she said she was cleaning house . . ."

"Very funny, Mom," Andi muttered, waiting.

"Miranda?" Dinah's clear voice might have come from upstairs.

"Aunt Dinah, Mom says you're having a great time."

"Incredible. And the meals! I think I've found every ounce I ever lost," Dinah said. "Your mother says you're cleaning. Don't. Just relax and let the dust accumulate. What was that?"

"Lily. She's watching the birds outside and—"

"—she pounced and conked her silly head against the window. How is Her Majesty?"

"Wobbling a little, but mostly fine, since she's taught me who's boss. Trifle, too."

Andi couldn't imagine how to explain she'd hired a ghostly horseman to tend the animal, so she didn't.

". . . ungodly bill . . . tell me the Sparrowgrass gossip."

"Let's see. Gina's third column ran in the Owen Canyon paper, Gertrude the Great Dane spent most of a night here"—Andi heard Dinah laughing—"and Rick's finished whitewashing the house."

Silence spun on so long that Andi wondered if they'd been disconnected. "Hello?"

"Rick Aragon painted Heart's Ease?" Dinah sounded shocked and a bit annoyed.

In the aftermath of Jason's death, had Dinah forgotten? Or had Rick lied? "*I'll put it on Dinah's account*," he'd said of some homely item. Had he lied to Jan as well?

"Well, yes." Lord, what would this mistake cost? Hundreds of dollars or thousands? "Jan said you hired him before you left. She said you wanted the job started as soon as I got here."

"I thought Cisco and one of his friends . . ."

"Oh, no." Andi grabbed her temples and pressed. Hard. Maybe she and Lily could share a bottle of aspirin.

"It did need doing," Dinah said.

"And it looks great, but if you weren't planning on paying for it, let me kick in"—Andi bit her lip and squinted her eyes closed—"half?"

"Don't be silly, Miranda. Rick does that sort of work during the summer and between terms." Dinah sounded as if she were convincing herself. "I just wanted Cisco to have the money. The boy needs a push in the right direction."

"Cisco helped. Rick's helping him train, too, so he can try out for the football team."

"Rick is quite the big brother to troubled boys," Dinah mused. "Cisco isn't the first.

"I don't mean to sound sarcastic, dear. Jason had this conviction that Rick was entirely self-serving, and I guess I started believing him. We lost contact with folks those last months, and it struck us as odd that Rick kept visiting long after our friends had the good sense to leave us a bit of privacy.

"Jason called him a vulture, said he was cozying up to us, just like he had to Sadie before she died." Dinah's chagrin carried over the miles. "And we couldn't help noticing how kind he'd been to the Smiths, before the Crest burned down." Dinah's sigh carried quite clearly. "He had a disadvantaged boy working with him that summer, too. Gina always thought Jimmy—no, Jeremy, that was his name, *Jeremy*—had something to do with the fire."

Andi bit the inside of her cheek. Dinah's grief was too raw for Andi to speculate that Rick took interest in the old and dying because of his study of thanatology.

She shuddered, then realized Dinah stood under the Mexican sun, waiting.

"Tomorrow I'm cleaning your basement," Andi said. "That's the least I can do for the mistake."

"No, no, no," Dinah said. "Don't attempt to make sense of that basement. Not a soul but I—and maybe not even I—can tell the treasures from the trash."

Relief sluiced through Andi, until Dinah added, "But there's something else you might do."

As Lily left off stalking, Andi sank to the floor and leaned her back against the couch.

"Anything," she said. "Tell me, Aunt Dinah."

"Is there any way you might rent me your condominium for the rest of the summer?"

"Rent? I'm living here absolutely free—"

"—working your fingers to the bone."

"Not exactly—but sure, stay there." Andi wondered if Dinah could tolerate sirens, the drone of passing cars, buses, and the challenge of accelerating into the fast-moving traffic on Third Street each time she left the narrow garage.

"A permanent move might be the answer. Seclusion doesn't appeal, with Jason gone," Dinah said. "Speaking of seclusion, here comes the end of mine. Not your parents, dear," Dinah whispered. "The ship's social director, wearing an ungodly chrome whistle and an eager-beaver smile. If I don't dodge, I'll be dragged off to a Tecate tiddlywinks tournament. *Adios!* Don't forget—''

Static foamed over the line, then there was a beep and a dial tone. Andi hung up, wondering what it was she shouldn't forget.

Yesterday's run and today's stretching had conspired to make her legs cramp, but if she wanted to finish the downstairs today, it meant she should wash the glass chimneys from every light fixture with ammonia before lunch.

She did, and polished every inch of wood furniture with lemon wax, before drinking down a gallon of the sun tea, straight from the pitcher.

Lily's hiss coincided with the clang of the copper drainpipe. Something hit the back wall of Heart's Ease's once, then again, measured and deliberate.

Fortified and furious, Andi slammed out the front door, shouting, ''What the hell do you think you're doing?''

Chapter Eighteen

Rick planted his feet more firmly on the rungs of the ladder as the silly little bitch came roaring around the side of the house, mad enough to spit. Apparently the effects of the roofie's hadn't been permanent.

"Relax," he said. "Dinah's precious copper drainpipe is fine. I still say you'd be doing her a favor to have me replace it with galvanized steel."

Her face was smeared with dirt. A black smudge marked her cheek.

"You're knocking down my swallows' nests."

"Didn't want you to have to do it."

She paced a few steps and he saw only the top of her head until she looked up, hands on hips, with a scowl.

"I wouldn't have. They're not hurting anything and I love watching them. At dusk, they go down to the creek and eat insects and get mud—"

"—which looks like hell on my new whitewash." He kept his tone reasonable.

"It's not *yours*. Dinah didn't want you to do it in the first place."

Shit, how had that come out? Andi's lips flattened together. She hadn't meant to say that and he recognized her flicker of fear. That, plus her getup—it looked like the bib half of a pair of overalls—sent a charge through him.

The thrill didn't last. Cobwebs clung to her red bandanna and one wisp squirmed on the breeze. He shuddered. He had no use for a messy woman. Even in bed.

No use except the Graveyard Rose, he reminded himself and tried to soothe her.

"They shouldn't be hanging around, anyway," Rick said. "Their eggs were gone when I did this the first time." He struck the hoe at the nearest nest laughing.

"Then they must have had babies. Rick, stop it."

She said it tough, as if she were bossing around a high school boy.

He swung the hoe again. "I don't think you're cut out for country living, Andi."

"Get down now."

A shudder telegraphed up through his legs and he grabbed the ladder. Down below, she gave it another kick.

"Andi, you could hurt somebody."

"It's going to be you." On the side of the ladder, there was a lever for raising and lowering the extension. She'd started fiddling with it. "Don't test me."

Rick came down, careful not to stomp her fingers, though it would've been a pleasure.

"Look, honey—"

Wrong. She coiled up as if she'd smack him.

"Andi, we're only talking about some old mud nests. They'd desert them in a few days anyway, then things would just dry up and fall down on your head when you're out picking blackberries."

"No, we're talking about Dinah's property and your right to screw with it." Her eyes hardened with conviction. "You don't have one."

What did she *think* she knew? Noah and Blake had both been over here, sniffing around. A sheriff and a lawyer. Shit. In a second she'd write him a check for services rendered and send him packing.

No good. Renetta had been funneling him money from the Hanging Tree's cash register, but it wasn't enough to live on. He needed that box. Soon. Once Renetta's husband got his bank statement after the July Fourth weekend, old Ralph would notice that a fair number of deposits hadn't made it to the bank.

Rick had four days to set his little insurance fire, find that box, and get the hell out.

"I'm sorry if I seemed pushy. To tell you the truth, I was working off some steam. Can you believe they're canceling my thanatology class in favor of standard English? 'Lower-than-expected sign-up for the fall semester,' they say." He stuck his hands in his pockets, counting on her nice-girl up-bringing to make her sympathetic.

Andi just stood there, vibrating with outrage over a damned birds' nest, when she could've nailed him for a lot worse.

He hefted the hoe in both hands. She should've seen it as menacing, but her expression didn't change.

"I'll just take this back down to the basement."

"You can leave it," she shrugged, so stupid it apparently hadn't occurred to her to wonder how he'd gotten the hoe from the basement in the first place. Stalling, he pretended to swing it like a baseball bat, then leaned it against the house.

The bathroom floor. He opened his mouth to say he would just measure to see how much replacement tile he'd need, then stopped. The bathroom floor was his excuse to drop back by, anytime he felt like it. He wouldn't give her a chance to refuse.

"I was just trying to keep things tidy, so Dinah'd have one less thing on her mind."

"I think she's selling, anyway."

Andi wasn't a good enough actress to hide how that pained her, so Rick shook his head with sympathy.

Perhaps he would spare her the misery of selling Heart's Ease. Once a fire started running, there was just no telling which direction it would burn.

• • •

The dust cloud from Rick's departing van had settled when Andi realized she'd lost her zeal for cleaning.

Droplets lashed her legs as she moved a sprinkler on the side lawn. Vines of Virginia creeper covered the back gate and she made sure they got sprayed before she headed back into the house.

Damn Rick Aragon, anyway. She had plenty of daylight left for tackling the upstairs, but he'd wrung the enthusiasm right out of her.

She walked through the great room and out the sliding-glass door onto the back veranda. She could have brought iced tea, if she hadn't drunk it all. She could have brought a sandwich from the groceries that she'd bought this morning at Gina's, but she wasn't hungry. The feeling that pulled her out to gaze over the ravine was yearning.

It rose like a plea. *Kit.* Once before she'd done just this, and he'd appeared, astride Trifle. Now Trifle dozed in her paddock, growing lazy without him.

Please, Kit, don't be gone. Like a teenager with a crush, she wanted to carve his name into a tree or inscribe it over and over in the margin of notebook paper. *Kit, I really tried to find it.* No matter how hard she willed it, nothing moved on the path through the trees below.

How many hours in a woman's lifetime were spent watching for a man? Over the centuries, men's clothing had changed from buckskins to blue jeans and their errands had changed from hunting dinner to driving to the mini-mart, but women still watched from windows, porches, and doorways, waiting for thudding hooves or flashing headlights.

And then she saw him.

Bare-chested, Kit broke from the cover of the trees, holding one arm stiff.

"Kit!"

Lord, Miranda, you're not fifteen. Exert some self-control. Let the man get within hearing distance before you make a fool of yourself. *Oh, Kit.*

He'd heard. Even more than his alert posture, some movement of his arm told her.

His chest and lean belly were incredible, carved like hardwood. But why on earth was dignified, starch-ruffed Kit walking through the forest without a shirt?

His vault over the stream initiated screams and a great flapping of wings. An eagle or some other bird of prey clung to his wrist.

Hawking. Once, Kit had mourned his loss of the sport and made some joke about her squeamishness. Squeamish wasn't what she felt now.

He looked beautiful. Male, strong, and—beautiful. He would hate the word, but when Andi tried to modify it to *handsome* or *splendid*, sun glinted silver on his black hair and he strode with a grace that conquered uneven ground and unlaced shoes. He *was* beautiful. She couldn't just stand and stare for another minute.

So she ran to him.

"Careful." His eyes met hers, but he crooned to the bird as Andi rushed through the back gate.

She stopped. The bird's torso was no bigger than a paperback novel, but her wingspan, as she beat the air with feathers marbled brown and black, was impressive. Hooded in black, she hissed and hopped.

Still, Andi watched Kit. At first, he gave no sign how he felt. Then came his faint smile, prideful because he'd caught the bird—or because she'd come rushing to meet him.

"I thought you'd left."

"I tried." He stepped past and Andi followed.

"Then—are you stuck with me?"

When he didn't answer, fear yanked her fantasies away.

As they approached Trifle's corral, the mare bucked in celebration. The bird fluttered and stepped from foot to foot.

As Kit waited for her to quiet, he turned to Andi. "I heard you calling and I could not stay away."

It wasn't resignation in his eyes. And it wasn't amusement. She couldn't interpret his expression. That Kit Gallatin was helpless against her longing seemed impossible.

"Kit." She wanted to know more, but he made a silent hushing motion with his head.

"I'd like you to help me."

"Tell me how," she said, and for a paper-thin slice of time she thought he'd kiss her.

"The lawn mower handle," he said. "Does it come off?"

They weren't the words she'd longed for, but she closed her eyes in thought. "I'll have to look, but I think there are screws or bolts or something."

"To make a perch," he said. "So I can set her down."

And have your arms free to hold me.

"Look, I can saw it off if I have to," Andi said. "That machine's on its last summer."

"Good. Get it."

It turned out, the handle was clamped in an iron channel and she needed neither screwdriver nor wrench to work it loose. Andi burst back into the stable.

"Ta-da!" She displayed the handle to an explosion of feathers and flapping. "Sorry."

"Don't rush her." Kit's voice wasn't angry.

And you, Andi thought. *Would I be rushing you if I wrestled you into the straw, or upstairs to your cot?*

She swallowed and tried to look away. His lazy attention—watching her, watching him—made it impossible not to walk into his arms. But she couldn't. He had a wild animal strapped to one of them.

Andi let her attention relax, but only a bit.

Oh, God, how far gone was she when a man's collarbone aroused her? She wanted to kiss him there, where it cupped a vulnerable little scoop of skin, and *there*, where symmetry stopped.

"How did you break your collarbone?"

"Rough play," he whispered. Then he added, "Why don't you get me a shirt?"

So much for helping. As she climbed the stairs to his apartment, she blushed so completely her cheeks hurt. She'd never been distracted by a man's physique. Never—but this was Kit. And now he'd sent her away for staring.

Lord, what had she done, that last night, to make him leave?

She didn't ask. She snagged his feed-store T-shirt and brought it down. When Kit motioned her to set it aside, she did, then sat in the corner while he jammed one end of the mower handle into a hay bale, then padded it with a burlap feed sack.

While he worked, Kit whistled the same low notes, then urged the hawk to step from his black-wrapped hand to the perch.

Could a bird be brave? Blindfolded, would the falcon step off into darkness because Kit asked her to?

The bird shifted from foot to foot. Andi saw that he had used a shoelace to tether the bird's feet a few inches apart. His other lace made a leash that he'd tied to the perch.

Kit settled into a crouch, talking to the bird.

"There, lass, it's not so bad now. Straw and scents of home and some company. Even if she is a horse."

Kit didn't look away from the bird as he reached a hand back to get his shirt. The muscles over his shoulders were fretted with light seeping through the barn door. He pulled the shirt over his head, then yanked it down to meet the top of his jeans.

Kit's voice remained a gentle singsong and it took a moment for Andi to realize he talked to her.

"Now we sit," he said. "We wait as long as it takes her to become calm on her perch. I don't know how long it will be, but watching is important. If she should bate—just fly off the perch—the jesses would hold her. Hooded like that, it's likely she'd hang upside down, beating her wings until she died of fright."

Andi stayed quiet.

"I wouldn't want that to happen," Kit added.

"Of course not," Andi answered, and the falcon did exactly what she'd feared. She took wing, stopped short with a cruel jerk and hung flapping upside down.

"There, lass." Slowly, he righted her. "Wasn't that a mistake, now?"

Andi braced for a recriminating glare, but once he'd resettled the bird and crouched nearby, he lifted a shoulder as if such accidents were to be expected.

"And now for dinner. It's only the second time I'll be feeding her," Kit explained. He reached into a cloth sack fashioned of more black cloth, and Andi finally recognized it. He'd shredded his favorite black shirt to make the hood, sack, and the wrapping to protect his arm from the bird's claws.

The bird stiffened as Kit made a squeaking sound, sucking air through his lips, sounding something like a distressed rodent. Which was, she learned, the point.

"Now, we play mousie." Kit held meat in one hand. With the other he stroked his index finger over the bird's toes. He squeaked again and before he finished, the falcon's beak slashed down.

He met her with the meat, but she didn't seem to savor it. She stayed stiff, but when Andi saw the red slashes the bird's suspicion had cost him, she supposed the pair had made progress.

Both heads tilted as Andi rose, edged toward the barn wall, and lifted a leather gardening glove from a nail for Kit.

He slipped it on before feeding the bird a second course.

"Another mousie come to call," Kit coaxed and Andi smiled at the childish lure.

This time, feeling the tap of leather, the bird grabbed with one talon as her beak flashed down. Again, Kit was ready and now the bird seemed to relish the tidbit.

Andi's foot was asleep. As she flexed it, Kit mouthed, "You can go," but Andi shook her head.

Let him find the Graveyard Rose and Kit was gone for good. His kind expression and tolerance were like the eerie calm of a man who'd decided on suicide. With the decision made, stress slackened. He could afford to relax for a little while.

She'd had seven days without him. That was enough.

"She's settling nicely now," Kit crooned. "I should think if someone invited me for a civilized cup of tea, I might appear—barring disaster—within an hour or two."

Andi's heart catapulted high in her chest. There was every chance in the world she would make a fool of herself this afternoon. She could hardly wait.

• • •

A civilized cup of tea. Andi whipped through the shower, toweled off, crisscrossed her hair into a braid over one shoulder, and jogged upstairs, naked. Dodging Lily was like trying to do that Philippine stick dance, where they pounded bamboo poles on the ground, then tried to slam your ankles between them.

The sun still shone, but the house had cooled. They'd take tea on the front veranda, at the spindly white table.

Andi shimmied into a poppy-red peasant blouse. Without a bra. Miranda Fairfield was no bimbo, to use Cisco's vernacular. She was a woman with a mission. She meant to keep Kit with her for as long as he could stay.

She took the blue corduroy shirt from her closet. She longed to see it on him, but had no idea how to present it.

"Hey, I just happened to notice you wandering around without a stitch on above the—"

She'd think of something. Meantime, she hesitated between a black broomstick skirt and jeans. *Civilized.* That's the key word, Fairfield. She pulled on the skirt and sandals, then searched the pantry for tea.

Dinah's pantry held several tins of tea. Andi compared the printed descriptions and selected the one which sounded most robust, then put water on to boil and considered Dinah's two teapots. The smaller one was prettier, but there was something in the figured design which reminded her of India.

Since she didn't want thoughts of Sarah to cross his mind, Andi left the small teapot on the shelf and warmed the big white one with hot water.

But any Anglophile knew that "a civilized cup of tea" didn't mean just *tea.* As Andi whirled toward the refrigerator in search of delicacies, there was a bleat.

"Well, Lily." She scooped the cat into her arms and received a bite as punishment for her enthusiasm. The cat leapt down, shook her fur free of Andi's scent, and twined between her legs.

"I see, you'd rather just rub white hair on my black skirt."

On one plate, Andi arranged five Dancing Goat macaroons and a dozen foil-wrapped chocolate kisses from Brown's grocery. She layered fresh red lettuce, ruffled edges out, on another plate and added tiny triangles of the pesto pizza. It smelled incredible.

Not Claridge's, but not bad.

Outside, a late-afternoon breeze rustled the cottonwood's leaves. The cloud-skeined sky was as blue and white as the gingham cloth she fluttered over the veranda table and even the dandelions, devilish-thick next to the walk where she'd routed them two days ago, looked cheery.

Andi peered back toward the barn. No Kit.

She picked two orange daylilies, and though she couldn't find a vase, she found a cache of about a hundred old green Coke bottles and used one to hold the centerpiece flowers.

Andi bent to arrange them. Half-listening for the teakettle's shriek, she didn't hear him tread the veranda stairs. Kit announced his arrival by standing very close behind her, hands clasped on each side of her waist.

"Kiss me, please," were the words he uttered, but Kit's hands made it clear this was no polite request.

Chapter Nineteen

Kit loosened his grip just enough that she could turn to face him. While his hands stayed linked around her waist, Andi leaned back against them. Looking up, she saw his reluctant affection.

"What sort of maid are you," he asked, "trusting a ghost not to let you drop right through his arms?"

"You won't let me fall." She leaned back further and reached so her hands rested on his shoulders.

"And are you so easily gulled," Kit said, "that you'd let a ghost kiss you?"

Because he knew the answer, she let the moment build. Kit's jaw hardened as her hands moved over the muscles at the base of his neck. His chest caught a breath and held it, until her fingers grazed skin. And then, he shivered.

"If a ghost said 'please,' I don't see how I could refuse."

His jaw stayed set, his breathing quick.

"If you're trying to prove you're more patient, it's no contest. I've really missed you." She tugged Kit's neck.

His lips descended so slowly, she smelled traces of burlap and bird on his clothes. But his face smelled of wind.

I thought you'd left.

I tried.

Where had trying taken him?

She didn't care. By the time his lips closed on hers, she gasped, shocking him into action. Two kisses slanted over her mouth, first one way, then the other, all pressure and no invasion. When her longing heated into passion, he felt it.

Blatant and demanding, Kit pulled her hips against his and kissed her so hard that Andi felt her lips cut by her teeth. Or his.

He was no shrinking, fading ghost. His strength would allow him to do whatever he wanted. Instinct half-turned her from this onslaught, but he didn't release her.

"I won't hurt you."

His tone said just the opposite and his fingers' pressure at the small of her back induced languor which slowed her battle against momentum taking her too far, too fast.

"You're—not going anywhere." She cursed the ambiguous words and her cowardice.

Damn, she wasn't afraid. She'd felt overpowered, but that was probably natural. She'd never allowed herself to learn the rules of an affair. Once, Kit had been willing to teach her. *It's bloody well time you were with a man and it bloody well better be me.* Were there more erotic words in the language? But now Kit had loosened his hold and Andi slipped a few inches away.

He raised a hand to his face. "Along those same lines, it's probably best you know, I had to cut my beard before coming to you. With an actual knife. My beard hasn't grown in centuries."

Andi fisted her hands, resisting the need to stroke that beard, smooth and harsh like some wild animal's coat. But trimmed, before he came to her.

The ghost she couldn't kill, the man beyond her curse, had trimmed his beard. And his physical response, flagrant as he pressed against her, was no illusion.

Andi took a breath and tried to speak, but no words could untangle her combination of elation and fear. After all, no other woman—sane woman, that is—had considered the wisdom of losing her virginity to a ghost.

A shriek erupted in the kitchen.

"Time to prove you can brew a proper cup of tea." He made a half bow and his arms opened.

"You bet," Andi said, and though she should have felt like he'd opened an escape hatch, she only felt cold.

"Should we move this to the barn, maybe? If your falcon bates—that's the word, isn't it?—how will you know?"

"She was dozing when I left. She should be fine." Kit straightened a sterling fork in line with a knife. "If she falls, she'll scream. The whole bloody town will hear her."

Kit's uncharacteristic fidgeting made Andi as uneasy as the effusive praise he'd lavished on the outlay of tea things. Even more curious was the fact that he was drinking tea and nibbling a macaroon.

Above the neck of the tan T-shirt, Kit's throat moved as he swallowed.

"How do you do it?"

He understood at once.

"As I do anything else requiring me to hold shape." He waggled both eyebrows.

Cute, but something hid behind this humor.

When she didn't respond to his lecherous allusion, Kit tried to explain. "It's a sort of . . . unconscious concentration, like breathing." He reached across the table and his thumb rubbed the frown line between her eyebrows. "If you quit breathing, you'd soon notice and recommence. If I quit holding the tea, it would dribble on my shoes. It's that simple."

"But then, you can't enjoy it."

"Not exactly. It's sort of a"—he tilted his head, musing—"detached appreciation."

Andi tapped her fingers on the table, concentrating on each as it struck. Little finger, ring, middle, index. If she and Kit made love, she didn't want his *detached appreciation*. Little finger, ring—wait. He couldn't *exactly* enjoy food, he'd said.

Doubt left the door open just a crack, and if she could tempt him with food, sex should be easy.

"Try this." Andi reached, hand steady, for the cheesiest piece of pizza. "Lower that skeptical eyebrow, if you please, and open your mouth."

When he didn't, Andi touched his firmly closed lips with her index finger and rubbed the seam between them.

He glowered. She tried to recall the expression about tweaking a tiger's tail.

"It's not poison, Kit, only pizza."

"Miranda, let me remind you, I am not a peasant. A French cousin of my mother's served a quiche very like this. I found the dish ordinary and overrated—"

When his scornful tongue lay exposed by the word *overrated*, she plopped the pizza on it.

He actually blinked with surprise. Then he chewed.

"But—" His eyes lost focus.

He reached for another. This time he was completely still, apparently savoring all four cheeses and the piquant basil. His cheek bulged as his tongue hunted for more.

"Have they improved the formula, do you think?" Andi moved the dish out of reach, so he'd concentrate on answering.

"Give me another, witch."

"Feeling a flicker of 'detached appreciation,' are we?"

"More." Kit snapped his fingers.

"Oh, right. *That* might work." Andi considered throwing the pizza to some starlings clustered on the driveway.

"Miranda." Kit's voice was level and faintly desperate. "I tasted it distinctly."

"Um-hmmm."

"It was—better than 'detached appreciation.' "

"Yes?"

"And it is, most probably, due to you that I can enjoy many things, now."

She rewarded him with the rest of the pizza. His smile boded well for so much. Summer nights in the bed upstairs. Tramping side by side through flame-colored leaves in autumn. Baking him a super-deluxe-combo pizza, from scratch, and snuggling into his arms before a winter fire.

Dreamily, she watched him demolish a paper napkin as he cleaned his fingers. Then, as if he read hope in her thoughts, Kit broke in.

"There's no cure, Miranda." Kit held his hand a foot above the tabletop. He let it drop straight through to rest upon her knee.

Andi reached under the table, captured his hand and squeezed it. "You'd tell me if there were, wouldn't you?"

He hesitated.

Andi scooted away from the table, away from him.

"Do you want to die, Kit?"

"Miranda—" His voice was weary. "I'm more than four hundred years dead already."

"No. Don't give me that. You're what, twenty-eight? Thirty? And you're healing from ghosthood. I know it's impossible, but you can smell violets and hold me and eat pizza."

She stood, fuming, then leaned forward, palms on the tabletop. "That's a miracle."

He might have been carved from the pillar behind him.

"Kit, the way things are going, you could live another fifty years. You could have children."

"By all that's holy, Miranda, you have no reason to believe such a thing."

"I have no reason to believe any of this." Her shout and wide-flung arms sent the starlings flying. "I'm sick of wondering, of arguing, but I'm feeling pretty damned fearless. Let's see if this works."

It took a moment to realize Kit was laughing. He cleared his throat, then managed, "See if what works, exactly?"

"Nothing's funny here." Andi jammed the table toward him and walked toward the house.

Silently, he was at her elbow, turning her back from the door. If he was insulted, outraged that she'd assaulted him with a tea table, those things were all mixed with desire. His black eyes had turned smoky.

"Mistress Fairfield, am I to understand you're daring me to make love to you?" He held her upper arms. "Be sure."

His fingers stroked the tender inner surfaces. "This time, I fear I can do it."

She nodded. Kit's chin raised a notch and his eyes widened.

"Yes," Andi said.

If the sun dropped to swallow them both, it would feel like this. Yellow-orange blazed behind Andi's eyelids as he kissed her, cupped the back of her head with both hands, backed her over the threshold, into the cool house. Inside, the sun burned even hotter. His thumbs skimmed her cheekbones, funneled down her neck, past her breasts and back up again.

No bra. Her mind searched for a shred of shame, but the heat flooding from the palms of his hands washed down her torso and her mind lost.

His hands explored, lightly. His kiss nudged her lips wider, but he barely touched the surfaces inside. Exquisite teasing made her catch his tongue with hers, then grab his shirt to pull him closer.

Kit's hands left her breasts to trace the channel of her spine, and the red silk blouse made the sensation slick and so sharp that she eased forward, away from his hands, into the wall of his chest. She crushed her breasts against him. If she pressed harder, would they stop demanding he hold them again?

"I've never known a maiden so forthright in her desires." He kissed the side of her neck, then nuzzled the sleeve of her blouse further down her shoulder. "Still and all, you are a maid." He nipped the top of her shoulder. "I'll go slowly."

"Kit." There was no begging this time. She heard warning in her own voice as she tugged the T-shirt out of his jeans, thrust her hands up as far as his shoulders, and let her fingernails rake down.

"Easy, Miranda."

He bent one knee, but that was their only stop on the way to the floor. A rectangle of light fell through the open door, but the feverish heat came from Kit pulling her blouse from the black skirt, over her head, off—then pausing astride her, still holding the blouse as if the sight of her skin held him too stunned to move.

She closed her eyes, and he was beside her, turning the length of her to match him, kissing her as she pulled his shirt up over ribs that were a glory to touch, over that collarbone she'd longed to kiss, and now did.

"I wanted to do this." Andi brushed her lips there, until she reached the bump in the bone. "What kind of rough play?"

"The quintain smacked me from the rear and then Barrett stepped on me."

She sighed and rubbed against him.

"You didn't think—" Kit loosened the drawstring at her skirt's waist. "*Did* you think I meant rough play with a woman? Sakes, Miranda, I'm not that sort." He did a quick survey of their scattered garments, the rug shifted out of place on the wooden floor, and added, "Usually."

He eased the skirt down, baring her hipbone to his touch. She kept her eyes closed, her face pressed against his chest, and breathed of him. If this man was not real, nothing was.

His fingers left their circling and pulled the skirt back up to her waist.

"Kit?"

"Shhh." With one arm he cradled her against his chest, while his other hand dipped to the hem of her skirt.

He grazed the flesh behind her knee, and reflex made her reach her leg across his. He followed her thigh, up, and then his hand lingered at her hipbone, as before.

She opened her eyes and found him staring. Had she truly thought those black eyes cold and bottomless? They held a recognition that this was more than grappling in the sunshine.

"You make me glad, Miranda."

The reverence in his expression stayed behind her lids as her eyes closed again. Shy, excited, she couldn't think as his hand followed the hemline of her panties from her hip, across her belly and lower. Her head fell back on her neck as his hand cupped her.

Their breathing mingled, water pattered on grass outside,

her muscles trembled with waiting, and she surged against him, wanting more of this secret touch.

"Conquered but not subdued, lady?"

Her hands shook as she touched his face. "Don't stop."

His hand moved convulsively, and she heard him swallow. "In a minute." He stroked the silk of her panties. She couldn't remember what color they were. "You need a minute."

"I don't."

In the instant his eyes believed her, her world grew hazy. She blinked, willing away her mind's reluctance, which suddenly blended with a scream.

At first she thought of a fire engine. An image of Noah chopping down the door with a fire ax. Except the door was open. And she recognized that shriek.

"Your hawk—"

Kit surged forward, pulling one of her ears against him, covering the other with his hand.

"She's going to die if—"

"Let. Her. Die." Kit might have turned to steel and clamped her in a vise.

"She's helpless." So close—all that excitement turned to misery. "Hanging upside down." Tears, not just for the bird but for this whole hopeless tangle, choked Andi. "I'll wait."

"God's bloody nails," he said, but the sound might have been the wind moaning as it closed the door with a slam, because she lay on the floor, alone.

The setting sun cast a coven of shadow trees on the ceiling. Andi watched them bend and menace and shake their rattling leaves. They were dampening her spirits worse than Kit's desertion.

Wind slipped through the windows, bringing autumn smells. She heard loud rustling. Swallows, maybe, in their mud nests under the eaves, or Lily, padding up the staircase. She thought she'd remembered to close the closet door in Dinah's room, but maybe, in her delight over finding the denim drudge dress, she hadn't.

Though it wasn't really cold, Andi reached across the

floor, grabbed Kit's T-shirt and pulled it on. She closed her eyes, burrowing in its warmth, except it wasn't warm. It was Kit's.

He'd look great in the blue corduroy shirt, but would he welcome the gift? As Andi walked upstairs, Lily bounded out of the master bedroom. She'd probably left the closet open, after all.

Kit's anger, as he'd vanished, hadn't been for her.

"No big deal," she told Lily. "A little setback."

Kit was healing, without his heart. She would keep looking for the Graveyard Rose, but she'd begun to wonder if it was an obstacle instead of an asset.

Andi slid the skirt down, thinking how Kit had scooted it down past her waist, how her pulse had pounded in her throat so she could barely draw breath. She yanked it the rest of the way off and picked up a pair of jeans from the floor. Not exactly fresh, but perfectly suited to sitting in the barn, watching a falcon snore.

She shivered and circled the bed to shut the bedroom window. Still drafty. Andi stared at her own open closet. If the secret passage to the basement hadn't been boarded up, she'd think the wind seeped in from there.

She took a hanger from the closet, slung her skirt across it, and peered around. No, the secret door had been boarded over. The nail heads glittered just inches apart. She lifted Kit's new shirt out and arranged it on the bed, but before she could step into her jeans, the phone began to ring downstairs.

"Good exercise," she told herself, then gave her closet door a push, grabbed the blue shirt and her jeans, and jogged back downstairs.

She couldn't have been more surprised if Lily had handed her the telephone, but she recognized the voice right away and felt flustered by her state of undress.

"Mr. Sterling?" Andi held the receiver against her shoulder, while she worked her jeans up.

The principal of Lincoln High School, a man who'd rarely remembered her name, who'd referrred to female teachers as "sugar," "honey," or other confections—in direct disregard of school district sexual harassment guidelines—had tracked her to Sparrowgrass.

"How are you getting along, Miss Fairfield? I hope the time off has settled your nerves—know what I mean?"

"I'm fine."

Saying her nerves had never been *un*settled was on the tip of Andi's tongue, so she bit it. If she said that, she'd add that his "know what I mean" was a faculty joke.

"It's so nice of you to look me up, Mr. Sterling."

"Of course. When Mimi mailed the registration for my curriculum-planning conference at a local j.c., she mentioned that Owen was near the village you'd moved to. Sparrowgrass was such a lyrical name, know what I mean? And who would know better than the one who addresses your checks."

Check, she thought. *Singular.*

She didn't say it, since Cal Sterling would take it as criticism. Her principal's sole qualification for leadership seemed to be seven straight winning seasons as varsity football coach at a Palm Springs high school. And he was always looking for a tackle out of nowhere.

"Owen Canyon Junior College?" Andi asked. It was only coincidence that Mr. Sterling's conference was at the college where Rick taught and coached.

"Yes, Owen. Small, but a nice phys ed department, know what I mean? I've been running their track every morning. Leaving tomorrow, though, and I did want to take this opportunity to ask if you were planning to return in the fall . . ."

"I am," Andi insisted, then raised her voice. "I miss the kids."

She did. Besides, being acting mistress of Heart's Ease didn't pay, and local employment opportunities for ladies with master's degrees were sparse.

"Took a drive over your way with a principal from Manteca, who said we could get decent baked goods. They're feeding us in the dorm, and dorm food hasn't improved in the last twenty-five years."

"I know what you mean," Andi interrupted, relieved that

the stranger who'd asked Noah's buxom assistant about her was Mr. Sterling.

"So," his voice veered from the phone, then came back, louder. "Will you be under a doctor's care if you return?"

It was all Andi could do to keep from jerking the receiver away from her ear to stare at it. Instead, she slowly zipped her jeans and snapped them. Okay, maybe he had her confused with some other "cupcake."

"Mr. Sterling, I absolutely will come back." Andi tried for tact. "I know you had a lot on your mind toward the semester's end. Perhaps you'll remember that I didn't ask for medical leave. You suggested I take it. I was out only one day last year. With flu."

"I didn't forget, Miss Fairfield. Disruptive to the educational process. The uh, sensual, uh, *sensational*, that is, nature of the accident was bound to interest students, you know what I mean? Couldn't have talk like that. Not over one of my teachers. But, if you're sure."

"I'm sure."

"Living out in the sticks alone, well, a city girl might imagine things. Wouldn't want it to lead to, you know, a breakdown."

"Mr. Sterling, I'm healthy as a horse. In fact, I've been caring for one all summer." Andi allowed herself a white lie to save her job. "And renovating an old house and gardens. I even have my own Weed Eater."

Sterling's grunt of approval jetted straight to her eardrum. "Good for you, honey. See you in September."

She hung up as Lily pounced from floor, to couch, to the telephone table.

Andi knew it was time to sit down, sort out all the clues and coincidences, knit them together, and present her conclusions to Noah Lincoln.

She watched Lily arch her back and rub against the lampshade until her eyes closed in pleasure and the lamp teetered, ready to fall.

It really *was* time to be sensible, but her stomach fell away at the memory of Kit astride her, regarding her body with awe.

Lily yowled and batted a paw in Andi's direction.

"You're right, cat. I just saved my job. That's enough sensible behavior for a day."

Andi didn't waste time going upstairs for shoes. She left the lights burning, ran out of the house, and gloried in the dew on her toes as she sprinted toward the carriage house and Kit.

Chapter Twenty

The falcon dangled upside down, where she'd quit fighting the jesses. The inquiring tilt of her head told Kit the bird was only tired, not dead.

"Poor daft thing." Kit reached to stroke the ruffled feathers and jerked back a bloody hand.

He pulled on the leather glove before righting the bird on her perch. Shrill cries accompanied flailing wings and a knife-edged beak that slashed at the void beyond her hood.

"All is on the hazard, eh?" Kit squatted in the straw, watching the falcon's fury. He, on the other hand, felt fine.

His happiness had little to do with Judith, for so his imagination had named the bird, and much to do with Miranda.

What had happened? What had changed?

Miranda would give all of herself, but he'd known that for days. And yet, how different those moments on the veranda had been from the ones in her canopied bed.

Last time Miranda had claimed to love him, but her eyes had been glazed, almost blind with carnal pleasure. A mood devoutly to be sought—nonetheless, today had been better.

This time her eyes of Swanfort blue had been filled with him.

"Come, lass." He nudged the falcon's feet and made the squeaking sound that signaled his approach. "Would you try sitting on the glove, then?"

Judith made a halfhearted slash, then extended a talon to shove his hand aside.

Not so, modest Miranda.

Most often, she could be caught covering even demure bodices with a well-placed hand. He'd seen her do it first at the fair, when she hid herself from Rick. Around Cisco, a mere boy, she'd adjusted a proper shirt collar by closing buttons to her chin. And she forever tugged down the legs of her short pants. And yet, today, before their civilized tea had cooled, modest Miranda had let him gape at her breasts.

Passion-fired, they'd taken each other to the floor. But lust carved out only a small share of the memory. She'd tucked her leg over his with possession that spoke of belonging. She'd touched his collarbone's bump in worry. And more than sunshine gilded Miranda's face as she looked up at him looming above, ready to plunder.

Yet she must know he had naught to give.

She could expect no worldly gifts, no name of import in these raw times, no children either, though she'd ventured half a pinch of hope.

His tender feelings didn't scatter, as he remembered her fingernails scoring his back, and the most marvelous words a man in rut could hear—"Don't stop."

Ye gods, the irony!

Miranda believed he was healing, and so he hoped. But he feared death was like amputation. Healing couldn't restore all that had been.

"Let's see if this works." He chuckled aloud to the falcon, still not sure why it amused him so. As a prelude to love-making, it was not romantic.

Miranda made a fit sparring partner for a choleric ghost. What harm in telling her he admired her? If he must stay, bound by his hidden heart, would it not be bittersweet to show her his esteem? Not love.

Perhaps the nature of love had changed. In his time, love was something wished for but never expected. One might be just as likely to find, of a morning, a diamond in the toe of one's stocking. And even in these love-besotted times, the most sentimental fool—which he decidedly was *not*—must admit the heart was the seat of true love.

Judith started out of a doze. Trembling, she regarded the world she could not see. It was more than the scent of rain on the wind. It was Miranda.

Kit knew he was a rogue for playing Peeping Tom, but he did. Through silver twilight, Miranda tiptoed on a lawn wet from all her sprinkling. She came quickly, her expression full of news. A garment swung from her hand, but she tucked it beneath her arm and bent to study something small.

A red beetle dotted with black, paddled vainly in a flooded leaf. Braving the spray, Miranda offered it her smallest finger as a ramp, then stepped out of the sprinkler's course and held the insect aloft.

"Ladybug, ladybug, fly away home." She blew, drying its wings, until the creature soared away. She stared after it a moment, then strode toward the carriage house.

"What tidings, love?" He materialized behind her.

Miranda yelped, stepped on a stone, and stumbled. She hopped on one foot while holding the injured one in her hands. An instant before sympathy came, Kit mused that such flexibility could be put to fine use. Then he swept her into his arms and scolded.

"There is, I suppose, an explanation for your barefoot state?"

Miranda sighed as she leaned her head into his shoulder. As she nodded, her braided hair scrubbed against his chest.

"I was in a hurry to bring you something."

"Yes?" Kit warned his extremities to stay solid and his mind to stay focused.

"Your shirt," she said, giving her shoulders a small squirm.

Indeed, she wore the shirt he'd left behind. He found its dampness and Miranda's clear lack of underpinnings fascinating. Still, since he didn't want to bruise her bottom by having his arms melt beneath her, Kit ignored the damp patch spreading over one obviously chilled nipple.

"You're a fair hussy, aren't you, Miranda?"

Face rapt and unashamed, she waited until he stopped just inside the barn door.

"Only with you."

"Ah." He set her on her feet and turned away. He adjusted Judith's jesses and avoided any hint of appearing smug. "Else a man would ask how you're still virginal."

He heard her lips part and a little gust of breath as she tried to answer, then faltered. When he turned to face her, Miranda stood uneasily in the straw, her cheeks stained red.

"I've told you all about that. Why I—haven't. If you're trying to make me back off, you'll have to do better than that."

"Whyever would I want you to 'back off'?"

"You don't, really." Miranda grasped her temples and rubbed. "You're in the habit of being a pain, I suppose."

Mayhap she was right, but he could hardly agree.

"And since you deserve to suffer for it," she said, "here's your present."

"Present?" he asked.

She held it spread over her chest, fingers holding its cuffs.

"A gift, from me to you," she said.

"But why?"

He took the fine piece of stitchery from her. A sort of corded velvet, it would sit well on a man's shoulders. The color, too, pleased him. Grayer than Swanfort blue, but he'd always thought his ensign's hue rather flashy.

She pressed her fingers to her head once more. Damme, but he'd like to loosen her plaited hair. He'd wanted that on the veranda. He'd longed to see the cinnamon skeins spread across her breasts.

"A *like* token, okay?" Miranda bristled when he stayed silent.

Just when he'd convinced himself that she'd forgotten his rejection, her sarcasm made him wonder.

"I'm sure ladies have given you keepsakes of a far more intimate kind," she said.

"No. That's far from true." Kit lifted the shirt, and as he slipped into it, he realized Miranda was staring. These rough times had robbed him of manners.

Never fashion's fool, he'd scorned lead paints and powders to pallor his skin. But now he was brown as a farmer. After shredding his shirt to make Judith's hood, he'd stayed on the cliffs until his torso was sun-touched. If pressed, however, Kit thought he might say Miranda was not put off. So why did she turn away before he finished closing the buttons?

"You're not feeding her my quail." Miranda pointed at the meat bag.

"Not yet," he said.

Only her expression said she objected.

"It's a fine shirt and I will hold it dear," he said, smoothing a hand down the opposite sleeve.

"Good," she said, but a frown still marred her brow.

"What's wrong, Miranda?" He took her hand. "Other than the minor vexation of being courted by a ghost and stalked by a madman, I mean."

"Just a headache," she began, then seized on his words. "Are you courting me?"

"In a witless and clumsy fashion, I suppose I am."

With their hands still clasped, Miranda kissed him. It was a tender kiss which did not deserve a sinful response. He touched his lips to her hand.

"I can tend that head pain, if you'll allow me," he offered.

She gave him a considering smile, then bowed her head, abandoning herself to his hands.

Kit took up the dark blue scarf she'd left in the barn before and twisted it.

"First, release the braid," he said. "I marvel that you didn't think of it yourself."

Her eyes narrowed, but she stood there face to face with him, refusing to give in to ill temper.

"I had other things on my mind," she said.

Plait loosed, Miranda forked her fingers through her hair until it was a rippling mass around her shoulders. It smelled of perfumed soap. He wanted nothing more than to bury his face in it, then nuzzle through to her neck.

He turned her to face away from him. As he stood behind her, aligning the scarf across her brow, she reached back and gave his thigh a friendly pat.

Lust sat flammable on his skin. Her touch ignited thoughts which were truly obscene. But she was counting on him for aid.

"The snugger I knot it, the sooner the ache will fade."

"Yank that sucker tight," she ordered.

He covered the snort of a laugh. He found these sudden cracks in Miranda's ladylike manner quite amusing.

As soon as his hands left her, she moved away, as if she would leave. He wanted her to stay.

"In truth," he raised his voice as she reached the doorway, "telling what's passed since I've been away, *that* will likely relieve your pain the most."

Her silhouette was dusky, as if she, too, could fade away. That foreboding, and the fact that Miranda usually spilled her thoughts with abandon, troubled him. Was it his ghostliness or his arrogance which kept her silent? God, he wanted her to stay.

"Have your old posies bloomed? I thought I smelled roses as I came up through the ravine."

Miranda shook her head, looking dejected.

"Listen," he said. "Frogs croaking down by the stream."

"And crickets starting up for the night."

For no sensible reason, the twining night sounds closed his throat with melancholy.

Miranda looked back over her shoulder, as if sensing it. "Don't leave it all behind."

"Ah, Miranda." He would make her no promises, but he would hold her. He sat on the third step leading up to his rooms. "Come here. Help me sit watch on this bird and talk to me for a time. Turn around." He pulled her to sit on the step beneath him, held her shoulders steady with his knees and stroked her temples with faint touches.

"Tell me truly what's passed. I vow I'll not bark or fade away."

It did not surprise him that Rick Aragon had made a travesty of their friendship. With the listing of afflictions, Miranda's spirits sagged. Clearly she saw that Aragon, and not the boy Cisco, was to blame.

" 'sblood Miranda, let me kill him."

"For scattering underwear?" She twisted in the grip of his knees. Her lips were level with his breastbone. "Why don't you just have him drawn and quartered?"

"We have but one horse, and we'd need to tie each extremity to—"

"For crying out loud, Kit! That's a little severe."

"Shh. Turn around, Miranda. Draw in three even breaths and hear me." He waited, and faith, she obeyed. "Killing may be severe for scattering undergarments, but what will he do next? Aragon is in your house in the dark, when you lie abed, Miranda. He's terrorized you with your past and you haven't given way."

This time when she turned to face him, she twisted in a most uncomfortable manner, but her frightened expression made him wonder if she felt the contortion. He did not relish the next words, but they must be spoken.

"That order you gave him today, to quit this place for good—what is that but a challenge? Were you a man, how would you meet such a defiance?"

He didn't say *rape*. He didn't say *murder*. But both thoughts flitted across her face.

"If I could find the damned box, I'd give it to him."

"I would not allow that."

After all these centuries, he didn't know what magic tied him to the box. Opened, it might send him to eternal rest, to drifting dust, to the clutches of devils.

"We might, however, allow him to believe so."

She untwisted herself and faced the barn door, relaxed between his knees as her fingers tapped each other.

"Then I could tell Noah and we could track Rick, see what he does with it—sell it, probably—and Noah could arrest him. Although, not if I just outright gave it to him, that would be no crime, so I'd have to devise some—"

"Sakes, Miranda, stop your trittle-trattle." He shook her shoulders. "My way is much simpler."

His gentle grip melted her. Miranda's legs slid forward and she leaned back, head in his lap. Ye gods, the encompassing love in her eyes proved Miranda his.

"If you kill him, you go to jail," she said. "I want you with me."

Her words' testimony matched her eyes'.

"And so I will be with you. Every moment until he's no longer a danger. I have been a soldier, and a good one. My skill was never bested until a traitor took me from behind. I will be your guardian, and if you don't have faith in my skill, believe this: Twice, I've lost to the house of Aragon. This time, I will not stop until Rick Aragon suffers the disgrace his ancestors earned. I will not lose again."

Black despair belched a memory of the last time he'd needed to be a man. On the veranda, his forced flesh had failed him. But he was the best protector she had. He must not shake her confidence.

"I will not fail *you*, Miranda."

He placed his hands on each side of her face. Upside down, Miranda's expression should have been comical. In fact, it was too tender to bear.

"Off to bed with you," he said. "I'll stand guard."

"But, the bird—"

"Her name is Judith, and she will be on her own this night. At daybreak I'll set her free."

"Her wing is injured, you said."

"Nonetheless, she can take her chances as she would have had I not found her."

"But you did. You can't throw her back now."

"Whyever not?"

"Because it's cruel."

"I am heartless, Miranda, and it will serve me well in fighting Aragon. Even if Judith stays, I can't sit with her every hour. It would drive us all mad. Even the bird."

"Fine, but tonight I'll stay with you."

Waves of heat might have invaded the drafty barn. If not

for his gelding's performance on the veranda, he'd have had her upstairs and deflowered in a trice.

"Very well, go to my bed. Nothing will happen."

With a hop, Miranda reached high enough to encircle his neck and pull his face down to hers. Her whisper was so fierce and low, it took him moments to understand.

"I want something to happen."

Andi butted her lips against his. On tiptoe, given their height difference, it wasn't easy. And though Kit returned the kiss, they were clearly back to detached appreciation.

"Sorry I got a little pushy."

His sigh gusted against her hair, and he clapped her on the seat of her jeans to hurry her up the stairs.

"I only wanted you to know. In case you couldn't tell. I liked, I mean I *really* liked—"

"An' it please you, lady, I would speak of other things." As he bowed her inside the carriage house, something marred Kit's arrogance.

What had she done now?

He *had* desired her. Lying on the great room floor, he had dominated her and she'd loved it. Her blood hummed at the memory. And the way he looked at her right now made her cross her arms over her chest. The passion hadn't been one-sided, and she could think of only one reason he wouldn't want to start all over again, right now.

Andi meandered toward the table. His manuscript lay where she'd left it. He watched her as she tried to remember the moments before Judith's scream.

She hadn't felt him ebbing, but she remembered the moment when she'd felt her eyes go blurry with wanting him. Perhaps it hadn't been her eyes.

"To bed, mistress."

"It can't be later than eight o'clock."

"Did I ask you the time?"

Andi sat cross-legged on his cot and patted the space beside her.

A chill breeze ruffled the curtains. Andi chafed her arms.

"It's been the strangest summer."

"Indeed." Kit knelt beside her, pulled the window closed, then lowered the latch in place.

She appreciated the protection, but she couldn't help thinking Kit was overreacting.

"I can't imagine Rick would strike at a window two stories up. Not when I'm with you."

Kit gave the latch an extra push, then settled beside her.

"A smart man plans for the enemy's capabilities, not his intentions." Kit said it soberly, draping an arm around her shoulders.

"We're not talking about war—" Andi began.

With a quick shift, Kit moved Andi's shoulder to level her across his lap. "Nor, necessarily, enemies." He grinned down at her. "But plans can diminish the element of surprise."

Andi wiggled and Kit gloated. Somehow both her arms were trapped beneath her. He kissed the tip of her nose, just because he could. Those eyes she'd once thought harsh had turned teasing. Of course he was insolent and arrogant, but out of millions of women over hundreds of years, he'd come to tease her. Andi wanted it to last forever.

"And this is supposed to make me feel safe?"

"Do you?"

In spite of the chill wind and the increasing patter of raindrops, Andi thought of Sarah. Kit's manuscript had put Sarah in a place of torrid, clinging heat, but the doubt in his voice had come from Sarah the ungrateful wretch who'd sent him away, even though he'd saved her child.

"Of course," she said. "I've always felt safe with you."

"Mistress Miranda, may you blush as a liar."

"I *have*. Well, maybe not always, but ever since—"

"—I materialized, drank poison, and"—Kit looked a little guilty—"ejected your seducer."

"*Seducer?*"

"Suitor, then?"

"Yuck. He's about as appealing as"—Andi fumbled for the name of something slick, blond, and stilted—"a mannequin."

"And yet he's handsome."

"So is a mannequin, but I wouldn't cuddle one during a rainstorm."

She wanted to hold him. She wanted to crush against him and feel him pull her closer still. Instead, they rearranged themselves with both heads on the pillow, face to face, and it was enough.

For a moment, Kit's eyes closed and his lashes lay black and thick and vulnerable.

"Sarah was an idiot." Andi bit her bottom lip. Kit looked so suddenly distant, she wished she could take it back.

"So, you read the pages I left you."

"Every one, back to the beginning."

"And what I wrote was so filled with disrespect that you think Sarah mentally deficient?"

"Maybe not, but emotionally lacking. You saved her baby and she threw you out. For crying out loud, Kit, the woman had no—"

Heart.

Kit nodded. Both heard the echo of a word unspoken. How many times had she talked around that word?

"I was far from tolerant then, and that's how I wrote it," Kit said. "Now, I blame the influence of Aragon."

"Don't make excuses for her. She doesn't deserve it." Andi saw Kit's wry smile. Was there a way to soothe a wound that was that old?

His solution for the current Aragon was simple. Murder.

"Kit, how did that first Aragon die?"

He drew a breath, held it, and shook his head as he exhaled.

"You don't know?" Andi felt an edge of excitement.

"How would I?" he chided. "Arabella didn't mention him. By the time I surfaced in India, his story had been molded by his heirs." Kit frowned. "What is it you know, Miranda?"

Given modern libraries, generations of master's theses and the Internet, a Spaniard who'd committed treason in the age of Elizabeth shouldn't be tough to track.

"Nothing, for sure, but Kit, I'm a teacher and a darned good researcher. I know how to find historical information."

She swallowed. "I can't promise anyone wrote about him, but if someone did, the college library in Owen is bound to have the resources we'd need to find out how he died."

"It matters naught."

"But wouldn't you like to know? What if he was never unmasked? What if everyone bought that story his descendant had engraved on the box around the Graveyard Rose?"

Kit drew in a breath with a hiss.

"What if he died a traitor's painful, grisly, tortured death?"

"That might be worth knowing."

Andi felt satisfied and a little drowsy. Kit told her more details of the accident that broke his collarbone, and more about a young nobleman's training in combat and in dance. He extended his forearm and lay hers atop it, explaining it was part of a dance called Alemain and considered rather daring. He claimed not to know the song "Greensleeves," and yet when she sang it, in a high piping voice of which she was only a little ashamed, she heard Kit swallow.

"Ah, that," he scoffed. "Too slow for true dancing."

Andi yawned. "I don't want to go to sleep. This is so—" Again she yawned. "Interesting."

"In a moment, you'll have me telling about Scots witches gathered on a heath, flinging toads into a cauldron."

"Is that—?" She struggled to part her eyelids.

"Nonsense. Your upstart player knit them out of dreams and deception." Kit rocked her. "Close your eyes, Miranda. I'll tell you more another night. It's not the last time. I promise you."

Cocoon-safe and warm, Andi slept. Only once, when Kit's warmth stole away, did she hear him leave, move about the barn, then return to check the latches.

Probably she dreamed that Kit stood peering out the window. And even if he did, it was probably imagination which made her think the reason he stood so far to one side, just beyond the window frame, was that he felt someone watching.

Chapter Twenty-one

The Dark Ranger night vision scope was the best toy Rick had ever owned.

He lowered the eyepieces and rested his forearms on his knees. Sitting right here on his own porch at one A.M., he could prove that Miranda Fairfield, for all her prissy ways, was getting it on with the guy in the carriage house.

If they'd stayed on the grass to do it, he could've watched. But even five hundred bucks worth of high-density plastic and aluminum couldn't give him the ability to look through walls. The Dark Ranger did the next best thing, though, amplifying light up to thirty thousand times, so he could watch all that went on at Heart's Ease.

Well worth the price. It would've saved him the soggy knees he got from peering through Andi's back window. It might have shown him Noah lurking around that night he'd damn near gotten cornered in the basement.

The scope had by God earned back its price tonight by showing him Christopher Gallatin was no ordinary opponent.

Rick glanced at his watch. Gallatin was walking patrols at odd hours. It had only been thirty minutes since he'd last appeared outside the barn, patted the horse, then vanished.

Yeah, *vanished.* Rick raised the binocular-style scope and swept the area. The illuminator had picked him up three times now. Once at dusk and twice after nightfall, which was pretty damned interesting, since Gallatin was, by all signs, a ghost.

The cold spots in the house and the frigid air in the carriage house, should have been a tip-off. Twice tonight Rick had been focused right on Gallatin when he vanished. The house behind him, the clothesline in front of him, and the blackberry hedge had stayed put, but Gallatin evaporated.

Rick elbowed the black cat away. A gift from some student, Rick hadn't even named it. He kept it around because Renetta said it suited him, but the animal shifted for itself, eating mice and lizards.

Paranormal activity was easier to accept the second time. Tonight he was willing to believe Gallatin was a ghost, but when old lady Williams had come back to check out the house he'd stolen from her, it took him days to believe.

He'd just finished the last coat of varnish that turned the place from a 1940's fishing shack into a glossy A-frame, when he'd seen her. No glowing red eyes or clanking chains for Sadie Williams, just that ratty green bathrobe, fuzzy slippers, and old-fashioned metal curlers in her hair.

Even after teaching thanatology, he needed extreme suspension of disbelief to see Sadie as a ghost.

Unnerved, he'd looked up spells taken from white witchcraft and voodoo and stopped short of Satanism when he heard about a local priest known for his skill at exorcism.

Father Paul wasn't quite a Catholic priest. He'd been barred just before ordination. A Jesuit colleague had confirmed tales that "Father" Paul had been practicing exorcism without a collar. In addition, he'd ignored the church's edict that a priest diagnose the possessed and identify the cause before healing the victim. Father Paul didn't mind a little skulduggery or working alone. He fancied himself a godly ghostbuster.

On Sadie, Father Paul's magic had worked just fine. Of course, Sadie Williams's ghost had meant no harm. She'd only checked out the improvements on her cabin. Even after death, she believed what everyone in Sparrowgrass believed: She'd died of a heart attack.

Gallatin was different.

Sadie's wispy arms had trailed behind her like scarves. Gallatin had lifted Andi's wineglass and smashed it on the hearth.

Sadie's ghost seemed bewildered. Gallatin radiated hatred.

"Yeah, well, let him think he's a badass," Rick muttered to the cat determined to curl atop his feet.

When Gallatin met up with Father Paul, he would have a nasty surprise.

"Get lost." Rick scooted free of the purring cat, checked his watch, and raised the scope.

Shit—he'd missed him coming out.

Two o'clock in the morning, and Gallatin crouched at ground level between the two back windows. He wouldn't find what he was looking for in the dark.

"C'mon, c'mon, do it." Rick focused tight enough to see Gallatin's shirt wrinkle. The ghost stood and surveyed the yard. He gazed up at Andi's bedroom window and, finally, across the ravine.

Gallatin wasn't tied to Heart's Ease.

Jason would have mentioned a ghost. He'd wanted one, badly. During his last weeks of life, Jason had been flying on morphine. One of his favorite topics, as they'd sat sipping contraindicated Cutty Sark under Dinah's disapproving eye, had been his starring role in a New Orleans vampire film. *Heart's Ease* had gotten Jason into big money and the occult. The combination inspired him to build Heart's Ease, complete with secret passages perfect for haunting.

The old coot thought it was like hammering together a birdhouse and hanging it in a tree. If you build it, they will come. Maybe he'd gotten his wish.

If Gallatin wasn't haunting Heart's Ease, he was guarding something, searching for something, or seeking revenge. Research showed that ghosts and fetches didn't crop up for no reason. Rick would bet Gallatin was guarding the Graveyard Rose.

It explained why the antique box remained hidden, why even Andi couldn't remember where she'd stashed it.

Rick sat silent. Gallatin's malevolent spirit had a man's physical power. Nothing would keep him from floating across the ravine and grabbing Rick's throat.

Gallatin's ghosthood had forced Rick to readjust his image of Andi once more. Ghosts didn't have sex with mortals, they possessed them.

Did Andi realize what was happening to her? One quick way to find out was to bring on the priest.

"There," Rick said it on a sigh. "Gone—again."

He'd seen enough.

Booting the cat aside, he climbed the stairs to his alcove. The room welcomed him. He would be sorry to see it reduced to a pile of ashes, but it would serve a higher purpose. And the plan was sweet. He'd researched it in the college's fire science library, taking notes and rearranging details until there could be no whiff of arson.

He would get his collections out first, of course, and hope the blaze swept toward Heart's Ease. Exorcising Gallatin should help Andi remember where she'd hidden the box. If she was still recalcitrant, he'd extract the information with pain, then kill her. He'd have to make sure she lived long enough that her lungs were full of smoke, so she'd be ruled a victim of smoke inhalation.

Whether or not he found the box, he would take the collection of Vincent Price paintings hanging in Jason's bedroom.

Damn, I'm good, Rick mused. The destruction of his house would explain why he'd finally made his long-discussed move to San Francisco. Only, he and Renetta would be screwing their brains out in a Chicago penthouse with a lake view, courtesy of Sharif, one very rich collector of antiquities.

Rick unlocked the filing cabinet, empty except for the scope's Cordura case and a voice-activated tape recorder.

Rick always recorded conversations with Cisco, so he could track the information he fed the kid. Usually, it was just enough to keep Cisco in trouble.

Rick considered it fate that he'd had the palm-size recorder in his sweatpants pocket when he'd caught sight of the jogger in the Los Padres sweatshirt.

While Cisco did wind sprints, Rick had spent thirty minutes trotting along with the stranger, b.s.ing about pulled hamstrings and ripped Achilles tendons. By the time they got to Rick's technique of using moleskin on blisters, the guy was his buddy for life.

Walking laps to cool off, Rick happened to mention the one person he knew from Los Padres. Cute but unstable— gee, what was the chick's name?

"Don't tell me it's Miranda Fairfield."

"Yeah, that's it!" Rick hadn't faked delight over the guy's guess.

"Good reason to be unstable," the guy had said, still trying to catch his breath. "Lost her job."

"No, really? Hmm. That's not what I heard. It was something kind of—" Wobbling his hand back and forth with his brows raised, Rick had baited the guy.

"Well, yeah. That's why she lost her job, know what I mean? Rumor has it—"

Minutes later, Rick learned that one of the ambulance attendants had a son at Lincoln High school. That son had spread dad's corny joke about lacy pink lingerie scattered at the accident scene.

Rick zipped the scope into its case and closed the drawer. The guy in the Los Padres sweatshirt claimed to have heard it all from the kid, but Rick wondered. Would an outsider know Andi hadn't been canned? This guy said she was only on leave.

The best part of the whole scenario had been telling Cisco the pink underwear story so he'd blush and act guilty next time he saw Andi. Sure enough, she'd been in town the morning after. By the time he'd lurched into Rick's van, Cisco had stammered, sworn, and pounded his fist against his thigh for three miles.

As planned, Andi suspected Cisco. Her little hissy fit this morning had only been hormones, but it had made him feel downright unfriendly. If the wind cooperated, it would cost her Heart's Ease.

Rick locked the file cabinet and turned to his desk. From the lower right drawer, he took an assortment of spell implements. He chuckled, pleased by the balance of high-tech and primitive weapons.

Chanting snatches of Latin, he arranged the green candles and incense, cinnamon, nutmeg, and juniper, which would evoke money spirits. Solemnly he wrapped gold cord around dried marigolds and mistletoe and knotted it tight for success.

While the herbs and flowers smoldered, he pictured Gallatin suffering. In a haze spread by Father Paul's swinging censer, Gallatin's mighty frame would dwindle, just like Sadie's had. Gallatin's ruthless eyes would melt to the consistency of pudding. Finally, he'd expire with a sound like the one you got sticking a switchblade into a tire.

Rick had counted Sadie's exorcism as a once-in-a-lifetime kick, but he must be living right.

Andi hummed a joyously loud "Greensleeves" as she burrowed under her canopied bed, gathering a notebook and pen for her library foray with Kit. When she smelled coffee, she smiled.

Her first ever all-nighter with a man, and she'd awakened alone. No hard chest to lean her cheek against, no male legs tangled with hers, not even a warm spot on the sheets, but Kit had greeted her as she opened the door and descended the stairs to the barn.

Brushing Trifle's sweat-darkened coat, he explained he'd already taken the mare for a run.

Kit hadn't touched her, but he'd watched, making her aware of her every gesture. Yawning, pushing her hair from her eyes, futilely smoothing her mass-of-wrinkles shorts—he caught every movement.

He'd also promised that after he'd coaxed Judith onto his glove for food—a process which could take minutes or hours—he would accompany her to Owen Canyon College.

Kit had paused then, curry comb stilled on the mare's back, and mused, "Oh, how I hope he died screaming."

And now her bloodthirsty Earl of Swanfort bustled around in the kitchen downstairs brewing coffee. Andi held on to the bedpost. Eyes closed, she prayed. *Please God, let him stay*. It couldn't be sacrilege to want a good man saved.

Thunder grumbled beyond the mountains and Andi caught herself in a self-conscious chuckle. If that was God's answer, it sounded like "Well, maybe."

Judith screamed from the barn and a flight of sparrows exploded past the bedroom window. Lily didn't give them a glance as she stalked into the room, fur puffy as a dandelion, and jumped onto the bed.

"I didn't mean to leave you alone all night." Andi pulled on a yellow skirt and tucked in a white sleeveless blouse. "If that's what you're sulking about." As she buckled on sandals, Andi gave the cat a sidelong glance. She'd seen Lily do that puffball routine only once before, around Rick.

She hoped the Owen Canyon College library didn't require special credentials to work in the research areas. She supposed she could cite Rick as a reference. He might even be on campus with Cisco.

Andi brushed her hair. It snapped with static, following the brush, but she managed to catch it at her crown and twist it into a coil. The sky outside threatened rain, but it would get good and hot first.

How had Kit learned to make coffee, she wondered as she passed through the stained-glass rainbows on the stairs. She stopped in the bathroom, pawed through her jewelry box, and tied on the plain amber bead.

"Surely you had servants to—" Andi stopped in the kitchen doorway.

The man in pressed khakis and oxford-cloth shirt wasn't Kit. Rick Aragon, his hair slicked back, his jaw so smooth it had probably been plucked free of whiskers, offered her a china mug of coffee.

She took it automatically then set it down on the counter so hard it slopped a puddle. She'd left the door open and he'd just walked in. In some Sparrowgrass houses, he'd have gotten shot.

"What are you doing here?"

Rick tried to appear casual. "I only came by to apologize for knocking down the swallows' nests. I should've guessed you'd be softhearted about animals."

Softhearted. Lord, the word was everywhere.

"I also wanted to take another look at that bathroom floor, maybe get it done when you're out sometime." He nodded toward her armload of notebooks. "Wouldn't that be nice to come home to? And I also wanted to mention I have a friend who collects relics. He said he'd pay two hundred fifty dollars for your Graveyard Rose."

"But they only cost twenty-five." Andi felt her pulse throbbing in her fingertips. Kit was right. Her Graveyard Rose was the real one, and Rick knew it.

"Seems like the artist struck the mold." Rick stared at the last drops of coffee dripping into the pot. "She's not making any more, so those in existence have increased in value. Nice coincidence that Sparrowgrass was her last stop, huh?"

Coincidence. Andi felt the danger.

"Since he was pretty pissed that I wouldn't part with mine, I told him I'd see if I could acquire yours."

"I don't know where it is. I wouldn't sell it if I did. And you can forget about the bathroom floor. It's not likely to fall off the house this week. Now, thanks very much for the coffee, but I'm about to leave."

"Aw, Andi, I know you might be feeling a little self-conscious about your relationship with Gallatin, but I'm no gossip." He slid his hands into his pockets. "You're an adult woman. You can do what you like." He gazed at her with puppy-dog sincerity. "I'm just sort of sorry you didn't pick me."

In his haste, Kit didn't open the front door, but Andi heard him condemn the door harp to eternal damnation before he strode into the kitchen, wearing his blue corduroy shirt and an air of menace.

"She didn't and she won't."

Rick didn't turn to face Kit. The only sign that he was unnerved was in his pockets. Andi saw his fingers fist, creating unsightly creases. Still, he wore the expression of a man with an ace in the hole. Almost as if he'd guessed the truth.

Andi felt the kitchen tighten around them. In this whole hot, humid little town with a thunderstorm brewing, there were only the three of them.

No sane person would believe Kit was a ghost, but Rick taught that macabre class. Even if he knew, what could he do about it?

"I know what you are."

"I doubt that." Kit stepped smoothly between them. Andi couldn't see Rick, but she saw the line of Kit's shoulders, relaxed and ready. "Aragons never recognize gentlemen. Honor is a concept foreign to them. Their native tongue is treachery."

If Kit had meant to provoke a fight by slurring Rick's family name, he failed.

"Even if I don't have the strength to oust you, I know one who does," Rick said.

I'll call my big brother, Andi thought, mocking. But she didn't want them to be fighting. She only wanted this over.

"I'll escort you to your car," Kit said, then led the way.

Andi let them go. Not that she didn't mind being shuffled aside as if this had nothing to do with her, but because she knew her presence would only escalate the battle. Besides, the front windows were open and she had every intention of listening.

Of course, Kit was the first to speak and he didn't underestimate his opponent's knowledge.

"If you do indeed 'know,' then you know also that you're powerless to stop me from snapping your neck here and now, before you have another chance to harm Miranda."

"I know that if you were successful—and specters *do* have a habit of dematerializing at the most inconvenient times, don't they?—you'd leave Miranda, a woman with a proven history of instability, with a body to explain."

Andi felt hot with humiliation. She should throw the coffeepot at him, or the potted geranium, but her hands shook, until Kit's sneer stopped them.

"Sirrah, you live in a uncommon soft century to believe I couldn't dispatch a single corpse." Kit made a curt gesture, as if shooing a fly. "Take yourself off now and prattle threats to your pupils."

Chapter Twenty-two

"Humanely strangled!" Kit's hiss sounded through the library.

Two students, heads together at a nearby table, looked up. One giggled nervously.

"Wait a minute." Andi scrolled down through the microfiche. "That's just one man's version."

She stuck in another sheet of the plastic film. Same time, different author, but again, a grain merchant named Throckmorton wrote of Aragon's death in nearly identical terms.

Born Catholic, but loyal to Elizabeth, Throckmorton had worked to stir up England's Papist enemies to illegal acts.

"An agent provocateur?" Andi muttered, but Kit had turned to stare out a window.

He'd found Throckmorton's archaic English less troublesome to decipher than Andi had, but the account of Richard Aragon, half-Spanish traitor to the queen, had held no comfort. And there'd been no mention of Christopher Gallatin, Earl of Swanfort.

The library's tinted window gave a greenish pallor to the quad, to the lowering clouds, and to Kit.

Andi skimmed the rest. Aragon's end sounded horrid enough. A trial, defamation, conviction, and strangulation by a bribed guard before the public burning.

Poor melancholy ghost. Andi lay her hand over Kit's. Misplaced by time, mishandled by one who loved him.

And she *did*. From God's viewpoint, as He peered down from a cloud, Kit must appear a poor choice, but for some reason He'd allowed it, so Andi took heart.

Kit carried the directories, microfilm, microfiche, and bound papers to the reference desk. As Andi checked them in, he waited politely. A single outburst had been his only protest. Andi took that as a warning.

Squinting against a dusty wind, she led the way to the student union patio and picked a table with a coral-striped umbrella. She had to shout over its flapping.

"It isn't enough, is it? But he died a traitor. Everyone knew what he'd done."

"I'm glad of it."

A pair of mallards, on a stroll from the campus pond, waddled past with a tailwind. They probably wondered where summer had gone.

Andi folded her hands. Her brother, Will, claimed well-intentioned prying was her worst flaw. When something went wrong, Andi wanted to fix it. Immediately. She would question, dig, and meddle until the recipient of her help felt more like a victim. This was no time to intrude on Kit's emotions. She practiced looking patient.

The ducks came back across the patio, pushing their beaks against the wind. As they quacked their displeasure at the Friday selection of crusts and crumbs, Kit leaned forward.

"There is no list of those who would have stopped him. These scribblers take note of Aragon, a traitor, a Judas. But there is no glory, nor word of praise for the good men.

"It is not *right*, Miranda. A man's name is all he leaves behind. When that is forgotten, when there are no sons to carry on, what does he have?"

"You have another chance."

"Pity I'm not in the mood for carousing," Kit sneered.

She gave the sting no time to hurt. "I'm not talking about

breeding sons. I'm talking about your book.''

''That book was a pretense from the start.''

''And yet you kept writing it.''

''As a diversion, while I tried to find my heart.''

''And you left it behind for me to read, so I'd understand.''

''Very well, if you must examine my faults, I confess to vanity.'' His fist struck the table. ''The worst of that vanity bade me believe Walsingham, Elizabeth's spymaster, when he assured me *I* had the skills to catch a traitor.'' Kit infused the words with melodrama.

''Walsingham, whose duty was deception. Can you think of a less likely man to trust? But I did, oh, most assuredly, when he credited me with talent.

''A horseman, a soldier, a scholar, he called me, praising a mind more than sharp enough to send messages inscribed in orange juice. Yes, a quill dipped in orange juice writes with a marvelous invisible ink. Did you not wonder why my hand shook as I cut the orange that day?

''How I embraced the role of spy. With Devereaux and Raleigh at odds over the likelihood of a traitor with troops hidden in Scotland, I chose Raleigh's side.'' Kit touched his left earlobe and Andi noticed a tiny scar. '' 'sblood, what a young baconbrains to wear a pierced ear like Raleigh's pirates!''

The image claimed Andi's mind, and she imagined Kit wearing an earring inscribed boldly for a man. This man.

The wind off the college lake could have been the blast catching his hair as he rode a thundering warhorse. The flapping of the umbrella overhead could have been the buffeting of his queen's ensign, held aloft in glory. She wished she could take him back to brag. Kit's adventures had taken him farther than Raleigh had dared to dream.

''Raleigh was an atheist who cared naught for Aragon's papistry.'' Kit flashed her a confiding look. ''He wanted to make his goddess take the tumble and thought this victory would make her ripe for tupping.

''Yet none of them—Walsingham, Devereaux, Raleigh— none are to blame. I'd placed half my trust in Aragon. I didn't quail when Barrett joined our troop.'' Kit's hand rose to where his heart had been. "My naive young brother. Well, at least he lived.''

Pity mixed with Andi's exhilaration, but how she wished for a classroom and students to regale with living history of Shakespeare's time. Kit noticed.

"Does this excite you, Miranda? My deception and my death?''

"Not that part, never, but—the rest? You bet it does.''

Kit's indulgent smile forced her to explain.

"You know, all the court intrigue, and Raleigh trying to kiss the queen—''

"Oh, our Walt did a fair bit more than that, I'll wager, but he kept his arrow nocked, since his target was the Crown.''

Cold skepticism displaced Kit's longing. As his hand reached toward her, Andi refused to shrink away. But he only let one finger graze the amber bead.

"Time's come round again.'' He withdrew his hand, slowly. "It did not work out so well, last time.''

Was it a quotation or another of Kit's melancholy musings? Well, she wouldn't give in to either.

"Kit, you were actually there. It's fascinating.''

"You're easily amused, love.'' He heard the word as she did and pushed his chair back with a screech. "That being so, let's go have a look if Judith's managed to hang herself.''

Andi held Kit's arm and sun seeped between the clouds as they hiked to the Volkswagen's far-flung parking spot.

"No skipping, Miranda. Keep a more sedate pace, if you please. Or cease towing me along.''

His bicep's swell beneath the corduroy made her swing him around. From a distance, it probably looked as if they danced on the vast asphalt parking lot with wild mustard pushing through.

"Miranda, what is this, now?'' He stopped short and frowned.

"This is me, falling in love with you.''

Kit caught her nape and pressed her face against his neck.

He said nothing as he rubbed his chin against her hair, but Andi knew the smell of hot tar and summer would always remind her of this.

"I tell you my tale of woe and it sends you into ecstasies. This does not bode well, Miranda."

For what? "Bode-ing" at least assumed a future. As they walked the remaining yards to her car, Andi didn't ask, but her hands shook as she groped for the key to unlock the door. Kit stood so close beside her, the top of her head knocked against his jaw.

"Sorry."

"Don't apologize, lady."

His sly tone made her quit fumbling and look up.

"One advantage height has not lost is this." Kit drew a finger along the scooped neckline of her blouse. "A tall man can delve into the bodice of any wench he fancies, if only with his eyes. And I am far more fortunate than that."

Speechless, she bumped him aside with her hip and climbed into the car. After three tries, the key fit the ignition. Four miles later, her grip on the steering wheel loosened and color flowed back into her hands, but her veins still hummed when they drove past the Owen Canyon drive-in movie.

After two hours spent with the hawk, Kit had ruined Dinah's gardening gloves and worked himself back into a funk.

"... owls screeching and they'll make of you a tasty snack ..."

"Are you threatening that poor bird?" Andi stayed in the doorway when she noticed Judith was unhooded.

Kit squeaked at the bird, and Judith's yellow eyes turned back to the meat he offered.

"She feels no fear from my threats," Kit crooned.

Judith's head moved in sharp nods as she ate.

"Soon I'll give her a last bite, and she'll have gotten her good from me. Watch and you'll see her wing's healed. I could free her tomorrow."

The falcon huffed as Kit replaced her hood, but this time, when she batted her wings, she didn't flinch.

"One more bite—there, lass—so she doesn't associate the hooding with the end of her meal."

Andi smiled. It didn't sound to her like he was going to part with the falcon soon.

Now that the bird had returned to her perch, Kit faced Andi as she lifted the blue aluminum baseball bat from its hook.

"Do you mean to thrash me?" he asked.

"Do you deserve thrashing?" She rested the bat on one shoulder.

"I suppose it depends on your point of view. Were I your father, I'd say most definitely. He does expect you to wed?"

"Of course."

Kit's expression wavered between pride and frustration. "A man doomed to disappointment," he said.

"My father?" She watched Kit nod. "Oh, *really*?" Andi let the bat slip from her shoulder. "You think no one will want to marry me? Ever?"

He grabbed both her wrists with his right hand. The bat fell between them, and the stir created by Trifle and Judith was nothing compared to his assault.

"Miranda, I won't be clubbed over a misunderstanding." His free hand grabbed her hair and tugged her head back so he could plunder her throat. "Let me"—he said between kisses—"give you cause."

"There are other fish in the sea," she gasped.

The cliché must be a recent invention, for Kit's lips hesitated. Only for a minute, though, then his mouth was on hers. Andi's muffled noise of surprise stayed sealed by his lips as he drove her backward and her heels hit the bottom step.

"Other fish, are there?" Still clutching her wrists, Kit raised her hands over her head while his other hand sought the snap at the top of her jeans.

"No! " Her squeal startled Judith past bearing. Andi squirmed away as the air filled with straw dust from flapping wings. "No other fish," she laughed. He loosed her wrists and she linked her hands around his neck. "Only you."

"That's as it should be." Kit kept her pressed against him. "After what you said."

It didn't matter that he hadn't told her he loved her too. Not too much. His kisses said he wanted her love as he wanted her touch, and only she could give them.

With a jolt, Andi wondered if that were true. Good Lord, what if, in coming back to human senses, he could feel others' touch? What if they affected him as hers had?

Bolder than she'd ever felt before, Andi caught Kit's face between her palms, parted his lips with hers, and met his tongue.

"Jesus!" Kit's gasp sounded more prayerful than profane. His knee moved between hers and Andi's legs trembled. "I thought you'd forgotten. I was a rogue to answer you so, before. Forgive me."

If she could think. He was speaking of love, of the way she'd told him. . . . If only she could align thoughts to make sense of what he'd said.

"I never told you before."

Kit's eyes widened. "Very well." His voice pitched even lower. "If you withdrew it and offered it again, your love is so much the sweeter."

His solemn apology convinced her. Doubt and fear of the sort which had nearly paralyzed her after Domingo's death engulfed her.

"Did I?" she asked.

Sensing her fear, he nodded and kissed her.

"The drink clouded your memory is all."

"I wasn't drunk." Andi searched for another reason. "Even drunk, I would remember." Tears stung her eyes. "Kit, I wouldn't have missed that for the world! I told you—? Did you—?"

Her ribs flexed within his hug, and she returned it, thankful for his reluctance. When it happened, when he finally told her, she'd be *there*.

"You don't remember how I tried to silence you with kisses, and—more?"

"Kit!" Alarm slammed into her belly. "Did you take me to bed?"

"You're a virgin still. That's all that matters."

"No, Kit, really, I can't remember anything after you came in and chased Rick off." Andi pressed her palms to her temples, trying to force out a drop of memory.

And then she knew. "There was more than poison in that wine." Andi sucked in a breath at his narrowed stare. She'd planned to keep those sips secret. "I only drank a little."

"By all the saints' celestial suffering— Oh, shut up, you dratted bird!— Wretch!" He shook her shoulders. "When did you think to tell me you'd swallowed it?" He gave her no time to answer. "If we ever— If you—"

Kit held up a hand, paced the length of the barn, then came back to face her. "You lied to me."

"No, I didn't."

"You did not tell the truth."

She couldn't argue with that, but she leaned over and picked up the baseball bat again, determined to execute her plan. He held up a finger, cautioning her, even as her lips opened to speak.

"Lady, do not tempt me further. This may be an age enlightened by respect for womanhood, but I am sorely pressed."

"I know, but I have something fun for us to do."

"Fun."

"You're still angry with Richard Aragon, right?"

"Oh, no, Miranda. After mulling it over, I've concluded any man might make such mistakes and— You've never been beaten, have you, girl?"

"I'm going to ignore that." Andi stood on tiptoe and kissed him again. "Go get in my car, Kit. We're going back to Owen, where we'll play baseball, so you can smack the heck out of something. And then we're going to a drive-in movie to watch *Romeo and Juliet* and neck in the car."

"*Romeo and Juliet*. That's not some of your Shakespearean drivel, is it?"

"No."

"Miranda, I warned you about lying."

"It's not drivel."

Kit's sigh might have inspired sympathy if Trifle hadn't

echoed him by heaving a whuffling sigh of her own.

"Well, then, what is *necking*?" He looked willing to break his pout. "It sounds more appealing than Shakespeare."

"Kissing."

"Ah. And people do this in a public place?"

"Sort of. In cars."

"An amazing age."

"Try this for amazing. At the drive-in theater, there's a snack bar and besides popcorn—which I've been popping for the hour you've spent with Judith—they have pizza. Last time I was there, three kinds of pizza."

"Well, then, if it pleases you," he nodded toward the barn door.

"This is where you say 'Lead on, Macduff.' "

"Miranda, no." Kit forked his fingers through hers and kissed her cheek. "Whatever your shortcomings, I'd never revile you as a Scot."

"You are in sore need of education, Swanfort."

It would be an arduous task, trying to rid him of prejudice against Catholics and Scots and cats.

He lowered his face so near, his nose bumped hers.

"Don't despair, love. Bribe me with pizza."

Rick found pricking a pinhole in the lightbulb the most difficult part of his plan. Wearing rubber gloves—not that there'd be a thing left to lift prints from—he used an eye-dropper to squirt three drops of gasoline inside and plugged the photo-sensor night-light into the wall.

That done, he stripped off the gloves, dropped them in the grocery bag that held his two failed lightbulbs, then recommenced his almost silent whistling of "Louie, Louie."

For some reason, he'd been whistling the damned tune the whole time he'd been setting up the fire. Maybe it had to do with the ". . . we gotta go" line.

Bracketed by his thanatology collection, he and Renetta had celebrated their forty-eight hours' countdown in the back of the van. Weeks of going through policies to make sure he had fire insurance had him thinking in those terms, and when he'd called Renetta his "attractive nuisance" she'd turned horny.

Rick glanced at his watch and gave himself fifteen minutes to finish up, get in the van, and drive to Sparrowgrass to start building an alibi.

Pulling on a second pair of gloves, Rick decided his reputation as a neat freak was about to pay off. His pantry and carport were filled with carefully labeled spray bottles. He tested one in the kitchen sink, sniffed at the stench of gasoline, then adjusted the nozzle to mist furniture, carpet, and drapes.

Silent whistling turned to humming as he imagined the inept volunteer fire department looking for a kid playing with matches, a candle left burning, or a cigarette on the forest floor.

With no obvious source of ignition, they'd stand around watching the arson investigator search for slosh patterns against the walls or gas pooled in the pad beneath the carpet.

"No such luck, hotshot," he told the imaginary expert, then replaced the spray bottle, labeled "Lubricant," in the carport.

He couldn't have done a better job of remodeling the house as a fire hazard if he'd planned it.

". . . oh, no, we gotta go . . ." he hummed.

He considered his choice of wood-shingle roof and A-frame construction to be fate rather than luck. Either way, it added up to a house built like a chimney, with kindling on top.

This next part would be a little noisy, so he returned to the kitchen window for a final spy scope-out of the area. He turned the lenses toward Heart's Ease.

All was quiet, as if Andi were resting up for the little tussle they'd have later. That'd be after Father Paul came to call, so he wouldn't have any trouble with Christopher Gallatin.

"Three-thirty, vent time." He trotted upstairs, imagining Renetta doing a rhythmic interpretation of "Louie, Louie." Then he kept the beat himself, by kicking out an alcove windowpane.

The maroon drapes protected his foot and the vent would

pamper the oxygen-hungry fire. There'd be glass in the yard anyway, since the windows would blow out during stage three of the fire.

Scope around his neck, he dead-bolted the back door, went out the front, and locked it with a key. The next guy in would be slinging a fire ax.

Rick paused to consult his list. He'd worked his way down to the last five—no, four—items without a hitch.

3:30	vent upstairs
4:00	groceries—drop van
4:30	Father Paul
5:00-6:30	Miranda
6:45	Hangin' Tree

Now he'd head down to the grocery for bread and a quart of milk, his usual weekday purchases, then go drink a few beers at the Hangin' Tree. Who would notice that between those two stops, he'd double back to Heart's Ease? No one but Cisco, who would borrow his aunt's Suburban and drop him off.

The beauty of assumption was that anyone who saw Blake's truck would assume she was visiting Andi. And if Blake noticed the Suburban missing and reported it—bingo, Rick had a fall guy. Cisco, in trouble again. Poor dope probably never would get his driver's license.

Back at Heart's Ease, Rick planned to enter through the crawl space between the back windows and come up in the basement. One thing he wouldn't miss was getting stabbed by those blackberry bushes every time he wanted to get into the basement from the outside.

Once there, he would shake some sense into Andi until she talked. If she didn't, he'd move to plan two.

He'd had his eye on Jason's collection of Vincent Price originals, and he knew a few collectors who wouldn't quarrel over provenance papers. He might actually get more for the paintings. But that wasn't the point. Now that Gallatin was involved, Rick wanted the Graveyard Rose.

Whatever he walked away with, he'd be drinking at the Hangin' Tree by 6:45 and he would still be there, with plenty of witnesses, when shadows spread through his A-frame living room, dimming, darkening, until the night-light clicked on and—pouf!—instant inferno.

Rick walked down his carefully raked path. Soon it would be swarming with fire hoses.

"Sorry, Sadie," he muttered, but even he heard his lack of regret. He took one last look over his shoulder before stepping past the black cat.

Foolproof. Bulletproof. And what a kick to beat these redneck firefighters at their own game.

Shoulda cut me just a little slack on that entrance test, guys. He'd been able to do the damned pull-ups, but when he couldn't haul gangly Brother Wolcott down the ladder, they'd claimed he would be a liability.

Liability *this*, assholes.

All he had to do was wait for sundown.

Chapter
Twenty-three

For all that it was a child's game, Kit loved baseball. Not only did Miranda cuddle close so he could mirror her batting stance, but she pitched to him for three-quarters of an hour, while he pretended to beat blood out of a ball on which he imagined Aragon's face.

Baseball was a game of elegant simplicity. He nodded, Miranda pitched, he walloped the ball, and she ran like a retriever to fetch it. She'd been panting like one, too, until she called over two boys in baggy pants and outsized brown gloves. One each.

From the middle of the field, the taller boy considered Kit, then turned back to Miranda.

"Practicing for the majors? I don't think so."

"But *he* does." Miranda's voice dropped as she tapped her temple.

"Miranda! What are you telling those children?"

"Nothing, honey. Batter up!"

Let her babble. This sport required all the skill of the quintain, without the punishment of a sandbag swinging into his skull if he didn't duck.

Crack! Kit gloried in the impact. The shock slammed up his forearms and into his shoulders.

Because he'd tried to wield the bat like a broadsword, it had taken a few swings to get the knack. The stance required for lopping off Aragon's head had resulted in spinning the ball backward or toward his feet.

Then he'd swung at the level of an aristocratic castellan cheekbone and connected. The feeling, as Miranda had called out to him, was "sweet."

Flushed and loose-jointed, Miranda strode toward him. Her hair was fastened high and wound with something like yarn. It wagged side to side like a horse's tail.

The two boys bounded at her heels. The taller of the ill-mannered little louts had a mother who attired him in an older brother's breeches. Still, that didn't excuse a rowdy game of tag in which he placed his sweaty cap on Miranda's head, then dodged aside.

"Go back out," Kit motioned her away, but she kept coming.

"You're done for the day, slugger." Miranda reached toward him and he stepped back. "Kit." She said his name too patiently. "Put down the bat."

'Zounds, she might have addressed a mental defective.

"I've not finished smashing his arrogant face."

Miranda plopped down and leaned against the backstop. The boys, reeking of all-too-apparent pink bubble gum, loitered nearby. Miranda ignored them and peered past locks of hair that curled around her face.

"We need to stop, so we can get a good place at the drive-in."

"Just when it was my ups." The younger boy moaned disappointment. Kit would have echoed him had it not been unseemly.

"The drive-in's only a mile or two down the road," Miranda continued. "But it's built into the west side of Owen Canyon, where it gets dark early."

"That's totally cool," said the baggy one, "because you don't have to wait forever for the movie."

Kit's exhilaration flagged. He couldn't decipher Miranda's

words, though the child obviously understood.

Gravel scraped under Miranda's canvas shoes as she gathered herself to stand.

"My fate is in your hands." Kit bowed, but not before the baggy-pants boy offered Miranda his hand.

Miranda allowed herself to be hauled upright by the presumptuous pup.

"You got a problem, man?" The boy slung stringy hair back from his eyes and sniffed at Kit.

He met the child's eyes, thinking how foolish he'd been to let irritation show. Like Cisco, the boy was at an age where lust ruled good sense. Now, the little princox looked at Miranda's breasts.

"I have no problem." Kit slipped between the boy and Miranda, rested an arm across her shoulders, then tugged until her hip grazed his. "Unless you admired more than the lady's athletic prowess."

Warm from exertion, Miranda's arm curled around his waist. If he'd ever felt such satisfaction, it didn't come to mind.

"Yeah, whatever." The boy and his cohort sprinted across the field, having determined by invisible sign that they were bent on ripping each other's shirts off.

Miranda had left him to lower the car's convertible top, and Kit felt mystified. Why should he do such a thing, if the attraction of drive-ins was "necking"?

The heavily shaded canyon faced a huge white screen. Parking spaces lay so close together, he saw a woman with brownish rings beneath her eyes in the battered car to their left. She dozed, her head against the car frame. Though the compartment beyond her swarmed with children, she opened her eyes and smiled at Kit.

He quelled the impulse to offer her some of Miranda's popped corn, as one of the children spilled some out the car window. The smell of grain and salt tempted him, but Miranda had insisted that the traditional dish wait until the beastly *Romeo and Juliet* began.

In front of Miranda's car, a couple bundled in the rear of

a pickup truck. Their behavior supported Miranda's claim that drive-in intimacy was de rigueur, though he couldn't see how they'd get far past their thick trappings.

In addition to the sleeping bag tucked around them, they wore puffy jackets. When he and Miranda had stopped to buy gasoline at a rustic convenience store, the queued-up customers had gossiped of the week's unseasonable cold.

The clerk behind the counter had offered Miranda a chance to join the "snow pool." Apparently the area was famous for foul weather. It had snowed every month except July.

Nevertheless, a score of hapless fools had laid odds it would.

He'd discouraged Miranda from proffering a dollar from her meager store of bills, then surrendered to her madness when she wrote her guess as noon on the Fourth of July.

Miranda's belief in the impossible was limitless.

Still, even he felt the night's icy chill and worried about the consequences. He didn't fret over the ancient roses Miranda feared would fall to a killing frost. No, Miranda had trundled off to the drive-in's rest room to "freshen up." That worried him; perhaps it included swathing herself in puffy layers.

His skin continued to exult in her touch. And she delighted in giving it. Out on the baseball field, he'd spotted a golden dip next to her knee that begged exploration.

Kit considered the passenger-side latch of the convertible top. Leaving the top up would lend them privacy, but admitting his scheme was too brazen. And here she came.

At first glance, Kit rejoiced. Miranda had clearly sacrificed warmth for accessibility. Arms bare, legs covered only to mid-thigh, the dress showed a bounty of skin. Then Kit noticed there wasn't a button or a lace in sight. And the skirt—wasn't. As she climbed into the seat beside him, he saw that each leg was encased separately.

His wooing skills, though considerable, wouldn't allow him to reach her breast through the leg hole of this modern-day chastity belt.

"Stop frowning." Miranda chafed the gooseflesh on her

arms. "I'll take it back if you don't like it." Then her head cocked to one side. "No, I won't. I like it."

In spite of her dismissive tone, he could tell she was disappointed.

"It's a lovely shade of blue."

She reached for the thermos in the backseat and unscrewed its top. "Is it Swanfort blue?"

Warmth spread from his center to his fingertips. She'd bought it with no thought but honoring him.

"It is very like Swanfort blue." Kit lifted her chin. "But even more like your eyes, which I treasure far above my family colors."

"Wow." Miranda blushed as she sipped the drink she'd poured.

Kit steadied her hand and kissed her. "You taste of wild cherries."

"Cherry Kool-Aid," she explained. He noticed a faint rim of red around her lips. "We always used to have it at the drive-in. Want some?"

"You seem flustered, Miranda. Isn't it time for necking yet?" Kit glanced around. Now the spaces on both sides were filled, and every car but Miranda's had a metal box hooked on its window. Night had turned the sky deep lilac. He could count stars.

"I do feel a little nervous." She handed him her cup, attached the sound box, then fiddled with a knob. "I've never been to the drive-in with a guy. My father wouldn't allow it."

"A wise man." Kit watched the couple tangled in the truck. He tasted the drink and found it unbearably sweet.

"And then when Blake got pregnant here—"

"Wait. Blake, the mother with the mannish-short hair?"

"That's a secret, Kit. I shouldn't have told you."

"My interest does not lie in her morals, I assure you." Kit lifted his hips, gauging the width of the seat, then touched the emergency brake jutting between them. "She didn't tell you true, Miranda."

Her laugh spilled out like silver. "I think he had a bigger car. A Chevy or something."

"All the same."

"Too loud!" Miranda pounced on the blaring sound box and turned it down. "Wow, they're starting on time." She peered at the purpling sky, then settled back to watch the huge images. "Wait until dark," she whispered, drawing her fingers over the back of his hand.

"And then?"

"Shhh." Miranda kept her eyes fixed on the screen, but even in the dim light, he thought she was blushing.

Darkness inside and out. Rick sat at a back table near the rest rooms and watched the Hangin' Tree door open to admit another three volunteer firefighters. Beyond them, the purplish halogen light over Ralph's parking lot had come on.

Cigarette smoke hung thick, the jukebox thumped with deep bass and indistinct country lyrics, and five minutes ago he'd remembered why all the volunteers, even Noah Lincoln, had turned up here. He should have figured the tradition into his plan.

Each Fourth of July the volunteer fire department hosted a steak fry, followed by a safe-and-sane fireworks display. The night before, they always ended the bunting hanging and table arranging with drinks at the Hangin' Tree.

Rick hoped they tied it on good, although he could see two party poopers from here.

Noah Lincoln, looking dejected and nursing a beer, talked with Brother Wolcott. Talking to Brother had that effect on everyone, though the fact that he'd crossed the bar's threshold told the depth of his devotion to the fire department.

Just step into the hardware store on a slow day, and Brother would bore you with the newest fire technology and admit that fascination with fire was his sole vice.

Renetta trailed her fingers on the edge of Rick's table as she headed for the bar. A cloud of Tigress cologne swirled behind her. If it weren't for Chicago, he'd feel sorry that tonight would be the last time he'd see Renetta stroll by with her waitress notepad wagging from her back pocket.

Gina Brown, head of the volunteers' ladies auxiliary, bustled in, jabbering. Rick imagined the whoosh of flames spreading over his silver-gray carpet. Had Gina spotted a glow through the trees?

He listened intently, trying to block out the music and the click of cue stick on balls.

"And this year, Dr. Lincoln, I expect you to keep that huge mangy monster you call a dog away from the dessert table."

"D'you hear that, Gertrude?" Noah called across the room, and damned if there wasn't a woof from under the pool table.

Renetta was well rid of Ralph. Imagine letting a dog into your bar. The guy was just too down-home for words.

Rick fidgeted. It was time. Past time. If not Gina, who'd be the first to notice the fire and report it?

Probably not Andi. Although she could be back by now.

Rick was still pissed about having to jog cross-country back to Heart's Ease. Cisco had turned goody-goody, refusing to take his aunt's car, though Blake and Jan were in Owen, where they'd never know.

Once at Heart's Ease, Rick had seen no sign of Father Paul, so he had waited in the basement, ready to pop out and scare Andi into talking. When she hadn't shown by 6:25, he'd salved his temper by snagging two of the smaller Price paintings and stashed them in the van.

The only other thing of interest had been an official Owen County Sheriff's Department notice gummed to the front door of Heart's Ease. Atop that a blue note read, "Andi— call ASAP." The scrawled signature had been Noah's.

"Hey, there, Rick." Noah's slap on the back rustled the Owen Canyon newspaper Rick pretended to read. " 'Bout got that thing memorized?"

Rick flattened his hands on the table to keep from making a fist to jam in Noah's mouth. "Small-town Friday night," he said, shrugging.

"Tell me about it." Noah jiggled a paper straw in the corner of his mouth. He'd just about chewed the disgusting thing to a pulp. "I had to decide between the Owen County drive-in and making sure the gazebo will hold Sparrow-grass's esteemed string quartet one more year."

"Yeah?" Rick watched Renetta approach.

She gave Noah a playful wink. "Hey, Doc."

"Hi, Renetta. Do me a favor, will you, hon? Keep after Ralph about that blood pressure medication. He just admitted he can't remember it but three or four times a week. That's not enough."

"I'll do that, Doc."

Without blinking, Noah was back to small talk.

"Yeah, Jan and Blake and all their kids went in for back-to-back old and new *Romeo and Juliet*'s."

"Did Andi go with them? Thought I'd talk to her about ripping out that whole bathroom floor. I've got some time tomorrow."

"No, she and that gentleman boarder are staying close to home." Noah's voice didn't change, but his half smile made his comment for him. "They've got some injured hawk they're nursemaiding out in the barn."

So she'd be back soon. And Father Paul surely would have arrived by now. Rick almost rubbed his hands together. It'd take the fire a while to jump the ravine. He'd better get back over there and pay Miss Miranda a visit.

But damn, *why* hadn't Noah's beeper gone off? Or Ralph's emergency radio, sitting there, red light glowing that it was indeed functional. Rick figured if he sat here another ten minutes listening to country bullshit, he'd scream.

". . . believe she wanted us to feed the kids fettuccine instead of beans and weenies tomorrow night?"

Rick shook his head, hoping it passed for interest.

"Hey, did you ever give up drinking?" Noah asked, touching the end of the limp straw. "To keep thin?"

"No, one beer's my limit."

"I figured." Noah looked ready to head toward the bathroom, then he was struck by another thought. "Are you still thinking about taking that job in San Francisco?"

Rick smiled at Noah's perfect timing.

"You know, I'm considering it real seriously, Doc. The college just canceled my favorite class, and San Francisco City College is still after me to come on down."

"That'd be a great opportunity." Noah fiddled with the

squelch button on the radio snapped to his belt. "What d'you have to have to teach at Owen? A master's? I wonder if Andi Fairfield would be interested in applying for your job. She seems to like being back in Sparrowgrass."

Wasn't it just like these provincial hypocrites to pretend to care about a guy, when they were after something else entirely?

"I'll put in a good word for her," Rick said, and he would, even if Miranda Fairfield was in no shape to go back into a classroom ever again.

Noah had been gone only seconds when the emergency tone reverberated through the bar's cozy gloom. The garbled voice was covered by the rest room door slamming open and a dozen men surging toward the parking lot.

Brother Wolcott spoke into his hand-held radio and glanced up at Rick. Smoothing a hand over his balding head, Brother turned preacher for a minute, looking sympathetic.

Yes. Let me have it, Rick thought.

"Rick, you might want to hitch a ride on the volunteer truck. I'm afraid the fire's at your place."

Kit found the movie interesting, though the swordplay was slow, even if he allowed for the men being Italian. The horses stood too tall, and their hooves rang as if they wore modern metal shoes.

But the speech. Kit cleared his throat, damning the scribbler for his authenticity. The players' words made him homesick.

Kit reached for a handful of Miranda's popped corn. It was messy with butter but tasty.

"That one." Kit stabbed his finger toward the screen. "He looks very like Richard Aragon."

Miranda leaned forward so suddenly that the Volkswagen's horn beeped. "Tybalt?"

"Aye." Kit nodded. "Take this wretched stuff." He returned the cup. "It tastes like honeysuckle. Dreadfully sweet."

She quaffed the drink, screwed the top back onto the thermos, then watched him study the well-endowed Juliet.

"And does she look like Arabella?"

Kit bided his time, savoring Miranda's jealousy.

"The same complexion, but other than that, nothing like. My Arabella was a crone of seventeen."

She punched his arm and he ignored her, pretending fascination with an elaborately long love scene on a balcony.

"*Now,* it's time for necking," she said and met him with a claiming kiss.

She teased for only a moment, and then her lips parted and her mouth begged his invasion. He made her wait.

"You bear a fever, Miranda." He spoke against her lips, punctuating his words with kisses. "Not a petty one. Its onset was innocent, and now I blaze with it." His hands skimmed the crisp cloth of her dress. "But by the rood, what would you have me do, when you're sewed into your garments?"

She took his hand beneath her horse-tail hair, to her nape, set his fingers on the tiniest of latches and showed him it would descend.

"A zipper," she said.

Oh, and it *did* descend. A silent groan built within him as the zipper passed the base of her neck and bared the bumps of her spine.

"Forgive me, but I dare not ravish a virgin in this confinement." He could, mayhap, manage it, but it would pain them both and possibly damage the car.

"And have you ravished your share of virgins?" Miranda nipped the side of his neck.

"Never," he said, and it was true.

The purring he heard then did not come from the friar on the screen. It came from Miranda.

"Some people sit in the backseat," she suggested.

He'd noticed its more hospitable dimensions hours ago. Though it was no solution, it was an improvement.

"Yes." Kit reached across, opened her door, and shoved it wide.

Crawling and cramming his knees through the narrow slot behind his seat, he joined her.

In moments, far-off voices interfered with their embrace.

"Did you"—Miranda was breathless, as he wanted her,

so he stopped her words with a kiss. It worked, for a moment. "Did you hear someone call my name?"

"No," he said. A chorus of childish cries came again. "If you don't leave off thinking of other things, I'll feel quite wounded."

Miranda reached over his shoulder and rubbed a clear spot on the fogged window. In his arms, she started.

"Right next to us." Miranda choked back a titter. "It's Jan and Blake and all their kids. And maybe a dog. They're waving."

"Beshrew them all." He felt Andi return their waves. Straightaway she'd be worrying about her reputation.

"They saw us come back here, into the backseat," she said. "There's only one reason—"

"I can think of a dozen." He kissed her cheeks, the tip of her nose, and behind each ear. Through a contortion that turned his head fat with trapped blood, he craned his neck to kiss her knee. "But I would rather show them to you at home."

Miranda hesitated, clearly struck as, damme, so was he, by his use of the word *home*. Heart's Ease felt like home, and it was at Heart's Ease that he would make Miranda his.

Miranda cleared her throat. "Is the movie over?"

"How in heaven's name would I know?"

"Are they still alive? Romeo and Juliet?"

Kit squinted past his seat, toward the windshield. "They look lively enough. I can see his bare bum, Miranda."

"Oh, this is where it starts getting sad."

"We can't have that." Kit took her hand to his mouth and nipped the soft swelling at the base of her thumb. She trembled and he smiled. "Lady, won't you come home with me?"

Chapter
Twenty-four

With the rooftops of Sparrowgrass in sight, Miranda pulled over to allow the passage of a green Forest Service fire truck. Even with the Volkswagen's heater switched on full blast, the sirens' wail penetrated the car.

"I turned off the stove," Miranda muttered. "I didn't use my curling iron, and there hasn't been a fire in the fireplace for days."

At first, it simply appeared that the cloud bank that had obscured the western mountains had reversed positions. But the vapor glowed underneath.

"You've no reason to think it's Heart's Ease," Kit said it, knowing very well he sounded as nervous as she.

"Except *that*—" She took her hand from the steering wheel to gesture. "Is in exactly the right spot."

He tried to prove her wrong, by vanishing, checking the estate, and returning to this very seat. *He could not.*

By Christ's holy nails.

Kit swallowed, wet his lips, and closed his eyes to try again. In the early days he'd learned to disappear by curling

in on himself, then expanding his energy to blend with
Earth's vapors. He tried it now.

Nothing.

He leaned his head back against the seat and prayed. If he
could not dematerialize, if the letting go and fading, which
had become a reflex as natural as a sneeze, refused to happen,
had God declared him a new man?

Well, then, God knew Kit Aragon was a soldier, not a
man of philosophy. With a battle before him, he would fight.

If only Miranda would hurry. At home, Judith stood tethered by her jesses in the midst of an inferno. Trifle, too stiff
to jump her fences, would gallop in circles, surrounded by a
wall of flame. And that cat.

This fire reeked of Rick Aragon, and traitors never considered their casualties.

Once more Kit willed himself to vanish and find his way
through the ether to Heart's Ease. Once more he stayed solid
in his seat.

Miranda took a hard right turn out of Sparrowgrass, then
glanced his way. "Can't you—" She made a gesture. "Go
there?"

"I tried."

She turned to him. In the car's dim interior, her mouth fell
open. The tires stuttered off the road onto the shoulder and
his head struck the window. The sound made her jerk the
steering wheel back toward center.

"Can you drive faster?" he asked.

"Yes." She slammed her foot to the floor, and the car
jerked.

"Without killing us, I mean."

Miranda took a deep breath and held it. Killing *us*. He
heard his moronic question, but he didn't amend it.

"I think so," she said. "Hang on."

Oh, God, *oh, God*. Andi braked outside the gates of the
estate. The fire approached in a blast of burning pine. What
if it jumped the ravine and burned through the thicket up to
Heart's Ease? What if Dinah came back to a charred skeleton
of her home?

Before Kit jumped out of the car, Andi pulled a U-turn, pointing the Volkswagen out, so she could get back down the dirt road in a hurry.

What had Brother Wolcott said? Better hope there was no fire, since her narrow road would have to serve as exit and egress? Well, there were no fire trucks in her yard. The volunteers must be attacking the blaze at its source. She pictured the huge vehicles, engines laboring as they shouldered through the brush to the other side of the ravine.

"Stop now. I'm out." Kit slammed the door, then cocked his head at the sound of Trifle's neigh and galloping hooves. "I'll free Judith and lead the mare out." He walked away, still giving orders. "Drive back to town. Stay at the Dancing Goat, so I'll know where to find you."

Andi turned off the ignition, reached into the backseat for the backpack that had held their snacks, then dumped it and brought it along. It might hold a few of Dinah's things. Or Lily.

Smoke grayed the night. Squinting, she saw nothing beyond the back fence, though fire reflected from the bottom of the smoke, lending a weird radiance to the yard around her. Shouts echoed across the ravine. The fire must be at Rick's.

A shape emerged from the haze. Kit stood in front of her.

"Miranda, get in the car and drive away. I'll free Judith and the horse—even the bloody cat, if you insist—and I'll be right behind you. Now, go."

"Okay, but first I need to water down the roofs."

Trifle's neigh changed from high-pitched squeals to a deep, rapid chuckle. Andi had never heard the sound before, but she recognized terror.

"There's no fire on the roof," Kit said.

"That's just the point. If I wet it down, maybe the fire will jump right over us."

Kit's eyes narrowed. Would he force her, push her, and drag her to the car? His face had turned to that of a ruthless stranger, the sort of man who lopped off heads and burned villages.

And then they heard it.

Train-loud roaring crossed the ravine. Cold wind, quail rustling in the blackberry bushes, everything stopped.

Andi grabbed Kit's arm. She wanted to believe it was over, but the blaze was still hungry. It ate the forest with an innocent sound like a campfire nibbling at kindling.

"Look! Kit, my God, look."

High tongues of flame, satiny orange and soaring, reached above the smoke.

"Wetting the roofs may be wise. There are hoses for each of us. I'll get the carriage house roof, as soon as I free the bird. But—Miranda?"

Andi was nodding, turning away, "Yes?"

"If I come for you, you *will* go."

Andi didn't argue, she hurried. She turned on the faucet, grabbed the ladder, and slanted it against the house, amazed that its icicle-cold burned her fingers. Smoke pressed sulfurous gray around her as she climbed, hose slung over her shoulder.

Panic. It lurched from the pit of her stomach and grabbed her throat. She hadn't stood on the roof since she was thirteen. The roof narrowed like a church steeple. She wanted to lie flat and hold on. She didn't. She fought the need to gasp and suck in breaths of searing smoke.

Water pressure. Only a trickle pattered from the hose. She needed it bad. How long 'til she should give up? A cold torrent burst past her hands, strong enough to spray the shingles covering Heart's Ease. So where was Kit? Andi couldn't think, fight nausea, and swirling vertigo at the same time. She could only aim the hose and stay upright.

Judith saved her. With a cry of rejoicing, the falcon burst free, mounting straight for the heavens. She hit thick smoke, banked away, and rode the hot air currents up. With wing tips spread, she went gliding over Heart's Ease, over Sparrowgrass, aiming for the far mountains.

Andi blinked, stirred by a sight she would never forget.

So, she'd remember it later. Now, she had to squirt the roof and keep her soles flat on the slippery shingles as she edged toward the ladder.

Finally, she saw movement on the dark carriage house roof. Kit. The winds mounted. Oddly tropical in the frigid night, they bore away most of his shout.

"... arse out of here!"

A spurt of irritation and then, as she watched, Kit took a step, wavered, and sank.

"Kit!"

What if he'd fallen through a rotten spot in the wooden shingles? That barn was a hundred years old and while Heart's Ease wore a new roof, the carriage house didn't.

He braced his hands and pushed himself up, and then he stood. Andi sucked in a breath, thinking of Kit's poor leg, raked by verminous boards. Then she choked on smoke and the possibility that Kit was mortal.

Panting, she threw the hose off the roof, toward the grass below. While it fell like an awkward snake, she descended, feet finding each rung as fast as they could.

Kit. If he died, *again*, in this place and time, because of her, she'd know the truth. Three times was a sure thing, and the world would be better without her.

Melodrama, damn it. He wouldn't die, and she had a whole heck of a lot to do before she indulged in sentimental bunk.

Like drench the roses. Andi dragged the hose through the back gate, sprayed them as they bowed, then cranked off the faucet so Kit had more water pressure.

"I'm getting Lily. I'll meet you at the car," she shouted against the fire's roar. She snatched up the backpack she didn't remember dropping. "At the *car*."

Kit nodded and Andi ran for the veranda. She peeled a sales notice of some sort off the front door and let it drop.

The door harp bonged her entrance. How normal. And how silly that she'd never taken the annoying thing down. She closed the door firmly so Lily wouldn't slip out.

Something was wrong.

"Geez, Andi, d'you think so?" She mocked herself for flicking on each light switch she passed and blamed the smoke and hellish shadows for the vise of foreboding.

"Lily, here, kitty, kitty."

Andi spun at a creak behind her. Nothing. Damn, she'd been alone at night too many times to get freaked out by old boards torqued in mountain winds.

"Lily girl. Hurry, kitty."

A definite thumping shuddered the wall running from the basement to her bedroom. Not starlings. No, in spite of the nailed door, Lily had found a way to negotiate the secret passage. But why did it sound as if the cat were dragging a pair of shoes along with her?

An unfamiliar smell made Andi pause in the kitchen. Faintly chemical, like kerosene. No, it was smoke. Not the heavy, throat-clogging wood smoke from outside, but cigarette smoke.

"Or," she mumbled, "it could be insanity."

Close the windows. Tear down the curtains. Sprinkle everything with water. She should, but Kit was waiting. She slammed a window shut and called again.

"Lily!"

The cat cried from the basement.

I'm coming, kitty. Andi eased on the light switch outside the basement door. *Don't run and hide.* She turned the doorknob, lifted, and pulled. *Wait for Andi. She'll take care of you.* She left the door ajar and proceeded softly down the stairs.

The fitful overhead lights sputtered as she descended. Her hand clutched the river-rock walls for balance. At her age, Dinah really should have handrails installed.

The old sewing machine, the freezer, and the costume rack shimmered electric blue. Did a suit sway on its own? Was the draped mannequin facing half a turn too far to the right?

Three steps short of the cement floor, she saw a white tail slip beneath the last step.

Yes!

Outside, that freight-train roaring recommenced. Closer. Hotter. Kit, if you get out before I do, don't come back for me.

Time had run out. If Lily got away, she was on her own. Andi stepped off the final step, turned and eased into a squat. In the dark beneath the last step, she heard the cat purring.

Then she made out Lily, content in her makeshift den, curled around the Graveyard Rose.

Lily batted pencils off tabletops. Lily tapped earrings to watch them plummet off the dresser. Lily had trailed Andi to the washing machine the day of the Renaissance Faire. Andi remembered her eagerness to strip off the cigar-scented sheets draping Dinah's furniture. She must have gathered the Graveyard Rose with the fluttering armload. Then Rick had come. She hadn't started the wash until morning. By then, Lily must have pursued the tumbling box beneath the basement stairs.

As Andi reached for the silver box, the basement door creaked and she heard popping. *Popping?* Whatever it was wouldn't stop her from grabbing what Kit had searched four hundred years to find.

Lily complained as Andi slid the box away. The metal filigree felt warm, as if it welcomed her touch after weeks in the dank. Andi's thumb felt a dent, a broken piece of silver lace. Barrett had used the butt of a left-handed dirk to pound the metal from a sword hilt into a casket for Kit's heart.

It was true. And she could give it back to him.

Miffed with Andi's preoccupation, Lily emerged. Upright and attentive, tail curled to hide her toes, the cat watched Andi twist the backpack around and slip the box inside.

Perfect timing, except that when she moved to intercept Lily, the cat exploded into a spitting puffball.

"Give me the backpack, Andi." Rick stood at the top of the stairs.

"Nope." She shrugged the straps over both shoulders and squared them to balance the weight of the box. He'd have to dismember her to take it.

At first he was silhouetted against the upstairs light. Then Rick took a few rapid steps toward her, and the fitful light glared on his face. He looked sweaty.

"You don't really want it, Andi." The sound he made was too tense for a sigh. "It's safer with a collector who'll never meet Christopher Gallatin. You know what will happen when Gallatin opens that box?"

"Not a damned thing," she said.

"I'm afraid this is a poor time to champion logic." He took a long breath. "You can trust me on this subject, if nothing else. We all know what's in there."

Rick moved closer. The stairway was so narrow. Could she sprint past him? She'd have to shove hard, to slam him against the river rock. Even then, it might only enrage him. He didn't seem to have a weapon. He'd underestimated her, so a distraction might be enough. Quickness might conquer strength.

"Open that box and Christopher Gallatin will be right back where he lost his heart. On some foggy battlefield with Barrett astride his body, sobbing as he hacks out his brother's heart. Then he'll die."

Andi resisted Rick's story, refusing to give him an edge.

"Except," Rick continued, "for just an instant, the Gallatin you know will see it and feel it and regret ever meeting you."

Popping went off like gunshots, Lily darted between Rick's legs and Andi followed. Feint high, hit low. She rushed him, butted her shoulder against his, and socked him in the stomach.

"No!" Rick loomed, thrusting his torso into her face. The impact rocked her back as she was supposed to be shoving past him. She was trying to force her way by when she stumbled backward. She stayed upright, fingers clutching the river rocks, as darkness fell all over again.

The popping.

Flames in the power lines had doused all the lights.

Then there was a grunting movement, and Rick kicked her in the face.

A snap, tears, and distress signals of aquamarine rain flashed inside her skull. Reflex made her hands jerk up. Too late to protect her face, she grabbed Rick's ankle and cranked his foot far right. He screamed and fell against her right hip. She shoved past him.

"I'll kill you! Goddamn it! I'll kill you!"

Andi heard the spiderish pounce as he humped up the stairs on his belly. He made several at a time, straining to catch her leg. She heard him slip, strike rock, and tumble down the stairs.

She didn't stop.

A yellow glare—not lights but fire—lit the great room, casting shadows in unfamiliar places. She ran out, across the veranda, into the yard, toward the shine of her own headlights.

"It's about bloody time." Kit held the nerved-up mare in place. Trifle obeyed on the strength of training. Instinct would have spurred her well down the road.

That point would have proven that Miranda lacked good sense, if he hadn't felt the clutch in his chest.

Here she came. Just when he'd been about to take the rope coiled on Trifle's saddle, stride into the house, and drag her out at the end of it.

Relief didn't stop him from noticing her awkward side-to-side gait with the backpack pounding time or that wraith of a cat bounding behind her as she collapsed against the car door, wrapping her arms with trembling hands.

"Didagelily." The clogged and nasal quality of her speech mystified him but only for a moment.

"Of course you did, foolhardy wench. The cat's there between your feet."

Miranda was crying. But why?

She scooped the cat up from the dirt, juggled its claws away from her bare arms, and slung it into the car. As she threw the backpack after it, the Volkswagen's interior light showed blood. Not scratches. Blood streamed from Miranda's nose and smeared her cheeks. Her lips were slick crimson and a gout of it had marked her dress of Swanfort blue.

"What in God's name happened? From here, I saw the lights go out. Did you run into something? 'sblood, if you hadn't insisted on charging back in there for a stupid animal."

"I saw Judith."

"Oh, shut up, will you, Miranda? Get in the car and *drive away*. Your blood. It made me think—"

She swayed against the car and grabbed the mirror for support. "I left him in the basement. I didn't mean for him to burn."

God's bones. Aragon.

Miranda wept, but he couldn't comfort her. Not yet.

"Besides your face." Kit wedged the words from a throat hard with dread. "Did he hurt you?"

"I'm okay."

Kit nodded. Miranda couldn't hear him praise a God who'd confined him for four hundred years. She could guess he offered another four hundred in thanksgiving.

Sirens screamed closer, and lights gleamed from the foot of the driveway, half a mile away.

He would have Aragon before some poltroon rescued him.

"Can you drive past? I dare not ride Trifle by them," he lied. "It would be dangerous. I'll wait, give Trifle some space, and then follow you."

As soon as she nodded and slipped into the car, Kit wheeled the white mare on her haunches. She reared, fighting the pressure of his legs and the insanity of running toward fire. Still, he sent her back.

Beneath the sirens, Kit heard scrabbling at the back of the house. The quail had flown, long since. This sound had a desperate, human quality.

Miranda had not killed the last Aragon.

Kit reined Trifle through the back gate. Head tossing, the mare picked her way around the corner. The fire burned bright as ten thousand torches, lighting the khaki-clad backside emerging from the blackberries.

Aragon had saved him time, and a slog down the basement stairs. The villain was cursing and limping. One side of his face was swollen and discolored. He walked a few steps, then stopped to examine his scratches.

Trifle snorted and pawed the ground, alerting him.

"Get away from me." Aragon backed up several steps and Kit's spirits sank. Until now Rick had been a worthy enemy, but physical courage was not his forte.

"Oh, weak and puling boy, a disgrace even to your whipped-cur ancestors." Kit felt bile rise at the truth of it.

Then he thought of Miranda's blood. "Bested by a woman, you crawl out on your belly, expecting nature's mercy. Well done, Aragon. Better you beg mercy from fire, for you will have none of mine."

Aragon could not even be taunted into boldness. He bolted toward the woods.

Scorn counseled Kit to let him go, but he could not. The men fighting the fire had showed some mettle. They might risk worthy lives for this coward.

Kit pivoted Trifle on her hind feet and cut off Aragon's escape. He had a mounted man's advantage, but if he dismounted to even the odds, he might lose the horse.

"You've got no evidence." Aragon stood tall for a moment. "Of anything."

"Other than a blood-soaked woman and a man crawling out of her house, what sort of evidence does a ghost need, I wonder?"

Aragon shifted to the balls of his feet. They both heard laboring engines, shouts, and the clang of a truck colliding with the flower-twined front gate of Heart's Ease.

Aragon pulled a knife.

"Well done," Kit scoffed, but when Aragon lunged toward the mare's breast, Kit flung himself right, slipped to the ground, and sent the horse off with a slap on the flank.

Aragon moved with slow, untrained clumsiness. He swung the knife before him in wide strokes. Such an easy target. There was little pleasure in backhanding the knife out of Aragon's grip and less in watching him fall.

"Stand," Kit shouted. "Stand, if you be a man."

Aragon huddled, covering his face, and since Trifle had moved off only a few steps, Kit took the rope from her saddle.

If the swine would not fight, Kit could at least have the pleasure of leading an Aragon through the streets of town in defeat.

"This is your doing, is it not?" Kit nodded toward the fire as he looped the rope around Aragon's wrists. "And the priest? Was he yours too?"

Alertness parted Rick's misery. "Father Paul. He'll be

back, Gallatin, I've seen him work. He's the real thing.''

"I, apparently, am not.'' Kit let his words sink in. He would not try to explain, for he could not. "I'll not forgive you that delay. While he demanded that I speak devilish talk and walk through walls, Miranda could have fallen.''

Oh, now excitement mounted in the churl's cheeks. At mention of Miranda. Kit longed to kill him, but he would not go to hell from this lifetime, for the death of this fragment.

But the craving for violence wouldn't leave. Once more, before he cinched the rope tight in a handcuff knot, Kit tried to provoke Aragon.

"Before I send you on your way, I would know what other beastliness you've wrought.''

Aragon's blood was not so waterish that he didn't hear the dare.

"I screwed Mir—''

"Liar.''

This time he clouted Aragon full in the face. He used his fist, and it was no impervious, ghostly hand. Kit struck with a man's fist. The impact skinned his knuckles, scrabbled the delicate bones in his hands, and felt bloody marvelous.

Chapter
Twenty-five

Trifle's hooves clopped across the empty Hangin' Tree tavern parking lot.

Years aplenty had passed since Kit Gallatin had ridden horseback to a tavern door and rapped for the barkeep. In those days, if he'd dragged an Aragon behind his horse, Kit would have celebrated the night long. This time, he wanted rid of the blackguard so he could go to Miranda.

Trifle pulled at the bit, then twisted to nudge Kit's foot in the stirrup. It was past time to unsaddle the mare and rub her old sinews, but first Kit must surrender Aragon to Noah Lincoln.

Kit rapped again. He did not relish meeting the cuckolded Ralph. Still, relinquishing Aragon to Renetta's ill-used husband had a pretty ring of fairness. Noah Lincoln was entirely too evenhanded to be a sheriff.

"They're both volunteer firefighters." Aragon stood even with the mare. "No one'll be here."

Kit kept the rope taut as he looked down on Aragon. *This* was what Kit hated of Miranda's time. Cutpurses and cutthroats were no scarcer, but justice had turned mawkish.

When all was finished, Aragon would be alive.

Aragon's scorn had rebounded, and his energy was high. He had the stamina of a coursing hound. Even with a twisted ankle, the walk had not tired him a jot.

The door opened a foot, releasing smells of ale and peanuts and men. But it was a woman's dark hair that glinted beneath the streetlights.

"We're closed. Everybody's at the—" Renetta startled at the thick pall of smoke that lay on the streets. Then she noticed Aragon. "Rick!" Her tone melded shock and shame.

Kit might have told her Miranda had bashed Rick Aragon's head and blacked his eye, but he waited.

The door slammed behind her as she came outside.

Kit swung Trifle's hindquarters around, so he sat at an angle to these plotters. With his mistress at hand, Aragon could be dangerous. Already the traitor's eyes signaled her to act.

Renetta had the nerve, but Kit would wager the trollop served no man who couldn't serve her. She looked from Rick's bound hands, to Kit, calculating.

"Better not, madam."

She gave a small flounce, as if frustrated, but he thought it was playacting for Aragon.

"Might I use your portable telephone?" Kit had formed this strategy over the dark miles from Sparrowgrass. It seemed the surest way to keep Aragon captive.

"My cell phone? Sure."

Kit hoped that was indeed the implement he'd seen on Aragon's floor. It was a risk, allowing her to return to the bar.

With her hand on the door, Renetta flashed a considering look over them both, but Kit watched Aragon, not the woman. Aragon tensed, straining to convey something, but Renetta's bland expression made Kit think she'd already chosen to cooperate and keep her losses small.

As the door closed behind her, Kit considered the chance that he'd misread her completely,

"Aragon," Kit snapped, "if she returns with a weapon,

you'll learn how it feels to gallop down this street on your belly.''

Renetta might have heard. When she returned, she held the telephone out before her and didn't balk when Kit ordered her to stay at the door, then rode off a few lengths, with Rick in tow.

''911 Operator,'' came the voice on the line.

''I must speak with Noah Lincoln.''

''Sir, this line is for emergency calls only.''

''I have a burglar who attacked and injured a woman. He's trussed up, and I'm holding him for Noah Lincoln.''

''Sir, just to verify, you're calling from Owen Canyon, California, and you're . . .''

''Sparrowgrass.''

''Sparrowgrass, California, and you're holding a burglar who has assaulted a woman?''

''That's right.''

''Sir, are you in any physical danger?''

''Of course not.''

''Is the woman safe at this time?''

''Yes.'' Kit didn't have the stomach for much more foolery. The question made him hope that Blake and Jan knew some doctoring.

''The burglar is not armed—is that correct, sir?''

''Not anymore.''

''And the name?''

''His name is Richard Aragon.''

''That—excuse me, sir. That's the *intruder's* name? Richard A-R-A-G-O-N.'' Her fingers tapped quickly, transmitting the message, he thought. ''That's *A*dam, *R*obert, *A*dam—''

''Madam, there's no time to waste,'' Kit said. Let her make of that what she would.

''Your name and location, sir?''

''Sparrowgrass, California, as I said. Look, there are things to be done here.''

''Don't hang up, sir. Could you describe your location more precisely, so I can dispatch a deputy to help you?''

''I don't need any bloody help. I need Noah Lincoln to

take this capon off my hands. I'm in front of the Hangin'
Tree tavern.''

''And this is where the assault took place?''

''Madam, just send Lincoln.''

More tapping. Kit decided the system was futile. He had
no patience for waiting at Lincoln's office. Better to cut Aragon's throat with his own knife.

''Sir, would that be *Dr.* Noah Lincoln or Deputy Sheriff
Noah Lincoln?''

Kit didn't swear. He didn't grab his forehead in frustration,
though the action appealed. ''The deputy.''

''Sir, I can't patch you through, but I have Deputy Lincoln
on another line. Can you hold?'' The voice vanished, then
suddenly returned. ''Sir, the deputy is on the scene of a structure fire near your location. He will respond to the Hangin'
Tree bar, but he's asked me to determine who has Richard
Aragon in custody.''

Sigh. ''Christopher Gallatin.''

''That's C, as in *C*harles . . .''

''Tell him Kit Gallatin of Heart's Ease estate—''

''Sir, Deputy Lincoln overheard your outburst.'' Oddly,
the operator's voice held no reprimand. ''He's indicated that
Owen County Sheriff's Department, which is on holiday
staffing, will *not* be responding a regular deputy to your
scene. Deputy Lincoln says 'just keep holding Aragon' and
he'll be with you shortly.''

For ten minutes Kit had stared at the telephone's power
button. Now he pushed it.

Hellfire. He should have said he'd wait at the Dancing
Goat.

''When Lincoln gets here, please tell him he'll find his
charge tethered to the hitching ring in front of the Dancing
Goat.''

''But you just—'' Renetta began.

Aragon's eye had swollen almost closed. He blinked re-
peatedly as he protested.

''You can't go dragging me cross-country and parading
me up and down Main Street in the middle of the goddamned

night, then put me out on the curb for Lincoln to pick up like garbage.''

Trifle pawed at the asphalt, blowing impatient breath through her lips. Kit patted her neck, then glanced at Aragon.

''Whyever not?'' He wheeled Trifle toward town. ''Renetta, you understand what I've asked?''

''Got it,'' she said, ''But, oh, Rick, why don't I get your keys out of your pocket?''

She started forward.

''Stop.''

''It's okay, I only thought—'' Her tone turned too pleasant. ''Rick has an appointment tomorrow. And I could deal with his business associate, if I could get into his van.'' She indicated that it was a simple request. ''That's going to be really important, Mr. Gallatin.'' Her voice dropped to a conspiring purr. ''Rick has a little loan from my husband, and I think, under the circumstances, Ralph will want it paid back right away.''

''I've no doubt you're correct. When Lincoln arrives, tell him.''

Renetta started forward again. ''I'll just dip into Rick's pocket now and save us all a lot of trouble.''

''Later, perhaps.'' Kit put the mare into a trot. Aragon was hard-pressed to keep up, at first. ''I'm sure he'll look forward to it.''

''He'll go nuts when he sees you. He may kill Rick.'' Blake shepherded Andi toward an overstuffed chair by the front window.

Before she sat, Andi made sure the black backpack lay where she'd put it.

''I thought my face looked sort of okay.'' Andi shivered and pulled the backpack closer. The air was cold, outside the shower-steamy bathroom of the apartment over the Dancing Goat. ''What do you think?'' She took the ice pack off the side of her nose.

''It looks fine. I don't think it's even going to bruise, but in Cisco's sweats, you look fragile. I think this took a little something out of you, sweetie.''

"I'm just worried for Kit."

Melissa and the twins played with Lily on the braided rag rug. Blake and Cisco watched Andi, braced for more drama.

Andi sniffed and handed Blake the ice. She pulled the cuffs of the borrowed sweatshirt over her fingers.

"You can have those sweats." Cisco's hands stayed in his pockets as he shrugged. "The color's so gay."

"The color is *toast*, you moron, a very cool shade for guys secure enough to wear it," Melissa looked up to sneer at her cousin. "I helped Mom pick them out, so—"

"I tried Noah again," Jan bustled in from downstairs, bearing a cup of tea. "His service is still answering, so I guess he's still at the fire. Drink this."

As Andi sipped mint tea, Jan fidgeted beside her.

"I know you've never liked Rick," Jan said, "but are you sure you want to call the police? Couldn't this have been a misunderstanding?"

Andi shivered. Half her chill was from sitting outside the Dancing Goat, waiting for the Kerns to arrive home from the drive-in. Both Blake and Jan had held a sleeping twin and each had handed hers off to a teenager when they saw Andi's bloody dress.

In spite of that, Jan remained skeptical and Cisco silent. Even as Jan perched on the arm of the chair, Andi gazed out the front window. Main Street at midnight was empty and she had no energy to argue. Where was Kit?

"Mom, if I tell you some stuff that happened, like, way in the past, you can't get mad, okay?"

"I'll try not to," Jan said.

"I mean, you can't hold it against me, for my license."

Andi applied the ice pack, hard. Did she want to hear this? Did she want to do anything besides crawl into the safety of Kit's arms?

"Go ahead, honey." Jan sat stiff on the chair's arm.

"Okay, I know I'm, like, in charge of my own actions, but I think Rick was sort of using me."

Jan bolted up from the chair arm, arms outstretched.

"Mom, gol, get a grip." Cisco blushed. "Not like that. He kept going over stuff about Clint, telling me how women

can make a guy do stuff he wouldn't normally do." He nodded toward Andi. "And I, kind of, did that thing on the front
of Heart's Ease."

"The graffiti," Blake said.

"Not really, it was just painting over some letters as a
joke. A mean joke, maybe, but we were going to paint over
all of them the next day anyway."

Andi wet her lips. A boy with a good vocabulary, a boy
so clever at Scrabble, would see it that way.

"I didn't really think anyone would notice."

Adults were so dense, Andi thought, and gave him an en-
couraging smile. It hurt. She looked out at the empty street
once more. *Kit.*

"What about the flowers?" Blake asked.

"No, I didn't do that. Or break the windshield, or blow
the fuses."

"I didn't tell anyone about the fuses," Andi said. "Did
Noah tell you?"

"Rick did. And about the, you know, the underwear."

"The *underwear*?" Jan swallowed her dismay, then shook
her head. "Go on."

Cisco leaned against the wall, arms crossed as he stared
at his feet. "In Andi's accident, some of her— Mom, Rick
was, uh, getting such a thrill out of that, I—" Lips still open,
Cisco watched his mother. "It was like, *sick,* Mom. He was
trying to get me to do more things to get back at Andi, and
she's not that bad. I mean, she *can* play football, and I was
starting to believe you and Aunt Blake about her being okay,
in spite of Clint."

Cisco stopped, and his Adam's apple moved.

Blake stood at the window, staring down, giving mother
and son privacy to weigh each word and reaction.

Andi watched the twins curled up on the rug with Lily.
Dozing, Cami sucked her thumb and fingered the cat's fur.

"So, I did one last thing—moved Trifle out of her corral
and tied her upstream. That was the Tuesday after Father's
Day, and"—Cisco cleared his throat—"I felt like Dad was
looking down, all ashamed.

"After that, I didn't do anything. Really, Mom, Rick came

here tonight and wanted me to drive him to Heart's Ease. I know where the spare keys are, in that lame hide-a-key thing in the walk-in freezer, but I didn't go. I turned up the stereo really loud and didn't answer the phone either.'' With a grimace, he looked at Andi. ''Sorry I didn't hear you knocking.''

''You're a good boy.'' Jan hugged the son who stood inches taller than she.

Andi sniffed. Her throat ached and her right ear rang as if Rick had kicked it too.

''Could Kit be riding a horse?'' Blake asked.

Andi ignored the jolt of dizziness and joined Blake.

''See horsey . . .'' Cami reached out a drowsy hand.

From the window, Andi saw Trifle clopping down the street. Kit must be the rider.

By the time she got downstairs, without the shoes Jan admonished her to wear, Rick was tied to a hitching post.

Kit's eyes met hers as she flung open the Dancing Goat's door. He stood a few yards off, lifting Trifle's saddle.

''You're all right?'' Kit spoke before she could. His British inflection had never sounded so dear. The streetlight and heavy layer of smoke leached the color from his skin. He looked tired. He kept a hand on the mare's sweaty back and his gaze on Rick, but the single searching look in her direction said he'd worried.

''I'm fine.'' Her words came out on a frosty plume. How she wanted to grab Kit and wrap her arms around him, seeking more than shelter from the cold.

His hand was bleeding.

''Stay back, Miranda,'' he snapped. ''He may only be playing the eunuch.'' Kit's lips twitched as Jan and Blake and Cisco crowded the sidewalk. ''I suppose I daren't ask why we have the whole family gathered 'round.''

''I'm sort of, like, *involved,* man,'' Cisco snarled.

Jan made a reflexive move to quiet him, then stopped. Cisco's anger was aimed at Rick.

''Pardon me. You're right, of course.'' Kit pressed his lips together. Ice tipped his beard. ''Do you have a weapon?''

''What?'' Blake blurted. ''A *what?*''

Cisco seemed to straighten ten inches.

"Yeah." He detached the chain lapping from his pocket.

Jan moaned, but Kit treated Cisco like another man. Andi wondered how old his brother, Barrett, had been when Kit did the same for him.

"I tied him too blessed loose," Kit told Cisco. "Because he wanted to sit on the curb. As you see, he hasn't. Watch him while I tie the horse. Unless you'd rather—"

"I'll watch the son of a bitch."

Andi felt a shiver of warning. This wasn't a movie, where everything turned out all right, but Cisco didn't know that.

"Don't talk. Just watch." Kit led Trifle a half block away, to the next hitching ring.

Shake it off, Andi told herself. Kit could sprint that far in an instant. She'd obviously hurt Rick by shoving him down the basement stairs. Besides, Rick's hands were tied together. The rope was tied to the hitching ring. Five of them stood watching. What could Rick do?

Kit slipped Trifle's bit from her mouth. He was tying her bridle reins to the hitching ring when Melissa burst out of the Dancing Goat's front door.

"Where is she? Little monster, I got her dressed for bed," Melissa gestured helplessly at Blake. "And while I was getting Cody ready—"

Bundled in a footed sleeper, Cami dashed from behind Andi's parked VW and sprinted toward Trifle. To do that, she had to pass Rick.

He swooped over her. The short rope between his hands caught Cami under the chin and he lifted the struggling child off her feet.

"Keep back!" Rick shouted as Jan leapt toward him. "Back *off!*"

"Maaaa!"

Andi felt gooseflesh at Cami's strangled scream.

With nightmarish slowness Kit approached, step by step, watchful and fluid.

"You." Rick glared at Andi. "I want your car keys."

"They're upstairs, I—" Through the door, up the stairs someplace in the bathroom. The trip seemed too far.

"No, I've got 'em." Cisco stood closest to Rick. He pulled a knot of car keys from his pocket. "I was going to move it around back." He took a stride toward Rick.

But they weren't her keys. Her keys were upstairs.

"Kick 'em over here."

"Put Cami down first." Cisco dangled the keys.

"Look, kid. Don't pull any bullshit. Kick them over." Rick let Cami's sleeper touch the sidewalk as the keys jingled across the sidewalk, a yard from his feet.

"Mama! Maaa!"

"Shut up!" Rick jerked the rope but left Cami on her feet. His face contorted, and he blinked fiercely to see past his swollen eyelid. "Gallatin, cut me loose. From the post. Don't come any closer than that." He shifted his stare to Jan. "Make them listen, Jan. I don't want to take Cami with me, but I will if I need her for a shield."

"Please, stay back," Jan whispered.

No one told Rick he wouldn't get away with it. No one told him Noah Lincoln was on his way. He knew everything they did, and he was desperate enough to try anyway. *Except for the keys. The keys won't work. What will he do to Cami when the keys won't work?*

A rushing sound, like the release of a truck's air brake, made them all turn. All except Kit, apparently, because when Andi turned back, Kit had advanced a few steps.

"I said, no farther than the ring." Rick wheeled on Kit. "You may be safe, but this kid isn't."

Kit's hair had come loose, and his head was tilted to one side. *Trying to appear harmless,* Andi thought, but the lazy, low-lidded look countered the impression. Kit was watching for an opening. A single distraction.

Rick hunched over Cami as he bellowed at Kit. "Now cut the rope. You've got my knife, *cut it!*" He looked down, judging the distance to the keys. He reached out with one foot and winced. "Andi, get them. Not you, hero," he sneered at Cisco as the boy fidgeted. Rick nodded toward Andi again. "Do it—now."

Andi swallowed and took a step. "Okay." She tried to say it in a qualified tone, wavering, as if she had something to add. Two more steps. "I will, but here comes—"

Every head turned but hers. Andi dove, tackling Rick at the knees. Asphalt rushed up to meet her. Rick's knee caught her under the chin. *Damn the man.* Rick didn't fall, but he staggered and that was enough. Before she caught a breath, Kit and Cisco piled on. Cisco snatched Cami and rolled out of reach, but Rick had the knife. *How? How?* He yanked a handful of Andi's sweatshirt. It tightened at her throat and came up her torso, but only for an instant.

Rick's weight lifted away, twisting. Andi scuttled out of reach as Kit slammed an arm around Rick's ribs. And then Kit had the hand holding the knife. He bowed it back toward Rick's forearm. The knife clattered to the street and Rick's shout sharpened into a scream. Kit bent the hand back, farther and farther, at an unnatural angle.

Andi heard the bones break. They popped, and Rick flopped loose in Kit's grip. Face drawn with disgust, Kit thrust Rick forward onto the street and stood beside him, legs braced wide, waiting.

Rick's moan, the friction of his pants as he writhed against the street, and Cami's sobbing all pressed into Andi's ears. She pushed skinned palms against the street and gathered her feet beneath her to stand.

Blake helped, but her face was bent toward Rick. "You bastard." She glanced at Kit. "I'll get the gun."

"Aw, shucks." Noah Lincoln stepped out of the Dancing Goat with his revolver drawn. "Let me."

Chapter
Twenty-six

Blankets and borrowed parkas kept Kit and Andi from shivering atop the love seats on opposite sides of the Dancing Goat cafe. But nothing helped them sleep.

As Andi tried to doze, her mind replayed the incessant popping of the popcorn she'd prepared for the drive-in, the transformers exploding on the burning power line, the tiny bones ridging the back of Rick's hands.

Rick was probably still in the hospital. By morning he'd be in jail, if Noah's legal revelations, spilled out in a drawl as he tended Rick's broken hand, were accurate.

"You made a mess of this," Noah had told Kit. "Might keep him from grabbing kids and serving ladies cups of Rohypnol. Sorry," he said at Rick's yelp. "That too tight?"

Rohypnol. Andi listened to the metronome ticks of the grandfather clock and remembered a warning to high school students about "roofies," the date rape drug. Lab tests on the glass shard Noah had found on her hearth showed that Rick had slipped the drug into her wine. That explained her memory lapse too.

Across the room she heard Kit sling his knees over one

end of the love seat. He didn't fit. That was his excuse for restlessness. Her only excuse was a chattering brain.

Thank God, a search of Rick's van had turned up several of Jason and Dinah's paintings and papers connecting Rick with Sharif, a renowned trafficker in stolen art. How would she have explained to Dinah?

Worse, there was the fire. Heart's Ease—and even Rosencrantz and Guildenstern—were safe, but the old Williams place, according to Noah, was a "write-off," which probably was the way it had been planned.

"We're waiting on the arson report, but looks like Brother Wolcott's studying paid off." Noah's chuckle had turned Rick paler than before. "With the mess of glass layin' in the yard, we just naturally thought heat blew the windows out. For most, that's true. You could tell by residue on the inside of the glass. Brother, though, found a pane that was perfectly clean.

"When I left the scene, everybody was rollin' up hose while Brother pontificated about that window bein' knocked out before the fire started, to vent the upstairs and give the fire plenty of air."

With the concern of a physician, Noah had loaded Rick for transport to the Owen Canyon hospital. With the finality of a deputy, he'd slammed the door, complimented everyone's quick thinking, and apologized for taking Andi's VW in for fingerprinting and inspection.

By way of apology, he said it was plain as red paint that Professor Aragon wouldn't be returning to his job at Owen Canyon Junior College. He suggested that Andi apply, if she planned to stick around.

The grandfather clock bonged five A.M.

Andi wanted to stick around. At Heart's Ease, with Kit.

Kit thrashed again, and Andi sat up to see him staring across at her, his head supported by one hand.

"Hi," she whispered.

"Good morning."

Two simple words launched her into a fantasy of waking in his arms.

"I know it's a long walk . . ."

"And it's bitter cold," he added.

"But, what if we started for home?"

Kit crossed the room, untucked the blanket from beneath her chin, and kissed the space between her shoulder and ear.

"We'll be gone before anyone tries to feed us." His breath warmed her neck.

Andi's toes curled. She tried to form a thought worth speaking. Instead, she concentrated on standing up, and, in only a minute, they stood outside on the sidewalk.

Trifle greeted them with a nicker, and Kit rubbed the mare behind one ear. "I think she's too stiff to carry us both. Shall we lead her home?"

Andi nodded, remembering a man she'd thought heartless.

"Oh, wait. I can't go without my backpack." Andi twisted the Dancing Goat's doorknob. Of course, it had locked behind them.

"Leave it, love."

Warmth flooded the center of her body. No matter how tempted, Andi knew she couldn't keep the Graveyard Rose secret much longer.

"I've got to have it." She stared at the door. The rear entrance would be locked too.

She glanced over her shoulder. With the horse behind him, arms crossed and weight on one leg, Kit looked irresistible. On the other hand, she could guess how furious he'd look if she left the box behind and one of the twins opened it.

"It's pretty inconvenient that you can't just walk through doors anymore," she said.

Trifle followed Kit as he pulled Andi into his arms.

"Oh, lady." Under the horse's arching neck, he kissed her. "You'll take back those words. I promise."

Andi took a shuddering breath as he released her. Then the door opened.

"You guys getting an early start?" Blake, sleepy-eyed and barefoot, grinned. "I have to put coffee on. Want some?"

"No." Andi crept back inside. "Thanks, though." She grabbed the backpack from under the love seat. "Thanks for everything, Blake." She deserted the warm shop for the cold and Kit.

Wind had cleared much of the smoke, but as they walked toward Heart's Ease, they were surrounded by a haze of awareness.

Kit held her hand and his thumb stroked the thin skin over the veins at her wrist. He steadied her waist as they crossed the train tracks. And always, he watched her.

Today, Andi thought as her pulse thrummed louder. *Today.*

"It puts me in mind of Scotland," Kit indicated the murky morning. "That last day—"

His voice broke. Andi faced Kit in disbelief. He hadn't just stopped talking—his voice had cracked with emotion.

"I may have wronged you, even before we met."

"Of course you didn't." She wanted to hold him, but his expression held her off.

"The last sight I saw, as I lay dying, was a girl wearing a necklace of amber, like this." He lifted the bead from the hollow of her throat. "Her name was Miranda."

Chills spilled down Andi's arms. "But she wasn't me."

"No, she was a scullery maid with pale hair, only a wench that Aragon snatched from the Court kitchens. And she walked all the way to Scotland."

Kit's eyes closed for a moment. "She was making an ass of me. That's all I thought. Clinging to my leg so I couldn't mount my stallion. But she warned me of Aragon's treachery, and I—Christ."

Kit frowned. "You see, I didn't think to ask— It was another age, Miranda. Women and men . . . were different. He had her all those days, and I didn't think to ask if he'd harmed—*her*.

"But it wasn't you. Merely God's idea of a jest, and your necklace reminded me. The girl called it a griffin's eye." Kit tugged Trifle's rein and walked ahead. "She said it would bring me back to her."

"What?" Andi thought he'd stop, thought he'd turn those last muttered words around, and say something else. He didn't. "It would bring you back? *Kit?*"

"Silly," Kit walked faster. "To even recall such nonsense."

She sprinted, braid hammering between her shoulder blades, and still she couldn't keep up.

"Yeah," she called. "Might as well believe in ghosts."

With the gates of Heart's Ease in sight, Kit stopped.

"About that," he said. "Have you considered what might happen between us?"

"An explosion of sulfur, you think?"

Where had the assurance come from? She wasn't a bit afraid.

"I think *that's* unlikely," Kit admitted. "But if I'm not a ghost, what am I?"

"Mine," she said. Then she took Kit's hand and led him through the estate's wide-open gates.

Kit felt the fool for his confession. He blamed it on his brain's tug-of-war with his body. If he made love to Miranda, would he lose her? Only the act would tell.

Now, he fretted like a nursemaid over pieces of burnt bark and singed pine blown in by the fire's breath. Would they distress Miranda?

He need not have worried. She saw only her roses.

"Kit! Look!" She ran ahead, calling with delight so shrill that Trifle shied.

"I'm supposed to look for a five-petal cluster. One, two . . ."

Did she genuflect to the scrawny bush?

". . . five! That's what Jan told me. Oh, they're perfect. Look at that vivid color. Not scarlet, not orange. What would you call it? Sunrise?"

He had no time to venture an opinion. Miranda stood, shaking dew from her fingers.

"Everything else—the foliage and stems, Jan said, was consistent with Apothecary's Roses. Kit, do you know how old these are? Do you?"

"You're babbling, sweet," he said, but Miranda, practically dancing, was immune to mockery.

"Medieval," she said, smiling. "Even older than you."

He rejoiced in her teasing and in the gust of wind which made them pull their coats closer.

"Pity they'll get their bloody heads frozen off." He squinted at the fat-bellied clouds.

"Oh, I think they're tougher than that."

As she faced him with a saucy look, Kit couldn't deny her such simple glee. Even sleepless and slightly bruised, Miranda put the blooming rose to shame.

It was she who looked like sunrise.

If God was offering him this life, he wanted it.

His rooms were bitter cold, but Kit shucked off the borrowed coat and went to the closet. He took down comforters in green flannel coverings. Unlike a court lady, Miranda would accept a nest of everyday bedding upon his narrow cot.

A hundred times, he'd lusted for her. In the warmth of her canopied bed. In a wet red jersey which barely reached her knees. In little but sunlight, on the great room floor. But now that the moment was upon them, Kit felt humbled.

He smoothed the quilts in place, stalling. He'd never bedded a maiden. And this was a maiden he loved.

"How long do we have?" Miranda molded to the back of him, arms circled beneath his breastbone, hips nestled to his, so obvious in her desire.

"You were talking to Noah." Her words nudged his memory as her lips moved against his back, against the smoke-blue shirt she'd given him. "Didn't he say when they'd come to take formal statements?"

Her hands were cold through his shirt.

"Noah said he'd hold them off a day, because of the holiday. There's time enough, Miranda."

He heard her shrug off the backpack. He heard her jacket fall, but when he turned to face Miranda, she waited for him to lead.

He didn't ask if she was sure. It would have insulted the pledge in her eyes. He pulled her close and eased his hands beneath the fleecy sweatshirt. They smoothed up from her waist to shoulders, first fingertips, then fingers, then full palms, which circled without ceasing to her breasts.

He caught her small cry with a kiss. When Miranda's fingers wound in his shirt, her head fell back and her breasts pressed into his hands.

There was no need to urge her hips closer. She was there, answering, and Kit smiled. With Miranda, it was simple as that: He touched her breasts and her hips met his.

"Sit with me." He lowered her to the bed's edge and lifted her hands away. "Just a moment."

He began unbuttoning the shirt.

"I can't wait much longer than a moment." Her words made him fumble.

Kit tugged the shirt off over his head. Impatient and unsteady, he shoved the jeans down, unlaced the shoes, and swore at the tangle he'd made while she watched.

Except she hadn't. As he'd disrobed, so had she.

Pink and silver in the odd light, Miranda stood before him. How amazing, that with all her skin bared, Miranda's fingers were most erotic. Fisting and straightening as she tried not to cover herself, her small hands kindled heat which melted tenderness and desire into one thing.

Kit set his hands to her waist, pretending to steady her, though he felt just as shaken. It might have been the very first time.

At his silence, Miranda lifted her chin. Cinnamon hair streamed over creamy flesh, and she bit her lower lip. He had never asked heaven for a goddess. He did not deserve this one.

"I love you, Miranda." He held her shoulders. Though she shivered, he made her listen. "Carve it deep into your brain and your heart, too. Whatever happens, know that I loved you dearer than my life, dearer than the world."

"Kit." She wavered close enough that her breasts grazed him, and they held each other.

She repeated his name as they went down upon bedsprings which threatened to collapse. It didn't matter.

"Look at you. My God, Kit. You're—" She shook her head, and a lock of hair veiled one eye. He didn't push it away. There was something innocent and clandestine in her staring. "—beautiful."

Kit urged her down between the quilts, in case she recovered her modesty. Hand hidden by the quilts, he stroked the rise of her hip, the dip of her waist. His hand shaped gently to her breast.

"I'd learn of true beauty, by memorizing you, bit"—his lips sipped her nipple in and released it—"by bit."

Miranda's gasp ignited the hottest sort of love. Love, still, Kit thought wildly—as their mouths locked in a kiss which widened to a consuming battle—but love which took all and gave all.

The endless kiss gave him all he needed of flesh and love. Miranda's breasts flattened to him, her arms slid over his, her hands skimmed, explored, burrowed in the hair of his chest, beneath his arms, making a virgin's tour of male differences, and all the while she murmured at her discoveries. He stopped only one of them.

"No, love. Not—" Kit clamped her wrist and held it. Suddenly he knew that passion's greatest danger was not his disappearance but her curiosity.

"Let me," she insisted, then surged up, breasts brushing his collarbone, fingers straining to touch whatever they could from their captivity.

"Soon enough, Miranda. I promise."

He waited for fear to glaze her eyes as he eased over her. *Careful.* Watching for a single qualm, Kit spread his legs alongside hers. *Slowly, Gallatin, you ape.* He shut his eyes and pressed his forehead to hers, hiding unseemly pride. Miranda's eyes had shown no dread, but they'd spoken to him in a curt and primitive language. *Yes,* they said, and *go* and *now.*

Her stomach sucked in, and her hips pressed into the mattress. "Kit?"

Hellfire.

Miranda's tongue wet her lips and questions furrowed her brow. "Did I—is something wrong?"

He shook his head, stifling a groan. Even raised above her, taking his weight on his arms, the shaking of his head thrust him against her.

Not yet. Take this chat as a gift, a chance to seize control. Don't think of the softness of her thighs.

"Why did you look away from me?"

"I did?" His arms trembled and his voice quavered. He tried to direct a penny's worth of his brain away from thoughts of savage coupling. "I looked away, because when I look into your eyes, Miranda—" The depthless blue and darker starbursts around black pupils pulled him, telling him to fall forward, forever. "I want to be part of you—" Ye gods, no stopping now. Precious, precious little time. "—I want inside you."

There. He'd spoken words that a man kept locked up. He'd taken on enough shame to last the next four hundred years.

"Now," Miranda whispered.

"Minutes, I swear to you." He touched Miranda's breast and her head tossed in feverish response. "Only minutes."

Gentle kneading and fleeting touches made her hips arch. Each time, every time. She took up his rhythm, feinting back and forth, mirroring his moves until she forgot shy hesitation. Miranda rocked with a grinding need which startled him.

Timing, bloody timing, Gallatin. God, with his brain afire, he could not think.

When he reached down to assure himself, to gently verify her willingness, a sharp quaking consumed her. *What?* Miranda's wide-eyed gasp, her arms' trembling, shook them both.

A touch. But a single, sliding touch, and Miranda was exploding in his arms. She gasped and clutched him, surrendering to a blessed culmination like a *man's.*

"I love you, Miranda. I do love you," he whispered, but as he joined them, and her arms held him hard enough to hurt, Kit's mind was shouting with wonder.

No secrets, no pain, no hiding, and no fading away. Andi wrapped her arms around Kit's back as far as she could reach.

"Mine," she whispered.

As if that fierce possession drove him, Kit's muscles hardened and he surged into her a final time. She held him to her. *Please don't go, don't go, don't.*

He didn't. He stayed solid in her arms, head burrowed

beside hers. He caressed her shoulder with spent tenderness. She scooted down and cuddled against his chest.

Across the room, she saw bicentennial bunting by a window. She saw his manuscript still sitting on the table. Downstairs, Trifle rolled in fresh straw. Beneath Andi's cheek, Kit's heart beat thunderous inside his ribs.

It could be *her* pulse.

It could be an aftereffect of that incredible falling *up*.

It could be her imagination, but it wasn't. All the same, she must be careful, in case she was wrong.

"Kit," she began, not knowing what came next.

"I feel it." Kit took her hand to his lips and held it there, kissing each side and angle of it.

Twice she thought he tried to speak. Finally, he did. "I suppose you'll be wanting marriage now."

"I—" She swallowed her outrage in time to feel him chuckle.

"Even though I have no earthly goods, you'll hold me hostage with this act."

Bewildered, half melted by emotion, Andi watched him. Kit was joking. His lazy amusement must be part of lovemaking. Just because the man had a heart didn't mean he'd shed the habit of acting heartless.

"Not necessarily," she yawned.

"By heaven, you will!" He held her so she saw nothing of the world, except his eyes. "And quickly, and thoroughly."

"If you insist." Andi let her eyes close, concentrating on the layers of feeling, of longing, of need that began building all over again.

She would not think of the box.

"What is it?" Kit's tone was sharp, but he passed a hand, feather-light, down her back. "Have I hurt you? Where he kicked your face, it didn't even bruise. I—"

"It doesn't hurt, but I need to tell you something." Andi brushed Kit's hair back over his shoulder. "And I have no idea how you'll take it."

The cocky tilt of his smile puzzled her. She framed her

hands on his jaw and felt a little smug that she'd waited for him.

"I feel wonderful."

"That's all very well, but let's have your revelation."

"I need to get out of bed, to show you." She bumped him with her hip, but Kit didn't move.

"You know the way, love."

She eased over him, eyes on the black backpack instead of his broad chest. She tried not to feel, even when he held her above him.

Kit grumbled and released her. Once out of bed, Andi felt shaky. Suddenly her cheekbone did feel bruised. She pulled Kit's blue shirt over her shoulders.

After all these years, he would be disappointed by the box's contents. What could be inside besides cloth and a grisly lump?

The backpack's zipper sounded incredibly loud.

"What have you got, a snake? You don't look as if you relish touching it."

Last night it had felt warm. Now, the box rubbed a scuffed spot on her palm as she handed it to him.

"Well." Kit sat upright, shoulders against the window frame over the bed. A swathe of sheet covered his lap, but Andi knew he didn't notice, or care. "What shall we do with this, then? Drive to the ocean and heave it in?"

His puzzlement faded quickly.

"Why *now*, Miranda? You've had it a while, have you not?"

"During the fire," she said, but her mouth felt dry. "I had to give it to you. It's yours."

"I repeat, why now? Why not an hour ago, or never?" He might have spoken to a stranger. "What made you wait until I'd pledged myself?"

"Well, *un*pledge yourself." She pulled the shirt closer and crossed her arms. "I don't care!"

She stared at her feet on the red, white, and blue rug. She did care—and she hurt. He might have taken her heart for his own.

"Don't you?" He sounded like Kit again, but if she

looked up, she'd cry. "Miranda, please don't force me to unman myself."

She let her gaze rise high, as high as his beseeching hand. *Unman himself.* Did that mean admitting he was afraid? Or apologizing?

"I will throw myself at your feet if you insist, but you'll pay, later." Kit wore a boy's smile within his black beard.

"How are you going to get it open?" she asked. "Want to try a table knife?"

As simply as that, Andi suggested the desecration of a priceless historical object. She had no choice.

"All right," he said.

Kit's fingers made an opening through a weak spot in the Graveyard Rose. He wedged the knife through and levered it back and forth until a scrap of cloth, oiled to dark tan, appeared.

"It's not there," he said. "Something is, but not an organ 'skillfully preserved by an apothecary.' Isn't that how you told the tale at the fair?"

She wanted to tell him to hurry. She wanted to scream that suspense was simmering her stomach in acid, but it was Kit's ruined sword, Kit's heart, Kit's fate.

The wrinkled cloth had hardened. He had to crack it open, and then a ring tumbled into his palm.

"By God, it's Barrett's ring." Carelessly, Kit passed the sapphire embedded in silver to Andi. He continued tipping the box and shaking it. Finally, he crushed the stiff cloth until nothing could have remained hidden.

The ring was heavy and ornate but not very big around. Tarnish smudged the inscription. Andi held the ring in both hands, sheltering a second son's tribute to his big brother.

Kit gave up the search and took the ring back.

"Am I to believe this ring drew me down the centuries? Where the bloody hell is my heart?"

"Maybe he buried it after all." Andi thought of the dreadful woman who'd scorned a frightened young ghost. "Kit, Arabella lied to you. She—!" Andi shook both fists. "Barrett wouldn't have left his ring if he'd thought you were a traitor."

Kit turned the ring, frowning.

"What does the inscription say?" she asked.

"Some motto, or—" He looked up suddenly. "This didn't have one. It was just his bauble, not a family ring."

"But look." Andi turned the ring, rubbing a finger over the etching under the tarnish. "Is it Latin?"

Kit leaned close to the window. "French," he said, tilting the ring. "Very fashionable among idle younger . . ." Kit swallowed and stared at her. "It says, *J'ai cru*, 'I believed.' "

"He knew you weren't a traitor."

"Yes."

"Arabella is a big, fat liar."

"It would seem so. That explains why we found no mention of my dishonor at the library." With each word his face brightened.

"If we go back, we can look for a portrait of her as a double-chinned dowager."

Kit caught her chin in one hand and turned her face to the window. "What a becoming tinge of green."

"It's not jealousy! I can't stand it that she made you suffer all these years." Something outside drew her gaze. "Kit, do we have a black cat?"

"No," he said, but he barely glanced up from nibbling her ear. "It's some refugee from the fire."

"Well, he's making himself right at home. Oh, wow—"

Kit ignored her. "Let's have no talk of other wenches making me suffer." Kit caught her closer. "You're doing your share of torture."

"Kit, really. Look." She wrested loose and opened the window. Cold wind blew the curtains around them.

" 'Zounds, woman, you're mad."

"Isn't that a snowflake?"

"Ash, more likely."

"This cold? Kit, I've won the snow pool!" She laughed and let him kiss her quiet. Kneeling face to face with him before the window, she felt him ease the silver ring onto her finger.

"No, it's your brother's ring, Kit."

He closed his knees outside hers and leaned forward, pushing her back, sealing her lips with his, engulfing her ringed hand with his as well.

"Barrett gave it as an act of faith, and I give it to you. Every day, you made the sweet assumption that I was real. Your mind denied, but you believed, even when I was impossible."

Kit released her hand and gave her lips a glancing kiss. "Now, to echo a lady of my acquaintance, I must humble myself and ask, 'How long will you make me wait?' "

"Wait?" Andi trailed a brave hand down his flank and shivered before he did. "How have I made you wait?"

"You have not answered the vow I gave you, an hour past. On occasion, Miranda, I am not a patient man."

She looked up, past his broad chest and wide shoulders to eyes full of her.

"I love you, Kit."

He sniffed, shrugged, and glanced out the window.

"Paltry words, without actions, lady."

Andi reached up and pulled him atop her.

"I love you, Kit Gallatin, even though you're still impossible."

Then, though quilts slipped to the floor and wind blew through an unlatched, forgotten window, the carriage house grew warmer. Outside, summer snow was falling on roses.

About the Author

Tess Farraday is the author of four historical romances and magazine articles on topics from birthing rooms to bats. *Sea Spell* and *Snow in Summer* mark her entry into the field of contemporary romance.

Farraday lives in the foothills of the Sierra Nevada mountains, where she shares a one-hundred-year-old farmhouse with two children and her husband, an award-winning journalist.

Farraday's work has won Heart of the West, Romance Communications, and Phelan awards. She has a Master's degree in Journalism and entirely too many pets, including an heroic collie, a German shepard, and a bossy feline named Sherlock.